What People Are Saying

"Susan K. Field in *Eleanor's Song* has written the classic novel: a character we can cheer for, who has talents and flaws, who makes mistakes but we understand because she's young and she's lived with terrible wounds. It's a compelling read, a true page turner that unveils a strong woman resilient through trauma. Bravo to Eleanor and to her creator!"

— JANE KIRKPATRICK, AWARD-WINNING
AUTHOR OF *BENEATH THE BENDING SKIES*

"Field brings forth an historical tale of family, trauma, love, and determination ... The prose sings, and Field offers welcome insight into life's most vulnerable moments. Historical fiction readers will find this compelling novel of growth and perseverance one to treasure."

— *BOOKLIFE REVIEWS*

"… Eleanor's Song is powerful and intense with the emotions of women and children battered in the poverty of the Great Depression. While never excusing the abuse, Ms. Field refuses to fall into stereotypes by showing compassion for the men twisted by despair and the horrors of World War II."

— MARYJANE NORDGREN, AUTHOR
OF NANDRIA'S WAR

"This powerful, tender book immerses you in young Eleanor's remarkable life story during the Great Depression."

— KATHY CARLSON, ADVANCED READER

"Susan K. Field has written a fast-paced, suspenseful novel with well-drawn characters and spot-on descriptions that evoke time, place and emotions with great skill."

— JANE BESSE, ADVANCED READER

Eleanor's Song

SUSAN K. FIELD

FORSYTHIA PRESS

Print ISBN: 979-8-9882911-0-7

eBook ISBN: 979-8-9882911-1-4

Edited by Ariane Kimlinger, Owl Focus Editing

Cover Design by Gwen Patch

Formatting and Inside Design by Krista Harper

For more information about the author, see www.susanfieldwrites.com

Reader discretion is advised. Eleanor's Song is intended for mature audiences.

*For the women who have survived
and those who haven't.*

May your stories endure.

Prologue

1927

The women of Eleanor Owen's family cobbled together their hardscrabble lives. For them, history had a way of repeating itself. Like the confluence of rivers, their lives intersected; adversities flowing from one generation to the next. The night of December 13, 1927, when three-month-old Eleanor rode in a car driven by her mother, Margarete Bowerman Owens, was no exception.

Sweet, innocent Eleanor babbled. Bubbles formed at her pink lips as she lay swaddled in blankets within a wicker basket wedged between the floorboard and seat. Only her blue eyes, rounded cheeks and tufts of blonde hair were visible.

Margarete's one joy, Eleanor, already lifted her head and smiled when Margarete called her name.

Margarete pounded her clenched fist on the steering wheel, complaining to no one except Eleanor. "Stupid fool. Following too close."

From behind, headlights beamed into her car.

Margarete sped up, putting distance between the 1925

Ford Model T she drove and the car behind her. She and her baby were on their way to the Seattle train depot. Winter's nightfall veiled the winding roads as slate skies transformed into menacing torrents of rain. The car's wiper chattered across the windshield, barely clearing the waves of water, and bottomless dark enveloped them as they snaked along the river.

"Nobody on the road. And some guy has to tail me. In this squall." She drove faster and so did the vehicle behind, following closer. Perspiration beaded along her neckline under her wool coat. Her fear filled the vehicle. It seemed to ricochet between her and Eleanor as her shoulders trembled. She turned her head to glance through the rear window again.

Finally, the car's lights veered to the left. Margarete, a young mother of nineteen, blew out a sigh of relief and checked her wriggling baby. She reached out a hand to pat Eleanor. "All's well." Margarete wasn't as sure as she sounded, but she said it for Eleanor. She talked to her daughter like they were carrying on conversations because it swept away the loneliness.

She had scrimped together loose grocery change for the past few weeks and still had to borrow money from her sister for train fare from Seattle to Pendleton, and then to her mother's house in Weston, Oregon.

Margarete's Ford rumbled along the uneven road for several miles, causing her feet to vibrate through her shoes. She continued to chat about how much better their lives would be in eastern Oregon. "Or maybe we'll move to Boise, where it doesn't rain all the time. I can get a job. We won't be too close to mum but near enough." She quieted. "Definitely away from your daddy. You know, baby, if he found us, he'd make us go back with him." She rolled her left shoulder where it ached, and the fist-shaped bruise was turning yellow. "Or worse, clobber me till I'm dea—" She didn't finish, thinking that voicing it out loud could make it happen.

Headlights from behind once again glared into Margarete's car as a sedan came up closer to hers.

She screamed, "No!"

Before Margarete said another word, there was a loud crash. A jolt. Something sideswiped her car. Metal caved in. Her vehicle bucked. Careened right. Tires squealed as the car smashed into the wooden guardrail that ran the length of the riverbank. The machine pitched and knocked out post after post that reinforced the rail. The impact forced Margarete's body to thrust through the driver's window, propelling her sideways across the road. Glass slices crashed down on the concrete as she disappeared into the darkness with a shriek that scattered like shards.

In the ditch, Margarete's hair clung to her head, caked with mud. Her shoes had flown off, exposing her feet and ripped stockings. She lay still. Silent.

The Model T slid to a halt. Steam sizzled under the hood. Burning oil spewed smoke while rain dripped from the car's roof. The collision into the guardrails had ripped off half of the passenger door and left the back tires clinging to the road, keeping the car from falling into the river.

At that moment, a black sedan sped away from the damaged vehicle.

Eleanor wailed. Her blankets remained soft and dry, smelling of sweet baby powder, until the bitter night's raw storm poured through the broken windows and down onto her.

One

1932

Five-year-old Eleanor spooned a mouthful of oatmeal to her lips, savoring the precious droplets of honey on top. Heat radiated from the cookstove and mixed with the May air, creating an inviting wood aroma inside the kitchen.

In Weston, a small rural town in eastern Oregon near the Washington border, temperatures were often extreme. Winter snow flurries from the nearby Blue Mountains chilled Eleanor's skin to the color of flour. Winds whipped down the slopes, across the exposed grasses of the Columbia Plateau, and through the gaps in their house's clapboard siding. In summer, scorching heat seared the earth, causing water to dry, rocks to split, and dust to drift.

Eleanor stared at her grandmother through the kitchen window. At forty-five, Delores Bowerman held strict religious beliefs, worked hard, and possessed unflinching resolve. Feeding all the children, clothing them, getting them to church, taking care of the farm animals, and paying the rent on their dilapidated house left little for her to give as a single mother. In addition to Delores' own burdens, she had been raising Eleanor since Margarete's death.

Under the early sun, she stooped in the garden, wearing a once-white bandana tied around her graying hair. Over her calico dress hung a dingy apron, its edges flapping in the breeze. In one hand she held a tin cup from which she plucked seeds, pushing them down into the ground with her other hand and covering them with soil.

Uncle Ernst, the oldest of Grandmother's sons, turned the garden plot. His chestnut-colored hair was tousled, and his muscles rippled under his cotton work shirt as the hoe he wielded chunked with a rhythmic thud into the rock-hard earth three rows in front of Grandmother. Everything about him was tall, his height towering above the rest of the family. The hems of his dungarees nipped at his ankles, exposing his long legs, and his chiseled tan cheekbones made his face appear stretched. At sixteen, Ernst took on the role of man of the house.

Grandmother depended on her oldest son for essential everyday tasks: carrying buckets of water from the well to the house and splitting wood for their cookstove. She had depended on Ernst for the last six years, since his father had divorced Delores for another woman.

Mr. Bowerman had ended their marriage with little regard for his children, but left the farmhouse and the orchard to Delores out of guilt for his infidelity. However, she lost that farmhouse and land when she, like many others in the community, couldn't find work, so couldn't make the payments anymore.

Afterward, Grandmother rented their current ramshackle house and garden plot, where she not only relied on Ernst, but she also genuinely couldn't maintain the place without him.

Eleanor recalled with a smile when Ernst, several days

earlier, found her singing in the kitchen. He chuckled and gave her a protective hug. "Your song's so cheery, you sound like a robin." After that, he called Eleanor "little robin," which always made her grin with a small pride, like she really belonged. She welcomed this feeling because living with Grandmother and her children, Eleanor's two uncles and aunts, mostly felt like being squeezed in burlap. Rough. Severe.

That morning Eleanor finished her mush, swiping her milky face with the edge of her flour sack smock. After climbing down from the chair, she padded into the only bedroom in the house and hummed a tune. On the wooden plank floor, she huddled in a corner and played with her rag doll, Little Mary, made from material scraps. She had loved Little Mary so much her cloth arms dangled from single threads and her sewn-in blue eyes were frayed. Eleanor used a twig to stir pebbles she had previously collected and pretended to cook breakfast for the doll.

"Here's your eggs and cakes. Hope you like the heap o' honey on 'em." She fed her with the stick. Sunlight filtered through the bedroom window. She yawned, curled on the floor, breathed in the well-loved scents of Little Mary's cloth body, and dozed.

Moments later, Eleanor awoke and called out, "Mama? Mama. I'll find you." From outside she could hear Babe's cowbell clang as she grazed; while she rubbed her eyes to rid them of the crust at the edges of her lids. With her eyes cleared, Eleanor gazed up to the photograph of her mother. "I'll find you, Mama. And let you out." With curiosity and determination Eleanor's short legs clambered impulsively

13

onto Grandmother's lumpy bed. The metal frame creaked like the rickety barn door. On the wall hung a treasured colorized portrait of Margarete Owens, Grandmother's oldest child. At nineteen years old the photo had been taken only months before she died. Eleanor admired her mama's auburn hair, bobbed in a stylish cut, and she wanted to run her fingers through the curl sweeping behind Margarete's ear. She studied Mama's searching, pensive blue eyes; pink, high cheekbones; and sumptuous, full lips. She wore fashionable tortoiseshell-rimmed glasses and a sleeveless green and cream-colored dress.

"You're the prettiest lady I've ever seen," Eleanor murmured, though no one could hear. She was better looking than Grandmother with her gray hair, coarse knuckles, and hollow cheeks. And, even more beautiful than the preacher's lovely young wife.

Eleanor pushed onto her tiptoes, reaching as far as she could to get the portrait off the wall. She touched it, exploring the exotic wood frame that looked like tiger stripes. Glossy and smooth, it measured as long as her arm. Fingering the lines around the oval edge, her sweaty hands left several moist streaks on the decorative piece. She desperately wanted that photograph down. She grasped the frame, gently lifting it from the nail in the wall, easing it down to place on top of Grandmother's quilt. Minutes passed as Eleanor stared at Mama's face.

She begged, "Mama, come outta there."

Eleanor turned over the heavy piece, grappling with the yellowing tape and clips that secured the cardboard backing. She peeled the brittle cellophane strips and twisted the metal clasps until the back loosened. Hints of mildew and dust puffed up and tickled her nose, causing her to sneeze. She lifted off the thin cardboard and put it aside, then tipped the glass onto the quilt. Excited to let Mama out, Eleanor flipped the photo paper over, believing she could set her free from the frame and bring her dead mother back. Eleanor believed that after Mama came out, she would finally take her home. They'd be together. Just Mama and her.

No aunts. No uncles. No grandmother. Instead, a real mother.

Eleanor knew about death. She saw bugs die in the yard. She even glanced once when Grandmother caught a chicken, put it on the woodblock and chopped off its head. Eleanor almost vomited. Luckily, she had turned away before the blood spurted out of its neck.

When Grandmother told Eleanor that her mother was dead, little Eleanor frowned. She didn't fully understand as she couldn't remember Mama. She couldn't remember smelling her mother's life-giving milk; how she swaddled her in warm quilts; or how she'd sang to her sweet lullabies.

With widened eyes, Eleanor pressed her anxious lips to Mama's photograph. A kiss would wake her, Eleanor thought. What a disappointment for the five-year-old girl. The paper felt dry, not warm with life as Eleanor imagined. No young woman leaped from where she was trapped. No mother appeared happy to stretch out of her stale, frozen image, and hug Eleanor.

She pleaded. "I know you're in there. Oh ..." Her shoulders slumped. Her head flopped forward. A sob came from within her empty soul.

Meanwhile, the back door slammed, and Eleanor's eight-year-old Aunt Virginia dashed into the house and bedroom screaming. "Babe tried to kick me!" When Virginia saw Eleanor and the portrait in pieces, she stopped short and screeched. "Put that down! Now!"

Her shouts startled Eleanor so much she gathered up the

loose items and accidentally cut her finger on the edge of the glass. Droplets of blood smudged her smock and the quilt. Her lower lip quivered as she stole frantic glances at Virginia.

Would she tell Grandmother? Would Eleanor get another whipping with a switch from the apple tree? She fingered scabs on her legs, fresh from the last licking.

Virginia gawked at her. "Oh boy. You're gonna get it." Her frizzy braids jiggled as she laughed. "*Really* gonna get it."

Eleanor kept trying to put the photograph back into the frame, but in doing so, she smeared more blood around.

"What'd you do?" Virginia's buck teeth and thin lips curled into a menacing smirk as she shouted loud enough for Grandmother to hear her from the garden.

"Shh! I was getting Mama."

Virginia snickered again. "Your mama ain't in there. She's dead," she said, rolling her eyes. "What a dummkopf." Virginia mocked Grandmother whenever she spoke the old language; but that didn't stop her from using the German insult on Eleanor. To Virginia, the arrival of her younger niece had interrupted her order of life. Eleanor was a disturbance who stole Grandmother's attention away from her. After all, Virginia knew she was kin. Real kin. Not somebody Grandmother took in.

Virginia's ridicule often targeted Eleanor, especially if her niece didn't hop out of a chair she wanted to sit in or if Eleanor sang to herself at night. The horrid, red-haired urchin, riddled with brown freckles all over her skin, pulled Eleanor's hair in secret or blurted her sour breath into the child's face. "Dummkopf, dummkopf! Nobody wants you. You ugly orphan!"

She trotted from the bedroom to the door and yelled, "Ma, come here. Look at what this imp did!"

While trudging from the garden and through the kitchen, Grandmother called out, "What's going on?" Grandmother's heavy, intent footsteps frightened Eleanor. When she reached the bedroom door and saw the blood and her treasured photograph in pieces, she scolded in a sharp voice. "Eleanor!"

Scared, Eleanor wanted to run. Hide. She cowered and pressed her shoulder into the hard wall as she shifted away from them. Sidelong glimpses at Grandmother made her realize Virginia was right. Instead of hugging Eleanor with empathy and lending an ear to her tale, Grandmother stomped straight out to the front yard.

Eleanor crooked her arm to hide her face. A loud snap of the apple tree just outside the door warned her. Grandmother marched back in, found Eleanor, lifted her dress, and whipped her legs with the switch. Whacking sounds made the whipping hurt even worse, and Eleanor wanted to scream.

Whack.

"This'll teach you right from wrong." Grandmother's voice snarled.

Eleanor closed her eyes tight and smelled the fresh sap of the stick.

"Sinful child."

Whack! Eleanor winced. Her skin welted and blood trickled down her thighs and calves.

"You're so careless. Never do that again. That's the only picture I have of Margarete."

"I—I'm sorry. I—"

"What a mess."

Virginia held her hands over her mouth. The brat giggled with a glee that stretched across her face.

Eleanor wanted to tell Grandmother that she was only trying to let Mama escape. Instead, she whimpered once and decided she couldn't cry because Grandmother would hit her harder. She had to be a strong girl; so she pressed her lips together, set her jaw tight, and wiped a single tear with the back of her hand.

She finally understood she'd never find her mother in the photo frame. Mama would never take her home. At that moment, Eleanor needed her mother even more. After that lashing, Eleanor hurt on the outside, but the pain festered inside, penetrated deeper. Lingered.

Two

1935

Almost three years later, seven-year-old Eleanor opened the back door of Grandmother's house and entered the kitchen after walking home from second grade. Since the portrait incident, Eleanor did what she could to avoid whippings, which meant always trying to do what Grandmother told her and keeping away from her aunt whenever possible. Though, shying away from bossy Virginia was harder, and Eleanor still occasionally got in trouble because of her. Her legs revealed the tell-tale welts.

The aroma of bread dough rising in the kitchen set Eleanor's stomach churning. She imagined eating the whole loaf with thick slabs of butter, but that would not happen because there was little to spare. Bread, milk from their Jersey cow Babe, last summer's canned spinach, and a few eggs were all the family had for their dinners. It seemed even the chickens were hungry and less productive that winter of the Great Depression.

"How was school little robin?" asked Ernst.

Eleanor hesitated before answering and looked around. Usually when she came home from school, Grandmother hovered in the kitchen, washing in the stand-alone zinc sink, cooking, or mending clothes. Ernst spent his days looking for work, any job that would help the family afford to stay in their house. However, that day Grandmother and Ernst were sitting at the table, which was unusual. Instead of working, Grandmother, in her yellow house dress, clutched a letter in her calloused hands, while Ernst, in his tired blue coveralls, held the letter's envelope. The tea kettle, one of Grandmother's few luxuries, clattered an aggravating hiss on the woodstove, heating water for a hot cup of Postum. This was Grandmother's favorite since she didn't drink caffeinated beverages.

Eleanor recalled one of Grandmother's constant reprimands. She'd quote straight from the Bible. "Idle hands are sinful hands." The two of them sitting quietly in the kitchen in the middle of the afternoon looked like idle hands. Like sinning.

Or maybe there was trouble; Eleanor imagined that they had to move again or maybe someone had been hurt–or worse yet, dead.

Eleanor's footfalls into the room were slow and slight. She finally answered Ernst. "It was good. Tilly and I played together."

Grandmother, whose face held wrinkles like a newly plowed wheat field, waved her arm and barked an order to the child. "Get along. Do your chores."

Eleanor tiptoed toward the bedroom, but instead of changing into barn clothes to tend Babe, she lingered, eavesdropping by the doorsill.

"One thing's for sure," Ernst said, his voice wavering, "if he's coming in two weeks like he says, we need to protect her." Uncle Ernst was like that—often looking out for Eleanor.

"What you getting at?" asked Grandmother, dropping her inflection with a sigh.

Eleanor sensed the weariness in her voice. She pressed one ear hard to the wall to hear better.

Ernst spoke with tight, agitated words. "Look, it's like that Charles Lindbergh baby."

Eleanor knew about the Lindbergh baby because Ernst brought home day-old newspapers from which he read to them about the case of the famous aviator and his kidnapped son. The January news told of the "crime of the century" and the kidnapper's trial. Eleanor wondered why Ernst and Grandmother were talking about that story.

"I don't want her hurt. We got to warn her. If he wants her and you write back to him and say no, we'll have to watch out for her," Ernst said. "Haydon's a scoundrel. He might try to steal her away. That's what I'm talking about, like that Lindbergh baby." He started whispering, and she had to strain to hear. "And you remember what Haydon did to our dear Margarete."

"Hush." Grandmother's remark had a decided snap to it.

Haydon? Eleanor realized they were talking about her father. Pulling her coat tighter around herself, every part of her body stiffened, except her right foot, which started thumping nervously up and down. She peeked around the corner.

"He's not fit to take care of her." Grandmother's voice hissed like her tea kettle, and she shook the letter so hard it rustled.

"He's got the law on his side."

They sat as the silence loomed, brooding as midnight. Sour heat flipped in Eleanor's gut as she ducked out of sight.

When Eleanor was younger, Grandmother had told her, "Your father couldn't take care of you. That's why you live with me and my children."

However, one day Eleanor overheard Grandmother whisper to Ernst. "Haydon's a drunk. He was a no-good brute to Margarete. Downright mean."

In the shadows of heavy green and gray walls, Eleanor glanced into the bedroom and back to the kitchen for a man— her father—who could be lurking. A tremble ripped through her body.

A chair scraped the kitchen floor. Grandmother heaved out a heavy sigh, got up, and plodded toward the cookstove. "My dear Margarete ..." her sad voice trailed off.

That evening, after Eleanor put away the supper dishes, Grandmother told her to sit down. Her tone took on a solemn, slow measure. Ernst joined them and sat near Eleanor.

Virginia followed Ernst, stuck her head in, and scrunched her lips into an ugly face. Eleanor looked the other way while Grandmother waved her arm impatiently at Virginia.

"Go. Find something to do. Now!" She left no room for argument.

Virginia scampered away.

In Grandmother's hands she held a piece of paper and an envelope. "I got a letter today from your father. He wants you to live with him." Her voice sounded wary.

"Ma's going to write and tell him no," said Ernst, whose innocent expression pleated into an adult frown as he tried to assure Eleanor.

She didn't really know who Father was. But if he was mean and a drunk, then Eleanor didn't want to live with him.

~

As she walked to school the next day with her aunts and youngest uncle Mattias, her thirteen-year-old Aunt Anna gave her a warning. "You gotta watch out. Your daddy says he's coming. And I don't want him to snatch you up." Her lean arms grabbed and held Eleanor tight.

"Ah, knock it off," said Mattias, who was fifteen and walked with a limp. "Quit scaring her. She's just a child. And afraid. You got big ideas in that thick head of yours. And a wagging tongue."

Anna protested, shaking her head so her ash brown hair flew from one shoulder to the next. "Uh-uh."

Of course, any time Virginia, the youngest of Grandmother's five remaining children, could be antagonistic, she chimed in, sneering at Anna. "Do so."

Eleanor didn't like their bickering. Anna meant well by trying to comfort her. But it was Mattias who shooed away both girls with his arm that always trembled, and took her hand. Eleanor sidled up to him as his warm grasp calmed her darting eyes, soothed the flips in her stomach, and quieted the unrest that flooded her.

However, the disquiet surged again when she walked home alone from school. The smell of her fear seemed to rise from the fields. Jump out from the trees. She told herself she had to keep watching.

Six weeks after Haydon's letter and Grandmother's refusal to send Eleanor back to him, Grandmother received a summons from the Brentwood County Court in a city over 200 miles west and about thirty miles north of Seattle, Washington. She and Eleanor had until March 12 to travel and appear in custody court.

They arrived at the depot in Pendleton on the Sunday before their appearance. The tall stack of the train engine belched thick smoke, clouding the air with a hot, sooty smell. Amid the clatter of other passengers dragging trunks on the platform and the conductor calling out, Grandmother's orders bellowed, "Follow me inside. We have to buy our tickets."

Minutes later, Ernst, who had borrowed a car and driven them, boosted Eleanor up so she could reach the Pacific Mountain Lines train steps. He kissed the top of her head goodbye, then she and Grandmother boarded for their journey to Seattle. From there, Father would drive them to Brentwood.

"I don't want to." Eleanor squirmed and jumped back when her feet touched the vibrating floor of the idling train. "The floor's going to shake apart."

"Nonsense, child. Keep up with me."

"If I walk on it, I'll fall … fall right under the train," Eleanor said, her voice insistent.

Grandmother's firm grip squeezed Eleanor's hand as she pulled her down the aisle to a hard, wooden seat.

"Get settled. It's a long ride." Grandmother stowed their brown satchel underneath the bench. Soon the train lurched forward with metal-on-metal screeching. Eleanor pressed her hands to her ears and flinched as the great whistle pierced the morning air.

About an hour into the trip, Eleanor grew bored. She popped out of her seat and darted to the other side of the train car to look out the windows. She played games with the quick passing view. If she stared straight out the window, the scenery blurred into brown, green, and brown again as they passed trees and shrubs. If she focused in the distance, the snow-covered hills looked like giants' toes covered with white bedsheets. Tired of watching the landscapes, she rocked

Little Mary, or kicked her legs back and forth, making shuffling noises with her shoes against the gritty train floor until Grandmother scolded her. With the rest of her time, Eleanor fretted about her upcoming court appearance.

"Will my father be there? What's going to happen? What's a judge?" Eleanor asked Grandmother in rapid-fire succession. Rumbles from the train shook her from her toes to the pit of her stomach. Eleanor's fear rolled in circles with each bump on the track.

Grandmother blew out a sigh, pinched the bridge of her nose between her thumb and first finger like she did when she worried. "I'll be there."

It occurred to Eleanor that maybe Grandmother didn't know what would happen either. What had she told Eleanor several times? "Just remember. If they ask who you want to live with, don't say your father. You'd be making a big mistake."

Eleanor had to remember what to say in court.

Eventually, she settled, resting against the thin window ledge. In this quiet moment, across the aisle, a baby suckled under a blanket. The mother hummed a sweet tune to the baby while its smacking lips gulped her milk. When the baby cooed, she shared the poignant moment with her husband.

"Look John, he's smiling at you." The mother's graceful fingers pointed at their son.

The man turned and lovingly gazed at the infant.

A girl, about the same age as Eleanor, slept with her head on his lap.

Once when Eleanor peeked over, the father stroked the girl's curly hair. His hands were clean, unlike her uncles' whose fingernails were filled with grime from the chicken coop, Babe, or grease from their tinkering.

Gazing back out the window, Eleanor flinched when

Grandmother jerked and snorted loudly in her sleep. In her lap lay the Holy Bible, open to a passage.

Eleanor longed for a mother's pleasing voice to sing to her and a loving father to pat her hair. She touched her own head, fantasizing about Mama caressing away her worries. But all she felt was her straight, braided hair.

Soon, the rhythmic clack, clack of the train quieted the pounding chaos Eleanor felt in her mind. She dozed. When she woke, the Peter Pan collar of her moss green dress was soaked with sweat, having had a fearsome dream where Grandmother had left her alone by a road. From that point forward, Eleanor sat still. She didn't want to upset Grandmother, on whose good graces she relied. She knew Grandmother was taking this long trip because of her, even though she couldn't afford it.

When the train pulled into the depot, its wheels and brakes squealing, Eleanor dashed out of her seat.

Grandmother arrowed steely eyes at her.

"I'm just trying to see the trains. Look. They're all lined up on the tracks."

"Sit down."

Eleanor turned away from Grandmother and scowled. This would be the first time seeing Father since she was a baby. She didn't remember how he talked, how he moved, or smelled.

Her body shivered. "I'm scared. I don't want to go," Eleanor said and stamped her foot on the floor. Her protest faded into the commotion as Grandmother quickly grabbed their satchel and tugged her wrist while the other passengers got up and carried their cases down the narrow aisle.

Stepping down from the train, Eleanor couldn't stop her shoulders from shuddering. Her insides spasmed, leaving her breathless. Grandmother and she walked into the station lobby where whiffs of sweat, scuffed leather, and dust drifted among the travelers who crisscrossed the sizable room.

Announcements over the loudspeaker pierced her ears in a cacophony of echoes.

Grandmother scanned the area. "Haydon's going to meet us. I don't like it, but he has a car. He's taking us to your Aunt Bernadine's so we can stay there."

Eleanor remembered her oldest aunt, Bernadine, her husband Mike, and their baby Phillip because they visited Grandmother during the summers. Eleanor had never stayed at anybody else's place before and wasn't sure she would like sleeping in their apartment. Her breathing shortened into quick pants, but Grandmother interrupted her worried thoughts.

"There he is." She pointed to a man with a pudgy face whose gut hung over his belt.

He stood at the refreshment counter, leaning toward a young lady. Tilting his head back, he opened his mouth and laughed above the noisy clamor.

He was loud and Eleanor didn't like what she heard. They headed toward him; Grandmother's sturdy shoes clomping on the stone floor.

"Haydon." Her sharp tone warned Eleanor that Grandmother was exhausted from the journey.

He turned his head toward them.

Eleanor stood stiff as she watched this barrel-shaped man approach, wearing a striped suit, with a full sandy-colored face, and broad shoulders.

On his head sat a gray felted Fedora hat, and his slick brown hair was nothing like her light brown hair. When he bent down to greet Eleanor, she shied away. His head loomed large—bigger than Grandmother's enamel dish pan—and his breath stank.

"Well, well. Aren't you a scrawny thing?" He chuckled at his own joke and tousled her hair with his thick hand.

Eleanor didn't know him and didn't like strangers touching her. She thought of the father who had affectionately patted his daughter's curls on the train. Her father was nothing like him. She cowered away from his towering height, and her knees wobbled.

She looked up from her shoes and out of politeness said, "Hello."

Father huffed with flaring nostrils. "That's better."

From the station lobby, they all walked outside into the sharp night air to Father's big black sedan.

The lights hanging on the building shone enough that Eleanor could see her reflection in the car's polished fender. Haydon opened the door so she could climb in the back, and Grandmother seated herself in the front. The cool, soft leather felt like butter tasted—smooth and creamy. Plush fabric lined the inside roof. She fingered the slick metal around the window, trying to avoid smearing it with her grimy hands. Although the car gleamed and felt like luxury, its putrid smell nauseated her, especially after Father flicked a cigarette from its box and struck a match until it sizzled. She didn't like the smell of it. Since no one in her family smoked, she wasn't accustomed to its blue-billowing odors so close to her.

Eleanor yawned, tired from traveling all day. But even though exhausted, she still gawked at the sparkling lights and lofty buildings; many of which were taller than the grain elevators back home. Father drove away from the depot parking lot and onto the glistening wet streets. Broad boulevards turned into neighborhoods lined with houses. Before long, it became silent as they traveled away from the excitement and onto a dark, two-lane road.

They finally arrived at Aunt Bernadine and Uncle Mike's

apartment building. Father lifted Eleanor out of the car. She squirmed, trying to wriggle out of his grip.

When Grandmother and Eleanor reached the apartment, Bernadine opened the door. As they walked in, Haydon told Eleanor, "I'll see ya tomorrow morning at ten so I can show ya the town."

Grandmother's head whipped around, and her unwavering eyes stared straight at him. "She's staying here with me."

Haydon spread his shoulders, like a general squaring off to a private. He met her resistance with a guttural laugh. Eleanor glanced from Grandmother's stern face and folded arms to Father's smirk.

"Ahem." He cleared his throat, "I *am* her father."

Grandmother's flushed face squeezed into a scowl, and she tried to shut the door, but Father stomped his foot down on the threshold, stopping it. Holding her body against the door, Grandmother was adamant as she spoke to him through the narrow space. "Eleanor will stay with me until the court date."

"You forget. She's mine. I'm picking up my daughter tomorrow."

"You must not remember. You wanted her to live with me. You said you were too busy to take care of your own baby. You'll see her in two days."

His snort mocked as he turned and walked away. "Tomorrow!"

The apartment walls shook when Grandmother slammed the front door. The ordeal between Grandmother and Father caused Eleanor's legs to give way and she slumped into a chair.

≈

The next morning, pounding footfalls headed toward the front door. From the sound of the gait, Eleanor guessed they were Father's. He knocked. "I'm here."

Uncle Mike, a short and stocky man, opened the door. Grandmother's face flattened and a rush of red marbled up her neck.

No one spoke.

"I'm goin' to drive her to Seattle." Father broke the silence. "I'll be takin' good care of her."

Grandmother's jaw tightened as she leaned her body forward. She squinted straight into Haydon's face. The two of them looked like dogs eyeing each other before a fight.

"Be back by noon." Grandmother's words, like someone's elbow in another's side, jabbed with contempt.

Eleanor couldn't help but feel even more nervous.

"Eleanor, get your coat on." Grandmother leaned down and whispered in her ear. "Mind yourself and be careful around him."

Father and Eleanor left. Her arm shook as she waved a weak goodbye. Driving around the city sounded fun, but not with him. Once she settled on the front seat, she slid her body as far from him as she could. The engine revved.

He first took her to his house about five minutes away. They walked across a sidewalk, onto a paved pathway lined with shrubs on either side, then into a neat, white bungalow with green shutters. His house, larger than the one-bedroom shack Grandmother lived in, harbored the mustiness of closed doors. Half-opened curtains hung in front of two windows, letting in only a sparse light. When her eyes adjusted, she saw that two dark wooden chairs stood tall and elegant at a round, polished dining room table. In the sitting room sat a low, sleek table.

Eleanor thought her father was rich. He had to be, to live

in a place with matching furniture, plush rugs, and wallpapered walls.

"Here. Have a seat." His voice filled the house as he pointed to an olive-green couch.

Eleanor sat and tucked the full skirt of her dress under her thighs. Shifting her weight from side to side on the deep cushions, she ran her hands along the velveteen nap and created dark and light swaths of rivers on the fabric.

"Not bad, huh?" He surveyed the room. "This is the house me and your mum bought just after you was born. I've lived here ever since." He cleared his throat. "Ever since the accident … you know."

Eleanor nodded, although she knew only a few details from snatches of information she had overheard about Mama dying in a car accident.

"Here," he pointed up a staircase, "let me show you your bedroom."

Eleanor lifted herself from the sofa and followed him. Her thoughts collided. She remembered the afternoon she came home from school when Grandmother and Ernst had been sitting at the kitchen table and Ernst had said: *"Haydon's a scoundrel. He might try to steal her."*

She took a step backwards, down one stair—away from him—in hesitation, like she found herself at the edge of a deep well. She told herself to stop. Turn. Run away. But in obedience, she kept climbing until they stood in a dormer attic with slanted ceilings and a window overlooking a porch. Beige wallpaper with pink roses and green vines decorated the room. A blue blanket hung over a single bed, and a pillow with a white case lay on top of it.

"This is yours," her father said.

"For me?"

"Yeah."

Next to the pillow lay a tin spinning top, painted with red diamonds and yellow polka dots.

"Go ahead. Try it. I got it for you."

When he talked, Eleanor tracked his bushy eyebrows as they lifted and lowered.

"Thought you'd like it."

"Thank you." Eleanor didn't reach for the top, but rather stepped toward the staircase to put distance between herself and her father. She glanced around the spartan room, and then they left. Like a relieved puppy, she scampered downstairs. Her caution lightened, but only enough to slow her pounding heart.

Haydon and Eleanor sat at the kitchen table, and in a moment, he popped up and returned with a wooden chest about the size of Grandmother's sewing box. After he set it down, his fat fingers fit a silver key into a hole and opened the lid. Red satin cloth lined the chest and inside were stacks of silver coins. He handled a few silver dollars, lifted them, then let them fall and clatter into a pile.

Eleanor counted the stacks. One, two, three, four, five, six … Before finishing she said, "Golly, that's a lot."

"Here, you can have two of 'em."

The first coin, solid and cold, weighed heavy in her sweaty palm. The second clinked against the first. She had never seen two silver dollars, let alone held any, and she slipped them into her dress pocket.

"I have lots more. That's why I want you to live with me. I can take care of you better than yur poor old granny." He turned his head toward the kitchen window and looked at Eleanor out of the side of his eyes. "And, if you tell the judge you want to live with me, you can keep 'em."

"Really?"

At that moment, his grin disappeared. "How about we go

for a spin? Show you the city. Then, I'm gonna get you some nice clothes. And how 'bout some toys too?"

"Uh-huh." Her jumpy right foot thumped. She wondered if he planned to kidnap her. Should she bolt out of the house? Try to run away?

Father led her to his car parked on the paved street in front of the house. They got in and Father started to drive.

"I'm a hardware delivery driver. Do you even know what a delivery driver is?" He snickered. "No, I guess you ain't got none in them two-bit towns you live in."

Eleanor didn't like his kind of laugh and didn't think he was funny.

"I deliver lumber and supplies to people who bought 'em. That's how I make my livin'." He added, "But I make most o' my money playing poker … I mean playing games and selling spirits."

Spirits. Finally, something Eleanor recognized. She knew about The Holy Spirit from Sabbath and camp meetings where church members received the divine touch. So, Father had The Spirit in him. He must be a God-fearing man then. Holy and churchgoing. Like the preacher in his pulpit on Saturdays. Although, she couldn't figure out how a man could play games and earn money because Grandmother never allowed them in the house. They were sinful. She thought Father must have a special game.

Soon, Haydon launched a plea. "I know you don't know me real good, but I'm your daddy. Your old granny, she don't love you. Why, look at what you're wearing."

Eleanor looked down at herself, embarrassed by her dingy dress, Virginia's floppy hand-me-down shoes that were too big for her short feet, and socks with holes in the heels revealing half-moon shapes of her pink skin.

"I can buy you lots o' new clothes. You're my daughter,

and I want you livin' with me. I'd treat you real special. See, I'm gonna run for mayor and one o' my buddies said if I wanna get elected, I need to show I'm a family man." He turned the steering wheel to round a corner. "We can drive around when I'm not working. Maybe take you on one of my deliveries. Then, you can go to school. I hear it's a good one, just a couple o' streets from my house. You'd like that, wouldn't you?"

Eleanor would like that, she thought, because she enjoyed reading and figuring sums. Walking just a few streets sounded much better than the mile from Grandmother's house to the school in Weston.

He waited for Eleanor's reply, but her mind circled in confusion. Father wanted her and so did Grandmother.

He blurted out. "What's wrong? The cat got your tongue?" He eyed her. "Well … what do you say?"

Without thinking, Eleanor agreed. "Swell. That'd be swell."

When they reached a department store, Father boasted. "This is the fanciest shop in the city. Just like I promised."

The store glittered with bright electric lights, glass cabinets, and polished floors. Eleanor's mouth gaped open as she looked around. She had never seen or smelled anything so grand. Fragrances of flowers in ornate glass bottles dazzled like in a palace, making Eleanor dizzy. The first thing she did was bump into a lady who wasn't real, even though she wore clothes and shoes. Eleanor hunched her shoulders and covered her face, wanting to hide after her blunder.

She and Father meandered around counters where women's hats, adorned with lace veils and long feathers, sat on fake heads. They then climbed a wide staircase until they reached the second floor.

There, a woman swished girls' dresses along a wooden bar. Under the rack near the lady's feet, two children laughed.

One called out, "Not it!"

Eleanor secretly wished she could play with them.

After some searching, Father selected three dresses and a gray coat with a black velvet collar. In the shoe section, Eleanor hid her feet as she pulled off her scruffy shoes and exposed her holey socks. She slipped on two brown T-straps, and they fit. Best of all, they were brand new. With her toe to the floor, she pivoted her foot from right to left, admiring the smooth leather and thick soles.

"Those look good. I'll take 'em," he said to the clerk. To pay for her shoes, he pulled out a money clip, bulging with bills. He waved his arm upwards. "The toys is upstairs." He reached out and clutched Eleanor's hand.

But she didn't like his thick fingers around hers. She stared hard at his hand. Once her foot lifted off the last step of the staircase and onto the third floor, she squirmed and slipped her hand out of his grasp.

"Go ahead. Look around."

Eleanor's head spun. *Toys!*

She scanned up and down, right to left. So many Eleanor had never seen. She skipped a few steps with delight.

Father laughed and then turned his attention to the salesclerk.

She slowed and began searching. Here were dolls, brown teddy bears, boxes of trains, puzzles, sacks of marbles, wooden doll houses with delicate furniture, building blocks, balls, tops, and play cars. The packed shelves mesmerized. Among all the splendor, one item caught her attention. She stopped in the middle of the aisle and stared up; high on a ledge was a pink box with an exquisite doll inside. She looked to Father, ready to ask him for help to get the doll down, but he was talking and laughing with a saleslady at the counter.

A passing clerk found Eleanor admiring the doll. "Her name is Madelaine. She's a real cutie, isn't she? Would you like me to show you?"

Eleanor nodded wide-eyed. The woman reached to the top shelf, lifted the box down and placed it into her open arms. She fell instantly in love.

Madelaine. Her face with delicate features matched the musical sound of her name. She was the most beautiful dolly Eleanor had ever seen.

Staring at Madelaine through the cellophane window on the box, Eleanor twirled. Her braids flew in tandem, and her heart flipped as she looked at the doll's bright blue eyes. They blinked! Really blinked. Madelaine's light brown hair curled around her smooth, pink cheeks. Eleanor hugged that box, wanting to tear off the cardboard, pull Madelaine out of the package, and cuddle her. She imagined playing house with the precious doll, dressing her up, taking her to her favorite tree in the afternoons, and singing to her at night.

Father ambled over and selected a few more toys: a red rubber ball, a wooden puzzle, and a blue toy car. He paid for all the new toys and carried the packages out under his arms.

Eleanor squeezed the box with Madelaine and her dreams inside.

On the ride back, Father asked, "That was fun, wasn't it? You can have all them things. They're what you always wanted, aren't they?"

"Yes." Eleanor thought about all of her new things. A wool coat with a soft collar. A pair of shoes—the first she could ever remember that didn't have holes in the soles stuffed with cardboard to protect her feet from the snow and rain. Three dresses, one frilly with lace. New toys. And Madelaine.

Maybe he wasn't a bogeyman like Grandmother said. Eleanor's mind swirled. She finally uttered, "I love my dolly."

"Good. You can have her and all the rest of the stuff. You want to keep 'em, don't ya?" Father's voice softened like a sweet song. "If you want these, you can keep 'em. You just gotta tell the judge you're gonna live with me." He drove the car onto a wide street. "See, if you tell the judge you want to go back to your granny's rat hole, I'll take the stuff back." He glanced at her. "Understand?"

Eleanor didn't understand. But she could tell his words didn't sound like a song anymore. They resembled a mad dog barking, so she cautiously answered, "Yes."

Before returning Eleanor to Bernadine and Mike's apartment, Father stopped at his house. He carried the packages upstairs. "Bring that doll and the money I gave ya."

Eleanor trudged up the stairs. At the top, she clung to the box with Madelaine, rocking it in her arms. Before she let her go, she kissed the clear covering, set the box gently on the pillow, and turned her head away before she cried. Next, she tossed the coins on the bed where they clinked together.

"They'll be here tomorrow when you come home with me." Father's words didn't reassure her. Her knees buckled. Her stomach knotted with emptiness because his promise didn't feel genuine.

Tuesday morning meant Grandmother and Eleanor had to go to court. Eleanor picked at her breakfast. The thick mush tasted dry and lumped in her throat.

"Finish up," said Grandmother, "we need to leave soon."

After they cleaned their dishes, she and Grandmother walked from Bernadine's apartment to the Brentwood County Courthouse. March gusts, blowing in from the Puget Sound, slanted the late winter's rain into their faces. Amid the briny air and fish tang, white sea birds screeched as they flew in one direction, stopped in mid-flight, then darted another direction in the chaotic winds. Grandmother clutched Eleanor's hand so hard her fingers ached. She tried to wiggle out of the tight grip, but that made Grandmother clench her hand even closer to her body. As they climbed the steps to the massive building, Eleanor couldn't tell if Grandmother was mad or if she felt scared too.

With her sleeve, Eleanor wiped away the remaining rain drops from her face as they hastened down a long hall, reaching the court in time. She and Grandmother took a seat on one of the empty wooden benches. Father stood on the other side of the room smiling and winking at her as he watched her sit down.

Eleanor turned away from him. Dark wood paneled the walls. Two flags hung on posts in front of the musty smelling chamber. Only the three of them sat in the impersonal space. Waiting, Eleanor grew impatient until the judge strode in with his black robe flowing. Everyone stood, then sat down again. This time she tucked both of her hands under her thighs, willing them to stop shaking.

Although the judge said things she couldn't figure out, she understood one thing for sure; Eleanor had to tell him who she wanted to live with.

Grandmother. Or Father.

Eleanor gulped hard when the judge commanded that she and Grandmother walk forward to his bench. Eleanor's footfalls on the polished wood floor echoed with each step. She shivered so much her teeth chattered. Grandmother stood by her.

When the judge, sitting high above them, asked Eleanor who she wanted to live with, her mind churned like a summer dust devil. Although Father scared her, she wondered, did he love her? Did he really want her? Could Eleanor have a proper life with him? A normal life? A dad and maybe even a mother someday?

Why did Grandmother warn Eleanor to stay away? She knew children were supposed to obey their parents. In sabbath school she recited the Ten Commandments. "Honor thy father and thy mother." She no longer had Mother to honor, and she didn't know Father. On the other hand, he had just bought her fine dresses and clever toys. He had a fancy car, nice furniture, and actual silver money.

Eleanor's mind swayed back and forth between two worlds, the one she'd been living in and the one she was supposedly being offered. Her current life with strict Grandmother: Aunt Virginia's mean temper, Grandmother's whippings, and the old, leaking shack they lived in wasn't great, but there was a familiarity to that life. Even a few good times. Like the summer before when the family had climbed the grassy slopes of the Blue Mountains to pick wild lupines. When they planted rows and rows of vibrant sunflowers for the family and birds to eat. When they gathered around singing hymns together in the evenings: "How Great Thou Art," "Sweet Hour of Prayer," and "All Creatures of our God and King," Eleanor's favorite because she could sing about the sun, moon, and clouds. While she stood deciding, she didn't hear any music, but rather heard her short, hard breaths. She peered up and over the tall, wooden bench to see the face of the judge, a stranger to her. Eleanor had to reveal her private feelings, make a decision she didn't think any of the kids at her school ever had to make. The silence in the room throbbed in her knees, heart, and ears.

Eleanor drew inward. She didn't pray to God. Instead, she silently asked Mama what to do. But Mama didn't answer.

Eleanor looked at the judge, then glanced at Grandmother standing at her side. Turning her head, she found Father's face as he perched on the edge of the seat. She focused again back on the judge, inhaled, and revealed in a timid voice, "I want to live with Grandmother."

The gavel pounded at the end of court, drumming in her ears so loudly she barely heard the judge pronounce, "Mrs. Delores Bowerman will now serve as the legal guardian of Eleanor Owens."

Grandmother blew out a sigh of relief and gave Eleanor a brief hug.

Father huffed and stomped out of the room. His heels struck the floor, rumbled like thunder, and ricocheted from wall to wall inside the chamber.

Eleanor's knees gave way. Dark spots spattered in front of her eyes. Grandmother steadied her, and then they both walked away.

He didn't even say goodbye. Tears nearly flowed, but what good would crying do? No Mother. No Father. Eleanor's shoulders slumped under the weight of his stinging anger.

On the train home to Weston, Eleanor wanted to shove the visit and the courtroom scene into the back of her mind and never think about them again. Try as she might, she couldn't. So, she gripped Little Mary. She wasn't Madelaine, but she was more precious to Eleanor than the frilly dresses. More valuable to her than all of Father's silver dollars. More loving than her own Father. Eleanor adored Little Mary and would never trick the doll to love her.

Three

1936

As time went on, Eleanor's daily life occupied the emptiness that had filled her after the court date. Shortly after their return, the family moved from Weston because Grandmother could not pay the rent. They returned to Millston, where they had lived before. Both towns had views of the mighty Blue Mountains and were in the Columbia basin where farming flourished. The house in Millston was dreadful. Still reeling from the Depression, Grandmother couldn't afford any better. The outside walls leaned. The ceiling sagged. Worse yet were the odors of rot rising like waves from the floors. The first time Eleanor walked in the front door, her eyes burned and she had to plug her nose.

Instead of just one bedroom, there were two. One for Grandmother, Anna, Virginia, and Eleanor, and a small one for Ernst and Mattias.

The farm house was close enough for Ernst to walk ten minutes to his first job at the Spencer Lumber Mill, and near enough that Grandmother could take in the laundry of the lumber mill owners, Frances and Peter Spencer.

Grandmother and her family had met the Spencers at the local church. Even though the Bowermans were scorned for being poorer than poor, and for Grandmother being a divorcee, the fine-looking, young couple would always acknowledge them at Saturday service, asking after Grandmother's family and their well-being.

As a result, Eleanor invariably gave the pair a cheery hello.

Likewise, Grandmother respected and trusted their kindness. Mr. Spencer gave a fair wage to Ernst, and Mrs. Spencer was generous when she paid for the laundry work.

Every time she came to pick up the clean clothes and linens from Grandmother, Eleanor skipped to the front door, happy to welcome the brunette-haired woman with a rosy complexion as she climbed out of what Ernst called a luxury car—a Lincoln.

"We have your wash all done," Eleanor said with a grin spread across her face.

In turn, Mrs. Spencer would give Eleanor a piece of hard candy and compliment Grandmother. "You sure do a fine job of ironing Mr. Spencer's white shirts."

Soon Mrs. Spencer—Fran, as Eleanor came to call her—grew fond of Eleanor and began inviting her to their home for afternoons and overnights.

During her first visit, aromas of Fran's simmering chicken and dumplings drew her into the kitchen. "Mm. Smells good. I'll help set the table." When Eleanor lifted three of the porcelain China plates, she wondered if she should have undertaken this task; the plates were delicate and nearly translucent. Eleanor thought better, put two of them down, then carefully carried only one piece at a time in her hands.

On a different evening, Eleanor played hide-n-seek with Mr. Spencer, who insisted she call him Pete. He was handsome with brown hair parted on the side and combed-down smooth. He wore pressed white shirts with ties, some even matching his gray eyes.

After Eleanor bounded down the stairs to the basement game room, she crouched under a table, covered her eyes with her hands, and counted out loud, "One, two, three …" to ten.

Pete came downstairs searching for her. "Let's see. Is she under the table? No!" He continued looking. "Is she on the shelf behind the games?"

Eleanor squelched a giggle. "Of course, I'm not on the shelf."

"Ah, I hear someone." He stooped, curled his fingers and thumbs into make-believe binoculars, held them over his horn-rimmed glasses and exclaimed, "I found you!" They were so different from Grandmother. They played with her, and Eleanor liked it so much she sometimes laughed until her side ached.

"Here, let me show you some things." He opened the glass door of a display case along one of the walls, picked up a gray, bumpy rock that was cut in half, then bent down to Eleanor's eye level. "We found this one on a rockhounding trip." He put it in her hand. "It's a thunder egg."

Curious, Eleanor fingered the outside shape of the rock, and the cut, smooth surface that showed the minerals within. "It looks like a lake inside."

"Each thunder egg has a unique pattern," Pete explained as he handed her a disc-shaped piece. "This one's jasper."

"It looks like painted branches." Eleanor turned the glossy rock over in her hand. "I didn't know rocks had pictures."

"Not all rocks do. If we went outside now and found a common gray rock and cut it in half, it'd probably be gray inside as well." He spread his arm out and made a wide sweep from one end of the cabinet to the other. "All of these are special." He selected another from a glass shelf. "This one's petrified wood. See its lines?"

Eleanor looked closely at the piece.

"Those are the rings of a tree. Millions of years ago this tree fell. Over time, it got covered up with dirt and other trees until it compacted into this fossilized rock."

"I see its rings!" Eleanor excitedly traced them with her finger. These rocks were mysteries. Each told a different story.

He reached into the cabinet and pulled out another. "I have a surprise for you."

"Ooh, I love surprises."

"When Fran and I went hiking last month, I found this." Pete's hand clenched something, and when he opened it, he revealed a shiny black object in the shape of a long triangle. "It's an arrowhead." He placed it in the palm of Eleanor's hand. Short grooves had been chipped from its edges. "That's a tip that Indians tied to arrows when they hunted. They carved them out of obsidian, like that piece over on the shelf." He pointed to a glossy, black rock about the size of his head. "During volcanic eruptions, mountains flowed with red hot lava and cooled into glassy rocks."

She cautiously reached for it, then pulled back her hand.

"Go ahead, you can touch it. Watch out though."

Eleanor handled the arrowhead carefully, feeling the point as sharp as one of Grandmother's sewing needles.

"And guess what?" Without waiting for her answer, he said, "It's yours."

"Really?" Eleanor pranced around the room, holding the arrowhead in her hand.

In her heart, she knew Pete's surprises and gifts were real, unlike her father's. Thinking back, Eleanor didn't regret her decision about choosing to live with Grandmother, because she knew Father's affection was fake.

Several weeks later, Fran came over to pick up her laundry. Eleanor was busy washing the breakfast dishes, observing how the steaming, soapy water reddened her skin from her fingertips to the elbows, while Grandmother sat in her rocking chair mending. When Eleanor heard Fran's car tires crunch the rocks and dirt in front of the house, she hopped down from the apple crate she used to reach the washbasin. As Grandmother got up, Eleanor ran out to Fran, wrapping her wet hands around her waist and breathing in her scents of kindness, like roses in a bouquet.

"Your clothes are all clean," Eleanor said, helping Grandmother gather up and carry the heavy baskets of fresh laundry to Fran's car.

Lingering outside, Fran gazed at Grandmother's garden. "Oh, how lovely. I see you're growing those beautiful coneflowers. I love them."

Grandmother beamed. "They're pretty in a jar on our table. But I dry them to make a tea that works as a remedy for when we've got a cold."

"I'll have to try that sometime." Fran nodded her head. Turning to Grandmother, she hesitated. "May I ask you something?"

"Yes."

"Pete and I wanted to know if we could take Eleanor with us on vacation in August. We have a cabin in the Blue Mountains where she'd stay with us."

After Fran's surprising invite, Eleanor held her breath, crossing her fingers behind her back, and wishing Grandmother would say "yes."

"Oh, please. *Please.*"

Grandmother stalled. She had a habit of frowning, as if she were constantly thinking of all the things that would go wrong. "I don't know… Anna's married. And now that she's gone, it's hard to get by." Not only had Eleanor's aunt recently married, but Ernst, who had already been promoted to sawyer at the mill, was now always at work. "If Eleanor goes away …" Her question trailed off while she smoothed her calico apron over and over with her right hand. "I rely on her to help around here." Grandmother stood silent for a long time.

Grandmother never asked Mattias to help with the household chores. And most of the time Virginia flat out refused and got away with her defiance.

Eleanor swayed from foot to foot, her heart thumping, impatient when Grandmother couldn't decide.

"It'll only be for a week." Fran pushed a curl of hair behind her ear. "We'll have her back before school starts."

"Well … I guess so."

Hearing Grandmother's reply, Eleanor jumped up and down and squealed all the way back to the apple crate to finish the dishes.

∾

It was mid-August and around seven in the evening when Pete, Fran, and Eleanor arrived hungry at the Spencer's two-story log cabin. As sun rays sunk in apricot bands below a glacier-rimmed ridge, Fran whipped up rice pancakes on the woodstove, and Eleanor breathed in the pancake's sweet aroma as they sizzled in the pan.

Fran let her pour rivers of real maple syrup over them and devour as many as she wanted. Pete smiled and winked at Fran.

How different life was with this loving, warm couple. At home, Grandmother worked all the time or read her Bible. She never fixed pancakes for dinner, and she never allowed Eleanor to eat as much as she wanted.

After willingly helping Fran wash the dishes, the three of them gathered around a pump organ. Fran's fingers glided across the keys while her feet alternately operated the two pedals. She played the ornate instrument with such gusto, the floor vibrated under Eleanor's shoes as they sang, "Ski-damarink," "Home on the Range," and "Polly Put the Kettle On."

Afterward, Fran said to her, "To think you've got perfect pitch. At your age. You should join us in the choir. Your voice is so fresh, you'd liven up some of those old ladies on Saturday mornings." In jest, Fran joked about the ladies, "And, they huffed, and puffed, until the whole church ran out of the building because they sang off-key." Eleanor doubled over with giggles.

"Here, let me show you something." Fran got up and walked over to a polished wood cabinet with a contraption on top that Eleanor had never seen before.

"What is it?" she asked.

"It's a gramophone."

"A what?"

"It plays record albums of music."

"How's it work?"

"I wind up the crank. It'll spin that plate, and when I put a record album on it, we'll be able to hear music. Let me show you."

"Oh, it's a music machine, right?"

"Right."

From a shelf Fran slipped out a square, flat paper envelope, removed a thick black disc, and placed it on the gramophone.

Eleanor ogled the dizzying record circling around and listened with fascination to recorded music that differed vastly from the songs her family sang. The words were unfamiliar, and the singers' voices were remarkably high and low in range.

"It's opera. Have you ever heard people sing stories on big stages wearing costumes like actors do?" Knowing Eleanor's background, Fran guessed that the girl had never seen anything even close to an opera.

Eleanor shook her head.

"Some are love stories. Some are about wars and revenge. This one's about a magic flute by Wolfgang Amadeus Mozart."

"It *is* magical." Eleanor listened, mesmerized. The instruments. The energy. Above all, the voices hypnotized. She wanted to stand up, let all the sounds race into her body in vibrating sensations. Let them soak into and absorb through her skin. She was riveted; she sat, didn't move, and hardly breathed for fear of missing something wonderful. Even the loud pounding of her heart couldn't overpower the thrill of the music. Goosebumps prickled Eleanor's arms while she listened to a queen terrify and enchant her at the same time.

She couldn't imagine anyone had the power to sing with such precision and passion.

From that moment on, Eleanor wanted to sing on a stage and wear a queen's costume. After the singing story finished, she sat and exhaled, out of breath as if she had watched it all in front of her eyes.

Pete had dozed off while the opera was playing so Fran patted his shoulder. "Wake up, honey."

He rose and poked at coals in the fire, letting the flames die down for the night.

Fran carried Eleanor's satchel in one hand and took Eleanor's hand in her other. Together they walked upstairs to the guest bedroom, where they hung Eleanor's dresses and coat on a rod in what Fran called an armoire. In her mind's eye, Eleanor pictured the beat-up box she used to put her clothes in at Grandmother's.

Fran turned down the blankets, tucked Eleanor into bed, and kissed her on the forehead.

Eleanor then wrapped her arms tightly around Fran's shoulders.

Once she blew out the oil lamp, Fran headed downstairs, leaving the faint smell of her perfume lingering in the air.

This is what it must feel like to have a mother.

Eleanor rolled from side to side in the enormous bed, enjoying the space all to herself. On fluffy pillows and under a thick comforter, she imagined living in a real home someday with someone who cared about her. Her fantasy drifted to a house with fireplaces and thick carpets in every room, while simultaneously the sounds of croaking frogs outside lulled her to sleep.

The next morning, Fran, who usually wore navy blue dresses in town, now sported fashionable shorts and soft tie shoes. "How about we go for a hike?"

Soon Fran and Eleanor walked out into the crisp air. Summer in the valley, especially August, throbbed with heavy heat. Up here, gentle sunbeams warmed the earth and glacial breezes freshened the mountain world around them. Over pebbled paths they trekked, on trails through maple tree thickets, and into tall evergreen groves. Soon they neared the edge of a meadow.

Eleanor unlaced her everyday shoes, pulled off her socks, and skipped across the glade of alpine grasses.

Spying a swell in the earth, Eleanor ran up it, straightened herself like a log, and rolled down. "Whee." Playing chase after an imaginary friend, she soon threaded her way around towering lodgepole pines and into a golden vale. Around another hill, she giggled, plucked pink wildflowers that made her sneeze, and gathered grasses into a bouquet. Hiding the flower gifts behind her back, Eleanor leaped toward Fran and gave them to her. "Surprise!"

"Oh, you're such a dear child." Fran inhaled deeply to smell the flowers' citrusy fragrance.

The two moved on and came upon a gathering of flat boulders where they sat for a while, listening to the squawky magpies.

"Look there." Fran pointed to a tree and whispered, "There … in the pine. A raven. See? Look how its wings shimmer—blue and purple."

Eleanor peered upward and searched the green boughs. "I see it. It's really big."

"There are lots of birds to admire up here. The ravens, owls, little towhees, flickers, hawks, and eagles."

Drinking in the spicy afternoon scents of the pines, Eleanor gazed at the soft edges of billowing clouds transforming from round puffs to shapes like bulky whales, then to angels, and finally to long, wispy feathers. With enthusiasm, she guzzled in the pure, vital air.

The next afternoon, Eleanor glided in a swinging chair on the veranda while Pete tied fly-fishing hooks. She asked, "How do you know so much? Like about fishing and the rocks you showed me in your game room?"

"I'm interested in a lot of things. Once I finished high school, I went to college. That's where I learned how to manage a business and about science, like rocks."

"And fishing?" Eleanor asked.

"No, I learned that from my father."

"What about Fran?"

"You mean, how does she know so much?"

Eleanor nodded.

"Fran went to the same college I did. She studied to be a teacher. We each went with a purpose, but we were also curious to learn."

Eleanor hadn't heard of college, but she wanted to learn too; about rocks and science and singing and teaching and maybe even about fishing. Fran and Pete always wore fine clothes and polished shoes that shone from a distance. They had a huge house and a log cabin, just for the two of them. They had plenty of food to eat. Eleanor thought back to Grandmother and her aunts and uncles. With an education, she thought that she could escape being poor. How she yearned to have a life where kids didn't make fun and laugh at her shoes and holey stockings. At that moment on the porch, Eleanor decided she wanted to go to college, so that her future would be like Fran and Pete's.

Fran sat next to Eleanor sipping hot tea from a China cup.

"You're drinking tea?" Eleanor asked with a timid voice.

"Mm-hmm." Fran lifted her eyes above the rim of the book she was reading.

"Grandmother won't drink tea. Or coffee. They're forbidden."

"Oh." Fran twisted her smile as if contemplating a troublesome problem. "The church does say we shouldn't drink tea or coffee." She placed the book, Agatha Christie's *Lord Edgware Dies*, on her lap. "Yes. That's what the church says. But me mum was a Brit. She grew up in England, and I've been drinking tea since I was a wee one. It's just something I've always done." She picked up her book again and added to her excuse. "Of course, in moderation only."

Later in the evening, the three of them gathered around the game table playing Chinese Checkers, a game they had taught her.

Plunk, plunk, plunk.

"I did it." Jumping over Fran and Pete's marbles, then moving her own players to the stars on the other side of the wooden board was one of Eleanor's favorite things. She giggled because she was close to winning the game.

Cool breezes from the mountains blew in through the windows, so Pete lit a fire in the stone fireplace. The pitchy wood soon crackled and warmed the cabin.

For fun, Fran popped popcorn over the fire, and Pete started getting silly. He tossed the hot popcorn in the air and tried to catch each morsel in his gaping mouth.

"Got it." He threw another up and passed the bowl to Fran. "Here."

Eleanor couldn't believe what she saw. Both were acting

like kids. Popcorn flew all over. Pete leaned to catch a wayward kernel, but it landed on his head. Eleanor copied him and missed. They all laughed, and she couldn't remember the last time she had so much fun. Lots of popcorn —food Grandmother would never allow her children or Eleanor to waste—lay scattered on the maroon and blue braided rug beneath them. Fran and Pete didn't seem to care about the mess.

After that, Fran grew serious. Her quiet face worried Eleanor, so she bent down and quickly started picking up the loose popcorn.

"What are you doing, child?" Fran asked quizzically.

"I'm cleaning up the mess. I don't want you to be worried —or mad."

"Oh, you're dear. You don't need to bother now." Fran motioned her hand in a dismissive wave. "We'll scoop up the kernels and put them in a tin to feed the birds. Anyway, we have something important to ask you, don't we, Pete?"

"Oh?" said Eleanor.

"You know we don't have any children of our own," she said.

Eleanor nodded.

"Pete and I cherish you." Fran was no longer serious. Her smile filled the room with compassion. "We want to know. How would you like to live with us?"

"Forever," added Pete.

Eleanor tilted her head, questioning what she thought she had heard.

Fran continued, "We want to adopt you."

"You'd become our daughter," Pete said, explaining.

The words "we'd like you to live with us" sounded like honey tasted. They sweetly echoed from one ear to the other inside Eleanor's mind.

"You want me? *You want me*?" Eleanor grinned, hopping up and hugging Fran, and then Pete.

After they swept up the popcorn and put away the game, the three of them headed upstairs to the bedroom to put Eleanor to bed.

Pete teased her. "Sleep tight. Don't let those bedbugs bite."

"There aren't bed bugs here, silly, just frogs." Eleanor giggled, rarely having much to joke about. But with Fran and Pete, joy tumbled out like burbling mountain springs.

Fran once again tucked her in the crisp sheets, stepped away, and blew out the oil lamp.

For the second night, Eleanor tossed from her back to her stomach, then flopped onto her back again. In the shadows, she followed the lines of the wooden paneled ceiling. If she tried to spread her arms open as wide as possible, she could never hold the fullness she felt in her heart. Fran and Pete's tranquil murmurs downstairs in the sitting room blended with her quiet thoughts, *"Pete and I truly cherish you ... truly cherish you ...,"* until Eleanor fell asleep.

Morning sunlight as soft as perfumed lilacs blinked through the windows. Because Fran and Pete wanted Eleanor, no morning would ever be the same. She walked downstairs where Fran peeled and chopped Gravenstein apples for an evening sauce. She gave Eleanor a slice. Sweet pleasures lingered after the first tart bites.

"Pete and I were thinking last night. We'd like to talk to your grandmother first about adopting you. When we take you home, I'll set up a time with Delores so we can discuss our plan with her."

"Okay." Eleanor nodded with a bit of hesitation about moving away.

Ernst, her favorite uncle, might be sad his "little robin" would be leaving. However, she only saw him at dinner and on weekends now that he was working.

Grandmother might be mad for a while because she wouldn't have anybody to help her except lazy Virginia. Eleanor wouldn't miss that brat at all.

In the end, Eleanor figured Grandmother wouldn't mind too much. There'd be one less mouth to feed, and she would be close enough to visit from the other side of the hill where Fran and Pete lived.

Fran reached across the table and gently patted her hand several times. How Eleanor had ached for that type of tender touch. Was her luck changing?

With eyes that danced, a skip in her step, and a wide grin Eleanor asked, "Grandmother will be surprised, won't she?"

"Yes, she will."

Four

1936

Eleanor had anticipated Fran and Pete's visit for six days. Before they were to arrive, Eleanor eagerly cleared the food and dishes from the table, and washed and put everything away. She swept the kitchen and main room floors, wanting everything clean and tidy.

That afternoon Virginia loafed around in the bedroom and Mattias tended to the animals.

Soon Fran and Pete knocked on the door and Grandmother welcomed them inside.

After the couple sat, Virginia nosed her way into the room and plopped herself on the floor next to them. Few guests visited the Bowermans in the evenings, so for them to come over was special.

Eleanor guessed Virginia wanted to hear the conversation, probably hoping for gossip; especially since the blabber-mouth often ranted and whined: "Why does Eleanor get to go and I don't?" Then a tantrum would follow: "I wanna go, *I wanna go!*"

Grandmother ignored her protests.

Eleanor knew the answers to Virginia's complaint. She had a mama. Eleanor didn't.

"You girls go do your chores." Grandmother waved her hand to whisk them away.

"We're done." Virginia pouted her lower lip.

"Well, go out and play," Grandmother said. "I'm talking with the Spencers."

Eleanor wanted to shout so everyone miles away could hear her joy. *I am wanted. I'm going to live with Fran and Pete.* She felt certain Grandmother would say yes, but she still squirmed like a worm in the vegetable plot. Eleanor kept her promise to Fran, though, and distracted herself from the enthusiasm swelling inside her, by wading between the corn rows.

Finally, Grandmother called out. "Eleanor, come here!" Her tone sounded pointed, like a sharp nail.

Eleanor ducked and pushed. "I'm coming. I'm coming." The stalks prickled her hands and arms as she eagerly rushed from the garden to the back door.

While Eleanor hurried, she spied the apple crate. After she came home from the cabin, she'd deliberately not unpacked, but instead, had stuffed another dress and sweater, and the arrowhead, into the satchel Grandmother had loaned her. She'd hid the bag on the back porch under that apple crate. Eleanor had thought herself clever, knowing no one would look there. She imagined when Fran and Pete came to get her, she would simply be able to grab the bag, hop into their car, and never look back.

Never look back. Eleanor had wished so much for that moment. It almost seared into her as she raced into the house.

Virginia trailed close behind.

Eleanor flung open the door, ready to be hugged by her new parents, only to freeze in mid-step.

Fran was crying.

Eleanor's stomach seized into a cold knot.

"Come on in." Grandmother beckoned, speaking in a muted manner.

Eleanor hung back, hands knotted behind herself. Something was wrong. Very wrong.

Without hesitating, Grandmother explained in one quick sigh. "You might as well know. You can't live with Mr. and Mrs. Spencer."

Eleanor stopped breathing. She clamped her hands over her ears and squeezed her eyes tight, locking everything inside of her, protecting her from Grandmother's words.

"I'm not your real parent. I'm only your legal guardian." In that moment, everything changed. "If you live with Mr. and Mrs. Spencer, I'd lose my guardianship. You'd have to go back and live with your father. That's the law."

Although Eleanor's ears were covered, she'd fully heard Grandmother's explanation and the muffle of Fran's sniffles. The chair where Grandmother sat shifted on the wooden floor. She spoke to Fran. "Only her father can agree to her adoption, and he never would."

Pete tipped his head slightly back as his eyes widened; while Fran opened her purse, reached in and pulled out a handkerchief. She dabbed her nose with the white linen cloth.

"Now please put your hands down and open your eyes," said Grandmother.

Eleanor didn't listen. She squeezed her eyes tighter.

"You know child, he never would." Grandmother reached out her hand and patted Eleanor's shoulder. "Remember how he stormed out of the courtroom?"

Eleanor took her hands down and screamed, "No! No! I don't believe you!"

Out of the corner of her eye, Eleanor watched Virginia charge to the door, where she then stood wide-eyed, watching the commotion.

"I don't believe you. You hate me." Eleanor's shriek filled the small room.

Of course, Grandmother didn't hate Eleanor. She had taken her granddaughter in when she needed protection. Care. A place to live in a God-fearing family, rather than with a drunken heathen.

Eleanor yelled at Grandmother, "Now that Aunt Anna's gone, you just want me here to clean, do chores—chores Virginia doesn't have to do. Like this afternoon."

"Stop! Must you cause trouble? Stop making a scene."

"You hate me. And you want to know what? I hate you. And Virginia." Fury, like oil, fed the fire inside of her.

"Eleanor—" Fran broke in softly. She stood up and enveloped Eleanor's shuddering shoulders with her warm embrace, giving her strength, even as her emotions spiraled further into a deep hole.

"We didn't realize, Mrs. Bowerman," said Pete. "We thought … well, I guess we thought wrong." He rose from his chair, his shoulders strangely slumped. "We'll be on our way now. Our apologies for causing this upset in your family."

Fran frowned, shaking her head. "Um. We misunderstood."

"We'd still like to … to have Eleanor visit us," Pete said, stammering.

Grandmother looked at Eleanor. Her eyelids drooped. Her shoulders softened as she sighed with an uncharacteristic gentleness. "Yes. You're very kind."

Fran and Pete strode to the door and out to their car.

Eleanor followed them, running out in front of their Lincoln. "No. No. Don't leave me! Please." She stood with locked knees, arms outstretched and tears streaming down her face.

Mr. Spencer stopped his car, climbed out and swept Eleanor up. Rocking her in his strong arms, he patted her back. "Come on, sweetie. We don't want to hurt you. We'll have you over again soon." He bent over and whispered into her ear. "Real soon."

In the middle of the night, Eleanor waited until she heard Grandmother's ragged snoring and Virginia's nasally breaths.

Since Aunt Anna had left, Grandmother slept alone in the big bed, but this night had been different. Grandmother let Eleanor have the single bed to herself while Virginia slept in Grandmother's bed. That arrangement suited Eleanor just fine. She hated sharing with her blanket-hogging aunt, anyway.

An indigo sky filled the view through the bedroom curtain. Eleanor wiggled her toes, then lifted the blanket away from her arms and legs, and carefully crawled out of bed. She kept her eyes glued on Grandmother and Virginia as she softly padded out of the room, hoping to avoid the creaky spot in the wooden floor. With nimble movements, she opened the back door and slipped out. Tiptoeing in her bare feet and wearing only her cotton nightgown, Eleanor lifted the apple crate and grasped the satchel strap. She sneaked through dry August weeds then onto the cool earth where whiffs of promise filled her. Illuminated by a gibbous moon, hanging as golden as a half-eaten apricot, she ran down the road toward Fran and Pete's house.

Someone trampling in the weeds nearby woke her the next morning. Daylight shone brightly overhead. Eleanor's gaze widened when she saw Grandmother and Ernst hovering over her, close enough she could smell his morning breath. She remembered. When running through the dark the night before, she grew tired, so had curled up on the ground inside a hollow of an oak tree. There she slept, using Grandmother's satchel as a pillow.

"What do you think you're doing?" Grandmother scolded, hovering over her with a wagging forefinger.

Eleanor didn't answer. She clasped her knees with her arms and became rigid.

Uncle Ernst scooped her up and cradled her in his long arms. Caught between a wish to wriggle free from him and run, or remain wrapped in his warm embrace, Eleanor settled into his soothing hold.

"Little robin, we've been looking for you nigh about an hour. We've been worried about you," Ernst said gently.

Grandmother picked up the satchel and brushed away dirt from Eleanor's nightgown.

"Now, why'd you go and do something like this? God put you in Ma's care for a reason. Don't you know she loves you? We all do."

Eleanor didn't answer. Instead, she tried to still the raw emotions in her stomach.

Grandmother reprimanded, "Never do that again." She straightened her back, lifted her chin, and then consoled Eleanor. "Now let's go home and get some breakfast." She stroked her coarse fingers gently along Eleanor's cheek.

Eleanor's chin dipped to her chest while her eyes looked up at Ernst's face. Her cheeks reddened, and she cried.

Five

1938

Eleanor continued to regularly visit Fran and Pete. She adored them; and even though eleven years old, she would still sometimes sulk because they couldn't adopt her. Once, she even thought of writing to Father to ask for his permission, but remembered how contentious that trial was.

Those memories reared up thick and complicated when Grandmother told Eleanor that she had to travel to take care of Aunt Bernadine.

"She had a hard delivery and she's hemorrhaging. If she bleeds too much ..." Her voice faded. "I can't even abide that thought." Grandmother shook her head with worry. "Plus, she's got the other two. They sure can't take care of themselves, especially that little Victoria. Spoiled already and she's only two!" During their conversation, it looked like Grandmother's frown was permanently stitched.

Grandmother snapped ends off from the freshly harvested green beans. "And your father's going to have to pick you up at the train depot."

"Father? No! Please. Not him." With the emotional scars of his trickery barely healed from years earlier, those wounds easily ripped open again; wounds Eleanor had never revealed to Grandmother.

"I don't like it either. There's nobody else to get you. Mike works."

"I want to go on vacation with Fran and Pete. Remember? They asked again."

Grandmother ignored Eleanor's question. "I can't go. Too much to do around here." She pointed toward the garden. "Ernst and I have scraped together three dollars to pay Haydon for driving you to Bernadine's. You'll take the money with you and pay him when you see him."

"But …" Eleanor realized if she said anymore, Grandmother would not hear, and her words would only tumble to the floor. She turned and walked away with a loud sigh.

The repetitive sound of steel-on-steel juddered Eleanor's entire body as the train sped west. Reflected in the window of the Pacific Mountain Lines coach, she followed the shape of her hair from the violet ribbon bow near the crown of her head to the end of her shoulder-length curls.

For a second time, she headed from Pendleton to Brentwood. Heat from the August sun radiated into the passenger car until Eleanor imagined she was sitting inside a large wooden coffin. Dribbles of sweat zigzagged down her forehead, cheeks, and neck even though she fanned herself with a newspaper she found when boarding.

The length of the train car included wooden benches on either side of the aisle. While the passengers rocked from side to side, it smelled as if stinking swine occupied the space. Breathing exhausted her.

"It must be a hundred and ten degrees in here," said one passenger who had previously taken off his suit jacket and loosened his tie.

"No. Probably a hundred and fifty," another said, grumbling.

"Even with the windows open, it's hard to get any air," said a third.

Eleanor tried to ignore them. Listening to their complaints didn't make the trip any easier. The power of their suggestions made her reach behind, where her fumbling fingers discreetly unfastened the top button on the back of her cotton dress. Only the top button though, because she would never allow herself to look improper.

Eleanor straightened her back against the uncomfortable bench, reviewing the instructions Grandmother gave her on how to care for Bernadine. She'd also given her the three dollars for Father. Eleanor carried them in a hand-stitched fabric pouch along with seventy-six cents for her expenses; her comb with three teeth missing; and a note listing Eleanor's full name, age, address, Grandmother's name, and Aunt Bernadine's house number.

"In case you get lost," said Grandmother.

The telephone number to the Brentwood Hardware Company, where Father worked, was written on another slip of paper. Eleanor wanted to crumple and toss it away, but Grandmother had said that he was the only one who could pick her up at the train station at six thirty in the evening.

The train whistle blasted and signaled its arrival in Seattle. The final jolt of the coach forced Eleanor to realize she needed to figure out what to say to him. More than that, she wondered: *Would he still be angry? What would he say to her?* Before she climbed down the steps, she peered over the crowd and spotted Father nearby, wearing a round driving cap with a small, stiff brim.

Eleanor called to him while walking in his direction. "Hello Father."

His head jerked back as if in surprise. "Well, look at you." His blue eyes examined Eleanor from head to toe and looked longer than she felt comfortable at the emerging bumps on her chest. "I woulda never seen ya. You look different, all growed up.

"I'm eleven, going on twelve." Eleanor proudly lifted her chin.

"My car's in the parking lot." He pointed beyond the station door. "Your Granny said she'd pay me."

"Right." Eleanor dug into the pouch and pulled out three one-dollar bills. "Here."

He took the money and her satchel while she carried her pouch. They walked in silence until he pulled his keys out of his pocket and tossed them up, catching them on the way down. "Here it is." He opened the passenger door for her, then tossed her bag in the back seat. "So, your auntie's had troubles lately. I hear you're gonna take care of 'em." He snorted. "Good luck. Those kids is always scrapping. And Bernie don't look good."

Two small, crinkled lines came together between her brows. *How did he know about Bernadine's condition?*

She asked, "So, you visit them?"

"Why sure. We's friends."

Bernadine and Mike were friends with Father? How could they be? Didn't they know Grandmother called him a drunk? A scoundrel? Evidently, Bernadine didn't see eye-to-eye with Grandmother's opinion.

"Yeah, that sad sack Mike's been trying to keep the whole lot from starving, but he's dumber than a meathead."

"Grandmother says he's working nights at the shipyards. That's why he couldn't pick me up tonight."

"Shipyards? Ha." Haydon laughed so hard he started coughing. "Shipyards, is that what they says?" He steered the car through the tall city buildings and streetlights. "He's workin' at the docks all right. Cleanin' fish guts."

"He doesn't build ships?"

"Hell no. He's barely makin' ends meet. I think all he's really doin' is cleanin' the crappers on them stinkin' trawlers."

Hmm. That isn't what Bernadine said.

When she and Mike and their two children visited Grandmother last summer, Bernadine boasted about Mike's new job. And he told the family at dinner one night that he was the first one hired when the ship building industry finally picked up again after the Depression.

While Eleanor looked away from Father, she clenched her jaw not knowing who to believe.

"Say, did you hear my wife's expectin'?" He looked at her. "Suppose you don't know, I got married last year. Her name's Winnifred. Winnie for short. You should come over and meet her."

"I'm going to be pretty busy at Bernadine's."

"Humph."

Eleanor couldn't decide if he grumbled because he thought helping Bernadine was impossible or if he felt rejected. During the ride, silence built like a rock wall between them.

Eventually, they arrived at Mike and Bernadine's. Father got out of the car then lifted her bag out and placed it in front of her aunt's duplex. Blurting a quick "bye," he left his daughter standing alone on that humid August evening as he sped away, disappearing around the corner.

She breathed a sigh of relief that he was gone.

Bernadine must have heard the car leave because when Eleanor approached the front door, she called out from inside the house. "Come on in. The door's unlocked. I'm back here."

Eleanor followed her voice. She hadn't wanted to travel to Brentwood, but when she saw her aunt, Eleanor realized it was the right thing to do. Bernadine looked like a mess. She lay covered in a twisted heap of blankets. With a face the color of ash, her dark skin hung below her eyes. And, when Eleanor entered the bedroom, the stink of Clarence's dirty diaper overwhelmed her so much that she scrunched up her nose. Curtains hanging on the only window were drawn, making the light faint. She saw Bernadine's hair matted against her head, and she was thinner than the last time Eleanor saw her.

"Thanks for coming. How was your trip?" With the back of her hand, Bernadine wiped hair from her face. "Good thing you finally got here. I just fed Clarence. He needs a changing. His things are over there." She pointed to a low wooden dresser.

Eleanor sighed, put her case down and walked over to Bernadine's bed where she greeted her with a clumsy hug. Afterward she changed the baby's diaper.

"Thanks. You're going to be a lotta help."

Taking care of Clarence; Phillip, now six; and Victoria— along with Bernadine and Mike exhausted Eleanor. She wasn't accustomed to waking in the middle of the night to change and rock a baby, let alone figuring out what to do when he exploded into bouts of screaming colic.

In the mornings, she learned how to grind and brew coffee for them, realizing her aunt no longer followed Grandmother's or the church's rules about drinking caffeinated beverages. Once a week Eleanor gave the older children baths, where she quickly gained the cunning skill of confining Victoria in the tub before she scampered out naked and ran around in a lark.

Bernadine's bleeding stopped after the second week. Eleanor held her aunt's arm as she began walking inside the four-room bungalow. By the third week, the household functioned smoothly. Eleanor organized their laundry, washing Clarence and Victoria's diapers every day in a basin of boiling water on the cookstove. Meals; such as mush, or bread and jam for breakfasts; potatoes and carrots for midday dinners; and stews like Grandmother taught her for the suppers, became easier to make with each passing day.

When Eleanor finished giving the children baths, she got down on her knees and scrubbed their moldy bathroom and kitchen floors with hot water and soap. Neither looked like they had been washed for months.

When Eleanor wasn't cleaning or waiting on Bernadine and Clarence, she sang nursery rhyme ditties to the children and played simple games with them like find the hidden spoon. They laughed and skipped around her, sometimes following her like puppies.

Uncle Mike noticed, and nodding his head one morning after returning home from work, he said, "I ain't ever seen this place lookin' so good." The bottoms of his coveralls were wet and crusted with something awful smelling like acrid grease. His thick hair shot out in tufts from under his cap, and fatigue covered his red-cheeked face. Even though he always looked rough after work, his demeanor was kind, and he often beamed a big grin. "Yep, I wish you could stay longer." He whispered in such a way as to keep Bernadine from hearing his comments. "Because your flapjacks is better than Bernie's."

"I can't stay. My school starts in two weeks. So does Phillip's."

"Oh, right." He nodded his head as if Eleanor had jogged his memory.

During the last week of her stay, Father stopped by every evening to have dessert and coffee with Bernadine and Mike before he left for his night shift. It shocked her. Didn't her aunt know Father had been mean to her own sister?

"Why don't you give 'im a piece of your birthday cake you made today," said Mike.

"It's your birthday?" Haydon's mouth fell open. "Why, I plum forgot."

Eleanor hung back from him.

"Come on," said Mike. "He's drooling for a piece."

Reluctantly, Eleanor approached Father and served him a slice of Depression Cake, a dessert she mixed together without milk, butter, or eggs because the ingredients were too expensive.

She then plopped a sugar cube into his coffee.

He asked her about school.

"I got all 1's for character on my report card, zero tardies, no absences, and 90's on my subjects. And my teacher promoted me to sixth grade."

"Well, ain't you clever?" Father said.

"I want to go to college and be a singer when I grow up. Maybe in Hollywood or … what's the name of that big city?" Eleanor touched her forefinger to her lips to remember. "Oh, yeah, New York City."

"Go to college? Don't you wanna husband? Kids?" asked Father.

Before Eleanor answered, Bernadine chimed in. "She's a good singer. She plays the organ and church piano without music." Her aunt looked at her. "You just got it in your ears, don't ya?"

"Guess so," Eleanor nodded, "I can play hymns without reading any music."

"Wonder where she got that. I can't sing for nothin'." To prove it, Father began crooning off-key.

"Good God, stop," Mike pleaded as he held up his flat palm. "You sound like a dying donkey." The adults laughed.

Three nights before Eleanor planned to travel back home, Father visited again. This time she served peach cobbler. While they forked in bites of the dessert, Father asked, "Hey, why don't you come over tomorrow night? Meet Winnie and stay with us before you go home."

"I… I can't." Eleanor shook her head. "I need to stay here for–"

Bernadine broke in. "Of course, you can. I'm feeling better. It'd do you good to get away from these squalling kids."

Eleanor agreed; the kids sure did cry a lot, and little Victoria was downright sassy, but her distrust of her father's intentions outweighed the need to get away from the kids.

"No. I really need to stay–" Eleanor tried to convince the

three of them once more, but before she could finish, Father insisted, "That settles it then. I'll pick you up tomorrow after dinner."

"No!" exclaimed Eleanor in disagreement, but by the time she uttered it, the three of them had started talking about some horse race. They bickered on while Father lit a cigarette and stunk up the entire place with its smoke.

"What ya gonna wager?" asked Mike.

"Depends on the odds," Father said. "The way I see it, Seabiscuit ain't got no chance. That's why I'm leanin' toward Ligaroti, Bing Crosby's horse. Sure as hell, I'll get my bet in before them horses fly outta the gate."

"Not Ligaroti. He ain't got experience." Mike's face flushed red as he protested and waved his arm at Father.

While they debated, Eleanor bit her lower lip, thinking of excuses to get out of going. None came to mind.

Mike and Bernadine yawned. Father brought out keys from his pocket, getting ready to return to his house. Eleanor grew more confused. Since she didn't come up with a good reason to avoid staying at her father's, she relented before he left. "I guess getting away for one night would be okay."

"Good, Winnie's been wanting to meet ya."

The next evening Father drove Eleanor around town. He showed her the hardware company where he worked, then passed by the harbor, where ships, tugs, trawlers, barges, and sailboats were moored, before turning onto the highway.

About ten minutes later, Haydon slowed and pointed to a stretch along the Brentwood River. "This is where your mum died. Did you know I was the first one there?"

Eleanor shook her head and turned away. She didn't want

to look where Mama had died. Instead, she pressed herself close to the door and stared at the trees, the bushes, the river. Anything but that horrible spot on the road.

"What'd you do?"

"I helped the police. I told 'em I saw her layin' in the bushes."

Eleanor frowned at him. "You saw her?"

Father glared at Eleanor across the front seat, and in a tone as hard as when he crushed his cigarettes into the ground, he said, "She was two-timing me. While we was still married. Can you believe it?"

Eleanor had learned bits and pieces of the story from Grandmother. But she'd never heard of Mama cheating or that Father had seen her in the bushes. Their conflicting stories weren't making any sense.

Silence followed, building that wall again. No more words were spoken between them for the rest of the ride.

Within minutes, he steered into a neighborhood and eventually stopped the car in front of a clapboard house. Winnie must have been waiting. As soon as Father got out of the car, she opened the front door, greeting them with one hand on her hip.

"It's taken you forever to get home." Eleanor thought her accusing nasal voice could be heard all the way across the street. "I've been waiting here for hours."

The first thing Eleanor noticed was Winnie's blonde hair. Brassy from a bottle is what Aunt Anna would have called it. Even though Winnie's hair was bright, her housedress was drab and worn. It bulged at her abdomen where a baby grew.

Father shouted at Winnie, "I gotta work late sometimes!"

What a strange thing to say. He hadn't worked late at all. The truth was, when he came to pick her up, he stayed talking with Mike and Bernadine, eating left-over peach cobbler and drinking coffee. She looked away but didn't contradict his lie. Eleanor had learned the hard way, from her aunt Virginia, not to interfere when someone fibbed.

Winnie introduced herself and scrutinized Eleanor up and down several times through round-rimmed glasses.

"Pretty dress," she said.

"Thank you." Eleanor swished her hand along the soft fabric. "My grandmother made it new for this trip."

"Hmm." Winnie nodded as if she approved. Her head tilted back ever so slightly as she peered down her button nose. "Haydon's talked about you."

Eleanor didn't know what to say, so she stood staring down at her shoes during the awkward moment. "I hear you've been over at Bernie and Mike's house."

Eleanor nodded. "I've been helping them. Clarence is a good baby, and Bernadine's feeling better now."

"Good." She nodded and then pointed toward the couch in the living room. "You can put your little bag down there."

Winnie watched Eleanor place her pouch on the rug near her satchel that her father had carried in.

"Here, I'll show you around, since you're staying."

Eleanor began to follow her through the two-story house. *Maybe this won't be so bad. At least this isn't the same house he lived in when he tricked me.*

Winnie started, "That's our bedroom back there." She pointed to the right. "Our bathroom. And here's the kitchen. Haydon got me a new icebox a couple months ago. It runs on electricity, but it can't nearly hold the butter and milk we need." Twisting her lips into an ugly grimace, she shrugged her right shoulder as though the appliance was not good enough. Eleanor imagined Grandmother's face lighting up if she could have an automatic icebox. Instead of buying ice and shoving the heavy frozen block inside the wooden frame, she'd be glad to store bottles of just-skimmed cream, thick hunks of butter, goat cheese, and eggs in such a modern contraption.

Winnie rambled as she walked around. "You sure got here during a devil of a hot spell. The weather's awful. Ninety-six degrees today is just too darned hot." She started up the stairs.

"Hear that?" Winnie asked and then eyed Eleanor with irritation.

She nodded.

An approaching train shook the house and blew its wailing whistle as it thundered by.

"It's a dad-gummed train. When he bought this place, Haydon didn't tell me about it. It runs along the river, a couple of blocks from here. Blasts its dang whistle just before bed and at two in the mornin.' Every night. Makes me so mad when it wakes me up." Winnie prattled at a rapid clip, hardly taking a breath between sentences.

"Don't know if you noticed," Winnie patted her waist, quieting her voice to almost a whisper, "I'm with child. Now Haydon's working late. Gets home at wee hours in the morning. What am I gonna' do if the baby comes and he isn't around?"

Eleanor thought about her question because she momentarily felt sorry for her. "Maybe Bernadine could help," she offered.

"Yeah. Maybe so."

Soon Eleanor lost interest in looking at the rooms. After they walked downstairs into the living room, Eleanor yawned, signaling to Winnie that she wanted to go to sleep. Getting up several times in the middle of the night and taking care of her aunt's family had exhausted Eleanor and left her as limp as a withered autumn leaf. All she wanted to do was lie down and sleep and sleep and sleep.

Winnie must have understood. "Okey dokey. Come on, Haydon. She's tired." She motioned to him to get up from his upholstered chair where he sat reading a newspaper, smoking a cigarette, and drinking something in a squatty brown bottle. "Go get the cot for Eleanor," she told him. "It's in the closet."

In what looked like a genuine token of kindness, Winnie fluffed a pillow, placed it on top of the cot, and suggested Eleanor sleep under the open window. "You'll be more comfortable. You might get some night breeze."

Eleanor thanked her and said good night. Once she climbed onto it, she believed she'd be dreaming soon. Instead of sleeping though, she tossed from her back to her side and to her back again for a while. As she stared out the window, too many thoughts from the past day crisscrossed in her mind, such as Father's version of Mama's death and his lie to Winnie.

While peering around the room, the late August moonlight peaked through the window, casting a dreary gray on Eleanor's things. On a mahogany chair lay her green dress, neatly folded at the waist with its sleeves tucked under the bodice. Her brown sweater, a hand-me-down from Virginia, hung on the back of it. Worn at the heels and nearly through the soles, her polished shoes touched each other and lined up side by side on the rug as if in a marching band. Eleanor did not want to be at Father's house, but studying her clothes created a sense of familiarity and helped her feel a bit more comfortable there.

The train rumbled by, waking Eleanor from a fitful sleep. She detected men's voices upstairs where a dim beam shone. Shadows seemed to hide secrets down the oak stairs and banister. As her eyelids fluttered slowly, drifting between groggy awareness and slumber, she wondered why there were men upstairs in the middle of the night.

"Shuddup." Eleanor heard Father's voice snap like a whip from upstairs.

She opened her eyes completely and stared through a haze of stale, reeking smoke at three men staggering down the narrow staircase as they laughed and elbowed each other. One of them wore a police uniform.

"Helluva game," a man with dark hair said, slurring his words.

Another wore his cap cockeyed and held his index finger to his clamped mouth. "Shush!" Then he started singing, "O Danny Boy, the pipes... the pipes they are a calling."

The police officer blurted, "Christ. Quit your groaning. Don't wake up Haydon's old lady or there'll be hell to pay." They laughed gregariously.

Eleanor couldn't figure out what was going on. Instantly, pulling the blanket over her nightgown to her chin, she almost stopped breathing. She remained motionless, afraid they would see her. The man with the dark hair, lumbering down the wooden stairs, tripped and tumbled forward.

Father muttered, following behind. "Next time I'm gonna get my money back from the son-of-a-bitch who stole it from me. I'm talkin' to you, Danny Boy. Five bucks." He shook his fist. "Five bucks you owe me and a bottle o' whiskey."

The three men left and father closed the front door. Outside, one kept droning his woeful tune; another laughed; and soon a car engine chugged, revved, and motored away.

Too tired to keep her eyelids open, Eleanor let them slide shut. She figured it was about two in the morning since she'd just heard the train whistle call in the distance. Meanwhile, in the kitchen, bottles clinked, water ran, and afterward the toilet flushed. Quiet blanketed the house, and Eleanor slept.

She awoke, startled, when she heard a belt buckle clink and seconds later the zip of pants. Instantly, an enormous weight crushed her.

Words hissed into her face. Hot breaths nauseated her. "I'm gonna be your first."

Eleanor recognized that raspy voice. She tried to scream.

Before she could, Father slapped his thick hand and barrel-round fingers over her mouth until his power mashed her lips into her teeth. Squirming did her no good. His muscular arms whipped away Eleanor's blanket. A monster hand groped under her nightgown, and his belly nearly suffocated her.

Reacting to the horror, Eleanor tried to bite his fingers and started grunting loud enough for Winnie to hear.

He snarled. "Shut up! Shut up or I'll…" Acrid stench frothed from his mouth.

Like a spring river rushing over its banks, fear flooded Eleanor. Her thighs hurt as he gripped them and pushed them wide apart. She shrank beneath him and squeezed her eyes tight.

His heinous savagery made her struggle, twisting until she tasted the hint of metallic blood in her mouth. He thrust his sweaty flesh repeatedly as he inched closer to her panties.

Eleanor tried to yell, "Stop! Stop!!" But her words came out muffled.

He kicked her shin. She willed herself not to die and rallied. A combination of fury and terror pulsed through her with each beat of her heart. She found two spots on either side of his broad shoulders and pushed him with newfound strength, then kicked his legs with her feet. Under her, the cot rocked and groaned. Father's huge body faltered, shifted as if falling to the right. But he grabbed the left edge of the folding bed and resumed his position.

Just as Eleanor attempted to push again, the downstairs bedroom door creaked. A grim light seeped from the bedroom where Winnie emerged.

"What the hell?" he sputtered under his breath. "Don't say nothin'," he demanded, rolling off from her and zipping his pants.

He called out to Winnie in a tense voice, "I'm a comin'." Tucking in his shirt, he said in a sweeter tone, "The boys is gone. I'm comin' to bed, honey." His ugly head twisted, and eyeballing her, he shook his index finger in warning. "Remember, not a word!" he fumed in a fiery whisper. His eyes, black and cold, bore into her soul, making her feel filthy and ugly.

Eleanor gasped bruised breaths, lifted herself to her elbows, then bolted upright. Vomit burned her throat, filled her mouth, and she retched all over the blanket. When Eleanor touched her lips, blood stained her fingers. In between silent whimpers and heaving sobs, she found the hem of her nightgown and tugged it down hard to cover her legs and toes. She then clasped her arms tight around her aching thighs.

For the rest of the night, Eleanor wanted to curl into a fetal position. But she sat rigid and watchful at their bedroom door for signs of him. She wanted to scream. Hit the walls. Flee. Block out the memory but couldn't. Instead, she started questioning and blaming herself.

Why didn't I stay at Bernadine's? I'm so stupid.

But how was I to know? I should always know something will go wrong when I'm around him.

Minutes passed. In Eleanor's mind's eye the attack struck

as quickly as flashes of August lightning. Again and again in a nightmare she couldn't stop.

~

At the first light of dawn, robins sang outside of the large open window. To them, nothing had happened. The world went on as usual—somewhere babies cried, men dressed for work, mamas made coffee and breakfast, trains traveled on tracks. To them, the day was normal. It was anything but normal to Eleanor.

Her own father had violated her with what vulgar Harry at school called his pecker. It was sinful.

Eleanor, full of frantic breaths, clenched her fists, wanting to hit his face; his big nose; fat stomach. She hated him. Without waiting until Father and Winnie woke, she tiptoed into the toilet and scrubbed her face and hands as hard as she could tolerate until her skin blotched red from the rough irritation. She wanted to be clean. Whole. Fresh. Not foul. But she could still smell his deceit. When she put on her dress, she saw purple and blue welts in the shape of fingers imprinted on her thighs.

Eleanor sat, unable to move after dressing. By the time Winnie got up, dragging her feet in pink slippers across the floor to the kitchen, Eleanor had already folded the blanket—hiding the vomit—and laid it on the cot. She packed all her things into the valise and was ready to go back to Bernadine and Mike's.

Winnie walked into the sitting room. "I'm gonna make some coffee. Wanna glass of milk?"

Eleanor couldn't look at her. Everything inside of Eleanor felt cold, empty. Her eyes stared at the brown floor where she sat. She shook her head while rising, then walked to her packed case.

"You okay?"

"I'm not hungry." Eleanor's words were flat. "I should get back to Bernadine. She'll need me this morning."

"So early? I'm not even dressed yet." Her shoulders shrugged. "I'll go wake Haydon."

"No!" Her voice exploded with rage. And shame. Eleanor took a breath to calm herself. She sat down and suggested in a tone as chipper as she could muster, "No. Let him sleep. He needs his rest. He works long hours." Feigning concern, she hoped her clever charade would convince Winnie.

"You're right about that. He's been working late a lot. Okey dokey, I'll get some clothes on and I'll drive you." She walked toward the bedroom and added, "How about we stop by Bernie's this evening so you can say bye to your daddy?"

Eleanor twisted her head and glared at Winnie. The thought of seeing Father made Eleanor sick. She didn't answer. Instead, she sat stiff on the edge of the mahogany chair near the front door. Arms crossed, eyes down, she pressed her swollen lips together, trying not to vomit.

Half an hour later, Eleanor walked into Bernadine's home. Her aunt wore a clean housedress with a muslin apron. The color in her cheeks had returned, proving she was recovering and regaining her strength. Phillip shrieked and chased Victoria around the front room while Clarence napped in a wicker laundry basket and Mike slept.

"Well, how was your visit with your daddy?"

"Swell." Eleanor lied. She vowed she'd never tell Bernie or Grandmother, because she wanted to crawl under a rock in embarrassment, feeling dirty inside and out, like she did something to cause the attack. If Eleanor told Grandmother, she'd scold her because talking about it was sinful.

She'd just say to forget about it. And to go on as if nothing happened.

Instead of describing Winnie's incessant complaints, Father's party upstairs with strange men, and his evil sexual assault, Eleanor scanned the kitchen, trying to switch off her memory of the previous night. Food-crusted dishes were stacked near the sink. "Here, let me help with the dishes."

"By golly, I'm gonna miss you. You been real handy around here. I can see why Ma wanted you to come." Bernadine smiled, then turned her attention to the children. "Hey you two, shut up. Your daddy's sleepin'." Bernadine cleared the breakfast table as she admitted to Eleanor, "At first, I didn't like the notion. You being so young and all. But you're a purty good cook, like Ma."

Eleanor twitched while Bernie talked a while longer. Words were trapped inside of her in the stifling August air. Hoping to hide her shame, Eleanor avoided eye contact with her aunt as well.

Water splashed into the sink as Eleanor shook powdered soap in. The caustic odor of the cheap detergent puffed upwards and burned inside her nostrils. At that point, she didn't mind. She didn't mind the smell or washing the dishes because it meant clean, and she wanted her hands clean. She wanted to wash all over; but that would have to come later.

"Say, I got something for you." A curl from Bernadine's hair bobbed and she walked toward her bedroom and brought out a scratched and dinged up wooden box. She opened the lid, riffled through papers, and pulled out a wrinkled, yellowed newspaper clipping. "You might be a bit young for this, but I kept the article about your Ma's accident. Do you

81

want it?" Without letting Eleanor answer, she shoved it into her hand.

Eleanor's wet fingers soaked the paper. Although it was thin, it seemed to weigh a hundred pounds. She wished everybody would just stop talking about Mama's death. Wavering between ripping it into hundreds of pieces or saving it, Eleanor stashed it in her pocket. "I'll look at it soon."

Six

1938

That next morning, Eleanor could not leave her aunt and uncle's place fast enough. While Mike drove her to the train station, away from that ugly town of Brentwood, she held no regrets whatsoever about leaving them and the children without any more help.

Eleanor never told Grandmother about Father. After her return, nightmares of his crushing weight and groping hands haunted her. Not only did she keep it secret, though, she grew angry at Grandmother for trusting Father to pick her up at the depot. Grandmother should've known better. Arranging for Father to drive her was a sin.

Grandmother's sin.

~

Several days later, on one of the last summer afternoons before school started, Eleanor stole away to the nearby creek, where she could find solitude. Sitting on the small bank, she got up the nerve to read the newspaper article Aunt Bernadine had given to her. With shaking hands, Eleanor unfolded the paper and read the detailed account of her mama's accident.

WEDNESDAY, DECEMBER 14, 1927
BRENTWOOD WOMAN LOSES HER
LIFE IN AUTO ACCIDENT
Wife of Delivery Driver Is Victim of Mishap
The Seattle News

BRENTWOOD, Wednesday, December 14—

Mrs. Margarete Bowerman Owens, wife of Haydon Owens, a Brentwood delivery driver, was killed last night when the car in which she was driving crashed on the highway near Brentwood River. Inside the car was Mrs. Owens' infant, who survived.

Brentwood County officials today were investigating the circumstances surrounding the fatal accident, which was said to have occurred when the car lost control skidding on the slippery surface, and crashed into the guardrail, splintering and knocking over 140 feet of fence. Mrs. Owens was thrown from the automobile and killed instantly.

With one or two witnesses to question, Deputy Prosecutor Terrance W. Grote said, "If responses from the remaining people to be questioned are the same as those obtained so far, I think Mrs. Owens was driving too fast on the slippery paving. There was no evidence of drinking. The car was badly smashed. It seems surprising the car could have hit the fence in so many places." Not only was Owens' automobile demolished, and the woman thrown fifty feet from it, but twelve six by six guard posts and the heavy timber fencing on them were shattered about the scene. "It appears to be an isolated incident," said Deputy Prosecutor Grote. Mrs. Owens' child was admitted to Brentwood General and released this morning when it was found the child's injuries consisted of merely a shaking up. The infant is currently under the care of her grandmother, Mrs. Delores Bowerman. The body of Mrs. Owens is at the Smith Funeral Parlor where services will be held at one o'clock, Friday afternoon. Burial will be in the Brentwood Cemetery.

Eleanor hadn't talked much since she came home from Bernadine's. After reading the article, there was one thing Eleanor *did* want to talk to Grandmother about—the accident. Was there something besides the weather that caused the car crash? How did Father get there so quickly? Unanswered questions lingered. All Eleanor wanted was the truth.

Her trembling fingers shook the piece of newspaper when she read about herself and her mother. She wanted Mama here so much. She gave a mournful sigh loud enough to scare away blue-winged dragonflies flitting on nearby rocks. Whiffs of moist earth rose from the mud banks while the creek burbled. If only everything was as clear as water. As easy as watching dragonflies.

Eleanor carefully folded the article and tucked it away. She got up convinced.

Mama didn't cheat on him.

Near summer's end in 1940, Hitler's blitzkrieg had invaded Britain. Eleanor, now thirteen, packed apple crates and cardboard boxes with Virginia because they were moving again; this time to live in Miss Ingrid Nelsen's cottage in Walla

Walla, a small town just twelve miles north in Washington. Only Eleanor, Virginia, and Grandmother were moving because Ernst had married, and Mattias lived with his brother and wife because they had an extra room in their rented home. That left the running of the Millston household and the cost of rent to Grandmother. Taking in laundry and sometimes nursing patients in her home was not enough to afford the costs.

As she labored to maintain their lives within their small community, folks in the nearby small towns became acquainted with Grandmother's nursing skills. When they could not drive through heavy snow or pay a doctor, they came to her. Money was scarce, so they bartered for her services with sacks of milled grains, sugar, dried beans, or sometimes chickens. She treated burns, stitched up wounds, and one day even set Seth Langley's dislocated elbow.

He came with his dad the previous winter during a January storm. "We nearly slid here," said Mr. Langley as they entered Grandmother's house. His twelve-year-old son, Seth, was holding his elbow, howling in pain. "Seth fell on the ice, and you can see here, his bone's out of place."

Grandmother examined his arm, up to his shoulder and down to his fingertips. Seth grimaced. She told him, "When the Good Lord created us, He made us flexible. I'll be able to fix you up in no time." Her hands, roughened from laundry, stroked his shoulder. "Now, I'm going to let you know what I'm doing. Nothing to be scared of." But before she said another word, she tightened her grip and gave a sudden, yet careful, pull to his forearm. A muffled *pop* sounded. The bones snapped back into place as Seth let out a yell.

Moments later he grinned and said to Grandmother, "You did it!" He stared wide-eyed at his elbow as if it were brand new.

"Well, I went ahead and put it right. Before you had a chance to get scared and jerk your arm away."

~

Based on news about Grandmother's skills, she was hired eight months later to nurse homebound Miss Nelsen, who suffered from a chronic cough and wheezing. Eleanor hated the idea, especially when she learned Virginia and she would have to sleep on an old, lumpy couch.

Before they left for Miss Nelsen's house, Grandmother and Eleanor woke up extra early and stayed up late for two days harvesting and canning corn, tomatoes, cucumbers, and squashes while Virginia flitted about with her boyfriend, Jim, a scrawny kid with pimples on his face like an adolescent, who had driven her around all summer on his motorcycle.

On Friday afternoon, hours before Sabbath, the kitchen had a pleasant smell of accomplishment. Grandmother and Eleanor had packed boxes full of glass jars with food that could last them through winter. Eleanor started singing the soprano notes and motioned to Grandmother to carry the alto tune of "Come, Ye Thankful People."

Come, ye thankful people, come, raise the song of harvest home;

All is safely gathered in, ere the winter storms begin.

As they cleaned up corn husks and cucumber peels, Eleanor enjoyed a few moments of harmony. During this bit of closeness between them, she was ready to ask Grandmother about her mother's death, but Virginia and Jim barged through the front door, letting it bang behind them. Their windswept hair and dusty faces gave way to grins and laughter.

"We just got married," said Virginia, holding Jim's hand.

"You what?" Grandmother's tone demanded rather than questioned. Her reaction surprised Eleanor because she rarely scolded Virginia.

"Got hitched." Jim's head cocked to one side.

"What about school?" Eleanor asked.

"We don't need school," said Jim.

Grandmother's stare fell, turning hard and cold as if she could not believe her daughter, whom Eleanor always believed was Grandmother's favorite, had made a drastic mistake. She mumbled to herself, but Eleanor heard her say, "What a nitwit." Her voice barked, directing her question to Jim. "What are you two going to live on? You don't have a job. Never even tried to find one."

"Don't worry. I'll get one."

As abruptly as they dashed in, they left again.

Outside, Virginia turned toward Grandmother and shouted, "I'll be back later to get my stuff!"

On Sunday morning, Ernst arrived in his car and helped Grandmother and Eleanor load their belongings. Grandmother, more irritable than usual, criticized Eleanor. "Hurry up with your packing. And don't make so much noise." She yelled like a stubborn mule. "Get in here this minute. Help me roll up this rug."

Eleanor guessed she missed Virginia. When she and Grandmother finished moving some of their things into Miss Nelsen's cottage and storing their furniture and other goods in her detached garage, Eleanor found Grandmother pacing in the kitchen and muttering. "How could she? My baby." With another step, Grandmother's tone changed to disdain. "What a knucklehead."

Within the first days of living in Miss Nelsen's so-called cottage, Grandmother and Eleanor scrubbed the house, which was nothing more than a one-story, two-bedroom place, filthy and full of cockroaches from years of neglect. Accumulated grease on pans smelled rancid. Heavy odors of must invaded the room from closets full of soiled clothing. And urine reeked from Miss Nelsen's bedroom.

Grandmother laundered clothes and linens, and set rat traps while Eleanor swept cobwebs from the ceilings and washed dishes and cupboards. Even though Grandmother had rented shacks and once even an old barn for their housing, she insisted on keeping them clean. Through the years, she was lucky she also had her own children and Eleanor to do chores.

About Miss Nelsen, Grandmother scoffed. "She doesn't know how to keep a house." But when Miss Nelsen, a former schoolmarm, whose family lived in Connecticut, became sick and infirm, her feeble condition prevented her from taking care of herself.

Although Eleanor didn't like living in her house, she pressed her lips into a sympathetic face because she guessed that Miss Nelsen had once entertained friends in her home. By the time Grandmother and Eleanor moved in, the frail woman, always coughing, with clothes hung loose over her bony shoulders, was likely a shell of her former self.

By mid-September, Eleanor adjusted to eighth grade, met new friends and teachers, and started studying Washington history. The autumn month rolled along mildly like the surrounding Walla Walla hills. However, by October, early winter winds struck. The storms of war in Europe blew nervous currents, surging ominously toward Ernst and Mattias after President Roosevelt signed the 1940 Conscription Act.

Thinking about the Conscription Act and the unknown, Eleanor wrapped her arms around herself. The unknown, an insidious fear she couldn't see or smell in front of her, caused her dread that Ernst would be sent to fight in World War II as the act required all men between the ages of twenty-one and thirty-six to register for the draft. Ernst was twenty-four, and Mattias was heading toward twenty-one.

Grandmother and Eleanor, along with Miss Nelsen, draped in a lap robe, sat bolted next to the radio, where it stood on a white crocheted doily and a walnut six-legged table. Beneath it the rug, once plush, was worn and faded. On October 29, each of them sat on the couch, staring at the radio speaker's tweed fabric as distant and brittle noises reached them over the airwaves. President Roosevelt called out the first lottery number.

"The first number is one—five—eight."

"I hope that's not Ernst's number," Eleanor said, squirming.

"Me too," Grandmother agreed, then circled her knobby fingers around her hands in a nervous habit.

At school, Eleanor's new friends proudly talked about older brothers and uncles eager to volunteer and join the military. Fervent patriotism bubbled up, and the need to fight the Nazis became one of the most discussed subjects.

Eleanor grew more uneasy each day because Grandmother's family had immigrated from Germany. She had been conceived there but was born in America.

One day Eleanor whispered to her so Miss Nelsen couldn't hear. "We have German blood in us, don't we?"

Grandmother nodded.

"Should we keep it a secret?"

"I'm American." Grandmother lifted her chin up and smiled.

"Yeah, but people might think we side with the Nazis. With your last name and all."

"I don't believe in fighting. And I certainly don't side with the Nazis." Grandmother's face paled, as if thinking about Eleanor's questions. "Just don't talk about it. Anyway, it's Ernst I'm worried about."

Eleanor bobbed her head in agreement.

Since President Roosevelt's announcement, Pastor Knight at the Walla Walla church preached about the difficult times.

When his voice thundered over the pulpit, Eleanor's shoulders shuddered. Her breath quickened when she pondered what might happen to her uncles.

"We're not war resisters. We do not refuse service to our country," Pastor Knight said, enunciating each word with distinction. "We are noncombatants. We refuse to bear arms."

His eyes slowly scanned the congregation. "I must advise you, especially you men, authorities will prosecute. Anyone who evades registration or chooses—as our faith decrees—to become a conscientious objector ..." He looked up.

His intense eyes and prolonged pause made Eleanor's stomach tighten.

"Or falsifies personal information..."

When Eleanor heard that, she blew out a sigh of relief. All was well because Ernst and Mattias had registered. Each had a serial number. They were safe.

The pastor continued and looked down through tiny round eyeglasses. He read from notes. "In theory, a man can appeal," he lifted his head and added, "but the Army won't let appeals for conscientious objection delay your draft, and this is what I'm concerned about."

A woman who sat in front of Eleanor sniffled.

"Our men might—probably will—face harassment, beatings, court martials. Even prison for adhering to our faith convictions. And you must know ... families of these men might also face harsh scorn. We were witness to those atrocities during World War I."

Court martial? The pastor's preaching sounded like a gnawing ringing in Eleanor's ears. She tried to stop listening in order to calm her shaking.

One Saturday in December, Eleanor rubbed her hands together. The friction warmed her fingers while she walked out of church on a windy, loden-gray day. It was almost noon. Eleanor buttoned her coat while Grandmother and she headed back to Miss Nelsen's. As they reached her yard, Ernst, with his wife Sylvia and Mattias, drove up in his jalopy.

"What a surprise," Grandmother said, opening her arms wide. "I wasn't expecting you." She grinned and hugged her oldest son.

"Ma," Ernst held a letter, "I got some news."

"Good, I hope." Grandmother's face lifted with what looked like anticipation.

"Not really." He sighed long and heavily. "I got drafted. They read my number." His body slumped while Grandmother leaned forward as though waiting to hear his next words.

The fear Eleanor previously hadn't been able to see or

smell became real. Visions of horror leaped before her mind's eye.

"Oh, no," Eleanor cried and drew nearer to him, putting her hand on his shoulder.

Soon they settled in Miss Nelsen's kitchen. Eleanor twisted the spigot, holding the kettle while water dribbled out of the faucet. She lit the cooking stove to heat water for cups of Postum.

Ernst spoke in a quiet voice, hoping that Miss Nelsen couldn't hear while in her bed. Holding the draft card in his hand, he said, "I got this form yesterday. I have five days—four now—to return it. It has lots of questions; like my job, my dependents, and a place where I can write to request exemption." Ernst's face furrowed.

Grandmother wobbled. Her eyes widened. In a tight whisper, she asked, "What are you going to do?" Her words sounded grave, deliberate.

Ernst shrugged and shook his head. "I'm not sure yet. I've got to work this out. One thing's for sure, if I claim conscientious objection, it's criminal. But I can't support killing."

Uncle Sam and campaigns urging men to do their duty and fight with rifles and bombs against the fascist governments clashed with the church's position. Silence sank in the kitchen like a heavy rock thrown into a deep well.

Finally, Grandmother broke the stillness. "Wars only bring wars." She lamented with her eyes closed. "And nations shall rise against nations. There will be no peace. It will all end in the battle at Armageddon," she recited, as if it would make the nightmare go away.

Mattias, who usually did not add much during family conversations, said, "I heard some guys are becoming medics. They're in the war. Just not carrying guns."

Ernst stared forward at a kitchen cabinet. Sylvia, his

young wife, hadn't uttered a word. She simply twisted her wedding band and occasionally dabbed her eyes with a rumpled white handkerchief.

"I'd do that," Ernst said optimistically. "But it still might be hard on you." He looked at each of them. "If I have to go to the front lines without a gun, the men might call me a deserter. Even a traitor. They'll hate me for my beliefs. That could get back to you."

"It's what God says," Grandmother said, defending her faith. "We'll stand by you, son. So will our church brethren." She placed her gnarled hand on his.

Impulsively and unaware of any consequences that might befall her, Eleanor exclaimed, "I don't care if people hate me."

"Yeah," Mattias agreed as he grasped the arm that always trembled.

Afraid Eleanor would never see Ernst again, she followed him around the house as he paced, to the front room, then back to the kitchen where she served him more cups of hot Postum and dished up a big heap of potatoes on his plate.

Days passed. Whenever she ate breakfast, Eleanor's foot jerked back and forth as she worried about her uncle. Walking to and from school, and lying in bed at night, she imagined the worst—Ernst in a prison with his head hung low and leg irons clanging behind him. Or, she envisioned him facing enemy fire, risking his life on the battlefields of Europe with nothing to defend himself. Eleanor shivered. Both images chilled her as if war blew its stiff winds on her neck. So, she decided to pray, which she rarely did anymore, except during church or with Grandmother before meals. Eleanor usually found that praying never did any good. Especially, when she had prayed for Mama to come back. Prayed Fran and Pete could adopt her. Prayed for her family to have enough money to eat. Yet, maybe this time, a prayer for Ernst might be answered.

Eleanor didn't want Ernst to kill anyone, but the church and God went against what America and other nations were trying to accomplish. She didn't want to be different from her schoolmates, teachers, or townsfolk. She wanted to show her patriotism. Maybe fighting was right. Perhaps the church was wrong. Anyway, why were boys sent to jail because of the church?

Overcome with circling questions, Eleanor frowned and didn't know what to think. Falling back on old habits, in bed that night she folded her hands, closed her eyes, and whispered, "God, please help Uncle Ernst. Keep him out of jail. Don't let anybody beat him up. Amen."

In the afternoons Eleanor usually went to the post box and brought back the mail for Grandmother. However, since Ernst's draft notice, Grandmother had taken on that task. Eleanor wondered why, figuring he'd probably drive to see them with news about his draft status since they only lived about twelve minutes away. Grandmother must have known he would write, though, because on December 24, a letter from him arrived. Eleanor saw Grandmother swallow hard. Her hands twitched as she tore along the envelope flap with a butter knife to open the letter.

Standing by her side, Eleanor held her breath while she read it out loud.

"Dear Ma and Little Robin."

Eleanor smiled momentarily and felt warm inside because he hadn't called her that nickname for several years.

"I can't afford gas to visit during this Christmas season. Besides, the roads are slick today. The Lord must have answered my prayers. I handed in my draft card and got a reply. They have deferred me."

Grandmother and Eleanor whooped and sighed. Grandmother continued reading.

"They wrote that I work in one of our country's essential trades at the mill. Lumber is needed overseas for the war. My classification is II-A. I'm exempt as long as I keep working. Sylvia is so full of joy and so am I. And we got more news."

Eleanor exhaled, almost sobbing. "More news?"

"He says more news," she snapped. "Now let me finish."

"We weren't sure the last time we were up, but Sylvia's in the family way. Have a happy Christmas and blessings be with all of you. Your son, Ernst."

"Oh, golly." Eleanor laughed and leaped around the room while Grandmother smiled and reread the letter over and over. Eleanor started singing, "Ernst is safe, Ernst is safe," to the tune of "Silent Night," one of her favorite carols. Finally, Eleanor exclaimed, "This is the best Christmas ever!"

Eleanor never knew if her prayer helped, but one thing was for sure: she could finally show her patriotism.

Seven

1941

After Miss Nelsen passed away, Grandmother and Eleanor relocated back to Millston, Oregon. Mattias moved back in with them because Sylvia and Ernst wanted the extra room for their daughter.

Eleanor was looking forward to the return as it would give her a chance to see Fran and Pete again. Although, with Pete's long hours at the mill, Fran's volunteer work organizing food and clothing drives, and Eleanor's increased school involvement, she was not certain they would actually have the time to visit together. War was raging on and affecting everyone.

The conflicts compelled Grandmother, Mattias, and Eleanor and the nation to listen to more radio news broadcasts. Eager for details yet deeply shocked, Grandmother and Eleanor both gasped when they heard about the attack on Pearl Harbor. Mattias shook his head as if in disbelief. They kept the radio on all that Sunday, and none of them hardly moved the entire afternoon. Grandmother covered her lap with a small quilt and swayed quickly back and forth in her oak rocking chair while Eleanor had to reread the same page of her text over and over because she was having difficulty focusing on her history assignment.

At school, Eleanor joined other girls after classes and rolled bandages for the American Red Cross to ship to the battlefront. She wrote letters to servicemen about the school's sports, news from eastern Oregon, and the top ten songs on the radio. Mattias helped Grandmother hang dark curtains over the windows. They turned out their one electric light and practiced blackouts at night.

When the U.S. entered the war after Pearl Harbor, the draft age decreased to eighteen. The unthinkable happened again: Mattias got his draft notice. He traveled to Spokane, where he was required to report. Grandmother and Eleanor's anxiety mounted as they waited throughout the day for his return. Late that night, he came home. Grandmother ran to greet him when she heard his footsteps shuffle through the front door.

"What's your news?" Gray desperation filled her voice.

His ashen gaze dropped to the floor. "I'm 4-F." Both his limp and arm tremor appeared more pronounced than when he had left earlier. "My leg and hand…" That was all he said. He did not have to say anything more. He was medically unfit to serve.

As months passed, Eleanor and others in the community waved their arms and said goodbye to boys who hadn't yet finished high school when they left to serve in the military. By June of 1944, young men were absent from stocking shelves in grocery stores, filling cars with gasoline at stations, and harvesting crops. In the surrounding agricultural area and businesses, vacancies left by the men and boys required women and girls to work at the fruit packing houses and canneries.

School closed a week earlier than normal that year for the pea harvest. Eleanor, sixteen, worked at the Fitzwater Pea Cannery. The company whistle's blast signaled the end of the Saturday shift. She had worked six days in a row. Grandmother had temporarily stopped enforcing Eleanor's Saturday Sabbath because the work was too important for the war effort. The fields of peas had to be harvested, processed, and shipped to the service men and women at the front lines.

The harvest was plentiful. *"A bumper crop,"* Eleanor had heard from one of the field hands.

"Plenty to feed every one of the boys fighting overseas," said Mrs. Greer, the warehouse supervisor. "Even mine."

Clanking machines wound down and quieted. Workers started shuffling out the doors and through the gate, toward their homes. Eleanor hung up her apron and hair net on a hook, then grabbed her purse. Glad to be done with the week's work and anticipating a day off on Sunday, Eleanor and two of her friends, finally finished with their ten-hour shift, decided to walk to town for a refreshment at the High-Hat Café.

Eleanor sat at the window next to Janice Metheny, her best friend, whom she'd met in home economics. In class Janice's nimble fingers tatted intricate lace while Eleanor's fumbled with a crochet hook and thread. Janice sewed cute bows and a pocket on her apron while Eleanor stuck herself with the sharp needles. But when they both went to choir, Eleanor was the one who could sing and carry a tune.

Corine Hosinski, another friend from high school, sat opposite Eleanor and Janice in the café booth. Her blonde hair and finely featured face made boys turn their heads in her direction. She never minded that kind of attention. Each of the girls had a straw in a five-cent bottle of Coca-Cola. In addition to abandoning Saturday Sabbath, Eleanor no longer cared about Grandmother's church belief that caffeinated drinks were sinful. She let the dark, cold soda sparkle in her mouth and fizz down her throat.

"Sure was hot today," Janice said, fanning her olive-skinned face and thick dark brows with her hand. "I nearly croaked in there." With her other fingers, she held a pencil over a crossword puzzle she was trying to solve.

"Yeah, I nearly sweat to death," agreed Corine. "How are you doing on that seaming machine?" she asked Eleanor.

"I hate it."

"Everybody does. It's dangerous," said Janice.

"But I like earning money. Making thirty-seven cents an hour. That's a lot. If I save enough, I can do something with my life." Eleanor didn't say what, but she knew the first thing she would do. Leave Grandmother's strict life. Leave behind the poverty they lived in.

"Something with your life? Like what?" Corine asked.

"Get married," said Janice, giggling. "Aren't we all going to?"

Corine smiled. "That's the plan, once the boys come home." She was already going steady with an Army Private stationed in England.

"Hmm, yeah..." Eleanor nodded, but was unsure if that's what she wanted. "I keep seeing U.S. Cadet Nurse Corps posters around. I'm going to send for the brochure on how to register." *That* opportunity had been percolating through her thoughts since school let out.

"Well, I just want Ralph to hurry and get home so we can get married," Corine said.

Janice added, "Well, when I get enough money, I want one of those dresses that shows girls' knees."

"They're adorable." Eleanor agreed. "I love the ones with shoulder pads, too."

"You'd look really smart wearing one," Corine said to her.

"Maybe. I'll have to wait. I have to pay ten bucks for room and board now. And I need enough to buy school supplies, too."

Janice scanned the crossword while Eleanor took a sip of her soda.

Corine leaned forward and whispered with her lipstick red mouth, "Don't go spilling the beans, but I peeked at the prisoners today. When they got off the bus."

"No!" Janice exclaimed.

"Really? The prisoners of war?" Eleanor pushed strands of her light brown hair behind her ears.

"Well, I didn't stare at them. I just took a quick look. Out of the corner of my eye."

"It's sure strange. Them being here," said Janice.

"Somebody's got to get the peas in. Might as well be them working in the hot sun," declared Corine. "Not many of our strong ones left."

With her pencil, Janice doodled at the edges of the crossword puzzle. "Yeah, they're scattered all over the world fighting."

"I heard they live in some prison camp in Walla Walla," Eleanor added. She lowered her head then whispered, "Do you want to know a secret?"

Corine nodded her head. "Do we ever."

"I listened to them during our break."

"The POWs?" Corine asked, raising her voice.

"Shh. You'll get us all in trouble." Eleanor's voice grew

quieter as she leaned in. "Yes, the German boys. I know we're supposed to ignore them. But when they were at their lunch—"

"You mean on the other side of that metal fence?" asked Janice.

Eleanor nodded. "After they finished eating, one of them started playing a harmonica. And they all sang."

Janice put her pencil down.

"Of course, I couldn't understand the words, but their song sounded lonely."

"How could you tell?" Janice asked.

"I don't know. The tune. It sounded mournful. Slow and lingering."

"Well, if you don't utter a word, I've looked at them too," Janice revealed. "To tell you the truth, I thought a couple of them were kind of cute. Too bad they're Hitler's men. Despicable."

Eleanor inhaled a small gasp at their confessions. She, too, had glanced, but had a different reason for looking. She wondered if any of those boys were distant cousins or uncles. Or, if they had killed someone she knew.

"I hate those filthy Nazis!" shouted Corine. "I mean, what if they kill Ralph?"

"Hush. We'll all get fired if anyone hears us," Eleanor said, turning her attention to Janice and the crossword puzzle. "What's next?"

"Okay. Here's one." Janice challenged the girls. "Seven letters. A kind of knot."

"Square," Corine chirped.

"No, dummy. That's only six letters," Janice said.

"Fun...ny." Corine's cynical reply was common between her and Janice. They were friends who aggravated each other sometimes so much they acted like cats hissing on either side of a screened door.

"Let's see what the knot ends in." Janice read the next clue. "Eighty-one down is five letters. A breakfast meat."

Corine counted her fingers as she spelled out, "B-a-c-o-n. It's bacon."

"I'll try it." Janice wrote in the letters. "That fits. If bacon's right, then the knot ends in 'n.'"

Corine lost interest and stared out the window. "Look. A serviceman's coming in."

The girls turned their heads as a young US Army Air Corps man entered, took off his hat that had covered his blond hair, and approached the counter.

"Maybe he'll talk to us," Corine said in a whispered tone. She waved at him. "Yoo-hoo. There's room here to sit with us." She patted the empty space next to her on the red leatherette seat as he approached their table. "We're cooling off after work."

"And trying to figure out a crossword puzzle," said Janice.

"Thanks." The young man scooted onto the booth next to Corine.

None of the girls stopped to introduce themselves. Janice just launched into another clue and directed it to the airman. "Can you solve this one? It's a seven-letter word; a kind of knot."

Corine interrupted with a syrupy voice. "He's a Fly Boy, not a Navy man. How's he gonna know about knots?"

"Pipe down," Janice scolded. "Well, what do you think? It ends in 'n.'"

"Hmm. Seven letters ... ends in 'n,' not a square knot or figure-eight." He lifted his index finger and declared, "Ha. I think I've got it. It's not a knot at all."

"Not a knot at all. What?" Corine looked confused; the side of her lip curled in suspicion.

"Have you ever heard of the Gordian Knot?"

"No," they all answered together.

"It's a symbol for a difficult problem."

"Well, that *was* a difficult one. How do ya know that?" asked Corine.

"I started to pledge for the Delta Sigma Phi fraternity before I joined the Army Air Forces. The Gordian Knot is in its seal."

"Oh, a college man," Janice commented. "His answer must be right." She wrote the letters in the spaces of the puzzle. "It fits."

The airman looked at each of them and asked, "So, what are your names? Mine's Jacob. Jacob Knudson."

"Corine."

"Janice."

"And mine's E-l-e-a-n-o-r." She hadn't tried to be cute or sarcastic, her answer just came out and surprised her as much as anybody.

"Touché." He smiled at her.

Shyly turning her head away, Eleanor caught a glint in his blue eyes.

"What are you doing here?" asked Corine, who now flirted by twirling her hair around her index finger as she spoke.

"Well, I just got here a couple of weeks ago. I'm stationed in Walla Walla, the training base." He glanced at the empty Coca-Cola bottles. "Hey, how about I buy the next round of sodas?"

They nodded and giggled because rarely did anyone treat them. Even though the Depression was considered over, money was still tight. Each of them had to work. Janice—

like Eleanor—contributed a share of her income to her family.

Corine saved money so that Ralph and she could get married.

Whiffs of hamburgers sizzling on the grill for customers' orders made Eleanor's stomach grumble because she hadn't eaten since noon. She sipped the last drops of her soda and said, "I have to get home. Help with dinner." She rolled her eyes in exasperation. "Do chores."

Jacob stood up. "I don't have anywhere I have to be. How about I walk with you for a spell?"

Janice urged her on. "Do Eleanor. Take him with you."

"Yeah," Corine chimed in.

Eleanor said to Jacob, "I have a ways to go. Uphill."

"For a few blocks. That's all. Because I need to get back to base soon."

"Okay."

Eleanor and Jacob said goodbye to the two girls as they left the café and ambled out into town.

"I came to look around Millston. Sightsee and all."

"Well. What do you see?"

"'Bout the same as I saw in Walla Walla." He pointed west toward the plateau. "More hills and valleys." Then he turned to the east. "And mountains."

"Those are the Blues. Snow lasts there all year. Glaciers, too."

"Yeah, we have mountains in Michigan, too, but they're more like your hills here," he clarified, nodding west.

"Oh, you mean bumps?"

"Yeah."

Their walking spell lasted about ten minutes around the main blocks of town. They headed down Cooper Avenue, where the movie theater, general store, and a Methodist church were located, then went onto 5th Street, passing the bank and post office, until finally turning west on Orchard Road, toward her house.

"This is where I turn for home." She looked up the road. "It was nice to meet you."

"You're not going to leave me here in the middle of town, are you?"

Eleanor turned inward into herself. Since her father's attack, she had shied away from boys. She hadn't had much occasion to be around them anyway, except in school and church, especially with Grandmother's strict rules about Sabbath. Going out on Friday nights was not allowed. Dances, picture shows, concerts, or dates–those were strictly forbidden.

Eleanor's right foot started fidgeting as she softened her gaze, then glanced down at the street. "My family's waiting."

"Well, can I see you again sometime? Say … next Saturday?"

"Umm …" Eleanor shrugged her shoulders, shook her head. "I'll be working." Then, without thinking it through, she blurted, "We'll probably be at the café again after work next Saturday."

"But wait, what if I can't get leave. Can I call you?" Jacob asked.

"We don't have a telephone."

"Hmm," he remarked, letting his shoulders drop. "I'm not giving up," he said with a firm nod of his head and a twinkle in his blue eyes. "I'll just have to get a leave."

A week later, Jacob found Eleanor with Janice and Corine at the High-Hat Café again. He walked her home, but she didn't invite him in. She stepped away from him, since she was unaccustomed to boys' attention. He was nice, gentle enough. But her mind reeled, thinking about what would happen, especially when his hand brushed against hers. Daytime nightmares of Father's forceful fingers wormed into her memory. The sinister sound of his zipper bruised her consciousness.

Late one July afternoon after Jacob bought Eleanor a soda at the café, they strolled along a path near the Little Walla Walla River. Honeyed fragrances of cottonwood trees meandered along with them.

"Boy, these hot days sure do make me think of home in Ann Arbor," he said with what looked like a pang of sadness sketched into his face.

"What's it like there?"

"Oh, it's a grand country. Lakes. Rivers full of fish. Forests. Farms. It's not too far from Detroit, so I've been to the city a couple of times."

"So, you were going to college?"

"Yup. Studying architecture." He gazed across the river. "I want to design famous buildings. But duty called. So, I joined the Air Corps. Maybe I'll fly one of those Corsairs soon."

"Sounds dangerous."

"That's what I'm learning."

"After high school, I'm going to join the U.S. Cadet Nurse Corps," Eleanor said with conviction.

Jacob looked straight at her with widened eyes. "Now that sounds *more* dangerous."

"I'll see. Last week I sent for a brochure. I should get it soon."

"You'd be in the thick of it. Too close to the front lines." He stopped in mid-step and frowned. "Really think about that before you join, won't you?" His deliberate tone revealed concern.

"I will." Eleanor turned away from the river. "When do you think you'll get another leave?"

"I'm finishing up my training. I'll be getting orders soon. This weekend could be one of my last."

Jacob was good to her. Like the slow rise of bread dough, he was unhurried. Kind and thoughtful. For days, Eleanor told herself to forget about her demonic father. In doing so, she had worked up enough confidence to overcome her hesitations. "Would you like to have dinner with us on Sunday?"

"Would I ever," he answered eagerly.

"I'll ask my grandmother and let you know in a letter on Monday."

"By then, I should know if I get leave."

"Sounds great."

On that last Sunday of the month, Eleanor finished cooking the dinner of lima beans in browned butter sauce and tomatoes. The kitchen bloomed with the scent of Grandmother's just-baked apple pie.

She went to freshen up by tying a spring green ribbon around her hair, while singing the first lines of "Together."

We strolled the lane together, laughed at the rain together.

Looking over her dresses, she chose one of her favorites —a butter yellow one with a fitted bodice and skirt, a crisp white lace collar, and tulip-shaped sleeves. She wanted to look her best for Jacob, who was fast becoming a good friend.

At work Corine teased her, "Jacob this and Jacob that. Soon Jacob will make you fat."

Sometimes her teasing annoyed Eleanor; she didn't like

the insinuation that she would end up in the family way. Like Anna. At sixteen, Anna had to get married because she was pregnant. Eleanor vowed that she was not ever going to end up in a situation like that. *Ever.*

Grandmother agreed to allow him over. After all, it was not uncommon for families to welcome G.I.s to church, picnics, or homes. Still, when the afternoon arrived for Jacob to join their dinner, Grandmother didn't appear too willing. Her folded arms across her chest and set jaw spoke volumes. When Jacob entered the house looking sharp in his uniform, she only nodded politely. But when he gave her a gift of a pound of sugar—an ingredient in short supply due to war rationing—her arms relaxed, and she grinned like a child with her favorite candy.

After cleaning up the food and dishes, Eleanor and Jacob sat on the broken porch step. In the evening breeze, they compared their favorite radio programs. The fragrances of the roses nearby created a mellow glow.

"'Adventures of Ellery Queen.' That's my favorite," said Jacob. "His clues keep me guessing."

"Mine is the 'Kraft Music Hall.' I like singing along with the tunes. And the Metropolitan Opera broadcasts. That's the one I like the best."

The two talked for longer. Jacob glanced at his watch. "Gee, I have to catch the last bus. And, if I haven't received my orders yet, would you want to go to a picture show with me next week?"

Eleanor debated her answer internally. Drinking Coca-Cola behind Grandmother's back was one thing, but going to a picture show was really disobeying Grandmother's rules. Eleanor did not want to let Jacob know that her grandmother still restricted her.

Eleanor replied, "Ooh. I'd love to. How about I meet you there?"

"You sure?"

"It'll be so much easier." Eleanor was trying to persuade him. "You won't have to walk clear up here. And, we'll have more time together."

"Okay. Next Sunday then."

On the following Sunday, after explaining to Grandmother she was going to visit Janice, Eleanor rushed to the theater. Eleanor hated lying. Deceiving was sinful. But wanting to go to a matinee picture show like Janice and Corine was not committing a crime. Eleanor wanted to fit in, be like a normal sixteen-year-old.

Jacob and Eleanor met at the front entrance. He looked handsome in his uniform and polished shoes. She wore a blue floral dress and had curled her hair with bobby pins the night before. When they stepped inside the theater, the opulence of the lighting and scarlet brocade curtains over the stage caught her attention. Her jaw slackened.

The usher, using a faint flashlight, guided them down the aisle to their seats. Once the overhead lights dimmed, Jacob reached over for her hand. She flinched at first, but soon relaxed and willingly nestled hers into his warm grasp. Sitting next to him on her first date made circles spin in her head.

The news reels started first. Everyone in the auditorium clapped during the introduction that showed patriotic brass bands and servicemen marching in formation. Before long, harsh music and noises exploded as Allied troops stormed the coast of Normandy in France. Eleanor shuddered. Her foot shook back and forth. Lights on the silver screen flashed. Bombs burst on train depots and cities. Eleanor squeezed her eyes shut because the sounds and the visuals in front of her were not like sitting in front of a radio. She could actually see what was happening, could almost smell the black smoke, and hear the screams of people dying in the streets.

After it finished, Jacob leaned over and whispered in her ear. "It's over. You can open your eyes now." He kept his lips near her cheek. "I've heard this is a good movie."

"I hope so." Eleanor's shoulders eased a bit and she soon relaxed and enjoyed watching Katharine Hepburn and Ethel Merman in the *Stage Door Canteen.*

When the movie ended, Jacob and Eleanor strolled toward the river, leaving the noises of town for burbling currents. Jacob broke the silence. "More guys from the base are flying over to Europe. One crew left for the Pacific."

A chill crawled up her spine.

"Well, I guess you know what that means." He stammered. "I ... I got orders too."

"Oh no." Eleanor froze. She had grown fond of the Michigan boy with hair the color of wheat stalk and eyes like a lake in spring.

"My first assignment's in Portland."

"Portland?" Eleanor blinked and clutched her chest with both hands.

"I'll be based there for some months so I can deliver planes from the factory in Washington to bases all around the country. You know, before they fly out on missions." He rubbed his chin with his thumb and forefinger. "I won't be going overseas. But my commander said that will come."

"That's great ..." Eleanor didn't finish the sentence. Jacob brushed her cheek with his lips. She then leaned toward him, and he clasped her hand. They walked on, his stride confident yet comforting, until they found an oak tree to sit under.

"I'll write to you," Eleanor promised.

He vowed the same. With his two hands, he cupped her face, speaking directly into her eyes. "Don't forget about me."

"I won't. I definitely won't."

After sitting for a few more calm minutes, they got up and strode toward town. Jacob veered right to catch the last bus to Walla Walla. Venturing forward about ten feet, he shot his head over his left shoulder and called out, "Remember me!"

"I'll be here." With a hollow void where her heartbeat was, and the smell of wariness in the air, she waved as her good friend stepped away.

Eight

1944

Although Jacob and Eleanor wrote to each other, she felt a space of regret between the past and future. She scolded herself: she should have been more affectionate and returned his fondness with kisses and hugs. Eleanor was not sure how to make it up to him, but she knew she would.

In the September of Eleanor's senior year of high school, she took a full load of classes, including chemistry, to get a head start before joining the U.S. Cadet Nurse Corps. She had not forgotten Fran's encouragement or abandoned her ambition to sing on stage; singing lived in her soul, as natural to her as breathing. But realizing that she did not have the money for college and music lessons, she'd simply changed her mind and decided not to make a living by performing. Besides, she knew that nursing was exactly what she wanted to do after reading the brochure for the Cadet Nurse Corps. Visions of helping servicemen paraded in her imagination. And by joining the Corps, she could get a college education —free from Uncle Sam.

~

On the afternoon of December 1, while snow fell and a stubborn wind stormed outside, Eleanor burst through the choir classroom doors and hummed a melody much different from her usual repertoire of church hymns and patriotic songs. Eleanor was instead practicing a song made popular several years earlier by Carmen Miranda, also known as "The Brazilian Bombshell," who performed in both nightclubs and movies.

Mrs. Halsey, the young choir teacher, chose Carmen Miranda's hit song "I Yi, Yi, Yi, Yi, I Like You Very Much" to be performed at the 1944 Junior-Senior Cotillion. Three weeks earlier, after she had competed against eleven other girls, Eleanor was selected by her teacher to sing the famous number. Following behind Eleanor was Janice, who took a seat at one of the wooden desks. When she learned that Eleanor was dressing up like Carmen Miranda, she offered to make a hat for her costume.

Mrs. Halsey, already at the piano, opened the fall board on the classroom's spinet. In a lilting voice she asked, "Are you ready?"

Eleanor nodded, glowing inside like a match struck just before it flared into a flame. This was her last rehearsal before singing and dancing the next night at the cotillion. She didn't consider herself a "bombshell" and certainly was not a nightclub performer like Carmen Miranda. Eleanor let her light brown wavy hair fall to her shoulders and occasionally wore red lipstick bought at the five-and-dime store, but that was the most stylish she could make her appearance. So, acting like Miss Miranda proved challenging. And Mrs. Halsey, with her stunning black hair and ivory skin, whom

Eleanor found to be much more glamorous, wanted this challenge for her talented student.

"For now, focus on the song. Take it from the top." Mrs. Halsey played the melody with her right hand and directed with her left. "One, two. One, two, One, two."

For this performance, Eleanor wanted her voice to sing of hope. Hope for her future as she neared graduation. Hope for the dreary mood of the nation during World War II. But all she could really hope for was remembering her dance moves while singing the lively song.

The solo. The dance. It all seemed like a dream. Although pride was sinful, Eleanor held her chin high. Her role included singing, dancing, *and* acting sexy. With her heart pounding, her chest didn't feel big enough to contain all her emotions. Vacillating between excitement and nerves—the kind that made her foot shake—Eleanor breezed through singing the melody and lyrics.

"Excellent," said Mrs. Halsey, whose smile showed she appreciated Eleanor. "That's why you're my best choir student."

"Swell." Janice clapped her hands in support.

"Now, let's see you add the dance." Mrs. Halsey, wearing a stylish long-sleeved green dress with padding at her shoulders, stood up to demonstrate. "Remember, when you sing the first two lines, you take one step forward on your right, step back with your left, and then slide right with one foot then the other. Side to side. Do that twice. When you get to the fourth line, *"My heart starts to beat..."* pat your heart with your palm. Hug yourself like your boyfriend's putting his arms around you."

Heat rushed up from her chest to her neck. She looked at the floor when Mrs. Halsey talked about boys and hugging.

The lyrics, "*you like my hips to hips-notize you*" were suggestive enough as it was.

"Boy, if my grandmother knew the words and that I was dancing, she'd make me stay home."

"Aren't you glad she *doesn't*?" Janice smiled slyly.

Eleanor nodded.

"Okay. One, two. One, two. One, two."

She sang a few bars, danced the first steps on the wooden floor, and fumbled.

"Try it one more time." Mrs. Halsey played the introduction.

"I'm all left feet! I can sing. But dance?" Eleanor shook her head and huffed out a sigh. "It's impossible." At that point, her foot *and* her voice started shaking.

"When you hear the orchestra play tomorrow night, it'll come together," Mrs. Halsey said in a calm manner.

"Yeah Eleanor. You're doing fine," Janice added with encouragement.

Eleanor took in a big breath and swayed with the syncopated rhythms. Then, she froze in mid-step.

"I don't know about this." Eleanor pinched her eyebrows into a frown as she turned towards Janice. "You know how she won't let me go out. It's so stupid! Dances. Picture shows. Dates. They're all forbidden. I mean, what seventeen-year-old has never gone dancing before? The only reason I get to go tomorrow night is because I'm singing."

Her good friend understood the predicament; if her grandmother found out, Eleanor would be in big trouble.

Most times Mrs. Halsey showed patience. But her next directive sounded less empathetic and more like an athletic coach with the snap of a firm ultimatum for Eleanor to conquer her fears. "Do it again, Eleanor."

Janice cheered her on. "Don't lose hope."

"I know I'm sounding like a whining child, but I'm getting the jitters."

Before she played again, Mrs. Halsey walked away from the piano to the phonograph on her oak desk. "Maybe this will help." She lifted the wooden lid. After pulling a 78-rpm disc from Carmen Miranda's "The South American Way" album, she set it down on the spinning table. "Dance along in your head with the record. Think about your moves." Amid the ticks and crackling sounds of the worn record, the three of them listened to Miranda's voice blossom out of the cloth-covered speaker.

"Ah," Mrs. Halsey sighed, tilting her head wistfully. "My husband and I danced to this song last year. Just before he left for France."

"France?" Eleanor asked.

Mrs. Halsey's expression wilted. "He's a medic. In the middle of the fighting. Near Germany."

"Hope he's okay over there." Eleanor inhaled a breath full of unpredictability. The war touched everyone. No one was immune. Everyone knew family or friends serving in the conflicts. What they did not know was who was going to come home afterward.

"I do, too." Mrs. Halsey stood up, lifted the needle, and took the album off the phonograph.

Janice piped up. "Well, this song makes me fancy Bill Norgren. I hope he sweeps me off my feet tomorrow night." Her brown eyebrows lifted in anticipation.

They laughed at the notion of Janice being swept up.

For Eleanor, time with her talented teacher felt special and it encouraged her to push even harder to achieve her goals.

Mrs. Halsey seldom talked about her personal life. In fact, an aura of mystery surrounded her. She didn't look like many of the other high school teachers with gray hair, long skirts, and disciplined scowls. Her porcelain skin dazzled the room with radiating light. She was not from any of the surrounding areas. Having read the certificate hanging on the front wall of the music room, all Eleanor and Janice really knew was that Mrs. Halsey had graduated in June of 1943 from the University of California. The two girls wondered how she ever ended up in a small town such as Millston.

Some of the students thought choir and music were easy classes. A place to goof off. On the contrary, their choir teacher maintained high expectations for excellence. Eleanor guessed that was why Mrs. Halsey noticed her, because she took the class seriously and tried her best. Another reason might have been that Mrs. Halsey once said to Eleanor, *"It's a pleasure having you in the choir. I see a natural singing talent in you."*

While Eleanor rehearsed, Janice continued to sew the hat. Neither she nor Eleanor had ever seen Miss Miranda in a picture show, but rather had ogled her photo on the album cover. She wore striking red lips, glamorous eyes lined in black, and one of her signature tutti-frutti hats made with tropical fruit mounded high. Using the photo as a guide, Janice fashioned Eleanor's fruit hat out of a stretchy black turban. Because of the war, real lemons and pineapples were scarce, so she attached artificial ones. She had gasped earlier with disbelief when Mrs. Halsey bought three *real* oranges and gave them to the girls for the costume.

Soon, Janice handed the hat to Eleanor. "The only thing missing is the banana. I'll put it on tomorrow night."

"That's adorable. You're such a lamb." Eleanor beamed and picked it up to inspect. Struggling, she tugged the heavy turban over her head. "I sure don't know how she ever danced with this thing." The fruit jiggled down over her left ear, and each of them giggled at the lop-sided headpiece. Laughing helped calm her fidgeting.

Mrs. Halsey led her through the song and dance one more time, then nodded at the end. "You did it." The girls whooped and clapped.

Eleanor was never quite sure how she mastered the dance that last time. Perhaps the laughing helped. Or the silly hat banished her nerves. Whatever it was, her head swirled in relief as her voice sounded clear, and her feet moved in the right sequence.

Mrs. Halsey and Eleanor took a break and sat down next to Janice, who handed them sections to eat from the one left-over orange she had peeled. The perfume of the fruit drifted throughout the room. Eleanor closed her eyes, breathing in the citrus fragrance.

She lifted the orange section to her lips, biting in slowly, allowing the juice to dribble down her fingers and chin. Her tongue tingled. The fruit sacs burst in her mouth, tasting like Christmas. As luscious then as it had been when she first nibbled into an orange's sweet flesh at eight years old. In the depths of the Great Depression that year, Eleanor's Christmas gift had been a paper package containing two peppermint candies and an orange. Even after the Depression, oranges were luxuries, something Eleanor looked forward to savoring on holiday mornings.

The three of them finished the orange. Janice and Eleanor grabbed their things while Mrs. Halsey gathered the sheet music and put it into her leather satchel. Taking her wool coat off the hook, she ushered the girls out of the classroom. "I'll see you tomorrow night. Now don't worry. Just practice at home."

"I will. I'm going to prove to you and myself I can master those dance steps." Eleanor waved goodbye.

Their footfalls echoed down the school hall while Janice and Eleanor talked about Bill and Jacob. At their lockers, Eleanor hung up the hat on a hook inside hers, while Janice chattered about what she planned to wear to the cotillion.

"It's rose-colored." She gasped with excitement. "It has fancy netting all the way to the floor. Can you believe it?" Her squeal filled the empty hall. "Full length!"

Eleanor pictured in her mind's eye how Janice would look. Wearing a floor-length gown would make her appear taller than her five-foot height. Also, her brown hair would complement the shade of the dress.

"Lucky you. And, lucky me." Lucky because she didn't have to worry about a gown. One week earlier, Mrs. Halsey had borrowed a long black skirt, a flame red scarf for a sash, and a lace blouse from the drama department for her to wear as a costume.

Janice and Eleanor walked home quietly while she practiced dancing in her head. The slope up the last rise to their houses was steep. The snow had stopped earlier, but in the approaching dusk the two friends had to buck the wind's angry gusts. As they climbed, Eleanor surveyed miles of dormant wheat fields along with pea farms below. The apple, apricot, and prune orchards smelled of yawning sleep, as if beckoning winter's long rest. When they rounded the corner of the road, Eleanor looked up at Grandmother's two-story house. A black truck was parked in the front yard. It was not theirs. In it was Grandmother's sagging davenport, her oak rocking chair, and Mattias' dresser. Cardboard boxes and wooden apple crates lay scattered in the muddy patch.

"This can't be!" Eleanor shouted.

"What?" Janice asked.

"Look. Our stuff." Eleanor pointed as if Janice couldn't see the furniture and boxes. "It looks like we're moving again. No!" Eleanor ran forward. "I'll see you later. I have to find Mattias."

Janice waved and walked onward to her home. Eleanor jumped over the broken porch plank. On any other Friday afternoon, Grandmother and Mattias would be preparing to observe Sabbath. The hours between Friday sunset and Saturday sunset were sacred. The electric bulb should be off, the lamps dimmed. Instead, light from oil lamps blazed through the kitchen windows and upstairs.

Eleanor tore into the house, desperately looking for her uncle. With Grandmother's rug rolled up and propped against a wall, the knot hole in the wooden floor gaped like the mouth of a hungry animal. Peering through the dust, the mattress where Grandmother and Eleanor slept together remained in the small alcove, which was nothing more than a lean-to. Rafters jutted out from the main room, revealing stains from last winter's snowmelts. Stains she stared at during sleepless, frigid nights when the wind whistled through the lean-to's cracks; where Grandmother would sleep curved around Eleanor, like two spoons in a drawer, in order to stay warm.

In the kitchen, the wash tub with sudsy water still sat on the side table. Nutty aromas of lentils filled the room as they warmed in a pot on the wood cookstove. It was not hard to find Mattias.

He groaned, pushing the kitchen table toward the truck. Mattias' right shoulder slumped. Premature wrinkles drew his face into shadowed lines. At twenty-three his right lip permanently sagged, even when he tried to smile.

"Mattias. What's going on?"

"We're moving. Ma even bought this truck here." Both his face and a muscle in his neck strained from the weight of the table. "Ma and I have work at a dairy." He heaved the table up onto the truck bed. "Over in Wilkes."

Wilkes was a day's drive to western Washington, just north of Portland, Oregon.

"And, if we earn enough, we're going to buy it." He climbed on the truck and shoved the table to the front of the bed.

"No! No! We can't!" Eleanor yelled, then ran inside and up the stairs to find Grandmother.

"Why?" Eleanor shouted in a burst of anger. She didn't stop to wait for an answer. She just kept shouting louder, even though the small dormer bedroom was upstairs, and Grandmother could easily hear her. "We can't move now. Don't you remember I'm singing tomorrow night? I'm almost done with…" She caught her breath when she reached the top of the landing. "My senior year ... I'm … I'm almost done. And I can't let my teacher and school down."

Grandmother, with wrinkles borne of adversities, stopped folding a blanket and lifted her head. The kerosene lamp light silhouetted her square, striking jaw. "You'll have to make do," she said sternly. "We're leaving in the morning." She turned her petite, yet strong, body away from Eleanor and went back to folding. "Now go downstairs. Dish up your supper. Sabbath starts soon and you'll have tomorrow morning to pack."

"I won't go!" Eleanor insisted. Then several thoughts popped into her head. "Let me stay with Janice. Better yet, Fran. Just until May. Please."

Grandmother didn't reply. Eleanor knew that Janice's family couldn't take care of her, and Fran and Pete were preoccupied with their business.

"You're coming to Wilkes. That's all there is to it," she said, resolved.

Eleanor started to panic. "Does it even have a school?"

"There's a school." She stacked several blankets in her arms, picked up the oil lamp, and started down the stairs. "But you won't have time to go. You'll be working the dairy with us."

"Work the farm? I have to finish." Eleanor's voice unraveled and grew louder. "You don't care if I graduate, do you? You just want me to end up like your girls. Married. Pregnant. And poor." Her voice grew as ear-splitting as a scream. Pacing back and forth in the small room, she intentionally called out to Grandmother in hopes of hurting her. "In fact, you don't care about me at all! Never have."

But Eleanor cared. She cared enough to want to earn a diploma, to enlist in the Cadet Nurse Corps. *Where can I stay? How am I going to finish school?* Eleanor had no answers. Feeling resigned, she sighed loudly while her shoulders slumped forward.

Smoke from the lamp hung, drifting through the empty room. Looking out the window, Eleanor saw the sun slip below the horizon. Shafts of the last light weaved through the paned window. Near the house, two maple trees stood bare, their branches painting marbled shadows on the gray walls. In the gloaming, Eleanor smelled grit. Jagged. Unforgiving. And, not yet settled after the commotion of moving furniture.

Nine

1944

On Saturday morning, Mattias drove west away from Millston. Snow flurries blurred the windshield while silent, ragged sobs clouded Eleanor's thoughts. By evening, driving December rains met them as they arrived in Wilkes, over two hundred miles away from where her high school was.

After the three of them moved into the farmhouse, she stole away from the chaos of furniture jumbled in corners, crates on the floors, and linens piled on the kitchen counter. She found one of her boxes and unpacked her stationery and a pen to write a letter.

December 2, 1944

Dear Mrs. Halsey,

I'm so sorry I missed the cotillion. As I'm writing this to you, it's seven o'clock and I'd be there singing now. But this morning my grandmother moved us to Wilkes, Washington. I didn't know we were leaving until last night when I got home.

I couldn't telephone you because we don't have a phone. I couldn't even go over to Janice's to let her know. I'm sad I let you and the school down. I hope you can understand. I really wanted to sing and dance.

I want you to know you were one of my best teachers. I will remember all that you did for me.

Sincerely,

Eleanor Owens

Tipping her head, Eleanor listened, hearing in her imagination how the orchestra warmed up their instruments by practicing scales. The lyrics of the song repeated like a scratched record in her memory while she wrote her second letter to Janice. Her heart ached, sinking with heaviness. Remembering the fun they had together made her feel even more miserable. Eleanor no longer had any reason to sing.

She could not understand why Grandmother didn't tell her sooner. A resentment larger than her heart festered inside. *Grandmother really hates me.* Eleanor couldn't forgive Grandmother for moving them in the middle of her senior year.

Once in bed, hours after the cotillion was over, Eleanor's head nodded and her eyelids wilted. Yet she forced herself to stay awake long enough to write to Jacob, and to Fran and Pete, about her move.

Bawling cows woke Eleanor the next morning. She wondered what the herd looked like, but knowing she would have time enough to look around, she lingered in bed. Warmth on the opposite side meant Grandmother had just gotten up.

Eleanor went downstairs and fixed her eyes on the toilet in the bathroom. That was one good thing about the move; they had their first indoor toilet. Though the biggest surprise was the telephone hanging on the kitchen wall. Eleanor's breath quickened as she gazed at the rotary dial and black handset. It, too, meant a step forward.

This is the best house we've ever lived in. Maybe this is why Grandmother made us move.

Come Monday morning Eleanor got dressed for school. Grandmother, ready to walk out to the barn in boots and a heavy coat, met her when she walked downstairs.

"Where are you going?" asked Grandmother with a snap in her voice.

"I worked yesterday."

"I told you. The herd is too big for Mattias and me."

"But I'm ready for school," Eleanor responded, incredulously.

With a stern expression, Grandmother pointed upstairs to the bedroom. "Go change," she ordered, seeming to grow larger, like an animal facing a foe. Eleanor could smell her insistence, hard and callous.

For days Eleanor missed school. She cleaned ten-gallon milk cans, disinfected cows' teats to ready them for the next milking, and shoveled manure, heavy with ammonia odors.

By Thursday, Eleanor found Mattias and Grandmother napping, Grandmother in her rocking chair and Mattias on the couch.

Eleanor washed grime from under her fingernails and her hands, then scrubbed her face. Afterwards, she changed into school clothes, then nodded her head with firm determination, believing that Fran would approve. *She'd want me to finish school.*

So, she wrote a note and left it in the kitchen.

I'm going to register for school.

When Eleanor returned, Grandmother was stirring a pot on the stove while Mattias sorted papers and receipts on the table.

"Yum. Smells good," Eleanor said, entering through the back door and breathing in the savory aromas of creamy vegetable soup, one of her favorite smells.

"Where've you been?" Grandmother asked with a snarl like a feral dog.

"I wrote a note."

"I saw it. And you're not going. Seems you can't stay out of trouble at school."

"Meaning what?" Eleanor put her hands on her hips. "I've never been in trouble. And I get good grades."

"Trouble." Grandmother repeated. "I'm talking about that performance the other night. You were going to be dancing, weren't you? Tsk. Tsk. Sinful! You're living under my roof and you're helping us."

"I won't … I mean … I will. I'll help. But only until I leave for school in the mornings. And on weekends."

Grandmother squinted while adding handfuls of canned, chopped morels to the pot.

"I start tomorrow." Eleanor turned and headed toward the stairs.

"Eleanor!"

"Ma. Let her go," said Mattias.

"Stay out of this," Grandmother said.

"Stop badgering her. I have a say in this farm, too. And, I say she goes. We'll manage by ourselves." He turned and said to Eleanor, "Can you help in the afternoons ... sometimes?"

Eleanor nodded and mouthed "thank you" to him.

Walking upstairs to the bedroom to change her clothes, she remembered the instances when both Ernst and Mattias had sided with her, and she appreciated their help during difficult times with Grandmother.

Over time, letters from Fran and Pete sustained Eleanor. Even though commitments demanded their attention, Fran encouraged Eleanor. "Stick to your dreams," she wrote. "Finish school and get an education. The Cadet Nurse Corps sounds like an excellent plan. And we're both very proud of you." She even sent her an Agatha Christie novel to inspire her. The gift came with a note written in Fran's elegant penmanship: "My dear Eleanor, if a little old lady like Miss Marple can solve mysteries, you too will be able to find the clues to help achieve your goals. Don't give up."

That's what Eleanor loved about Fran—her good sense and messages of hope.

When Eleanor returned from school one afternoon, a letter from Jacob lay on the kitchen table. She hugged it for several minutes, inhaling his bold spicy scents from the page.

6 Mar 1945
   Dear Eleanor,

It's happened. I got orders for the Pacific. I'm leaving Portland on 19 March. I'm coming up to see you one more time. I'll take the 1:45 bus and get to your place by dinner on Friday the 15th. I'll have to go back the next afternoon. I can't wait to see you next week.

XOXO,

Jacob

"I got orders." His words ignited fear. Eleanor's right foot started jerking up and down in dread that her good friend would soon be in harm's way.

On Friday, Eleanor waited on the front porch where the midday sun hinted of approaching spring. Around four thirty, she recognized Jacob's fast-paced gait in the distance. Wrapping her sweater around her shoulders, she ran to meet him.

He hugged her tight, and as Eleanor hugged back, she said, "I'm worried about you." A gust ruffled his hair. "I don't want you to go."

"I don't want to leave *you*. But I must." He braced himself as if a gale of unspoken fear blew through him. "I had to see you one last time before I left."

"Where are you going?"

"You know I can't say."

"Oh, right. I shouldn't have asked."

At dinner with Grandmother and Mattias, their conversation revolved around the war. The bombing of Dresden. The Marine Corps landing on Iwo Jima. Before long Eleanor's shoulders hung limp from the tragic discussion. She perked up when Jacob changed the subject.

"How's the dairy business lately?" Jacob asked, wiping from his lip a dollop of the golden applesauce served for dessert that Grandmother had canned the previous summer.

"We bought it!" Mattias announced loudly, clasping his hands together and waving them like a victorious prize fighter. "We made enough money. Bought it lock, stock and barrel." His smile beamed. "The house, barn and the whole herd, of course."

"The Lord's been good to us. It's been a good move," said Grandmother.

"Well, we've worked like fools. All of us," Mattias said, looking Eleanor's way. "It's a far cry from what we used to do."

Grandmother shot up from the table, walked to the wall, and took down a framed document. "We were upgraded to a Grade A Dairy." She held the certificate over the table to show Jacob. The blue in her eyes twinkled while some of her wrinkles smoothed; Eleanor couldn't remember the last time Grandmother grinned.

"Means we get a better price for milk," Mattias said. "That helped us turn a profit."

"Great. I know how much work it takes to run a dairy. One summer I was a hired hand on one near our home." Nodding his head as if in approval, he said, "You know, I thought I wanted to design big, fancy buildings. But I've been thinking of buying a farm instead. It's good, honest work." Turning toward Eleanor, Jacob changed the subject again. "How about you, Eleanor? How's school?"

"Chemistry, ugh." Eleanor rolled her eyes. "I'm sick of trying to remember the periodic table and formulas. It's no wonder I'm having a tough time. I missed three months of Mr. Proctor's class. And I started behind in Washington history, too. But I'm keeping up."

After Grandmother and Mattias left the kitchen, Jacob and Eleanor cleared the table and washed the dishes.

"Say, I remembered a Portland map for you," he said to her.

"Thanks. Let's put it out here," Eleanor said, pointing to the table. "I want to find my way to the recruiting office."

As Jacob pulled the map from his pocket and unfolded it, a gust of adventure seemed to swirl around the room.

"Where's the bus station?" She studied the map. "That's where I'll start."

He pointed to its location. "You'll see a clock tower above the train depot. It's next to the bus terminal."

"I have the address of the recruitment center. It's at the city hospital."

Jacob pointed his finger while Eleanor held her hand over his. "See here? You'll walk from downtown. If I remember right, it's through an industrial area. A rough part." He exhaled as though he were frustrated. "I wish I could walk you there."

"Oh, I don't think I told you," Eleanor responded, "Janice wrote to me last month that she wants to come too. We're joining together, so we'll be okay," Eleanor started to fold the map, hoping she had reassured him. "Gee, I'm so excited. Just a few months now."

Jacob nodded, then gently smiled and suggested a walk. "It's not raining, let's see if we can spot some stars."

They put on their coats and left out the back door. Frigid air gnawed at Eleanor's neck and fingers. As she inhaled it, she caught traces of approaching spring lilacs, lingering above the odors of the barnyard and river. They walked away from the barn.

"Look, there's Cassiopeia." She pointed to the sky. "See the 'W' up there? That's her. And there's Orion's belt."

"Where?"

"The three stars in a row."

"How do you know all this?" Jacob asked in wonder.

"My Uncle Ernst taught me. We'd sit outside in the summer, and he'd point out the constellations. I guess he learned from Grandmother 'cause she likes to look at the stars, too." Eleanor spun around to view the whole sky and opened her arms wide. "I love how each one sparkles, kind of like they flicker hope. Don't you think?"

"I have something ... sparkling for you." He clasped her hand and guided her toward the earthen dikes separating the pastures from the Columbia River. Reaching into his uniform pocket, he brought out a velvet jewelry box.

Even though a new moon shed little light, Eleanor could see.

"Eleanor, I love you." His hands shook, opening it. "Will you marry me?" Inside, a diamond ring glistened like droplets in the distant universe. He slipped it on the third finger of her left hand.

Eleanor's mouth gaped open. Composing herself, she said, "It's beautiful. And ... I ... I love you too." She then took two steps away, drawing her head back when the words "I love you" tumbled out. They were new. She had never said them before. She didn't exactly know what love felt like. Sure, he was a good friend. But love?

Her mind bounced back and forth until it settled. She stepped close to him, finally convinced that the warm glow inside of her was, indeed, love. Eleanor could feel it from the warmth of the band circling her cold finger, then answered, "Yes."

He whispered with a stammer. "I know ... I haven't asked your grandmother. I couldn't wait ... I had to know from you first."

"Pshaw." Eleanor waved her arm.

Thinking back to the first week after they moved to

Wilkes, Eleanor still yielded under Grandmother's control. But when Mattias told Grandmother to stop badgering her, he became an ally. From then on, she felt less restricted. Besides, Virginia had eloped before her junior year. Anna got married when she was pregnant at sixteen. Neither one had asked for Grandmother's permission.

And Eleanor was different from her aunts. She would have a respectful wedding with a man she loved who could provide a good life for her.

"You don't need Grandmother's approval. Neither do I. But I ... I think I need some time. I still want to join the Nurse Corps. Get an education. Do you think we could wait a little?"

He looked away; his face crowded with disappointment.

Eleanor immediately regretted asking. It was not Jacob's disillusionment, it was the fact that she caused him hesitation, frustration. And just days before he was shipping out. Eleanor had hurt him by saying she needed time.

He sighed. "Maybe this war will end soon."

To lighten the uncertain mood, she said, "Let's not talk about you leaving or the war. It scares me. Let's think about how wonderful our lives will be."

He nodded his head, and they started ambling back toward the house. When Jacob asked for Eleanor's hand, Mattias looked up from his whittling while Grandmother's eyebrows rose and her mouth fell open. "Well, well. Why, yes," she said with a grin. After Jacob's first gift of sugar, she doted on him, always making him apple pies when he visited. "To think, I'll have a new son-in-law."

"Here's my ring." Eleanor showed Grandmother and Mattias her left hand. The single diamond on the thin band glittered with promise.

Mattias stoked the flames in the brick fireplace. Somehow, the room appeared smaller than it had that morning. The furniture looked shabbier. The walls were duller now that Eleanor envisioned new horizons ahead in her future. Soon, it was so hot in the room, she didn't know if it was from the fire or her excitement. To cool herself, she walked over to the upright piano Grandmother had purchased since buying the farm. Eleanor played its chipped and missing keytops while singing church hymns along with Jacob, Grandmother and Mattias. Eleanor sang soprano, Grandmother a harmonizing alto, and Mattias and Jacob were both tenors. Their quartet filled the house with a glow brighter than the darkness plaguing the world.

Grandmother retreated to bed. Mattias went out to the barn for one last late-night check of the herd. Then, in order to spend as much time together as they could, Jacob and Eleanor braved the moist night air with another walk toward the river.

Ten

1945

Principal Vander announced the news over the school's loudspeakers.

"Hoorah! The Nazis surrendered," shouted teenagers throughout the school. The clamor of voices and the smells of victory echoed in the halls. Teachers joined in and cheered along.

Eleanor chanted too. "Hoorah. Hoorah. Germany surrendered."

Walking to her class, Eleanor bumped into the boys' flailing arms as they whooped and clapped each other on their backs. She joined the girls clumped together, hugging joyfully. Others were jumping up and down in circles. Glee resounded louder than a thrashing machine during a summer's wheat harvest. Adding to the commotion were the hallway bells. Clanging. Alerting the school that first period was starting. Soon, the shouting and cheering subsided; students shuffled into their seats.

On the chalkboard of Mr. Lyon's classroom was the date

May 7, 1945. He settled the students. "Quiet. Quiet." Loosening the knot of his tie, he said, "Wow! What a day. Hoorah!"

Caught up with the excitement, Eleanor stood up and burst into song– "*Oh say can you see…?*" Her classmates and Mr. Lyon joined her in singing the National Anthem until she reached the last word, "*brave*," which she sustained long after the others ended.

The teacher applauded. "Marvelous, Eleanor. Thanks for that inspiring start to class on this historic day."

"Gee, what a voice," said one boy. "I didn't know you could sing like that."

"Beautiful," said a girl who sat next to her.

When Eleanor arrived home, the spring rains that had lingered into May, made the mud spongy and slippery. She watched her step, so she didn't slide in the muck. Grandmother and Mattias were in the barn getting ready to milk the herd.

"Grandmother! Mattias!" Eleanor shouted, carefully rushing toward them, where they stood with a couple of Holsteins inside the barn. She reached them all out of breath. "The Germans… they surrendered!"

"We heard." Mattias' palsied arm trembled. "The neighbor came by about an hour ago and told us."

"It's wonderful, isn't it?"

"Maybe now some of the men can come home," Mattias responded.

"Like Jacob," Eleanor said. Her heart lifted and she began to sing again.

"Yes, Jacob, too," Grandmother agreed.

As each day passed, nearing closer and closer to graduation, Eleanor's emotions mushroomed. She could hardly contain her excitement until she learned she needed a wristwatch with a second hand to join the Cadet Nurse Corps. Eleanor hadn't expected that requirement. Uncle Sam funded the training, books, and uniforms, and even paid a stipend each month, but a watch was not supplied. She had not earned any money since her summer work at the cannery and didn't have the five dollars to buy one. Eleanor came up with the idea to ask Grandmother for a loan, so the next day, she found her in the barn. "Grandmother?"

"Uh huh." Grandmother had her attention focused on one of the cow's hooves. To Mattias, she said, "This heifer's lost weight." Fanning her nose to rid the obnoxious smell, she added, "Her foot stinks."

He carefully lifted the cow's leg, causing her to bawl. He examined the claw, probing gently, and feeling along her coronet. "Hoof rot. You can smell it, too," he said. "This rain sure is causing havoc. We'll have to separate her from the rest."

"I'll wrap her foot with Epsom salts. Maybe that'll heal the infection," said Grandmother.

Eleanor stepped closer and interrupted them. "Grandmother?"

She turned to Eleanor. "Can't you see we're busy? This cow's got an infection."

Eleanor needed her attention, but they were too involved in the herd's health. An infection in one cow could spread to others and decrease milk production. And a heifer was too valuable to let an infection spread up her leg. Grandmother's extra work, mixing Epsom salts with water and wrapping the infection several times a day would be difficult. The method was not a guaranteed treatment. Eleanor knew better than to disturb her when she was treating one of the cows.

It was not until four nights later that Eleanor tried again. After their dinner of meatloaf made of cereal, cottage cheese, and eggs, the evening was quiet. Grandmother read her *Holy Bible*, and Mattias whittled a piece of pine to steady his tremor while Eleanor played the piano.

When she finished her piece, Eleanor looked up from the keyboard to grab her grandmother's attention. "Grandmother?"

She looked up over the tops of her new wire-rim reading glasses.

"I graduate pretty soon. In a week and a half. You know how much I wanna be a nurse. Well…" Eleanor took a deep breath to bolster her courage, "I need a wristwatch with a second hand to join the Corps." The piano bench felt harder than usual under Eleanor's thighs as she squirmed. "I … I don't have enough money for it." Eleanor braced herself because she had never asked for money. "I'm wondering, could I borrow five dollars?"

Grandmother eyed Eleanor with a squinted scowl. "Five dollars?" Irritation, like a raw blister, filled her voice. "I don't have money for a watch."

Even Mattias, with wide eyes and raised brows, looked up at Eleanor.

"But Grandmother, just a loan. Five dollars. I'll pay it back. I promise."

She shook her head. "You'll have to find a job. Earn the money like we do."

"The other kids are getting gifts for graduation. I know that's out of the question." Eleanor started pleading. "I paid you last summer when I worked at the cannery. I've helped you with the cows. You know I haven't worked since last summer. Please. Just five dollars so I can buy a watch. It's not fancy. In fact, I saw one at the five-and-dime. And I'll pay you back fast after I get my first check. It's a lifetime opportunity. And after I leave the Corps, I'll have a good job to help you out financially."

Grandmother returned to her reading. Disapproval inched into every wrinkle as she shook her head. "You'll have to earn the money. That's all there is to it. And," she said, "you shouldn't have bought that new dress for your graduation. You should've saved your money."

In a huff, Eleanor popped up from the piano bench and stomped upstairs. She sat on the bed against the wall, holding a hand-crocheted blanket under her arms for comfort. She sighed loud enough for Grandmother to hear downstairs. "I'm glad I'm leaving."

Grandmother yelled, "It doesn't do any good to pout!"

It was true. Pouting didn't help. And Eleanor, on impulse, *had* bought a new dress, a special one for her graduation ceremony. But she hadn't realized then that she needed a watch. With her head hung low, she dug under the mattress and pulled out her dingy white money sock. Eleanor counted. Four one-dollar bills, two dimes, one nickel and four pennies. $4.29. Enough for the bus fare, but not enough to buy a wristwatch, too. She threw the sock against the wall. The sound of it thudding and falling to the floor infuriated her even more.

Before Eleanor went to bed, she jotted a quick letter to Janice and let her best friend know of her delay. Eleanor had to make do on her own. There was only one thing she could do. Find a job. Fast.

Eleven

1945

Several weeks passed. Grandmother and Mattias slogged in their mucky boots and work clothes from the barn to the back door. From the side yard, Eleanor waved, following them inside as she returned home from school and the first day of her new part-time job as a clerk.

"Mattias picked up the mail. You got a letter. Looks like it's from Janice," Grandmother said.

Eager to read it, Eleanor ripped open the flap of the envelope. "Hope she's not mad at me. Because I have to wait."

June 7, 1945

Dear Eleanor,

I can't believe we finished! Graduation was last night. Yay! No more books! We missed you. But I have terrific news. Bill proposed to me. I've decided to stay here and work at the cannery again. I won't be joining the Cadet Nurse Corps with you...

Eleanor stopped before reaching the end. Her shoulders

slumped like two anchors were weighing them down. "Well, that's swell," she said. Her sarcasm revealed her deep disappointment as she let the letter drop to the table.

"What is it? Good news?" asked Grandmother.

"No." Eleanor's tone bit the kitchen air.

While she plodded upstairs to change, Eleanor calculated she had to work two weeks more before she could earn enough to buy the watch. Meanwhile, graduation was three nights away.

Principal Vander announced over the microphone at the school's podium, "Eleanor Owens." She strode across the stage, her shoe heels clicking on the wooden floor. Nearly fifty students sat in folding chairs. Triumph, smelling as sweet as Grandmother's berry jams, flooded the mood in the gymnasium. Shaking her hand with the principal and accepting her diploma, she couldn't help swelling with pride. She'd graduated! After accepting her diploma, she sat down. The names of the other students the principal called simply jumbled into noise. She was too busy reading and rereading the fancy lettering on her diploma to hear the principal's announcements.

This certifies that Eleanor Owens has satisfactorily completed the necessary requirements of study as prescribed by school administrators and is thereby presented with this High School Diploma. Dated the Fourteenth of June 1945

Eleanor became preoccupied with thoughts as she stepped back in her memory, recalling all the things she had done to make sure she had been successful in school. Despite moving to different towns almost every year, she kept her grades up. Changing schools and starting over in midyear with new classes and new teachers meant she had to work even harder. Saying goodbye to friends. Meeting new classmates. Defying Grandmother's orders just months before when she registered for high school, so she could graduate and get one step closer to escaping her current life on the dairy farm.

There she sat. The first in her family to graduate. But Grandmother was not there. Mattias had dropped Eleanor off at the door, then returned to help Grandmother with another sick cow. Eleanor sighed, tilting her head to one side with regret that they were tending the cows instead of watching her graduate. She squeezed her lips into a resolute face. She was not going to let their absences ruin her celebratory spirit. Nope. Eleanor had goals. Ambition. She knew she would not allow anything to interfere with her plans.

Two weeks later, Eleanor had finally earned enough money and a little extra. She squeezed together in her hand the left-over money she had after buying a watch; eleven one-dollar bills and a quarter. She proudly glanced at the watch's second hand as it swept around the dial. She liked hearing its soft tick as if it were the backdrop rhythm of her life, giving her a sense of purpose.

On the following Monday, July 2, she stood before the clerk behind the Greyhound Bus ticket booth. From her purse, she withdrew money. Even then, she was so excited that she could hardly open her hand to pay for the ticket.

Soon Eleanor traveled south along the highway to Portland. Finally! On her way to her dream. Becoming a nurse. College. A goal that kindled a bright light, one she had held in her heart since her vacation as a child with Fran and Pete in the Blue Mountains.

Eleanor imagined relieving pain and fear among the troops. Assisting doctors with surgeries and wound care. And after that, she would work in a clean hospital where she could bring comfort to children and to elderly people too frail to walk or feed themselves.

Yes. She knew she would be a good nurse.

The bus engine grumbled and coughed black exhaust as it crossed the Columbia River bridge. As they approached tall city buildings in Portland, she spotted the train station tower and its clock.

Within minutes after leaving the bus, Eleanor's pace quickened along the city streets. Soon the hospital came into view. *There it is.* Gazing around the multi-level brick building, she spotted two nurses strolling nearby. They looked so important wearing their smart uniforms, white caps, and shoes. Eleanor traced each of their steps as if they walked on hallowed ground. Looking at their faces, she imagined the pride they must feel glowing inside of them.

Eleanor opened the hospital door with confidence, feeling like the luckiest girl in the world. A high school graduate, engaged, and soon-to-be nurse. As soon as she entered, her nerves jittered amid the acidic smells of hospital antiseptics. She walked into a room on the left of the hallway, where posters promoting the nursing corps covered one wall. Other posters showed Rosie the Riveter, "Do the Job He Left Behind," and "For a Secure Future, Buy War Bonds."

A middle-aged woman, wearing a regular civilian dress, sat behind the desk and packed papers into a box. Eleanor squinted at her, wondering why she was not wearing a uniform and curious that the center was not full of young women.

Eleanor smiled as she introduced herself. "Hi, I'm Eleanor Owens. I'm here to register."

The woman's head tilted back as she asked, "Register? You mean for the Cadet Nurse Corps?"

"Yes." Eleanor nodded. "I have my diploma and a watch with a second hand." She lifted her left arm to show the watch.

"Oh dear, don't you know?" The woman looked at her with a cocked head and a worried brow. "We closed registration last Friday."

Eleanor didn't understand. "But you still have posters up."

"Those just haven't been packed yet." She looked down and shuffled more papers.

"That can't be. Are you sure?"

"Sure, as can be. Since Germany surrendered, there isn't the need for as many nurses."

"Can't you let me register?" Eleanor pleaded. "It's only one day later."

"I'm sorry. The forms are packed. The Corps has already closed centers in most of the states."

"No. No!" Eleanor wailed, unraveling like a tumbling skein of yarn. Stepping backwards until her back found a wall, she slumped to the tile floor. Chaos like atonal sharps and flats collided in her mind. "Closed? How could that be? My dreams ... school ..."

"You, okay?" The woman approached and reached out her arm. "Here, let me help you."

Eleanor shook her head and touched the cool floor with the palm of her hand. "I'll be fine." Hoisting herself up, the words *I can't believe I missed it by one day* screamed in her mind. Dreams like a dropped locket sinking in a bottomless lake eluded her.

After leaving the recruitment center, Eleanor became numb. Empty. Her feet weighed heavy, like they were stuck in mud, because the time it took for her to walk just one block seemed like hours.

Now what am I going to do?

Twelve

1945

For the next several days, Eleanor's failure tormented her. When she wasn't working, she walked around aimlessly in circles inside of the house. She paced to the river back and forth, and once summoned enough energy to yell out, "No! No! No!" But most of the time, she shuffled along the top of the dike feeling nothing. Wondering what to do.

Grandmother doesn't care. But Mama might've.

Fran and Pete might have cared, too. But Eleanor didn't want to bother them, as busy as they were keeping lumber shipped to the warfront. Besides, she didn't want to reveal to them how foolish she had been.

I was so stupid to spend my money on a new dress. I could've had enough to afford a watch.

A day late. I can't believe it.

By Thursday of that same week, Eleanor acted on impulse and quit the good part-time clerk job she had been lucky to land before graduation.

Later that day she jotted a quick letter to Jacob, letting

him know she missed the Nurse Corps recruitment. Then, she telephoned Virginia, who during Eleanor's senior year, had twice in letters begged for Eleanor to come babysit her two daughters and live with them in Millston.

While Virginia prattled about the hot weather, Eleanor remembered how she had successfully taken care of Aunt Bernadine and her family five years ago. Now at seventeen, she was more mature and could easily help keep Aunt Virginia's household going. Breathing out a sigh of relief, this situation would be better and safer because she would not have to worry about her father visiting. She would not have to worry about his filthy attack.

Thus, during their conversation, Eleanor agreed to take care of Virginia's girls on some evenings and Sundays, and pay her aunt and uncle ten dollars a month as rent.

The next morning, Eleanor waved goodbye to Grandmother and Mattias as they headed for the barn, then walked to the Wilkes bus depot carrying two cardboard boxes of her things. By that evening, she had moved into the front room of Virginia's single-story two-bedroom apartment on Sixth Street, and soon made a bed out of the sagging sofa.

On Monday, Virginia introduced her niece to the office manager at Fitzwater Fruit Packing Company where she worked. Eleanor was hired and started logging outgoing shipments at the loading dock. Earning forty cents an hour, she planned to save money. For what, she was not sure. A room in a boarding house? A used car? She wanted to go to college, but that was too expensive.

All that first day of work, her dreams drifted away as if toward an empty shoreline. Her face hung with a distant gaze while she spent hours arguing with herself—like singing off-key without accompaniment.

Sizing up her options, Eleanor could continue working at

the packing company. Or maybe get a job at Pete's lumber mill.

That is, if I had the nerve to ask him. I haven't even called, because how could I show my face to them?

She thought of Jacob, and his words, *"been thinking ... of buying a farm,"* hammered in her mind. Once he returned, then what? Marry and go live with him as a farmer's wife? Step around barnyard muck, shovel manure? Find herself in the exact life she'd worked so hard to avoid?

No. Jacob was a great guy, but Eleanor didn't want to endure that.

One evening, after standing on the hot, grimy dock at work, comparing the fruit packing lists to the correct purchase orders, Eleanor rallied enough energy to walk to the nearest pay phone. Rummaging through her purse, she found Janice's phone number, then inserted a nickel into the coin slot.

"Janice? It's me. Eleanor." She listened to Janice on the other line.

"Eleanor? Is that you? How are you?"

"I'm okay. I'm living here again—with my aunt over on Sixth Street."

Janice's enthusiastic squeal was so loud that Eleanor had to hold the black receiver away from her ear, but hearing her friend's genuine surprise brightened her mood.

"That's great. I want to see you." Without taking a breath, Janice nattered on. "Oh gosh. I have so much to tell you. Bill's and my wedding is going to be next month. Then he's gonna be shipping out on the twentieth. I can't even begin to tell you how scared I am that he's leaving."

"Hopefully, he'll be okay, and he'll be back before you

know it," said Eleanor, trying to cheer her best friend. "I'll be around, and we can get through it together." Eleanor breathed slowly, thinking about Jacob who was somewhere in the Pacific Theater.

"Say, how's Mrs. Halsey?" Since Eleanor was back, she wanted to visit and apologize to her former music teacher for missing her performance.

"She's gone. She left right after school let out. Her husband came home injured. And last I heard, she moved back to California."

"Oh," Eleanor said with a long sigh.

"She missed you at the cotillion," said Janice. "Everybody did."

"You're kidding. You mean everyone missed me? Really?" Eleanor put her hand to her chest. "Well, how about we meet at the High-Hat on Saturday after work?"

"Sorry. Bill and I are going skating."

"You're going skating? Gee, I wish I could go. But I probably have to take care of my aunt's girls."

"Well, see if you can get out of it."

Eleanor scrunched her lips, wishing she did not have to watch Virginia's two daughters.

"Try," coaxed Janice. "Really try to come. Okay? I know we'd have lots of fun."

"I'll try. If I *can* get away, I'll meet you at the rink at seven. If I can't, then I'll call you later."

"Be there!" said Janice. "Bye."

The phone line clicked, and Eleanor listened to the dial tone until she, too, hung up the receiver.

∿

When Eleanor entered the Riverside Skating Rink for the very first time, the organ music—an exhilarating march—filled the large space with horns and drumbeat sounds while skaters circled the rink on an oak floor.

Earlier, she had convinced Virginia that she needed a bit of fun after her disappointing setback, missing her opportunity to join the nursing corps. Surprisingly, Virginia relented because her husband, Jim, had already planned to take the family to visit his parents in Spokane.

By the time she laced up her white skates, the organist was playing a jaunty tune. With one foot coasting in front of her other, skating was easier than the dance steps she'd learned for the cotillion, but her shaky knees and waving arms still made her feel like a fledgling learning to fly. Gliding and listening to the music helped lift her mood, though.

In the crowd, she found Janice and reached to grab her hand, saying, "I'm a bit wobbly, but I love it!" Sashaying round and round the rink helped her forget about her loss for a while.

While Janice and Eleanor skated side by side, a dark-haired man zoomed by them. He spun around, skating forward and backward with precision. Veering close to her, he nearly bumped into her right skate.

She teetered, and losing her composure, she called out, "Hey! Watch it."

Janice giggled and, over the din of the whirring wheels, shouted out to him, "Yeah, she's just a beginner!"

He sidled near her. "Sure was hot today, huh?"

Eleanor ignored him.

Janice nudged Eleanor. "He's talking to you."

"I don't care. He's a show-off and nearly tripped me."

The man, who looked to be in his early twenties, skated around again. This time he asked, "Fun place, isn't it?"

Eleanor, thinking this man was far too impressed with himself, turned her head away and glided the other direction, hoping that was the last of him.

Near the glassed-in organ chamber, an alarm bell clanged, and lights blinked the "Couples Only" sign.

Janice and Bill linked arms and skated together. Others either found a partner to skate with or moved off the rink.

Eleanor skated to the benches near the coat check counter and sat down. The show-off with dark hair stood nearby until the bell rang and lights flashed the "All Skate" sign. She moved cautiously back into the lanes for the last song. The hum of rolling wheels ended too soon.

Outside the arena, after the skating session ended, Eleanor and Janice stood with Bill around his car. The young, arrogant man, whom Eleanor had tried to avoid, stood near a post behind the group.

Whispering to Eleanor, Janice said, "It looks like Mr. Handsome likes you."

"Oh," Eleanor said, shrugging her right shoulder, "I hadn't noticed." But she had. During the session, he had been flirting with his smooth wheeling. In the parking lot, she glanced at him as she hid her hands behind herself and twirled her engagement ring.

He smiled and winked at her in return. Approaching, he said, "You could use some help skating. The next session's on Monday. Let's meet here at two o'clock."

"Can't," Eleanor said, rolling her eyes.

"I'm a good teacher."

"I work." Eleanor tried to ignore him like she had all evening.

Bill interrupted. "Come on Eleanor, Janice and I are leaving. Let's go."

"I'm on leave for the week. I'd sure like some company. Where do ya work?" he asked.

Growing impatient too, Janice swayed from one foot to the other, then blurted out, "The Fitzwater Fruit Packing Company. Now, let's go."

"I'll find it. See ya after work," he said, tipping his head and walking toward the south of town.

"What about Jacob?" Janice asked.

"Well, what about him? You're the one who blabbed where I work."

Monday's work shift ended with the whistle blasting. Eleanor half expected the boy wouldn't find her; and strangely, her other half wanted to see him. She walked out of the building and sure enough he stood there, leaning against the gate. Her fingers raced through sweaty wisps of hair that flopped onto her face, and she wished she had time to wash, brush her hair, and change into a clean dress.

The first things Eleanor noticed about him were his eager smile and his Navy uniform. She had not known he was a Navy man, nor acknowledged that he was so handsome.

Looking at him, her stomach tossed like she had told a lie. Eleanor moved her arms behind her and slid her ring from Jacob off from her left third finger. Letting it drop into her dress pocket as discreetly as she could, guilt gripped her chest. What about Jacob? What had happened to her? Her eyebrows raised because of the sensations she told herself she should not be feeling. After all, she was engaged.

Scattered emotions barraged her thoughts. For a moment,

Eleanor wondered why she did not love her fiancé like Janice loved Bill. Then she bargained with herself. *That boy is just in town for a while. I didn't do anything wrong at the skating rink.*

Everything in Eleanor's view faded away. All she noticed was the boy. Their gazes met. Intertwined. She studied his wavy black hair, his large brown eyes reflecting a mystery. A hidden allure scrambled her reasoning. It was not his muscled arms or fetching looks. It was his confidence, which she'd first perceived as arrogance, floating effortlessly in easy syncopation over the skating rink floor, leaning casually on the cannery gate.

So immersed in looking at him, she did not even realize he held a bouquet of flowers. Red roses! They were almost impossible to buy because everything was in short supply and rationed.

"Hi," he said over the noise of workers hurrying to get home. He waved, then walked to Eleanor and handed her the roses.

"They're beautiful." Eleanor stopped, taking a whiff of their sweet fragrance. Under their heady scents were his smells of earthy autumn with crisp breezes. He had a freshness about him that made her raise an eyebrow in curiosity.

"I found you."

"Indeed, you did." She touched a velvety petal on one of the roses. "Thank you for the flowers."

He nodded. "My name's Dick."

"Nice to meet you. I'm Eleanor."

"So, if we can't go skating, how about we get something to drink?"

"I only have about half an hour because I have to get home."

Eleanor and Dick walked three blocks to a one-room

grocers, where he bought two sodas. From there, they walked across the street to the city park—the same park where Jacob and Eleanor had once strolled. Under the shaded canopy of a locust tree, they sat on a bench. She propped the rose bunch against the back of it.

"I'm here for a week," said Dick.

Eleanor nodded. "I haven't seen you around before. How'd you end up on leave here?"

"My parents, kid sister and brother live south of town." He dropped his eyes, then grew quiet. "And we just buried my other brother up there." He pointed to the cemetery on the hill. "Eddie. He died in the Philippines. Took a mortar to his chest." Dick squinted against the sun as if he were trying to spot the fresh dirt of the gravesite.

"How awful. I'm sorry." Eleanor shook her head and frowned. "Too many are dying."

"My ma took it real hard this morning. Ed was just two years older than me." Dick clenched his jaw as his shoulder twitched. "I remember one time when I was a kid, I got lost in the woods. I walked 'round and 'round for hours. Up and down this creek."

His eyes followed and glared at children playing and squealing on the park's swing set in front of them. "Nothing looked familiar. Finally, Ed and our hound tracked me down. Brought me home. He was like that, you know. Always there. A good brother." He rubbed the back of his neck with his hand and then struck his other clenched fist against the bench. "Now he's gone." Shaking his head, Dick's dark eyes narrowed as he slammed down his fist again.

While listening to Dick's story, Eleanor put her hand to her forehead to stop the dizziness she sensed. The tragedy of it all overwhelmed her.

He took a breath and continued. "When Japan bombed

Pearl Harbor, I wanted to fight. I tried to fake my age, but couldn't get in."

No longer on the swings, one of the children punted a ball toward them. Dick stood up to pick it up, then kicked it, nearly hitting the girl. "Nuisance kids!" he yelled.

Eleanor waited patiently as Dick sat back down on the bench. His pain had turned into anger. "Anyway, I wanted to bomb those bastards. On the day I turned eighteen, I enlisted. I hate 'em even more now they killed Eddie."

"How terrible. I'm sorry you lost your brother. That must be so hard, especially since he was someone you relied on. I can see why you're angry."

Dick nodded and once more glared up towards the cemetery.

Eleanor followed his gaze where Al Compeau, also there, was buried a year ago after being shot down while flying over England.

"So, your family lives near here?" Eleanor asked, guessing they owned an orchard or wheat farm. "What's your family's name?"

He relaxed his face. "Messer. My real name's Richard."

"I've lived in lots of different towns. I've never heard of your family. Did your sister and brother go to school here? I probably know them."

"No. They just moved here."

"Maybe I'll see them around then."

"Maybe."

Dick took a drink of his Coca-Cola. "I was lucky. Since I was a kid, I've always been fixin' things. I wanted to work around planes and that's what I got assigned to. I'm an aviation machinist on the USS Bennington. My tour started on the East Coast. Even went on liberty in New York City. Then through the Panama Canal. From there, we shipped to Pearl

Harbor. It was winter. And, you know what?" He looked at her with a teasing smile.

"What?" Eleanor listened intently to his story.

"It was hot. Hot as can be. Can ya believe it? In the middle of winter." He tipped the bottom of the glass bottle and finished the drink. "Man. What a place. The blue water. Sun. From there, we shipped way over to the other side of the world."

The playing children left with their mother. Above them a robin chirped while her fledgling, awkward and vulnerable on the lawn, tried to find its flight. The female cucked, then chirred to warn the baby of danger.

"I have less than a year before I get out. Then, I'm gonna start my own company." He nodded his head. "Yep, an aviation company in California. Maybe I'll work for that big plane factory in Burbank for a while. Make big money. Then start my own business." He nodded his head once more with determination in his eyes. "Yep, I'm gonna be rich!"

Eleanor liked that he had such a grand plan. His zest for life piqued her sense of adventure. Sure, Jacob was nice and had a plan, too, but farming didn't appeal to her. She glanced at her watch; it was half past six. "I've got to hurry. I have to get back to put my cousins to bed."

"Stay with me longer."

"I'm sorry, I can't." She quickly stood up, picked up her purse, and said, "I've got an arrangement with my aunt and her family."

After an abrupt goodbye, Eleanor hurried to her aunt and uncle's home.

~

Each evening after work, Dick met Eleanor at the fruit packing company gates. By Thursday, she had come to expect him. As soon as she stepped out of the confines of the lot, he grasped her hand, pulling her toward town. "Let's go this way. I'm takin' ya to the picture show."

Eleanor returned his enthusiasm by folding her fingers around his. She couldn't resist his offer and accompanied him. "My aunt will be hopping mad if I stay out, but ..." She shrugged her shoulders as if she didn't care, then smiled in his direction. "Let's go."

On the way to the theater, Dick and she meandered around town and talked for the next hour. He wove his dreams into a colorful tapestry, one she could see herself intertwined within.

She shared the story of her recent predicament. "I can't believe it. I missed signing up for the nurse corps by one day. One day!"

"That's stupid. They should've let you sign up."

"I asked, but the lady said no." Eleanor shook her head as if in disbelief. "I'm ... I'm so mad. And sad at the same time."

"That's bureaucrats for ya. Hey, why don't ya walk away from your troubles for a while? You won't be giving up, just takin' a break."

"Hmm. What do you mean?" Eleanor tilted her head in thought.

"Just don't worry about it. Do something different."

"I guess so," Eleanor said in a resigned tone.

After they arrived at the theater and settled into their seats, Dick pulled a small sack out of his jacket. He leaned over and whispered into her ear, "Guess what I got for you."

"Hmm. I don't know," Eleanor muttered back.

"Come on, guess."

The picture hadn't started yet, and the wall lights still shone, so she played along. "Okay, a box of rocks?"

He reached into the bag, brought out and opened a pink box filled with chocolates. Six sumptuous milk chocolate candies were nestled inside. He picked one up and caressed the creamy sweet to her lips. Eleanor bit in.

"These are scrumptious," she said, smiling.

With chocolate still lingering on her lips, Dick kissed her. His full lips did not hesitate. Instead, they spoke of his ambition, and she liked the way his lips tasted hers. The lights dimmed and the screen lit up.

When the main attraction started, Dick turned and kissed her once more, then held her hand for the rest of the picture show. After leaving the theater, they slowly walked around town. Heat from earlier in the day rolled off the paved streets into groundswells. Shops and offices were closed for the evening, and only a few necessary lights glowed. They passed in front of a church, and Dick's shoulder appeared to spasm.

"What's wrong?" Eleanor asked, worried.

"I don't know. It's the war. That damn ship that keeps rocking in the middle of the ocean."

She couldn't figure out what he was talking about.

"Maybe it's because I'll be gone in a couple of days." He froze in his footsteps, pivoting abruptly toward her. "Eleanor, let's get married." His eyes jumped with excitement. "I need you. I don't want to go away without having someone to come home to." He dropped to one knee. Holding her hand, he proposed. "I—I don't have a ring yet. But will you marry me?"

"Really?" Eleanor pulled back from him in shock at his bold fearlessness. She had only known him for a few days. His energy electrified her, took her breath away. She believed they were like two stars streaking across the sky, colliding into one. Her skin erupted into tiny explosions popping all over her body and heat waves were rising up her neck. If Eleanor married him, she wouldn't have to put up with canneries or fruit packing houses anymore. No more eating dust at the loading dock. No more living with Virginia. No dairy farming. This would solve the problems of her future. She could eventually go to college in California. Eleanor wouldn't be giving up on her dreams, just taking a short break, like Dick had said.

Acting on impulse and abandoning common sense, she answered him with an ardent hug. "Yes. Yes, I'll marry you."

She stiffened, then heaved out a sigh as she thought about Jacob. He was a nice boy, but Eleanor had been immature in her relationship with him. When she had agreed to marry him, electricity didn't charge through her like it did when she leaned toward Dick and his cheek lingered on hers.

"Well, we should go tell your parents," Eleanor said, excited.

"Nah. They ain't around. They left the day after the funeral."

"And my grandmother lives on the other side of the state."

"That settles it. We'll drive to Lewiston on Friday. Get married before I ship out again on Monday."

Eleanor knew they could apply for a license and get married on the same day in Idaho, and Lewiston wasn't too far, being right near the Washington border. "That's a great idea. I can't wait." While Eleanor dreamed, twilight blurred into night.

Thirteen

1945

It was after ten o'clock by the time Eleanor walked into Virginia and Jim's house.

"Where've *you* been?" Virginia asked in a menacing tone. She scrutinized Eleanor up and down, from her tousled hair to her shoes, as if searching for clues about her whereabouts for the last five hours. She scowled. "You're supposed to be here. Babysitting these kids. That's the agreement. Not coming home all hours of the night. It's almost midnight for goodness' sake. We waited for you to put the girls to bed."

The July day had devoured every cooling cloud, leaving the earth scorched, the two-bedroom apartment stuffy, and her aunt's temper hot. When Eleanor went to the picture show in the afternoon, she had not told her she would be late.

Virginia squinted at her. Without a care about her anger, Eleanor kicked off her shoes and grinned until her cheeks ached. "Oh, Virginia. The most wonderful thing is happening. I'm getting married."

"I didn't know Jacob was home," she said, closing the door of the girls' room.

"It's not Jacob."

"Not Jacob?" Her voice swooped up an octave in surprise as she stopped in mid-step. "What happened with the two of you?" Virginia shuffled her bare feet along the planked, graying wooden floor. "You sure been showing off that ring he gave you."

Eleanor fingered where the diamond ring had previously sparkled. "Well, I was. Now I'm not," she said in a rush.

"You're not talking straight. Anyway, it's too darned hot to figure you out." Cigarette smoke drifted from the kitchen, stinking up the living room while Virginia fanned herself with her hand. "You're getting married but not to Jacob. Does *he* know?" It seemed as if acid dripped from her question.

"No." Eleanor sighed. "I'm sorry about Jacob, but I don't think I love him enough to marry him ... make him happy."

"You don't *think*? Don't you know?"

"Yes, I *do* know. That's why I'm quitting my job and getting married to another boy. I'm very happy. We're going to Lewiston tomorrow."

"Tomorrow? Well!" Virginia snorted then turned her back on Eleanor, stepping toward the kitchen where Jim sat. "A boy you know? When did you meet him?"

"Last Saturday."

"Saturday?" Virginia whooped and glared at her. "You gotta be kidding. You nuts?"

"Nope. In love." Weary of Virginia's skepticism, Eleanor walked toward the bathroom to wash for bed.

Virginia almost leaped into the kitchen. "Can you believe that whore?" she asked Jim.

Eleanor listened to their conversation through the thin, cheap walls.

"I heard. I heard. I don't care what she does," he said, loud enough to wake the children. "Just as long as she gets the hell out of my house. It's already crowded enough."

They started yelling, their usual method of conversation. "Sleeping with Jacob and now some new boy. What a little whore. All her life. Thinking she's special. But her daddy didn't want her, so we had to put up with her."

"You're the one who wanted her this time. Take care of the girls, you said. Well, she's here."

Virginia defended her decision. "Stop griping. She watched the girls Sunday when we went to Pendleton, didn't she?"

"Sure as hell, the two of 'em ain't gonna live here," Jim stated. "Jesus, we ain't got enough room as it is."

Eleanor's neck flushed with hot anger as she listened to them. She'd intended to pop around the corner into the kitchen to say good night and sidestep their argument because she didn't want either of them to kick her out then and there.

She tried to ignore their comments, but instead blurted, "For your information, I'm not a whore. I haven't slept with Jacob or Dick." Eleanor wanted to shout at them, yet she continued in a cool and calculated manner. "I came to live with you because you asked. For once, I thought you wanted me. Had a heart. Now I see you just wanted to use me."

The silence in the room was interrupted only by Jim taking a deep inhale on his Lucky Strike cigarette.

"I'll stay here tonight and leave in the morning. You won't have to complain anymore." Before retreating to bed, Eleanor wrote a letter to Jacob.

July 19, 1945
Dear Jacob,

I hope you are safe and well. I've heard malaria is bad there. I have something to tell you and I don't know how you'll react. Our plans to move to Michigan when you get back aren't going to turn out. It's hard for me to write this. You're nice and we had some fun times. But I was immature. I didn't know what love was, and I've met someone ...

Eleanor picked up her pen in the middle of it. She couldn't send it. Letters from the home front were supposed to keep the men's morale up. Correspondence was their lifeline. Sending Jacob news that she was breaking their engagement would demoralize him. It could endanger him and the men he served with. Eleanor ripped up the paper and stuffed the bits into her purse. She decided she would dignify him by telling him in person. Eleanor then wrapped the ring in a handkerchief and packed it in one of her two cardboard boxes that sat near the wall.

On Friday morning, Eleanor looked out the open window and couldn't help thinking that the cool breeze coming in from the north and the apricot streaked sunrise were meant for her and Dick. The night breezes blew the harvest haze away and now the air smelled new.

Eleanor finished packing. Dick arrived after seven thirty, driving a green sedan. A surge of energy sprinted through her. Finally, the strain of her disillusionment sloughed off, leaving her with something to look forward to, a purpose in life.

Dick rolled to a stop in front of the apartment, where Jim stood on the dirt drive with the hood of his old Edsel propped up. That piece of junk gave him more trouble than it was worth. Thick smoke spewed from the car's engine.

Eleanor hadn't finished dressing or cleaning the kitchen. Rather than rushing to greet Dick, she threw on her dress— the one she had bought for graduation—and then tied on an apron. Into the kitchen she dashed, still barefooted, to dry the last of the morning dishes and hurry the girls. Minutes later, the old Edsel's engine blasted a quick boom and began running. By the time Eleanor peeked outside again, Dick was knocking at the door. She ran to open it, expecting him in his Navy uniform. Instead, he stood without his jumper on, and his T-shirt was blackened with grease. Her eyes widened as she gasped.

"Don't ask." Dick shook his head and rolled his eyes. "Don't worry. I helped your uncle with that rattletrap. I need to wash up."

Eleanor sighed and pointed to the bathroom. "That way."

Dick and Eleanor reached the Nez Perce County Courthouse in Lewiston around eleven in the morning. He counted out the money and paid the clerk for the marriage license. She fidgeted, remembering her experience at the courthouse in Brentwood when Father stormed out.

"Yep, I've been here the last couple years. Watched a lot of kids get married. Mere girls and boys," the balding courthouse bureaucrat said, as if declaring a historical document. "Guess it's the war."

Dick and Eleanor nodded.

"Boys on short leaves and girls, well, sometimes in the... the family way. You know, marrying to avoid embarrassment."

"Well, we're in love," Eleanor said, raising her voice with emphasis. "I'm not in that kind of situation."

Their simple ceremony lasted less than ten minutes, and as they left the office, the justice called out to them, "Well, Mr. and Mrs. Messer, good luck to you."

Leaving Idaho, Dick drove them along the scenic Snake River and then through the small Washington communities of Pomeroy and Tucannon, toward Millston. "Well, how does it feel to be Mrs. Messer?"

"Wonderful." During the drive, Eleanor thought about Fran and Pete; how they would be happy for her that she was married and had a future. "I have two dear friends, Fran and Pete, in Millston. He went to college to learn how to build and manage his lumber company. He's very successful. You should go, too. You know, use the G.I. Bill, and earn a degree."

He said with a wisecrack, "Humph. I don't need no college. We're going to California, the golden state. I'm gonna make my own gold there."

Nearing the junction for a connecting highway to Seattle, Eleanor said, "We've got a long night yet, don't we?"

"Long night until what?"

"Until we get to Seattle."

"We ain't goin' there. I got a surprise for you."

"You mean we're staying at the Valley Hotel? What a dream honeymoon. I've never dared to set foot in there with all those rich people."

"Na. Somethin' better."

Eleanor's mind raced with possibilities, and she happily started singing the popular song, "Dearly Beloved," to Dick.

Tell me that it's true,
Tell me you agree,
I was meant for you,
You were meant for me.

Soon, Dick maneuvered around a couple of corners and parked in front of Hawk's Tavern, a low-slung, clapboard joint at the outskirts of Walla Walla. A carved wooden hawk with outstretched wings hung above the entrance.

"Why are we stopping here?" she asked.

"Ain't you hungry? Come on."

She followed him inside. A blue miasma of cigarette smoke sunk in layers from the ceiling, causing her eyes to burn. Hanging on the walls above the booths were stuffed hawks, along with various other mounted heads; an elk, a black bear baring its teeth, a cougar, and some coyotes and foxes. The stench of liquor crept along the filthy floor and coursed from the walls.

A waitress in a too-tight black skirt, carrying a tray of hamburgers on her shoulder, nodded to a booth in the back of the dim bar. "You can sit back there," she said.

Dick nodded in thanks and winked at her as the newly-weds walked to the empty booth in the corner. Eleanor was not sure she liked her new husband winking at the girl. She tried to ignore it as she skimmed over a slit in the black vinyl bench, lifting her dress to avoid ripping it, then settling near the grease-stained wall. Dick sat on the other side of a gray Formica table where sticky, summer flies buzzed around the menus caked with dry food. This was not what Eleanor had envisioned for her honeymoon.

"Let's have a drink to celebrate," said Dick, grinning.

Eleanor scrunched her nose. "It stinks in here. And I don't want to drink."

Dick didn't respond as Eleanor kept quiet, thinking to

herself that the evening would get better. In one quick move-
ment, he pulled out a pack of Camel cigarettes, flicked one
up, grabbed it in his lips then lit it. The biting smell of sulfur
suspended in the stale air.

The server strolled over and smiled. "What'll you have
folks?"

"We'll have a couple of burgers with fries, and make my
drink a bourbon press." He looked at Eleanor. "What about
you?"

"A 7-Up." Although Eleanor looked older, she was only
seventeen and too young to drink legally.

"Nothin' in it?" Dick asked, incredulous.

She shook her head, squinting at him. "No."

"Okay then. Okay." Dick yielded and spoke to the waitress. "Better yet, darlin' make mine straight up. We just got
married today."

"Congratulations." Her thick eyeliner and caked black
lashes belied her melodic voice and demure smile. Eleanor
surmised she was about her age and was required by the bar
owner to wear such an unbecoming skirt and gaudy makeup.
She probably worked in that seedy place for one reason: tips.
Tips from men too tanked-up to realize how much cash they
left on the tables when they staggered out into the night to
face their empty lives.

While they waited for their food, Dick ordered another
drink. Eleanor sighed. Then, she squirmed, leaning left
toward the greasy stains, tapping her foot against the wall in
exasperation.

Around midnight, the ash tray overflowed with Dick's
cigarette butts. Puddles of bourbon where he had spilled his
drinks spotted the table. Eleanor sighed audibly as she grew
increasingly impatient.

For the third time that evening Eleanor asked, "Dick?

When are we going to go?" Instead of an answer, he simply waved his hand at her in a dismissive manner. She excused herself to the ladies' room. When she gazed into the mirror, she saw what had been a lively, bright face earlier that morning distorted into a tight, morose expression. Even her hazel eyes drooped. Splashing cool water on her cheeks to freshen up, she felt better and justified that he was nervous. Maybe about shipping out again. Maybe about their honeymoon. After all, their courtship had been a whirlwind.

After Eleanor returned to the booth, Dick's loud speech slurred so much she couldn't understand him. His obnoxious rants caused other customers to stare in their direction. She gazed downward, curling her shoulders over her chest while her humiliation mushroomed.

In her most determined voice Eleanor told Dick, "I want to go."

"Nah. I still wanna shelebrate."

"Now!"

"No!" Dick blurted, anger twisting around his voice. At that moment, his head flopped forward and hit the table.

A man in the booth next to them intervened. "Hey, son. Looks like you need to go."

Dick didn't move. Rousing him to pay the bill appeared pointless, so Eleanor dug into her purse and paid it.

"I don't know what to do." Eleanor started jabbering to the man. "We just got married... it's our honeymoon... He said he had a surprise..."

"I'll help you."

"Thanks." She furrowed her brow in concern. "I hope he's okay."

"Yeah, he'll be fine. He's just drunk." The burly man got up and lifted Dick out of the booth. While he supported him, Eleanor reached into his pants and got the car key.

Dick yelled a clumsy "Goo-byee" to the bar's customers while she followed, wanting to slink out without anyone noticing. The considerate man rounded up Dick like a cowboy and shoved him into the passenger side. He sprawled out on the seat. Eleanor climbed behind the wheel, then thanked the man for his help and slammed the door.

"Um, where are we staying?"

"I dunno," Dick mumbled.

"Dick. Dick," Eleanor said, poking his shoulder for a better answer. He started snoring. "That's great!" she mumbled in disgust. She didn't have enough money to pay for a room, so she drove several miles to Virginia's. When they arrived, it was after one in the morning. Eleanor's anger-filled adrenaline gave her the strength to pull Dick out of the car and support him as he walked to the front door.

He stirred and bellowed, "Where'sh that cute little wait-ressh? I wanna 'nother drink."

"Shush. The last thing we need is to wake up my aunt and uncle. I don't want them to see you drunk."

"What tha' hell. Lemme go!" Dick yelled as she loosened her grip on him. "Oh shit, my head." Dick grabbed each side of his head with his palms.

Too late. A light was turned on from inside the front room. Wearing only pants and standing in his bare feet, Jim stuck his head out of the front door and shouted, "What the hell's going on? Get outta here before I get my shotgun!"

"Jim," Eleanor said, "it's just me. And Dick."

At that point, Virginia, in her robe, popped her head out of the door, too. Standing on the step, Eleanor couldn't ... she just couldn't admit to them that Dick was drunk, and they didn't have anywhere to go for their honeymoon night.

"After we went to dinner..." Eleanor said, taking a deep breath while she made up a story. "By the time we got to the hotel, our honeymoon suite was already full." With a dramatic flair, she waved her arm and added, "Can you believe it? Here Dick reserved the suite, and the hotel filled it. It was all a huge mess."

Eleanor hoped they couldn't see the lie emblazoned on her face. She never was a good fibber.

She said again, "We don't have our suite anymore." In the past, she would have stammered and asked if they could stay the night, but instead, she embellished the lie. "They're crooks. That hotel required Dick to pay up front. To think they filled it before we arrived."

Eleanor, hoping she'd convinced them, let Virginia and Jim have a moment to digest her whopper.

"Goodness. We'll just have to stay here," she went on, announcing her statement with a fluttery lilt. "I can assure you. It'll only be for tonight."

"Really?" asked Virginia, raising her eyebrows with suspicion. "The hotel filled your room, huh?"

Eleanor nodded.

Jim grumbled. "What a load of bull! That son-of-a-bitch's drunk as a damned skunk.

Eleanor froze. She couldn't hang her head low enough for all the shame that enveloped her.

"Please let us stay tonight." Her voice sounded softer than a mouse squeaking.

"Humph! You're probably both drunk," Virginia said, chiming in as she always did with a negative word.

"Oh, for Chrissake, I guess you can stay. He fixed that heap o' junk of mine this morning." Jim opened the door wide enough for Dick and Eleanor to pass.

Dick regained some of his senses and swayed through the door on his own accord.

Staring at Dick, Jim snorted. "Jesus. What'd you do? Drown yourself in whiskey?"

As they traipsed back to bed, Virginia said to Jim, "I told you. She's a whore and now a drunk."

Eleanor wanted to shout that she was neither, but their position was precarious; she could not jeopardize Virginia and Jim kicking her and Dick out in the middle of the night.

Dick plopped into a chair in the front room with his legs shot out straight, hands hung over the arm rests, and head flopped back.

Eleanor shook out the blanket she had folded that morning and smoothed it over the lumpy couch cushions, then turned out the light. Her shoulders hung heavy. The bold act she displayed earlier had faded as she said, "Here we are Dick."

Dick slit one eye open while she rolled her nylon stocking down her thigh and calf. Between his teeth he whistled a sloppy cat call. He muffled his words. "I love ya'."

"You sure didn't show it tonight."

"What do ya mean?" His voice turned hot and cold at the same time.

She shuddered at his harshness and turned toward him. "I don't want to fight. Not on our wedding night."

"Good." He stared at her with fearsome eyes. Eyes that unsettled her.

By the light of the half-moon, Eleanor unzipped her floral dress and lifted it over her head. Embarrassed, she clutched it to her chest, hiding her body.

Dick raised himself from the chair, unbuttoned his pants, and with one long stride lunged for her. He grabbed her with what seemed like the full might of his muscled arms.

Eleanor drew in her breath, gasped, and tensed. His hug was

tight, too tight. Instead of caressing her gently, his arms squeezed her, hurt her. Instead of tender kisses, his hard lips mashed into hers. Instead of murmuring endearments to her, he called her names she didn't like. Vulgar names that bad boys said below the football bleachers while sipping flasks of whiskey. She winced as he mounted her. Eleanor squeezed her eyes tight, trying to shut out the memory of five years earlier with her father on top of her.

Together they fumbled. In his drunkenness, Dick made fitful attempts.

Eleanor acquiesced in fright. As he penetrated and grunted, she bit her lip for fear of crying out in pain. After he slipped out of her, she choked out a tearful "Good night." She still hurt when he rolled over, slumped on the floor, and passed out. Eleanor distracted herself from the searing pain and unfulfilling lovemaking by watching a moth dive repeatedly against the front room window.

Fourteen

1945

The next morning, Eleanor folded up the blood-stained blanket; evidence that she was not a whore. She hid the spot only because Virginia would explode, knowing she would have to wash out the dirty blood. While Dick slept, she carried her two cardboard boxes, containing her clothes and personal belongings, out to the green sedan where she pushed them onto the back seat.

Dick woke, dressed, and practically ran to the car without talking to anyone. When he reached it, he saw her packed boxes. Yanking them out, he tossed them to the ground, then he climbed in behind the wheel.

"Wait for me!" Eleanor shouted from inside the house, trying to catch up to him.

"You're not comin' with me. I gotta get this car and me back."

"We need to find a place for me to live. In Seattle."

His answer to Eleanor consisted of revving the engine, forcing her to yell over the noise. "What am I going to do?"

"Guess you'll have to stay with your aunt."

She grabbed the passenger car door and opened it. "I can't. They won't take me in again."

"Damn it! Don't be such an idiot. If you don't know by now, I have to get to the base by tonight to ship out tomorrow," Dick said, exasperated. But seeing Eleanor's grim expression, he stopped the car and nearly jumped out, beckoning her to him. "Come here." She walked around the sedan, where he hugged her.

"I'm your wife. You need to buy a train ticket for me, too," Eleanor insisted.

Dick stiffened and broke away from her encircling arms. Before she was aware, he curled his arm and hit the side of her head with his palm. She landed on the ground with a thud, knocking the wind from her breath. While trying to gulp in air and pick herself up, Dick reached into his pocket and retrieved his money clip. He peeled five one-dollar bills and a ten and tossed them to the side of the road.

"You'll have to figure out what to do." He got back into the car, accelerated, and peeled out. Gravel sprayed as he sped away.

"But Dick! Dick!" She stood up, then stooped to pick up the money as she wiped away a tear with her other hand.

In her confusion, it seemed as if threatening clouds collided against a thick sky. One minute he loved Eleanor. The next he hated her. Panic twisted its talons around her. He had hit her. Hit her hard. She couldn't believe it. Asking herself over and over what she did to make him so mad, Eleanor imagined all kinds of answers—all of them her fault. She should not have expected to travel with him. She hadn't understood his plans. She *was* being an idiot, like he said. Though, walking back to the house, Eleanor reconsidered and admitted to herself and the heavens above.

I've made a terrible, terrible mistake.

There was nothing left for Eleanor to do in Millston, so she said goodbye to Virginia and the girls. With cool detachment, she shrugged her shoulders, picked up her dusty boxes, and walked away because there was no love lost between them. Eleanor never understood why her aunt hated her. Jealousy made Virginia ugly, even though as a child Eleanor had no advantages over her. Quite the opposite.

With a dollar that Dick had thrown her, she bought a compact of Max Factor powder at the five-and-dime. She slathered it over her swollen cheek, hoping nobody would see a purple bruise appear on her face. Around the corner from the store, Eleanor called Janice from a pay phone, and wished her and Bill well. She promised to write them, but doubted she could put even two words together to express anything that wasn't melancholy.

She had not contacted Fran and Pete since coming back to Millston. Although she wanted to hide in a hole, she decided to call them. Hearing Fran's voice, Eleanor's expression lifted into a smile, making her glad she made the call.

"We've missed you. Clear over there in Wilkes," said Fran.

"I've missed you, too."

Eleanor had reached Fran just after she'd arrived home to fix dinner for Pete, who was still at the mill.

Eleanor told her about her graduation ceremony, the bus trip to Portland, and how she missed the Cadet Nurse Corps recruitment by one day.

Fran was sympathetic. "Oh, dear. I know how much you wanted that. What are you going to do?"

"I don't really know." Eleanor sighed. "I'm going back to Wilkes. The town's bigger, and I can get a better job there.

Then, for sure I can save some money. Try to get into nursing school."

"Well, whatever you do, keep your chin up. You're a strong young lady. And smart too. I know you'll find your way. Just in case you ever need help, please let me know."

"Thank you, Fran." Eleanor knew she needed to say goodbye. "Take care and please tell Pete hi for me."

"I will, dear."

While walking a few blocks to the bus station, Eleanor repeated Fran's kind words: *"You're a strong young lady."* Words she'd never heard from Grandmother. Words she needed to hear and try to believe because she didn't feel strong. And certainly not smart, either.

Eleanor touched her painful cheek as she waited for a bus to take her from Millston to Pendleton, and eventually to Wilkes. Dick's slap had made clear that the Cadet Nurse Corps rejection was no longer her chief concern. No. She had bigger problems to worry about.

Because she had no place else to live, Eleanor reluctantly moved back in with Grandmother and Mattias, and quickly got a job. Within weeks, they celebrated the end of the war. And when Eleanor believed sending a letter to Dick wouldn't put other servicemen in danger, she wrote to him.

August 15, 1945

    Dick,

    I'm glad that awful war is over. We celebrated at home and with my friends at Kelly's Department Store where I work as a bookkeeping clerk. People came in and bought up almost everything! They were all so happy.

I don't think I ever told you the date, but today is my birthday. I'm 18.

I know you're not going to like this, but I want a divorce or annulment. I can't live with you. It's over between us. We should have never married. I am too young. I'll wait for your letter so I can go to a lawyer.

Eleanor

Eleanor waited and waited. She had to. She knew full well that a lawyer wouldn't file papers without mutual consent from Dick or without good cause.

September turned summer's corner and autumn approached. Eleanor, taking advantage of one of the last warmer days, returned home from work at the department store wearing a sleeveless dress and a pink hat. Inside the kitchen, in jars on the counter, the scent of three-day-old sweet, clabbered milk permeated the air. She breathed in the pungent aroma, knowing Grandmother was making a fresh batch of cottage cheese. When Eleanor walked through the kitchen she still marveled at the modern appliances—Grandmother's electric stove and refrigerator.

"Yum. You've been busy," she said to her grandmother who stood in front of the sink getting ready to pour the clabber into the square piece of cheesecloth. Before Eleanor walked out of the room, Grandmother wiped her hands on her apron, picked up a letter from the table and thrust it into her hands.

With one glance, Eleanor recognized it was Jacob's handwriting. Grandmother's blue eyes interrogated Eleanor over the top of her wire-rimmed glasses. Her gray eyebrows lifted as if curved into a question mark. She and Mattias knew about Eleanor's miserable mistake with Dick because on the very day Eleanor left with him to get married, Virginia did not waste any time writing to her mother about scandalous Eleanor and her drunken husband. As a result, Grandmother continued to make a point to Eleanor: *"Jacob needs to know about the mess you've made. Hmph. And with a drunk."* Both Virginia's letter and Grandmother's harsh remarks seared into Eleanor's heart.

To Grandmother's scrutiny, Eleanor said, "No, I haven't told Jacob yet, if that's what you're asking. I'm going to, though." Eleanor held his letter—the first she had received from him in five weeks. The various postmarks on the front cover made it clear why the letter was delayed. Jacob sent it to her in July in care of Grandmother's address, but Eleanor had moved to Virginia's and then back to Wilkes in that amount of time. Always before, she tore open his letters, anticipating his news. This time, she sank into the nearest chair. Grandmother's new electric fan whirred, cooling the sizzling summer afternoon. Its stream of air ruffled the thin paper in her hand while the herd in the barn bellowed, waiting for their evening milking.

Eleanor opened his letter, skimmed the black censorship marks, and read his message.

02 July 1945

My dearest Eleanor,

I miss you darling. I haven't had a letter from you for a long while so it must be the mail. It's slow getting here. I know you were disappointed with the nurse corps. Try not to let it bother you. Together we'll make our lives even better than we thought. Anyway, you won't have to work. I have a good job waiting for me at Carlsen's tire shop and I can earn enough money to buy our own farm. I have a good job waiting for me at Carlsen's tire shop and I can earn enough money to buy our own farm. The good news here is I'm finishing up with the fleet now that the war is over and I'll be heading back to the Portland base. I can't wait to see and hold you. Then, we can get married and make our home in Michigan. My family is eager to meet you. I've told them so many things about you. I love you.

    Yours,

    Jacob

After dinner, the night sky shed a fragile light when she rambled toward the dikes. Scorched grasses that had already sown their seeds began growing dormant and faded to the color of buff. Eleanor climbed around the summer's brambles onto the earthen mounds. While she walked on the dike's six-foot-wide flat top, the waterway coursed toward the sea and lapped its waves at the shore like brushes sweeping a snare drum. Whiffs of willow and sounds of the river some ten feet below jolted her back to the matter at hand. Since the war was over, she couldn't decide if she should write to Jacob and tell him that she was married or wait until she saw him.

Fifteen

1945

Mere days had passed when Jacob telephoned, surprising Eleanor that he had arrived home so quickly. Cheering and yelling in excitement that he was back on American soil, he shouted, "I've come home to marry my beautiful gal!"

His joy was so loud over the telephone receiver that Eleanor had to hold it away from her ear. Meanwhile, it took all her restraint to avoid bawling from her stinging guilt during their conversation.

"I'm borrowing a buddy's car on Sunday morning and will get to the farm about ten. I'll see you then. I love you, darling."

The following Sunday, Eleanor waited for Jacob on the front porch. Grandmother's yellow roses climbed up and over a wooden arbor, draping their sunny-colored blossoms into a ballet of fragrance. Next to them, dahlias stood tall and proud in burnt orange buttons and plate-sized maroon blooms. It had rained two days previous, greening up the sparse patch of grass in front of the house.

Listening through the open window, she hummed a few notes to a rebroadcast of the New York Metropolitan Opera performance of *Die Zauberflöte*. Young Mimi Benzell debuted her role as Queen of the Night, the same aria Eleanor heard when she vacationed with Fran and Pete years earlier. And the same music that had once inspired Eleanor to dream about a singing career. She never tired of listening to that enchanted opera, *The Magic Flute,* celebrating triumph over evil.

While she waited, Eleanor shook a bottle of red fingernail polish that she had purchased at the department store where she worked. Before painting her fingernails, she slipped on the engagement ring that Jacob had given her. As she brushed on the thick lacquer, her hands shook so much she spilled the bottle and smeared the polish. Thankfully, her nails had dried by the time Jacob arrived, honking the car's horn in quick succession.

When he stepped out of the sedan, Eleanor ran and cried out to him, "You're home! You're home." Though she was relieved to see him back from the war, her stomach seized into fits, like rocks knocking against each other. She was worried about how she was going to tell Jacob of her marriage, and also concerned that Grandmother or Mattias would tell him before she mustered up her courage.

In the distance, the barn door slammed shut as Grandmother's and Mattias' boots thudded on the dry, dusty earth. They must have heard the commotion and were rushing from the barn to greet Jacob, too. Soon, the three of them gathered around, congratulating him for America's victory and his safe return. Grandmother and Eleanor hugged him while Mattias vigorously shook his hand.

Sure enough, Grandmother eyed Eleanor with a squinted, caustic expression. Instantly, Eleanor pressed her expression into a shame-faced demeanor that she hoped said, *"Please don't say anything."* There was no mention of Dick, so Eleanor guessed that her grandmother must have decided to let her granddaughter break it to him.

While the four walked toward the house, Jacob said, "I've got stuff to finish at the base. But I'll be discharged soon." His face revealed the relief of a man who had been uprooted from his Michigan life and forced to endure the past years in terror, not knowing if he'd be one of the lucky or unlucky ones. He stood straight and held his head high as if trying to appear vibrant. However, like emotions trapped under ice—visible yet not crystal clear—his eyes appeared flat, dim. War had changed him.

When inside, he beamed as Grandmother steered him to the table where a hearty piece of apple pie waited. Even though sugar was still rationed, that's what she baked for him. Its sweet aroma smelled of homecoming.

The first thing she did was heap mounds of fresh whipped cream on his piece of pie. "You look thinner. Here," she said, "eat up."

He gulped down huge bites, ignoring the whipped cream smearing down his chin. Mattias roared with laughter at the sight, got up, and spooned almost the full bowl of cream onto Jacob's plate.

After dinner, Jacob invited Eleanor to an amusement park in Portland, about twenty miles away, that boasted a spine-chilling roller coaster and a glamorous dance pavilion.

"I'd like that," Eleanor said. She excused herself and changed into a sleeveless dress, all the while telling herself not to repeat her past mistakes and make the situation worse. She shuddered slightly at the thought of how he would react to her news. She wondered if his feelings were too raw yet from the war. Then, the thought occurred to her that if she told him, he might leave her at the park in disgust and hatred.

She wanted to delay the inevitable but admitted to herself, *I have to tell him. Tonight.* Eleanor had to believe she was strong, like Fran had said. She had to live up to it, persuading herself that she preferred telling him in person rather than sending a Dear John letter.

It was around four o'clock when they arrived at the park. Smells of hot peanuts, pretzels, and popcorn drifted through the crowds. On one of the last warm days, before the cool breezes of September blew, sunbathers swarmed around the swimming pool. On the main fairway, couples walked hand-in-hand. Young women showed signs of expecting babies. Children chased and shrieked at each other while fathers ran after them. It appeared to Eleanor, now that the war ended, everyone was trying to reach for the American Dream— success and prosperity. Eleanor had aspired to that dream, too. Although, she had not yearned for success so much, but more a rising out of poverty.

As they strolled along, their hands intertwined. Eleanor's worries smothered her as if in a tight cocoon. Jacob's kindness started chipping away at her confidence.

During the late afternoon, they rode on the miniature railway, shoulder to shoulder. Then the two twirled on the dizzying Merry Mix-up, rocked back and forth in the Ferris Wheel's bucket, and screamed while they careened down the tracks of the Big Dip roller coaster. The rides were a fun diversion from her difficult mission: breaking up with Jacob.

For dinner, they walked across the street to the Western Coffee Shop, then returned to the park while the evening sky played tricks with colors, transforming from blue to oranges to purples. Metal scraping, amusement rides banging, and people talking merged into a buzz of clatter outside the dance pavilion where they waited. Jacob reached the front of the line and bought two tickets for the Xavier Cugat and his Famous Waldorf-Astoria Orchestra concert and dance. A poster on the outside of the ballroom depicted a photograph of Cugat—in a white suit and black bow tie—with a slogan underneath that read, "The Rumba King."

Eleanor hesitated at the door. "You know I can't dance. Let alone rumba."

"Nonsense. I'll show you how." Jacob held her hand, then gently nudged her into the foyer.

In the grand ballroom, lavish chandeliers hung, reflecting glints of light in hundreds of crystals, while candles shimmered inside glass globes on white-clothed tables lining the sides of the room. Jacob found a round table where they sat and waited for the waitress to take their orders. Meanwhile, the band warmed up. Soon, curtains of gold velvet rose and behind them on the stage the orchestra players were wearing black tuxedos. Cugat, who filled his white tuxedo with theatrical showmanship, climbed onto a low podium, snapped his baton, and opened the show with his famous song, "Perfidia." The violins glided and the percussion patted a gentle rhythm. Jacob took her hand and kissed it, luring her to the dance floor. Soothed by the grandeur of the music and dazzled with the romance of the Latin tempo, Eleanor's tense muscles relaxed some as Jacob swayed and turned her with his hands. Even though she stumbled several times, Jacob moved her like a summer breeze on the dance floor.

At midnight, Cugat and the orchestra played a final song, and afterward everyone kept dancing right out the doors into the warm night.

Jacob's arm embraced her shoulders as they walked back to the car.

Eleanor had to tell him. "Jacob, let's stop for a while."

"Sure, darling. Getting tired?" He looked into her eyes. "You look exhausted." He guided Eleanor over to a picnic table under an overhead park lamplight. Long shadows blanketed the grass.

"I know it's late and we danced a lot. I think you've been working too hard." He smiled. "Soon, you won't have to work at all. I'll be taking care of everything."

"I am a little weary," Eleanor said, casting her eyes down. "Jacob, I have something to tell you. I'm so sorry for the mess I've made." She didn't want to, but a tear trickled down her cheek.

"Darling, you didn't make a mess on the dance floor. You were wonderful. There's no need to cry. I'm home now. I'm safe. We're together."

Eleanor couldn't finish what she started to say. That she was married. That she wanted a divorce from Dick. That she was truly sorry. That she was trapped.

They were together now, and she could read in his eyes how much he loved her. She thought back to the day he had said goodbye before shipping out. She regretted that she had not returned his fondness and remembered how she vowed she would make it up to him. Now was her chance. Eleanor decided she must return his affection. She owed it to him... before she told him.

His lips tenderly caressed hers. Soon, they edged their way to a secluded area within a grove of trees, where they sat on the grass.

She returned his kisses. "You've been so good to me."

Jacob smoothed his sport jacket on the grass; they laid down together.

She loosened and took off his tie, then unfastened the top buttons of his white shirt.

Over her dress, his tender hands explored her breasts.

Eleanor helped him take off his shirt.

Under her skirt, his finger inched up her legs without rushing. Without vulgar words.

She brushed her hand along his chest and down his waist. "You deserve this."

"Are you sure, darling?"

"Yes." She nodded, then moved her hand to help him slip off her lingerie.

Under the trees, they lay entwined like vines growing together, and made love.

Eleanor flattened her dress over her legs while he put on his shirt. Even though she let him make love to her because she believed she owed Jacob for being so kind to her, conflicting emotions battled inside. Her adultery tasted putrid. Because that's what she had just committed. Adultery. She hadn't premeditated her actions, but rather intended the opposite. Nonetheless, she'd sinned. Yet, passion and a sense of love for Jacob began growing in her heart, and she embraced him ardently.

Somehow, I have to get out of this marriage.

It was two in the morning when Jacob dropped her off at the farmhouse door. With his hand, he softly moved her head to kiss her. "I'll visit you as soon as I can."

"Jacob. I have to tell you—"

"Be still my dear." He put his index finger to her lips. "I'll return." He walked to the car, climbed in, and drove away.

The drone of the motor lingered even after he was no longer in sight.

Eleanor's courage had drifted away like smoke from a spent candle. She failed. It wasn't fair to him because he deserved better.

Six o'clock the next morning came fast. Eleanor tried to rush, but every step she took weighed with misgivings. Every other day she got a ride to work from Mattias, who drove to town to pick up their mail from a box in the post office. He was waiting for her in the car. Eleanor dashed outside, grateful for his patience.

A half-hour later, she finished recording the store's accounts receivables, and Stanley, her boss, had stepped out to make a bank deposit when Mattias entered the office.

Looking up from the papers on her desk, Eleanor said, "I wasn't expecting you."

"Eleanor, you got a letter," he said all out of breath. "I hurried over." He handed it to her with gravity carved into his expression.

Even though the war ended, Eleanor still received letters from a few servicemen who hadn't yet been discharged. But she knew Mattias wouldn't visit her at work with any of those. She took the letter and drew in a deep gasp. It was from Dick and postmarked from California. Her hands trembled so much she accidentally tore the letter in half. Her uncle stood by as she pieced it together and read it.

11 September 1945
 Dear Eleanor,

I'm back in Californeea. I tried calling. Nobody got the phone. I'm here for a while then I get discharged. Did you hear we bombed Japan? I'm coming up soon. The next time I call, I hope somebuddy hears the damn phone.

Your husband
Dick

"He's stateside already." Eleanor clutched the base of her throat with her hand. She struggled to breathe. Fear overwhelmed her—the same kind of fear she'd endured when Father molested her. "This can't be. This just can't happen."

"What can't?" asked Mattias. His tremors had increased since the move to Wilkes, and she worried about him. Perhaps the responsibility of the sixty head of cows, the early mornings, and the workload stressed him. Because of his condition, Eleanor tried not to bother him with her problems. At that moment though, she needed him and was relieved he waited there to listen.

"Thanks for delivering this. It's terrible news." She let the letter pieces drop. "I didn't realize Dick would be back so soon."

"The war's over. Guess lots of G.I.s are coming back," Mattias said.

"Yes," she agreed, then tilted her head. "That's odd. He didn't answer me about getting a divorce." Her right foot started to shake, and she felt like a fox ensnared in a leg trap, unable to break free.

Sixteen

1945

Eleanor glanced at the office calendar. Friday, September 28[h], was the last business day of the month and the end of Kelly Department Store's billing cycle. She and her boss, Stanley, stayed into the evening to finish preparing the month's invoices.

After closing the accounting office door, they stood briefly outside while Stanley remarked, "Man. It's almost seven. Sorry it's so late. Have a good weekend. See you Monday."

Eleanor waved goodbye.

Earlier that week, Eleanor had received another letter from Jacob, writing that he would be visiting her on Sunday, September 30. She counted the days. She had only two days to bolster her courage and figure out how to tell Jacob her predicament.

After the long hours of preparing customers' bills, she was tired and wanted to rush home. At the intersection, where she waited for a car to pass, a barrage of rain pelted down.

Soon the streets reflected the traffic and car headlights. Couples, caught unawares, dashed to the movie ticket booth for the seven o'clock showing. Others ducked under restaurant awnings along Third Street. As she crossed the street in the dense night, the autumn storm beat down on her black umbrella while she splattered through puddles in her galoshes. She suddenly heard a gruff voice hiss behind her. "Hey. You."

Eleanor flinched and turned around. "Dick?" She squeezed her shoulders together and hunched over as if to guard herself against him.

"I seen ya. You been waitin' for me, huh?" He loped toward her as his shoes pounded the road.

"I didn't know you were coming."

"Well, I ain't your lover boy if that's who you was lookin' fer." He stomped closer. Whiskey odors spewed from his breath.

"I wasn't looking for him… or anybody else." Eleanor backed away, holding the umbrella in front of her. She started trembling. "I'm just trying to get home."

In a quick swoop, Dick knocked her umbrella out of her hand to the sidewalk, and then pushed her against a building.

"You're hurting me."

"Ha."

"Let go of me." Eleanor's voice cracked. She wanted her words to be loud enough so passersby could hear. But they stuck in her throat, lost in the hammer of the heavy rain.

"Dick. I…I wrote you. I want a divorce."

"No!"

"I made a terrible mistake. I'm sorry."

"You ain't leaving me. Nobody kicks me out like a can down the street."

"Dick!" Eleanor tried to squirm away from him, but his arms pinned her torso to the hard bricks.

His mouth inched near hers. "You gotta remember, I can figure out wheres you live. Find your granny. And, that Uncle Gimp of yours. Why, I could break him with one swipe of my knife."

He let go with one hand and reached into his jacket, pulling out a knife about nine inches long, and flashing it in front of Eleanor.

Almost whimpering, Eleanor said, "Please ... Dick. No."

"You beggin' now?" He mimicked her by repeating in a falsetto voice, "Please Dick. Please Dick."

"Dick! I'm starting to feel sick."

"Sick, huh? I'll tell ya why you're sick. For wanting to leave me." His eyes squinted while his nostrils flared. "You bitch. You ain't gonna get no goddamn divorce. I tore up yer letter. If you try, I'll ki... You'll never see anybody again."

"You can't do that," Eleanor said, sniffling.

"I sure as hell can... and will. Now, you be a nice little wife and walk with me to that joint ahead. I'm hungry. We're gonna show everyone we're a happy couple. That everything's hunky-dory between us. You follow?"

Eleanor tried to sprint out of his reach, but he jerked her back.

"I'm a hero, damn it! Everyone loves heroes, and you're gonna show them guys in there you respect me fer killin' America's enemies."

After they entered the bar, Dick acted hateful toward Eleanor. "Oh, darlin' I missed you." He panted, forced his tongue into her mouth, and thrust his groin against her abdomen. His kisses tasted rancid, and he smelled of sweat and filth. She stiffened, embarrassed by his physical overtures, even though kissing and hugging homecoming servicemen after the war had become common. But he wrapped his arms around her shoulders so forcefully, Eleanor lost her breath.

The older men at the counter clapped as the couple embraced. Eleanor was disgusted by the satisfaction showing on Dick's face as they sat down at a nearby table to eat. Dick talked to the men while shoving messy forkfuls of steak and potatoes into his mouth. Eleanor picked at the food on her plate, unable to swallow even small bites.

"My ship stayed around Okinawa until they surrendered," he boasted.

A man sitting at the counter turned to Dick and said, "That's how we won the war. With brave lads like you."

While flexing his arm muscle, another said, "Yeah. We showed them."

Dick continued his story. "The ship's in Frisco now. They have to take her apart. She got purty goddamned beat up when a kamikaze bombed us. Gonna be scrap metal soon."

He scanned the place, as if checking that the customers were still following his story. From the looks on their faces, they were.

"I'm discharged now." He smirked. "Good riddance to ol' Uncle Sam."

They stayed the night in a cheap motel along the highway. Each time he touched Eleanor, she felt as dirty as she had when Father assaulted her. His mouth slobbered all over her face, leaving it sticky. His rough hands chafed her skin and held down her shoulders as he forced himself on her.

Afterward, he stripped the sour-smelling blanket off the bed and threw it on the floor.

"Damn, I'm hot," he said, waving his hand back and forth in front of his face while Eleanor shivered under the single sheet that remained.

Leaning back against the headboard, Dick lit a cigarette and pulled a drag; it flickered bright orange at the tip. Once done, he put it in an ashtray, got out of bed, and turned on a light.

Finding his coat on the floor, he picked it up and took his knife out of its sheath. "Ever hear of a Messer sword?"

She cowered and shook her head.

"Course not. Knights in the olden days ... they fought with Messer swords. I'm a Messer, and this one's mine. See?"

Eleanor looked away at the wall. She favored looking at *anything* instead of that awful knife.

"Look at me! Lemme me see your hands," he demanded.

Her hands shook as she reluctantly brought them out from under the sheet.

He inspected both. "Hmm. I see you ain't got that big fancy diamond ring on. What happened? You and lover boy split?" He feigned interest until his face turned into a vicious contortion. "And you thought I never seen that thing on your finger when I first met you. Well, watch."

Eleanor turned her head and gaped in horror as he picked up her purse from the chair, sliced through its leather handle, and threw it on the dingy floor.

"If you dare leave me, I'll cut you up like that bag ..." he stammered, "like this fancy coat." He lifted her new black wool coat and cut off the front buttons.

Plink. Plink. Plink. Eleanor, now even more frightened, stayed quiet as the buttons hit the ground.

"Piece by piece," he said, snorting a laugh that haunted the very cracks in the ceiling.

Seventeen

 ⟨ ∞ ⟩

1945

The next morning, Dick made Eleanor get dressed before dawn. He then shoved her out of the motel door and forced her to the bus depot where they stood until it opened.

Eleanor pleaded, "Dick. I need to go home and get my things, my clothes, before we go."

"No. You're comin' with me."

He bought two one-way tickets at the station window, and several minutes later they boarded a Greyhound bus to Klamath Falls, a small town just north of the California border.

They arrived late in the afternoon and moved into a stuffy one-bedroom efficiency room in a boarding house. The room they rented included a few cooking utensils, a sink, a wooden ice box, and a table with two mismatched chairs near the window. A bed, a wardrobe with one of its doors missing, and a small round table hugged the back wall. Next to the door sat a lumpy settee, covered in brown and gold upholstery, and an oak rocking chair. They shared an upstairs toilet with a couple in the room next door.

The following day, Eleanor begged Dick to let her telephone Grandmother to let her know she was okay and living in Klamath Falls. He grudgingly walked her to a nearby phone booth, where her conversation with Grandmother was shortened by his impatience and the cost of the long-distance toll. She never got the chance to telephone Jacob.

As late autumn approached the arid high desert, Eleanor parted the grease-stained curtains and peered out the small window. Honking black-necked geese flying over the boarding house caught her interest. Their chorus emerged in faint barks, became loud cackles at their zenith, then diminished into honks in the distance. Tracking their chevroned flight, she sighed and wished she could fly away with them. They were free while she was in a cage.

Next to the window was a two-burner hotplate. She turned her attention to the sizzling in the cast iron skillet and flipped over two pieces of bacon. She spooned out the excess fat from the pan so the strips wouldn't burn.

"Your breakfast is ready," she called over to Dick, who was still asleep. Waking up, he groaned.

The smell of the pork saturated all four corners of the room, causing Eleanor to become nauseous for the fourth morning in a row. She lifted the bacon out and placed the pieces on a scrap of newspaper to absorb the dripping fat. Placing two pieces of bread in the skillet, she fried them in the hot pan. Dick climbed out of bed. His hair lay greasy on his head; stubble covered his face. After ambling across the room, he sat at the table where she served breakfast. Bringing over two cups of coffee, she joined him. Steam rose from the black aromatic brew as she sipped it and secretly strategized.

He was going to go fishing. Finally! Time without Dick. After he found Eleanor in Wilkes, he had not let her out of his sight. Watching her as if she were his prey. With him out of the room, she could finally get away. Escaping was what she had counted on since he announced his fishing trip to her the day before.

He stuffed the last bit of bread into his mouth. Talking while he chewed, he said, "Yep. It's gonna be a great day fishin'." Walking to his clothes in the wardrobe, he pulled out his overalls and put them on. "They say chinooks are in the river. Fellas are landing big ones." He finished lacing up his boots, picked up his knife, and sauntered over the threshold.

Every time Eleanor saw that horrible knife, she shuddered, fearing he'd kill her.

"I'm gonna bring home a mess o' fish. You'll see. I'll bring home so many we'll have to eat 'em fer breakfast, lunch and supper." His grin radiated with enthusiasm.

"Fish sounds good."

Better than greasy bacon.

"Good luck," she said, trying to act calm as if she would be there when he returned. Her gut pitched for several reasons: anxiety, hunger, and an upset stomach she had been tending to.

Listening for his footfalls outside as he walked away, Eleanor dashed to the wardrobe. The one good door nearly fell off the hinges as she opened it. Grabbing her damaged purse from the bottom shelf, she stuffed it with her work dress she'd been wearing when Dick found her in Wilkes. Eleanor felt a twinge of regret that she couldn't wear her wristwatch with the second hand anymore; Dick had pawned it just days after they settled in Klamath Falls. While at the pawn shop, he bought her a pair of worn oxfords and a couple of ratty old housedresses, two sizes too big. One, she wore that day and the other she left hanging in the portable closet. She put on her black wool coat—minus the buttons—and fled.

Eleanor rushed down the stairs and out the front door toward the Greyhound bus stop, four blocks north of the boarding house. The town was bathed in white light, the kind that was too bright to hide in. So, she avoided the open sidewalk and crept close to a building in its shadow. Its rough red bricks scraped her knuckles.

Dodging to the next structure, a cramp seized her abdomen, causing the stale and bitter coffee from earlier that morning to rise from her stomach. She vomited, bile souring her mouth as she wiped her lips with her scraped knuckles while fixating on her condition. Even at eighteen, Eleanor didn't know much about pregnancy, but her woman's intuition had her reaching inside of the thick, wool coat and placing her hand on her abdomen. She was pregnant. She *knew* the baby was Jacob's and yearned to tell him.

Breathing heavily, she halted to consider her options.

What am I doing? I need to go to the police.

She pivoted around and headed away from the bus station and toward the police station to file a report against Dick. Starting to walk southward, a loud honk from a car alerted Eleanor to stop before moving in front of several passing vehicles. Waiting at the intersection while they drove forward, she reconsidered her decision.

If Eleanor went to the police, what would she tell them? That Dick scared her? That Dick destroyed her purse? Her coat? Ha! They'd laugh. Would she tell them Dick had threatened her? Who would they believe? Dick or her? Dick could cheat and charm his way to convince others to trust him. The police would consider her accusations as nothing more than a lover's spat. Her plan was filled with holes. She stood frozen, unable to move, sensing the weight of her situation, when Eleanor heard footsteps behind her. Dick's stomps ceased as his fingers closed hard around her arm. Her purse fell to the ground, spilling her good dress onto the sidewalk.

"You bitch! You tryin' to leave me?" he spat. "I been watchin' you go up and down the street like some whore." His eyes glared black, bottomless. He had tricked Eleanor.

While he tugged Eleanor toward the boarding house, she made up an excuse. "I was just going to the market. We're running out of food."

He yanked her harder.

A sick taste of failure flooded her. Like a prisoner caught after escaping, she acquiesced. Once Eleanor and Dick were inside the efficiency room and the door slammed shut due to his force, his fist whacked her. Black spots flashed in front of her as her jaw clacked, and she fell backward onto the bed.

"Oh, no you don't." He took off his jacket and threw it against the wall, thudding as it fell. Next, he seized the garbage can, its metal scraping the floor. Digging into the greasy newspapers and bacon drippings, he pulled out a foul-smelling handful of sopping coffee grounds. Brown streaks oozed through his fingers to the floor. He mashed the grounds between his hands, as if he were washing them clean, then flung the grounds at Eleanor and began smearing them over the blanket.

Her eyes popped wide open as she watched in disbelief.

He swiped more of the black slop on the sheets.

Too afraid to move, she lay on the cold, wet, and filthy bed until an hour later when he walked toward her. Eleanor cringed, covering her face with her right arm.

"You know I love you." He wailed, looking downward.

The reek of his tobacco breath exploded. He repeated, "I don't know what happened. *You* made me do it. You was leavin'." He whined in a subdued voice, sounding like a dog looks when rolling over in submission. "You gotta know. I can't help it."

Eleanor's voice escalated to a high pitch. "You can't help throwing coffee grounds all over? What's wrong with you?"

He didn't answer.

"You're lying." Shaking, Eleanor rose from the bed and stared at him. "Did you suffer some kind of shell shock in the war? Or are you just plain mean and sick in the head?"

He sat down in the rocking chair with his head hung and his elbows resting on his knees. "Don't know. So just quit your nagging."

He had just hit Eleanor, threw garbage at her, and smeared it all over their bed. His answer and wailing didn't excuse his brutality.

She pondered the incident for the next hour, then started to blame herself. *No wonder he went out of his mind. I made him mad.* When she climbed off the bed, she silently vowed to be extra careful because she had more to worry about than herself now. Eleanor had a baby to protect.

Eighteen

1946

All through the winter months, Dick and his knife overpowered her every move. He haunted her like a marauding vandal lying in wait. As a result, she lay awake for hours at night. Sleepless and afraid.

By February, snow drifts had frozen on the outside of the window and cold permeated their room. Drawing the curtains closed and retreating to bed—only to wake from daytime nightmares—became her daily routine. Overwhelming despair swelled in Eleanor like a gorged river in spring. While she filled the waist of her dresses, she couldn't summon any optimism, as if she had fallen into a pond and her blood froze. Moving her arms, even walking inside the cramped room did not alleviate her heavy dread.

Dick hadn't noticed the changes in her body. He had only grown more irritable.

So, one afternoon, Eleanor sat up and in her liveliest voice, announced, "Dick, I've got some good news."

"Yeah?" he replied with a sullen expression from where he lounged on the lumpy settee.

"We're going to have a baby."

"Really?" He frowned at her while he scrunched his lips in doubt. "You're joking, right?"

"No."

With her answer, his eyes brightened. His face lifted into a grin. "How do you know?"

"Well, you know how I was sick? Now my belly's growing." Eleanor wasn't confident he'd be gentle, and her heart seemed to throb near her throat. But she took a chance and patted her full abdomen, saying, "Go ahead. Feel the baby."

Surprisingly, he got up from the settee, hovered his palm over her stomach, then placed his fingers on her. Muscles in his face crinkled up, and she thought he started to cry.

"This is terrific!" He sat down on the bed next to her and started caressing her abdomen.

His touch made Eleanor cringe.

Shortly after, he popped up and began ranting, pacing back and forth. "How long've you known?" Before she could answer, he howled, "That's just great! How we gonna feed another mouth?" His rage ended with his hand beating into her shoulder.

Her protective motherly instincts ignited. She shot out of bed, stood over him with her hands on her hips, and scowling into her fiercest grimace, she took a chance and yelled, "Don't you ever beat me again! You'll kill the baby. Mark my words. If this baby dies, you'll be crazier than you are now!"

After Eleanor's demand, he didn't hit her. Although she was thankful she didn't have to endure his abuse, she stared at the walls, spiraling more and more into a blue-mood quagmire. The room reeked of shame, and every day, she felt disgrace for the mess she caused. She wrung her cold hands together, fretting about disappointing Fran and Pete, who had such hopes for her; and for believing Dick's deceptions. She frowned as her shoulders slumped forward, so full of despair, that when Dick left their little apartment, she no longer had any interest in getting up, packing, or trying to flee.

He'd just follow me anyway. She shook her head. *And I can't risk hurting the baby.*

Concerns for her baby kept Eleanor alive, even when she imagined using Dick's knife to end her problems. Steel, cold and decisive, the knife held promise of her relief. Yet, the baby kicked with life, forcing her to cling to wisps of hope.

Before dawn on the morning of June 8, Eleanor felt the first wave of cramps twisting around her back to her abdomen. She got up from bed, moving quietly so she wouldn't wake Dick. Trying to walk, she waddled to the rear wall and forward to the kitchen sink several times. Exhausted, she sat down on the edge of the bed when a warm flood streamed from between her legs and soaked the blanket, causing her to frown. Her head flicked slightly back at the sight, then she bolted straight up and touched her belly. She hadn't gone to a doctor during those months and didn't know what to antici-pate. And Grandmother hadn't practiced midwifery, so Eleanor had never been around any women who'd delivered. As though by some maternal instinct, she got up again and dressed without a sound. Just a few steps beyond the bed, she grasped the significance of her situation when a searing pain strangled her abdomen.

"Ahh!" Eleanor shrieked, waking Dick.

"What's goin' on?" he asked in a tone that was irritated.

"I'm having the baby."

In an excited frenzy, he walked with Eleanor while she struggled to the hospital. At two the next morning, she gave birth to a baby boy.

Within hours, Eleanor held him. She touched each of his fingers, counting them. She reached beneath the warm swaddle and breathed a sigh of relief when she found his ten toes. She examined him. His blond hair, fair complexion, and crystal blue eyes were Jacob's. Between rosy cheeks, the sweet lips that nursed from her breasts were Jacob's.

The next morning, Dick walked over from their boarding room and visited Eleanor and the baby. She forced a light-hearted voice. Pointing to the baby's face, she said, "See the smooth line of his nose? It's just like yours. His long fingers, they're strong. They show how he'll be athletic and smart."

Dick's head tilted, eyes squinting as if searching the baby for resemblances. His face hardened. "He's got blue eyes. I don't. And his hair is blond."

"Oh Dick. All babies have blue eyes when they're born. My hair was blonde, and it changed." She turned her face away in shame because she hated lying. Though, she had to… to protect the baby. If Dick killed her, the baby would grow up without his mother like she had. And then her son would be stuck with this horrible man, who wasn't his true father, raising him. Eleanor couldn't let that happen.

Her son needed a mother. A mother to nurture him. A mother to swaddle him in warm blankets. A mother to sing to him. A mother to raise him in a loving home. She didn't want him growing up as an orphan.

Dick left without any more questions, and Eleanor wished she could stay in the hospital room forever, surrounded by the cheerful, kind nurses in the bright, well-lit, safe room. While she forced herself to halt that impossible daydream, new emotions began to stir. Cradling her son, Eleanor rallied, as if the previous curtain of darkness and lethargy that had shrouded her for months had lifted. She sensed a renewal. Was it strength? Courage? Whatever roused her, she perceived an urgency.

Eleanor leaned her head down and whispered into her baby boy's tiny pink ear. "I'm naming you William, because Ernst's middle name is William, and Grandmother told me a long time ago that it's a strong name." She kissed his temple. "It hasn't been easy for me. That's why I want you to have a courageous name. Because together we'll have to be brave."

Nineteen

1946

Eleanor returned home from the hospital with weak legs. Little William nursed with vigor, and she beamed as his face filled out into pink, healthy cheeks.

During the next few weeks, Dick rarely worked. He found a few odd jobs that lasted only a day; though, nothing steady. Eleanor faced hunger again, but she needed food now more than ever because William needed nourishing milk.

"We need money for groceries," Eleanor told Dick. "You need to get a real job."

He always invented some lazy excuse. "Nobody's hiring," or "I'm not feeling too good today." Sometimes he would just respond in irritation, "Dammit, woman, lay off me, will ya!"

Then, on the last Saturday in June, Eleanor answered a knock on the door. Their landlady entered and Eleanor offered her a chair near Dick, who sat drinking his morning coffee. The portly woman held William for a few minutes, smiling at him and admiring the layette and blanket the hospital had given him.

She turned toward Dick. "I've told you before. My husband's going to dump all your things in the street. You have until Monday, the first, to pay your rent." As she got up to leave, she handed William back over to Eleanor, shaking her head and sighing. "We've let you stay this long because of the wee one. But no more," she snapped, her face showing an unyielding expression.

"Fine!" yelled Dick, slamming the door behind her as Eleanor gently set her son back down on the blanket on the floor.

Heat rose up Eleanor's chest to her neck as she folded her arms tightly in front of her. She didn't know how many months Dick was in arrears, but they had stayed beyond their good graces.

"Dick? How could you?" She scowled at him. "How much do we owe?"

"Shuddup!"

Eleanor's dark mood stirred, remembering an eviction that had forced Grandmother out once in Weston because she could not pay.

The landlady had riled Dick, so she had to be careful and change her tone of voice.

"Oh, Dick," Eleanor said quietly. "Can't you find a job so we can pay the rent? We can't leave now. William's only a few weeks old."

Dick stormed out, banging the door so hard, it rattled the whole room.

Before the landlord could kick them to the street, Eleanor packed their things, and they left the next day. They waited for the bus in front of The Depot Diner—a cafe and ticket station combined—on the main street in town. Holding William tight, Eleanor once more scanned the area for an escape route before leaving Klamath Falls, but there wasn't anywhere to run without Dick catching up to them.

Soon, the Greyhound bus arrived. Its motor idled a mind-numbing growl as the three of them boarded for Sacramento, and within minutes it drove away. Dick opened the window near them. A hot, dry wind—kicking up dust—blew in from the east. Eleanor shielded William's eyes with his blanket.

This marked Eleanor's fifteenth move in eighteen years. After Grandmother lost the farmhouse during the Depression, she had moved the family every time they could not afford the rent. At each new place Grandmother had found piece-meal work, but every single move had drilled deeper, making Eleanor wish more and more for a permanent home. Little William napped in her arms while she daydreamed of living in a safe place–without fear of Dick and without fear of eviction.

Dick fidgeted in his seat and once, when the bus engine backfired, he jumped and then ducked his head at the thundering noise. At the start of the trip he mostly talked to the window, mumbling garbled words. But then, a twitch in his face caused his right eye to blink incessantly, and he started blathering excited outbursts of things he was going to do when they got to California.

Minutes later, he prattled to no one except himself. "Can't wait. Start on Monday. I'll show 'em. Fix whatever they need. I'll be a big shot. They'll come to me and say, 'we need you over here to look at this motor.' Go there. They'll see what I can do. They'll say, 'you're a right, smart feller.' They'll take me to another machine. Give me a big fat raise. Make me foreman."

In front of them, a bald man swiveled his head and started

a conversation with Dick. The man's shirt and tie were too tight, and his face bulged as round and red as a beet. "I hear you're a fix-it man."

Dick turned from the window toward him. "Damn right. I been fixin' stuff all my life. Aircraft, engines, tractors, cars. Did it in the war, too."

"I was made a Corporal in the Great War."

"I'm a Navy man. Aviation machinist on the carrier *USS Bennington*. Was… that is."

The man nodded.

Dick continued. "Yeah, I fixed planes that came back to the ship all shot to hell." The jerking of Dick's eye stopped, and he grinned, as if his worries were waning.

Eleanor hadn't seen a smile on his face for months. He talked easily to the man who genuinely seemed to enjoy chewing the fat with Dick.

"We was one of the flagships. Was there when we bombed the hell outta Okinawa and sunk their ship, the *Yamato*. Maybe you heard about it?" Dick swiped his sweating brow. "Then, one morning we pulled up anchor. I got a new plane that day. Met my new pilot, Browning. He was a good Joe." Dick turned toward the window again as his voice grew agitated. "But I lost him. Lost him! Five planes went down. Lost him in a strafing run."

The corporal shook his head in sympathy.

"The blasts!" Dick's arms flailed and covered his head. "Watch out! Those damn blasts…" Moments later he lowered his arms and added in a more subdued voice, "He was a good Joe. A good Joe …"

"Damn shame. I lost buddies, too. In France," the man said. "But we beat the bastards, didn't we?"

"Yeah." Dick nodded, bobbing his head up and down for several long minutes.

Finally, Eleanor touched his elbow to bring Dick's attention to his overzealous and uncontrolled nodding. Dick paused for a moment longer and said with a lift in his voice, "My dad found me a job. That's why we's goin' to California."

"Good deal," said the man, twisting his body back into his seat. "I get off at the next stop." He called over his shoulder as he stood up. "Nice talking to you. Good luck, son."

After the bald man climbed down the steps and out the bus door, Dick resumed talking at the window. "My dad," his shoulder jerked, "got me a job." He shimmied his body toward Eleanor and said, "I ain't changed my idea of starting my own company. I'm gonna have a huge factory. Everyone workin' for me. I'll make big money."

"I didn't know your dad found you a job."

"Yeah, you'll get to meet him soon."

"Meet him? He's in California?"

"Uh-huh. They're waitin' for us. All of 'em. We's gonna settle in a nice house near the beach."

Eleanor's brows furrowed, suspecting he was lying. She wondered how that was going to happen when he hadn't enough money to pay the boarding room rent.

"No, a mansion. We'll have lots of kids. We'll have a little girl next." Dick's voice grew buoyant. He touched Eleanor's hand and smiled at the baby, gently extending his index finger to his fair, pink cheek.

About an hour later, Eleanor woke up and Dick was bouncing William; right on his knee and cooing to his tiny face as his crystalline blue eyes focused on Dick.

"You know what?" he asked while stroking the baby's face.

She shook her head.

"We match. His skin's the same as me. And, that fuzz, it's gonna grow black."

It was as if the baby had cast a spell on Dick. His comments relieved her somewhat, because he might forget about their differences and be kind to William. But the mother in her remained wary.

The bus bumped along on the two-lane highway, through rolling brown hills covered in oak groves, then into flatter valleys near Chico and Yuba City. As far as Eleanor could see, fields of vegetables were thriving under the hot sun. Orchards of honeyed air scented their journey to destinations she had never imagined.

As the afternoon wore on, the sun seared the air inside the silver bus and most of the passengers opened their side windows. A woman next to them beat a fan back and forth in front of her face. *Whip, whip, whip.* She made the air move in soft palpitations while streams of sweat ran down the sides of her cheeks.

Eleanor took off William's blanket, allowing his naked chest to cool in her arms.

Outside dirt swirled into the carriage, making it difficult to breathe. Congestion on the road ahead slowed the bus, causing the driver to yell outside, "Get out of the road!" Waving his left hand out of the window, he pointed his index finger to the field toward the right.

"Field rats!" shouted a man with graying temples from the front seat.

In the middle of the road, a dark-haired man with a mustache hurried toward the ditch. He ran in leather-strapped sandals and pulled a goat with a rope. He switched the animal's hind legs, steering it away from the cars and danger.

The bus stopped. Several of the passengers jumped out of their seats, moved to the side of the bus, and gawked.

Four young barefoot children scattered toward the edge of a nearby field while a woman tugged a wooden market cart along the ditch. Its wheels jostled over dried dirt clods and swayed the contents of the heaped-up cart from side to side. Secured by ropes and twine were wash basins, blankets, a small kerosene cookstove, stools, and a table.

One of the riders asked the driver, "What's happening?"

He answered, "Looks like a stupid goat on the road."

Some chuckled at the news. The man in the front thundered a rant. "Braceros! That's what those rats are. Braceros. Get them out of here. They're taking away our jobs."

Eleanor didn't know what the word *braceros* meant.

The man spit the word out, heaving it like an angry lumberjack wields a maul when splitting a stubborn maple log into pieces. Even though the inside of the bus was stifling from the summer swelter, the man's insults sent nervous chills up her spine.

The family's cart reminded her of the many times Grandmother moved them. Knotted ropes had held mattresses on car rooftops. Galvanized wash basins and buckets were stuffed in trunks or truck beds. Even Babe, the family's cow, got moved from one place to another. Eleanor shuddered, concerned about the children walking beside the road because she knew what it felt like to be poor and ridiculed.

Beyond the ditch was a field of ripened tomatoes. Men carried baskets full of the fruit as women stooped beside the plants and plucked the fleshy tomatoes from the vines.

The bus resumed its passage with another loud engine backfire. Dick reacted to the noise, jerking his head back while little William fussed; he wanted to nurse. Eleanor unbuttoned her blouse and shielded them with a stained, yet clean, cloth as she hummed a soft lullaby to him.

Twenty

1946

After hours on the bus, they arrived in Cliff Beach, a small town on the southern California coast. Eleanor wished for a cool refuge and a clean washroom. Instead, they climbed down from the bus into a depot smelling of dead fish and diesel exhaust. Sand and a few cigarette butts edged the inside walls. Outside, candy stuck to the wooden bench where she and Dick waited for his family. On the building, a colorful poster advertised a Fourth of July festival with live music, amusement rides, and fireworks. Any other time, the celebration sounded like fun. But this was not one of those times.

Eleanor shifted from side to side; the weight she had gained during her pregnancy was gone, so her bones ached from sitting on the hard wood beneath her.

Dick shot up from the bench and started pacing on the sidewalk with heavy, nervous footfalls, while she glanced furtively from left to right for an escape route.

Their last meal was the evening before at a greasy spoon

in northern California. "When are they going to get here? I'm hungry."

"They'll get here. Quit yer belly achin'."

"I need to eat so I can have enough to nurse William. He's hungry too."

About five minutes later, Dick's father arrived. "Hurry, get your things!" he yelled, barking like a snarling dog. He didn't make any eye contact with either Dick or Eleanor. "I already dropped off Clara and the girls."

Standing up, Eleanor extended her hand to shake his. "Mr. Messer. I'm Eleanor."

"Yeah, I know who you are." He nodded quickly, then ignored her and grabbed a box from the ground. Sticking out from under dragging, filthy pant legs were shabby boots, one with a hole on the top.

"His name's Russell," said Dick, picking up the last box of their meager belongings from the gritty sidewalk.

Russell's brown hair thinned at his crown and grayed at the temples. Not a handsome, distinguished salt and pepper, but rather a grimy color. His face showed about a day's growth of beard, hiding his sunken cheeks. His nose was crooked as if once broken, and his eyes—his eyes drilled with the same fearsome intensity as Dick's.

Eleanor looked away and made a mental note to stay clear of him.

Russell lumbered to a Ford sedan, opened the doors, and grunted. "Get in."

Dick heaved the last box into the trunk of the car while Eleanor crawled into the back and settled William on her chest.

When they were all in, Russell started the engine, accelerated, and tore out of the parking spot so fast Eleanor had to grip the edge of the seat to steady herself. Wanting more air, she cranked the knob and rolled down the window. She couldn't let her guard down, but the coastal breeze coming off the ocean provided a welcome relief after riding in the suffocating bus. Light winds blew strands of her hair while she watched the beat and song of the town. Passersby walked in carefree rhythm on sidewalks in front of quaint shops painted in bright colors. Beachcombers carried pails and shovels with children in tow.

Russell turned toward the sea and navigated streets where low cottages with well-kept yards were laid out in a grid of squares. All through the ride she kept track of the directions they traveled.

He drove by a three-story hotel with a royal blue awning and circle drive, where palm trees lined the entrance and terracotta pots with flowers flourished in masses of oranges, reds, and yellows. Just beyond the hotel, Russell steered the car toward the ocean onto a path—not more than a rut in the sand and not any wider than the car.

From this perspective, she saw the back of the hotel, where guests dined in an open-air restaurant. The ocean waters sparkled bright and clear as if sequins tipped the wave crests.

Eleanor gazed around, thinking that this could be a nice town to live in.

Russel drove on a wide, flat beach. Cars were parked near the water's edge, and families sat on blankets and ate from picnic baskets.

"I didn't know you could drive on the sand," Eleanor said, remembering only docks and wharves on the Puget Sound when she'd visited with Father in Brentwood.

"I'm staying on the packed sand," Russell replied as he waved his hand toward the ocean. "Not like them idiots. Leavin' their cars near the water." He laughed an arrogant chuckle. "What jackasses. When that tide comes in, well, there goes the cars."

Ignoring his sneers, Eleanor imagined better days when she could flick water into the air and play with William in the surf.

Russell continued heading north toward cliffs and hills of brown, the color of potatoes. "Them's the cliffs."

"Are we going there?" She stuck her head out of the window, straining to see ahead. "I don't see any houses. We've left the town behind us."

Russell just continued driving; his gaze didn't waver from the bluff ahead.

Dick had been uncharacteristically quiet until he scoffed, "We're taking a joyride. To see the ocean."

Though Eleanor couldn't see his face, she detected a smirk from his voice.

About five minutes beyond the beach access, Russell's car bounced and jolted over small rocks and low, bumpy mounds. In a cove ahead were two make-shift camps: one group of two shacks stood across a thin river and another cluster of four lean-tos were on the near side of it. Russell braked and turned off the engine. The camps were hemmed in by the cliff on the east, the river on the north, the ocean on the west, and the long beach to the south.

A young boy about eight years old, sun-tanned and bone-thin, bounded from one of the shacks over to the car as an older girl, maybe twelve, with ratty brown hair, set out a wash basin near a campfire. Eleanor could not understand why Russell halted the car at what looked like a rundown Hooverville—a shantytown leftover from the Depression made of cardboard, scrap wood, canvas tarps, burlap, and rusted corrugated tin. Or why a boy with chestnut curly hair ran toward the car.

"Dick! Dick! You're here," said the boy, yelling loud enough for Eleanor to hear over the ocean's surf.

"Why are we stopping?" Eleanor asked, squinting suspiciously.

Dick cleared his throat. "Um..." he stammered, "we're gonna live here 'til we find a house."

"What!" Eleanor shrieked. "I'm not living in one of those!" She jerked her hand up and covered her mouth, gasping in disbelief. "We need a house. An apartment. A baby can't live in a cardboard shack."

As Dick got out of the car, he yelled at her to "Shuddup!"

The wretched hut was much worse than anything she had ever lived in with Grandmother. A filthy canvas tarp hung over the entrance of a lean-to not much higher than Dick was tall. One side of it was corrugated tin and flattened gas cans hammered together. What had once been wood paneling—now patched with cardboard and fraying burlap—was the second side. Both sloped from the front until it reached thick vegetation in the back. It looked like something that had been belched up from the bowels of hell. Beside the hovel was garbage—cardboard, papers, heaps of empty tin cans, broken wooden crates, glass bottles, a smashed baby carriage, and other things rotting and unrecognizable—strewn among the drift logs, boulders, and wind-swept shrubs.

A woman with drab gray hair tied in a bun moved the front tarp to the side and limped out of the shadowed eyesore into the day. She crooked her arm over rows of wrinkles on her forehead and squinting eyes, as though she were shielding them from the bright sun. Shaking her index finger at the boy, she yelled, "Sam, get back here and help me!" As soon as her eyes fixed on Dick, she limped a quick step to him and wrapped her scrawny arms around his waist.

"Hi Ma," Dick said to her.

"Lord a mighty, we've missed you, son." She broke away from her embrace. "Come on. Sit fer a spell." She then called to the girl, "Betty, get Dick some coffee."

Betty ran to Dick with open arms. He swept the sunburned, barefoot girl up to his chest and lifted her above his shoulders, her legs circling around his torso as he twirled the two of them. "Whoa, you're not a baby no more," said Dick, almost out of breath. "You've gotten big."

Sam hopped up and down like a pop-up toy, trying to wrap his lanky arms around his older brother and Betty.

Dick hollered to Eleanor, still sitting with William in the car's back seat. "C'mon. Git outta there."

Eleanor reluctantly climbed out. Short, panicky breaths were all she could manage. With William in her arms, each step she took in the shifting sand weighed heavy with the fear of isolation pulsing through her. They were miles from town, and she felt the enormous expanse of the ocean and horizon close in on her. She was trapped. Whispering into his fuzz of hair, Eleanor promised, "The first chance I get, we'll leave." She then added meekly, "I'm so sorry, but we *will* get away."

Ma, as Dick called her, sat down on an upturned wooden orange crate near the fire, even though the day was warm. Sam settled down and dug in the sand with a stick, and Betty carried a cup of coffee to Dick.

"Hello," Eleanor said in hopes of making an ally with one of them. They stopped what they were doing and gawked at her. No one responded. The children peered with blank stares while Dick's mother gaped at Eleanor as if she were the oddest thing she'd ever seen. Their watching eyes made Eleanor squirm, and she wished she were invisible.

"I'm Eleanor and this is our son, William."

"That's Sam and I'm Betty," the girl said, scampering

over to Eleanor and pawing at William with her grimy fingers. "He'll be fun to play with."

Eleanor flinched, pulling William away. She didn't want any of them touching her baby.

Betty shied away and looked down at her feet.

Eleanor realized she had hurt the young girl's feelings. So, she softened and said to Betty, "Yes, he's a good baby."

"Clara, we're hungry," said Russell.

Eleanor looked at her. "Mrs. Messer, I'll help you with dinner."

A sky of indigo and a bracelet of stars held Eleanor's attention while Dick and Russell went to the camp nearest the stream. As Clara and the children crawled into the hovel, Eleanor shaped a bed out of newspapers near the fire. To protect William, she swaddled him tightly and settled him on her chest.

Before long, she could hear Clara shuffling cards and mumbling to herself inside the lean-to. Dick had told her about Clara's so-called gift of predicting the future. As far as Eleanor thought, Clara's fortune telling was nothing more than nonsense. Cards, and especially reading cards, were devil's play, according to Grandmother. Although Eleanor no longer believed in the devil, she didn't believe in fortune telling, either.

The fire crackled. Smoke blew Eleanor's way, but she didn't mind. The smell of embers rising into the air transported her to pleasant and fond moments with Fran and Pete in their log cabin where she had once been loved. Where Eleanor had snuggled between the Blue Mountains' alpine meadows and Fran's grace.

Eleanor turned to watch little William's suckling lips smack together. Her kiss skimmed his supple skin, and she whispered an apology. "I'm sorry son. I'm sorry I ever got us into this mess. I've been so stupid. I have no one to blame, but myself." She smoothed the blanket on his warm chest. "But we have each other ... we need to keep going."

Hours later, the Messer men drifted back into the sphere of the camp.

"We'll all drive over there tomorrow," said Russell, grasping the tarp and stooping to enter the shack.

"Sounds good." Dick took up a stick and poked at the fire's cinders.

Eleanor wondered where the two were going. Uncertainty washed over her, and she shivered.

Exposed, vulnerable on the sand, and smelling the briny debris near the water's edge, Eleanor pulled William closer to her, where they nestled like two birds in a nest. Not for long though, because she saw a rat skuttle near her head. Eleanor gasped, then lifted William on top of her breasts, trying to keep him safe from the vermin. Afterward, her night hours teetered between fitful sleep and wakeful worries.

Twenty-One

1946

In the leaden blue that appears before the coming of dawn, Dick's pacing woke Eleanor. His footsteps weren't loud, but rather a monotonous plodding in the sand.

The night's sea mist had dampened her hair, along with their blankets and the newspapers they slept on.

William was awake, resting with his eyes open, tracking with apparent fascination how his arms and hands waved in front of him. She smiled, relieved he was alert and unharmed. He was such a good baby, even sleeping longer through the night now.

Dick's shout interrupted her musings. "We need water for coffee." He pointed toward the river.

She rose, smoothed the wrinkles from the dress that she'd slept in and ran her fingers through her hair, trying to brush out sand. William started crying. She wanted to feed him before going to the river, but Dick would not stand for the baby getting attention before he did. So, she secured William inside a single piece of fabric that she slung around her shoulder and waist.

Scanning the camp, she found a bucket, then started walking to the stream. Fog, like woven gauze, capped the cliff and obscured the long beach in the distance. The silver ocean melded into the stone-colored sky as if they were one.

Muffled conversations came from inside a shack as Eleanor walked by. At the camp closest to the stream, a man in the shadows threw wood on his campfire, and sparks flew upward like orange jewels.

Strands of morning pearl and apricot began to streak the horizon. The river, which had been thin the night before, ran swifter. The depth of the water had risen, and Eleanor noticed that the ebb and flow of the ocean's tide influenced its volume. She veered away from the mouth of the river that would be salty and unsuitable for drinking and headed upstream toward a rock escarpment where water flowed freely. Melodies burbled as the flow poured over boulders, under dead logs and through thick foliage and grasses.

Eleanor took off her shoes, set William on the dry sand next to driftwood, and waded in. Balancing on round rocks below the surface, she surveyed the current to determine if she could wade through it. But she couldn't see to the bottom. Her shoulders dropped, realizing that crossing the river wasn't a viable way out. She then cupped her hands together to catch the life-giving liquid. After slurping a sip of the cool drink through her lips and into her parched mouth, she smiled. The water tasted pure. Almost sweet.

Above, the seagulls began their morning squawks. All the while, the ocean thundered, and the clamor momentarily reminded Eleanor of orchestral instruments: the surf keeping rhythm resembled a row of bass drums; the river streaming like flutes; and the sea birds calling out the bright bugling of cornets. The music momentarily comforted her, but she didn't let it lull her into complacency. Her eyes scrutinized the foreground, looking across the stream for an escape route, but the cliff jutted out, and she couldn't see around the other side.

Eleanor filled the bucket and was ready to carry it back to camp when two young girls swinging metal pails appeared from behind the rocky point. The taller girl looked like she was about ten years old and the younger one, who was maybe four, pointed at William. The girls spoke words Eleanor didn't understand. They chattered on, filling their pails with water, and Eleanor smiled at them. Their skin, the shade of acorn nut shells, shone in the first light. Sleek strands of their burnt-brown hair lay flat to their heads.

Eleanor spoke to the taller child. "Hi, I'm Eleanor and that's my son William in the sand."

They giggled.

Eleanor tried again, directing a question to the younger girl. "What's your name?"

The little one moved away, lifted the hem of her dress to hide her shy face and exposed her knees underneath. The older girl grabbed the little one's hand, then they ran off behind the jutting rock.

"Goodbye," Eleanor said, waving. Because they'd run behind the cliff after collecting water, she guessed there might be a road on the other side of the river.

When she returned to camp, she learned their mission was to find work. Eleanor tended to William's fusses and fed him while the rest of them drank their coffees. Afterward, she brushed her straggly hair down and put on another dress. With clean clothes on, she reckoned she might not smell too bad when she asked about a job.

∼

"That guy last night, Hank was his name...?" Dick paused, trying to recall. "He told us to drive inland. To McBride Road."

"Where's that?" Russell said, growling impatiently.

"How do I know? Just keep on driving. We'll find it."

As they traveled, Eleanor told them, "You can let William and me off in town." She suggested that for one reason and one reason *only*– she didn't know how, but she was determined to find a way to leave.

"We ain't goin' to town. We're goin' to Corbett Farms. Keep your eyes peeled," Dick said.

"Why there?" Eleanor asked.

"They's got work."

"I don't think a farm has much of an office or any planes to fix."

"They don't."

"Well, what do they have then?" Eleanor could hear the impatience creeping into her tone.

"Tomatoes." A second later, Dick shouted and pointed, "There's a sign for McBride Road. Turn left up there." Then, he turned his head toward her and said, "We're gonna pick 'em."

"Pick them?" Eleanor roared. "You've got to be kidding. Take me back to town! Now." Riding in the back seat with her were Clara and the children, who stared at her. Eleanor didn't care. Her anger—seething and solid—eclipsed her fear, and she pounded the top of the seat in front of them. She yelled again, "Take me to town! I'll get a —"

"Shuddup," Dick interrupted.

"... good job and we can get ourselves a place to live in. Besides, what am I going to do with William? He's too young to be out in the open."

Dick shrugged his shoulders. "Dunno."

He waved his left arm and flat palm through the air in a chopping motion, indicating to her to stop her questions and protests.

"Turn here," said Dick.

"I see. I can see it! I ain't blind!" shouted Russell.

Eleanor wanted to jump out of the car with William but knew she wouldn't get far on this dusty farming road. Besides, Dick's knife rode on the seat between him and Russell. Even if she and William managed to escape, Dick would catch up–he always did. And try as she might, she could not get his threat, *"cut you up ... piece by piece,"* out of her memory.

Occasional farm buildings dotted the two-lane road, the hills flattened, and peach trees grew in several orchards. On the ground under the trees, remaining peaches were spoiled and decaying.

Beyond the groves was an expansive farm plot. A small sign, painted in black paint and stuck in the ditch, pointed down a gravel road to the Corbett Farms. Russell turned down the lane toward a one-story barn. Dry earth swirled behind the car.

"I hope we're here early enough. Them guys says they only take so many pickers in a day."

"Well, let's see," said Dick.

The family got out of the car. Eleanor carried William, hugging him so intently he squeaked a tiny cry. Scanning the tomato field, she choked on her breath when her question about what to do with him became clear. Men and women bent over the plants, picking tomatoes, or carrying baskets to the end of rows. In the furrows were babies lying in the dirt, toddlers sitting upright, and older children helping their mothers pluck the fruit. All except the tender-aged children worked the field with the hot morning sun bearing down on them as heavy as despair.

Eleanor shot a burning glare at Dick and uttered, "How could you?"

They got in line at a table where a young farmhand, not more than a teenager, shoved a form at each of them and said, "Sign it." After they signed their names, the boy pointed. "Go over there. The field boss will tell you where to start."

Clara, the children, and Eleanor followed Russell and Dick, who both strode briskly to a tall man in a western-style cowboy hat. Dust covered his pant legs and boots. Blotches of red tomato stained his cotton plaid shirt and hands.

"Mr. Robertson's my name," he said, adjusting his hat up from his blotchy face and wiping his sweating brow with the back of his hand. He told the small group how to pick the tomatoes, in what rows to start, and the work schedule.

"Will ya have work for us tomorrow?" asked Russell.

"Depends on how you pick today. We pay by the pound. If you're good, you can come back. If not, we have others who'll take your spot."

"We'll work. You'll see," said Dick.

"Yeah, I've heard that before," he said, looking them up and down. He said to Eleanor, "I see you got a kid." His eyes glanced at William, but his gaze stopped on her breasts. "It's better without one. You can take it with you in the field. You just gotta remember, you're here to pick. This ain't no la-di-da tea party with the other ladies."

Already Eleanor didn't like Robertson. His lewd stare made her self-conscious, and she squeezed her lips together, stifling an irate remark—one that would have gotten her fired on the spot if she spoke it.

Dick trotted out with Russell and Sam to the first rows on the far side of the field. Clara, Eleanor, and Betty stopped closer in. Eleanor held William at her covered breast so he could nurse before she started. Clara and Betty were two rows away from her and already working.

She re-wrapped the blanket around William, ensuring a corner flap covered and protected his face, eyes and lips from the loose dirt stirring in the furrows and the sun's direct heat. Beside the bushy tomato vines, she tucked him under a thin band of shade, where the soil was cooler. While she harvested, she moved him along with her until the sun rose higher and the shade dwindled. He cried several times, but she had to carry on.

Once Eleanor filled a basket, she left him for short moments while she carried the heavy container to a wooden bin at the row's end. By the time she filled the third basket, her dress clung to her, and she smelled putrid. Dirt rooted under her fingernails. Dust swirled around her arms up to her elbows. Her teeth ground grit she eventually swallowed. Occasionally, she reached behind and massaged her back to relieve the spasms shooting up to her shoulders.

Dick yelled at them. "Pick more! Pick more!" Out of earshot from the boss and field hand, across the green rows, Dick shouted, "We gotta show that bastard boss we can pick fast."

"Shuddup. You'll get us all fired if Robertson hears you," snapped Russell.

In the afternoon, Betty came over to Eleanor's row and helped with William. When he fussed, she picked him up and comforted him.

"Thanks for your help," said Eleanor, genuinely grateful.

Betty had a knack for pacifying him and gently wiped dust off his face while cooing to him. In return, he waved his arms in front of him as if thanking her for the attention.

After twelve hours in the field, the field boss yelled into a megaphone, "Day's over." About twenty workers and Eleanor shuffled to the barn to get their pay. The men stood in the front of the line. Next were three women and their children. She followed them. In a huddle behind them were men and women who waited with their children until the white folks got in line. The ones at the end of the line resembled the family walking with their goat and cart along the highway.

The boss shouted at the families, "Get to the back!"

Eleanor didn't like that he forced them to wait behind. As she glanced at the rear of the line, she recognized the two girls she'd met earlier that morning at the stream. Until they were all in a line, she hadn't realized they were in the same field.

Russell stepped up to the table, where the farmhand announced, "One hundred, seventy-five pounds." He gave Russell bills and change.

Russell grabbed the money and counted. "Two dollars and sixty-two cents," he grumbled.

After a moment of figuring, Dick blurted, "Son of a bitch. That's less than two cents a pound." He stamped his foot to the ground like a protesting two-year-old. "In fact, it's only one and a half cents per pound."

Dick traipsed up to the table and held out his grimy hand, stained green from the tomato bush vines and leaves. "Shit," he complained, mumbling under his breath. "Two seventy-five. That ain't enough."

Russell elbowed him in the side as if to shut him up while they waited for Eleanor.

"Here you go," the farmhand said to Eleanor. "Not bad for your first day, and a baby too." His kid-smile and comment seemed genuine. He was surprised at how strong Eleanor was.

As soon as she received her one dollar and ninety-nine

cents, Dick, as quick as a whip, tried to seize her money with his tight grip. "I'll keep that."

Eleanor resisted, clenching her fist, and making a scene in front of everyone. "I earned it! I sweat for it! We need it for food."

Dick's eyes burned black. A muscle on the side of his neck bulged as he raised his other arm to smack Eleanor. In the end, he lowered it as she angrily released her earnings because his grasp was stronger than hers.

"What time does work start in the morning?" Russell asked.

The field boss said, "Six sharp."

"Well, guess we can come back. I didn't hear him say any different," Russell said.

"Yup," Dick concurred.

They walked from the field to Russell's car.

"They's cheating us. I know I picked more than they said," Russell complained. "I shoulda got paid more. The price of tomatoes in the store is lots more than two cents." He looked over to Eleanor. "What's it cost fer a tomato?"

"Hmm." Eleanor cocked her head, trying to remember. It had been months since she bought any because they were expensive. "If I recall, they're about ten cents a pound."

"Shit," said Dick. "Tomorrow we'll have to keep a watch out on that punk kid at the bin. He's shifty. All nervous like. Too busy to weigh our baskets right fer looking at them Mexicans—like they was gonna jump him."

The first thing Eleanor did after they pulled into camp was walk with William in a makeshift sling to the river. She washed herself as best she could, the swift current reviving her, and making her feel like she could breathe again. She cupped water and rubbed her hands together to warm it before touching William, but he cried, and goose bumps popped over his arms and legs.

"Oh, baby. It's cold. I know. Tomorrow night I'll heat up water for you. Tonight, I'm just beat."

When Eleanor returned to camp, Clara stood beside the fire, stirring a pot of pork and beans she had emptied out of three cans. Eleanor nearly gagged on the food. She had always enjoyed eating the kind of beans that Grandmother cooked. But these tasted terrible as they were mixed into the watery slop with clumps of indigestible pork fat and gristle.

After dinner Eleanor asked Dick, "Why are we working in the fields? Why aren't you applying at the plane factory?"

"We ain't livin' near the factory. And, if ya don't know by now, money don't grow on trees."

"Sure. We need money. But how much did we make?" She knew the answer because she had already calculated their combined earnings. "Four dollars and sixty six cents," she said with disdain. "You've got experience with airplanes. Use it. You don't have to do farm work just because that's what your parents do."

Even if Dick landed a good job, Eleanor vowed to herself that she'd still leave him. She just needed a chance.

"You gotta pick faster. I saw you dawdlin'."

"You heard the farmhand. He said not bad for my first day. Plus, I was taking care of our baby. We'll never be able to move from this dump on four dollars a day, let alone buy food. And the way I see it, there's just a few more days' worth of work at that farm before the tomatoes are all picked. Then what?"

Twenty-Two

1946

Following another long day in the field, Eleanor lay on her back in their beach camp with William on her chest. In the hush of darkness, she searched the cosmos and found the Swan constellation. Gazing at the pinpoint flickers helped her think of another time. She remembered, as a child during summer and fall nights, Grandmother and the family sat outside to cool off. Uncle Ernst pointed out the imaginary lines that formed animals and ancient mythical figures in the sapphire skies. He showed them the Milky Way, Big Dipper, North Star, Great Bear, Cassiopeia, and even the red planet Mars. One night, Ernst aimed his fingers at the Swan, a group of bright stars in the shape of two wings and a long neck. Although it was known as Cygnus the Swan, he liked to call it the little robin, after his nickname for Eleanor.

Sometimes, when only Ernst and Eleanor looked heavenward, he'd make up stories about Eleanor riding a little robin as it migrated south to a warmer climate or flew around the world to meet a mate. She cherished sitting side by side with him when the heat of those days rose from the earth, warming her legs, while smells of sweet purple clover and pungent fresh-cut hay drifted on the breeze. When her uncle shared his starry tales, the distinctive timbre of his voice was like a lullaby. Those stories had filled her with hope and guided her into the realms of possibility. Ernst was like a big brother to her. Smart, too. She chuckled, recalling impromptu ditties he had created.

She sang the two she remembered to William:

The little red robin
flew in a blue toboggan,
all the long, long way
to Guanabara Bay.

"Isn't that silly? I don't even know where Guanabara Bay is." She tickled under his chin, and he cooed. "Wait, listen to this one."

The little robin flew miles and miles to find her mate, only to see him perched on the front garden gate.

On nights after Ernst sang his made-up songs, Eleanor squealed, "Sing them again. Again." They laughed their cares to the heavens, and the stories he told made her wish she could fly like a robin to a world where nobody was poor.

She longed to see him and hear his comforting voice.

While Eleanor lay under the bowl of an inky and silver flecked dome, she wondered how he, Sylvia, and their daughter were doing? Eleanor had lost contact with him, Grandmother, and all the Bowerman family. Many times, Eleanor had wanted to telephone Grandmother, but Dick had forbidden any contact after that one brief call she'd made in Klamath Falls. Eleanor realized with a pang of sadness that none of them knew about her son, and she sighed.

Her groan must have been loud enough for Clara to hear

because she pushed aside the tarp, stepped out, and pulled up an apple crate.

"This is as good a time as any," she muttered.

Betty and Sam were sleeping. Russell and Dick were with other men at the camp nearest the stream. With the soft *brush–tap, brush–tap, brush-tap* on the crate, Clara shuffled her cards. A once-white, raggedy shawl hung over her hunched shoulders while she droned a monotone tune.

"I'm gonna tell yer future," Clara said, almost chanting.

"I don't believe in that stuff. I don't play them and don't like them."

"You ain't happy. I can tell. We'll find out what's ailing ya," she croaked in a raspy voice.

"I—"

"Hush," Clara interrupted, "don't be riling the spirits. I'm layin' the cards and listening to what they says."

Eleanor rolled her eyes and then set her sight again on the Swan in the universe above.

"You gonna sit up here? Or do I have to tell ya down there?"

"I'm staying here." William's soft breaths on her chest reassured her that he was sleeping.

"Suit yourself." The woman, who was in her mid-forties, appeared older than Grandmother, who was sixty. One of Clara's teeth was missing so sometimes her speech whistled.

"Yesh," she whispered, rustling like a sputtering teapot. She tapped another card on the wooden surface. "Hmm... bad omen." Clara's voice dropped.

Her comments unnerved Eleanor.

She mumbled something unintelligible, then lifted her head and lit her eyes on William.

Eleanor squirmed; she didn't like Clara staring at him. "Please don't."

"I'm trying to figure somethin' out." She slapped down another card. "Looks …"

Eleanor gulped hard. "Stop!"

Clara buzzed like an irritating sticky house fly.

"I don't believe in cards and fortune telling. It's Satan's work."

"Ha," the older woman said, crowing like a feral rooster. "Satan. God. They ain't got nothin' to do with us here. Is this how God wants us to live? If you ask me, we's in the devil's world here." She picked up the cards and put them in her dress pocket. "Wait till I tell Dick."

"Whatever it is, don't tell him. He'll just get mad." Eleanor sat up. "What's he doing over there, anyway?"

"Throwin' away our money. That's what them knuckle-heads are doing. Russell and I been picking along this coast fer near three years. Tomatoes here, putting in crops fer farmers in the spring. Picking strawberries or peaches in the summers. Then up t' Washington fer apples. Broccoli or grapes after that near here. And that idiot squanders our money on whiskey and betting. Can't never get ahead."

Eleanor didn't care about Russell spending his money on games. Dick was wasting their hard-earned money, which made her right foot jiggle in fury.

Clara got up, lifted the tarp, and looked in on the children. After days of them living in the hovel, a mixture of oily tar paper and human sweat escaped into the surrounding air.

Eleanor pinched her nose.

Clara sat and shuffled cards again.

"Please. No more fortunes."

"No, I'm just layin' out a game of Solitaire." Clara mixed the deck and said, "Ya know? We used t' farm in Arkansas. Corn mostly."

Eleanor turned her head toward Clara, surprised that she

was still talking. Since Eleanor had arrived, this was the first time Clara had said more than ten words to her.

"Maybe Dick told you already. We was livin' good. A house, land. That's where Eddie and Dick grew up when they was young. Until the Depression. Then, we lost it. Couldn't sell no more corn. Nobody had money. We couldn't buy seeds. Couldn't pay for the house. Started paying month to month for a little place. Russell was working for a fella, but that didn't work out."

The thin, bent woman snapped down a card and uttered, "And, now with Eddie gone, Russell's almost crazy. Not thinking. Don't care no more 'bout me or the young 'uns. Gettin' mean again like he was after we lost the farm. The boys, they was good then. Still, he whipped 'em so. Fer any small thing." She tightened the shawl around her shoulders. "He hit me too. The boys, they always came runnin' to help me.

"Mostly, Dick. He didn't like when Russell took it out on me or him. Told me he'd take care of me. Even when I got old. Knows that jackass takes all our money. Dick said he's never lettin' me die without a penny in my pocket. That's why he gave me the first red cent he ever earned." She tossed a half snort, half laugh. "Did during the war, too. He didn't want nobody to steal his money, so he sent it my way." She flipped over another card. "Cause he ain't very good 'bout keepin' track of it."

Eleanor was suspicious of Clara when she first met her, and she got irritated when the woman reached for her crazy cards, especially when she saw bad omens. But she could now feel a soft spot growing for Clara as some of her mistrust started melting. She almost got up to give her a little hug when she said Russell had beaten her, too. Eleanor had guessed as much. Watching Clara shy away in silence, and the children's guarded faces when they were around Russell, made Eleanor want to spit on him. Hard knots twisted inside of her—the same knots she felt with Dick. It wasn't Clara's fault they lost the farm, nor was she to blame for Eddie dying in the war.

Eleanor rubbed her stomach where those knots wound tighter. As calmly as she could, she asked Clara, "If Dick ever gives you our money, would you let me take care of it? I can help Dick... help him save his money. Then maybe we could get a place where all of us could live?" Eleanor tried to sound convincing. "I'm good at keeping track of money."

If Dick gave Clara their money, asking her for it would likely leave her feeling vulnerable. Penniless. But Eleanor persisted. "We need the money to buy food."

Clara moaned. Her sigh shook throughout her body, and Eleanor sensed her unease.

"Clara, please. We could keep it a secret for a while. Dick and I are married now. We have a child. Please. We would all live together ... somewhere we could cook and clean."

In the firelight, Clara shrugged her shoulders. "Well, he's keepin' it now."

"Just in case he finds out, I'll tell him it was my fault. That I took it from you." Eleanor waited for her reply. During the stillness between the ebbs and flows of the waves, she heard nothing from Dick's mother.

The men returned to the camp. Dick collapsed onto the blanket, reeking of liquor and sweat. Eleanor confronted him, even though he was drunk. "Dick, we need to go to the grocers tomorrow. Get something more than those awful beans. I'll get some bacon for you. I know how much you like it."

"Bacon?" he slurred. "Not just bacon. You're gonna git me a big, juicy steak. Potatoes and bacon. Yep, you're gonna buy all that," he snorted, "if we had money."

Eleanor gnashed her teeth, the tension in her jaw muscles bulged. "You've got money. I think you've been giving it to your ma."

"Whasht you talkin' 'bout?" His speech grew more garbled.

She stood up, anger filling her voice. She didn't care if she woke Clara or Russell. "Your ma told me that you gave her money. I suppose you still do. And mine, too."

He hoisted himself up from the ground, interrupting her.

Eleanor shielded her face. "I won't... I want to know where our money is and how much we have. Don't you remember? I was the one with a bookkeeping job at the department store. I know how to take care of money. Lots of it."

"For Chrissakes. Leave Ma out of this!" He gave Eleanor a hard shove to her shoulder.

She stepped backward from the thrust of his force, then immediately grabbed her painful shoulder. "Stop!"

"Yeah. Yeah. I'll give it to ya in the morning," he yelled as he stomped away from the camp.

After a sleepless night, she woke up and told Dick, "I want our money. You said you'd give it to me."

He pulled out his front pants' pockets. One pocket hung like a clown's floppy ear. From the other, loose change fell into the sand. She was positive he deliberately let the coins fall.

"There you go," he said, laughing.

She bent over to sift the sand through her fingers, finding what she could. She scooped up forty-four cents. "Where's the rest? I know you have a money clip."

He reached into the back pockets of his dungarees, pulling his hands out empty. He laughed even louder.

Eleanor wanted to clobber him in the head—for his lies, recklessness, and for starting to batter her again.

On the way to the tomato farm that morning, Eleanor wasn't certain, but Dick seemed to laugh all the way while Clara suspiciously cowered, avoiding direct eye contact with Eleanor.

The family picked on Wednesday and when they arrived on Thursday, the Fourth of July, the prior days' harvesting had nearly cleaned the field. Around noon, the field boss called an end to the picking to allow the remaining fruit to ripen. Most of the workers left the field while a few of them stood in line for their pay. Russell reached the pay table first, where he outstretched his palm to collect his money.

The farmhand stood up from the table and said something to Russell that Eleanor couldn't hear.

Russell yelled, "You can't do that!"

She wondered what he was bellowing about. The field boss walked up closer to Russell. His stature overpowered Russell's height by about four inches.

"Yes, we can. And we are. We need to make sure you'll come back and pick the rest of the crop," the boss stated.

"We'll come back," Russell shouted.

"Then, you'll get your pay tomorrow."

"That ain't fair. We need the money. Now." Russell's agitation changed to desperation as though someone was choking him.

Dick stepped up next to Russell and lifted his chin indignantly. As tall as the boss, Dick met Robertson eye to eye. "What's going on?"

The boss's voice boomed. "Everybody gets paid tomorrow when you're done." In the line, workers who were hired that morning grumbled among themselves, then left.

Dick stiffened and raised his shoulders like he was going to attack.

The farmhand spoke up. "Hey now. We don't want any problems."

"Listen bub. Won't be no problem if you pay us today. We gotta right to our money."

"You ain't got jack. Get out of here before I call the cops," hollered the boss.

Dick raised a clenched fist, hardened like an iron anvil, and waved it under the boss's nose. Robertson took up Dick's challenge and stepped forward, close enough their boots collided toe-to-toe.

"You got screws missing in that thick head of yours? I mean it. Get out. Now!" he roared, shouting into Dick's face just inches away. "Danny," Robertson said to the farmhand, "go inside. Call the damn cops."

After that threat, Russell grabbed Dick's shirt. "Cut it out, hothead." He then shouted to the boss man, "We'll be back."

Dick backed up and puffed out his chest, fuming. "Damned crooks. Crooks, I tell ya." He kicked the ground, a flurry of dust wafted as he walked toward Russell's car. Eleanor followed along with the rest of the family.

Even Betty complained. "That ain't right, is it Mama? We worked hard."

"What if they never pay us?" Sam chimed in.

"Both of you just shuddup," snapped Russell.

Dick warned, "If I ever see that jackass in town, I'll crack his skull."

Twenty-Three

1946

After the family ate canned pork and beans again for dinner that evening, Dick convinced Russell to drive them to town for the fireworks.

Before long Russell steered the car south over the sand, paralleling the shoreline, then onto the narrow pot-holed pathway, and eventually toward Cliff Beach.

Betty and Sam sat on the edge of the back seat. "I want to ride the big Ferris wheel," said Sam.

"I want to get some popcorn," added Betty.

Watching them, Eleanor smiled to herself, but suspected Russell and Clara would not part with their hard-earned money on such frivolous things.

"I can't wait," said Sam as he flopped his body back and forth like a fish on dry land.

The first thing Eleanor saw as they approached the town were two searchlights swinging bright arcs around the sky. Authorities had cordoned off an area where cars had already parked in two lines. Russell steered into a spot and all of them clambered out.

Dick sprinted ahead, touching every car—their fenders, taillights, hoods, and bodies. Eleanor watched as he carried out his bizarre ritual of handling surfaces: smooth metal, rough bark, fabric, plant leaves, gritty sand. She could not understand if it helped him to feel grounded, or if by fingering objects it made him think he owned them.

Betty and Sam screeched and ran to the amusement area where calliope music shrilled like a steam whistle. Russell and Clara followed the kids while Eleanor, carrying William on her hip, trailed behind Dick. Each step nearer to the stage, she heard the band music grow louder. She detected a steel guitar, drums, and a woman singing with a sultry, swing beat.

Lingering near the line of cars were two men. The face of the tall man was shaded by his cowboy hat. One of his pointed black boots rested on the front fender of an olive-green sedan, and one of his hands held a dark bottle of beer. His burning cigarette smoke swirled into the dusk. The other man, who was huge, filled his red plaid shirt with barrel-muscled arms. He slapped his hand on his thigh and whistled a catcall at Eleanor, which made the tall one laugh with a grating rasp.

She winced.

She finished snaking through the maze of cars and reached the sidewalk where Dick waited. A Ferris wheel circled in the twilight while vendors in stands hawked hot dogs, popcorn, and Cliff Beach's famous fried clams. As she rounded a corner, a stage strung with amber lights twinkled. On one side of the raised platform, a poster half as tall as Dick advertised the dance, featuring the Scott Tankersley Band and singer Eva Flynn. A few couples were already dancing on a square portable wooden floor in front of the stage. Others milled about while the children chased each other.

Soon, the other four of the Messer family joined them and they all sat down at a small, round table. Dick jumped up from his chair, pulling Eleanor out of her seat even though her arms were wrapped around William.

"Come on. Let's dance."

Eleanor had never danced with him. She recalled how he swooped and glided at the skating rink and wondered if he danced as well as he skated.

On the dance floor, all the women were pretty. Some wore the latest fashions, strutting around in fancy, strapless store-bought dresses and stepping lively in clean, polished heels. With her hand, Eleanor smoothed her cotton dress and tried to cover the frayed hem. Her shoes were scuffed, embedded with sand and field dirt. Her dingy white anklets looked dowdy compared to the nylon stockings worn by the other women. Eleanor felt ugly.

Yet, Dick wanted to dance.

"I've got William. I can't dance."

"For Chrissake. Give him to Ma," he insisted.

"Not now, he's quiet."

"Damn it. Why didn't you find somebody at camp to watch him?" Dick snarled over the noise and traipsed off toward the bar.

To comfort herself, Eleanor snuggled William and furtively looked down the fairway for places to run. Soon, Betty and Sam hustled off with a group of children, and Russell and Clara took to the dance floor. They were an odd-looking couple. Eleanor never imagined them dancing. At first Clara limped and Russell twirled her in stiff, jerky movements like their joints were rusty. By the middle of the song, they stepped together in fluid harmony.

A new song started. Clara and Russell shambled off the floor and sat down next to Eleanor while others moseyed onto the dance area. In the midst, Dick started dancing with a girl who looked about sixteen. Eleanor stared as he swooped and jitterbugged on his heels and toes while the girl shook her hips back and forth, making her skirt swish seductively, showing her upper thighs. When Dick winked and held the girl, she wished he would take off with her. Eleanor also wished Russell and Clara would resume dancing, so she and William could fade into the crowd and flee.

Dick and the girl kept at it through several numbers.

Betty ran by the table squealing and pointing. "Do you see Dick? Isn't he a swell dancer?" Not waiting for an answer, she ran off.

Indeed, he was a fine dancer. In fact, they danced so well that couples backed away, giving Dick and the girl more room. Bystanders started clapping with the beat as Dick and the girl, wearing peep-toe-shoes and a light blue sleeveless dress with a dark velvet belt, drew attention until the song stopped.

The next time it was Sam who zigzagged through the crowd and called out to Eleanor in a tattletale, "Dick's out there with another girl. Ain't you gonna stop him?"

The band leader, Scott Tankersley, announced over the microphone, "Did you see those two?" He directed the audience's attention to Dick and the girl. "Let's give them a big round of applause."

The crowd cheered. Betty stood clapping on the other side of the dance floor; her face lit with joy and fascination at Dick's dancing ability. Clara went to find Sam, who had scampered away toward the fairway. Russell, like a lookout guard with penetrating eyes, remained with Eleanor at the table.

After the loud acclaim for Dick and the girl, the band leader announced over his microphone, "They're so good, we're going to play a song just for them. Give them space." He counted the beats with his baton. "One, two, three, four."

After the first bars of the song, Eleanor knew it as "Sing, Sing, Sing with a Swing," a tune she had listened to on the radio. Caught up in her memories, she hadn't noticed the commotion until chairs crashed, tumbling against tables. A man pushed onlookers out of the way as he tramped his way toward Dick and the cute girl. Women gasped and couples scurried off the dance floor.

Eleanor stood up to see better and recognized the muscled man with a chest like a barrel as the one who earlier had laughed and whistled at her in the parking lot. The second man followed, adjusting the brim of his cowboy hat to uncover his eyes. Once he tilted up his hat, she saw him. The field boss, Robertson.

"Oh shit!" exclaimed Russell.

The boss from Corbett Farms shouted at the dancing girl, "Get away from that field rat!"

Dick clutched his arms tighter around the girl's waist. He turned to the tall man and snorted. "Who you callin' a field rat?"

"Git your filthy hands off my daughter," Robertson demanded. Facing the girl, he ordered, "Paula, I told you. Get away from that damned field rat."

Paula squirmed away from him. Dick lunged forward, caught her arm, and jerked her back. "I'm dancin' with the little lady, and I ain't no field rat. Leave us alone, you son-of-a-bitch."

Betty's expression changed from joy to wide-eyed horror.

The first man in the plaid shirt, a brute-sized fellow, scrutinized Dick whose nostrils flared as if he were struggling to breathe.

Russell stepped into the cleared area and yelled. "Leave 'em be, Dick."

"Get the hell outta here," hollered Dick to the field boss, "or I'll beat you to a pulp."

Paula jabbed Dick with her elbow, escaped and ran away in the direction of the amusement fairway. Dick feinted, jumped forward, then stopped short of the brute's broad reach.

Eleanor began trembling, not wanting any trouble. Someone yelled to call the cops while young couples fled the area. The band's music volume increased; the beat throbbed. At that very instant, a rapid fire of fireworks exploded into a crescendo over the town. *Boom! Bang!* Eleanor cringed.

Dick reached down to his boot and tugged. Within a flash, he grabbed his knife. It glinted under the amber lights. In response, the brute reached his right hand to his belt for something that Eleanor couldn't see.

Someone in the crowd shouted, "They got knives!" Shrieks from the crowd filled the chaos amid exploding fireworks and music.

The brute swung his fist at Dick's chin, who ducked, avoiding the blow. Then, the muscled man turned and ran into the dark toward the ocean. Dick twisted around and tracked him.

Eleanor had a hunch that Dick would follow because his temper would not let an insult drop. Dick dashed after the big man with the field boss on his heels.

Russell sprinted toward the fairway. "Clara! Sam! We gotta go."

The Messers scattered. Eleanor started running from the

dance area in the opposite direction, out of Russell's line of sight.

"This is our chance. We're getting out of here," she said to William as she already panted for breath.

But Betty, little Betty, broke away from the bedlam and ran after Dick in what looked like a blind rage. "Dick! Dick!" she screamed.

Eleanor yelled after her, "No! Don't follow them." She wanted to grab Betty's arm and drag her away.

Why is that girl acting so stubborn?

Then, Eleanor changed her mind. Betty either hadn't heard or ignored Eleanor, so she shrugged her shoulders and headed toward town and the bus stop to flee.

Half a block later, she halted in mid-step because a heavy guilt fell onto her shoulders, like a boulder crashing down a mountain. She searched the crowd for Clara and Russell. She couldn't see them, or Sam.

Betty was their responsibility. But Eleanor was the only one who saw Betty bolt from the crowd toward the fight. This moment was the perfect time to escape, but Eleanor couldn't let Betty run into the danger involved with the ensuing brawl between these three stupid men. Eleanor had made so many mistakes in the last year. She had lied, disappointed her family, and Pete and Fran. She had even committed adultery. She had to make up for her mistakes.

This was Eleanor's opportunity to make at least one thing right. Eleanor had grown fond of Betty and empathized with the girl. What kind of God-forsaken life would she have under the guise of California's sunny skies? In a filthy hole on the beach? Migrating from town to town, planting and picking crops? Clara tried to mother Betty, but Eleanor worried she suffered from Russell's abuse. Betty didn't deserve that, and Eleanor couldn't leave her out there to fend for herself.

Chasing after Betty was the right thing to do, but the wrong thing for Eleanor.

In the eastern sky, a crescent moon beamed its shaft of thin light, enough of a glow for Eleanor to see Betty's wispy hair bouncing on her shoulders, her arms flailing.

"Betty! Betty!" Eleanor yelled as more fireworks whistled and boomed above. Each explosion made Eleanor jump. Thankfully, a childish wonder appeared to still exist in Betty, because she paused to watch the blue, silver, and red sparkles march across the heavens. Carrying William slowed Eleanor, but she finally caught up to Betty.

"Dick's fighting. He's gonna' get hurt," Betty cried out.

"It's dangerous." Eleanor grabbed Betty's arm and pulled her into the shadows of nearby driftwood. "Can't you just go back? Now?" Eleanor pleaded, knowing that if Betty went back to her parents, Eleanor would still have the chance to escape with William.

Not listening to Eleanor at all, Betty squirmed, then broke free and ran ahead. "I got to stop them from hurting him," she yelled as she headed toward the three men racing north along the surf.

Against the backdrop of the white-tipped surf, Eleanor saw Dick stop in his tracks and brandish his knife. The brute's knife glinted as he lunged at Dick. They circled on the sand, around and around, both with their arms outstretched, knives pointed forward.

Don't be foolish! Let her go. But Eleanor didn't let her go. Exasperated, she rolled her eyes and, holding her son as tightly as she could, loped after the frightened girl. She wheezed out of breath by the time she caught up to Betty the second time. At that moment, the sound of a siren wailed, and a red light flashed behind Eleanor.

"See, the police are here. It's trouble." Eleanor yanked Betty down onto the sand within a patch of tall beach grass. "Stay down!"

From the dance floor, police pointed lights up and down the beach. Their beams illuminated the gray sand, dark water, and curling surf. Minutes earlier, she couldn't figure out why the brute and field boss had run away. At that moment, as Eleanor peered through the blades of grass, she witnessed why. The brute and Robertson wanted to fight out of sight and under the cover of the night when the police officers arrived. Their strategy worked because the officers' lights dimmed, and Eva Flynn started singing a new song.

After the bright glare, Eleanor's eyes adjusted to the dark, and she saw the big man charge. Dick leaped into the knee-deep water, separating himself from the two men. The brute advanced. Dick blocked him like a linebacker, pushing his attacker toward the waves. Dick cursed anyone who slurred him. Even more than being insulted, Eleanor's year with him had taught her that Dick despised authority. As she remembered what Dick threatened, *"If I ever see that jackass in town, I'll crack open his skull,"* every fiber in Eleanor's body tightened with the dread that he could and would crack Robertson's skull.

The brute got up. Together, he and Robertson charged after Dick. Water splashed on rocks. Waves thundered. Foam sprayed and more fireworks detonated.

From behind, Robertson gained on Dick. He grabbed Dick's shirt and ripped it. Then, he kneed Dick's back and circled his hands around his neck. The brute positioned himself into an advantageous spot, charged into Dick's gut, then sliced his arm and boxed his face.

"No!" yelled Betty as she escaped from Eleanor's grasp.

Dick stumbled and flopped face forward into the water, where the tide washed over his head. The two men fled north.

What a fine mess I'm in now, Eleanor lamented to herself.

She then tried to comfort William, who was wailing and squirming from all of the commotion. "Baby, we're okay. We're okay." She kissed his forehead and added, "You're a good boy."

She turned to Betty and asked, "Could you take William for a minute? So I can tend to Dick's wounds."

Betty used her arm to wipe away tears that smeared the dirt on her face and nodded. She opened her arms and took William.

The three of them rushed to Dick. Blood, as dark as the sky, pulsed from the deep slice in his bicep into the white froth.

Eleanor yelled at him. "Get up! Get up or you'll drown." He didn't respond.

Twenty-Four

1946

The sound of the ocean's pounding surf devoured Betty's nonstop wails over her brother's battered body.

Eleanor, worried that Betty was not fit at the moment to take care of her tender son, yelled to her as she pointed to dry sand. "Put William down over there." He must have sensed their despair because his three-week-old body started shuddering and his simple crying turned into a howling, distressed bawl.

Betty placed him away from the tide and returned to Eleanor's side. Turning Dick over onto his back was the first task. That's what Eleanor remembered Ernst did when he had saved a boy from drowning in the Walla Walla River. But how? How was she going to turn Dick over? Ernst was big and strong. The boy he saved had been small for his seven years. Dick was muscular and lay like dead weight, soaked from the surf.

Eleanor yelled orders to Betty. "First, we have to turn him over. Then, we have to get him out of the water. Listen.

Listen to me carefully." Eleanor grabbed Dick's shoulders and with Betty's help, they turned him over. "Now pull! You pull that arm and I'll pull this one. Pull!"

The two of them planted their feet into the sand and yanked his arms. They were able to inch his body out of the water.

"We did it," hollered Betty.

Eleanor shook Dick's good arm. "Can you hear me?" Blood and sand smeared his face. His injuries revealed puffy, swollen eyes that looked like a swarm of hornets had attacked him.

"Is he alive?" Betty asked.

Eleanor flattened her ear to Dick's wet chest. "I can hear a heartbeat."

"Save him. Save him."

Eleanor straddled him and with outstretched hands on his stomach she pushed down on his torso. "Push. Push. Push." She thrust down several more times, expelling water. Soon, Dick vomited a mixture of bile and gore, then groaned.

"Yes... yes... I think he's alive." He was alive, but Eleanor's rage inside flared like fireworks. She was so furious with him for fighting and putting Betty and her into this predicament. In between Betty's hysterics and William's crying fit, Eleanor heard Russell, Clara and Sam yelling as they approached.

Clara shouted, "What happened?"

Eleanor didn't take the time to answer. "Give me your shirt," she shouted to Russell.

He cocked his head as if in question.

"I need it to wrap around that bleeding on his arm."

Russell whipped off his blue chambray shirt and tossed it to Eleanor. Meanwhile, Clara stooped over Dick and wailed.

"Lord a mighty! Not this one. Not this one, too. Stay with us, son. Stay with us."

Betty gathered up William and soothed him while Eleanor ripped the shirt into strips of cloth. She held a strip to his wound. Blood streamed and soaked through the makeshift dressing within seconds. The bleeding was more serious than she thought. She worked with nimble hands, wrapping new strips around his laceration, then applying pressure.

"This should stop the bleeding," Eleanor explained to Russell and Clara. Betty stopped crying and stood wide-eyed, slack-jawed, watching Eleanor's movements.

Dick moaned.

Clara cried out, "He's alive!"

Even Russell softened and called out, "Praise the Lord."

"We need to get him to a hospital," Eleanor said.

"I'll get the car... drive it down here as close as I can," Russell yelled as he started running toward town. He stopped for a moment and turned his head back. "Betty. Sam. Come with me," he insisted. Betty passed William to Eleanor. Her son quieted in her arms.

Cool night breezes blew in from the sea and dried Eleanor's sweaty arms while Clara and she waited for Russell's return. William's short breaths fluttered like a bird's wings. Eleanor sighed, having lost her chance to escape. She could have gotten away. But, what else could she have done? She couldn't let Betty get hurt. She couldn't let the girl watch her brother die.

Clara sat rocking back and forth on her haunches. Eleanor walked to the ocean's edge and soaked a strip of the shirt in the salt water. When she returned, she dabbed Dick's nose and face, knowing full-well the salt water would sting, yet heal.

Dick groaned in the front seat on the ride back to the camp. Russell decided Dick wouldn't go to the hospital.

Eleanor persisted. "He needs a doctor."

"I got my mind set. We don't want any trouble. Them doctors will call the cops. Then, what do ya think will happen? Dick'll be in the slammer in no time flat."

Eleanor tried to remember how the whole thing started. "The field boss and that big brute started it."

"No. Dick was messin' with that girl. He shoulda minded his own damn business." He turned to Dick and spewed his anger. "And then you, you stupid cock, you grabbed your knife."

"That cut on his arm … it's a bad one. It could get infected," Eleanor said. Dick needed nursing, but none of them could help. Clara would, no doubt, summon her cards for divine healing, while Russell would ignore him. That meant Eleanor would have to nurse him, and she didn't want to.

Back at the camp, Clara and Russell insisted that Dick hide under the cover of the lean-to. Eleanor crawled into the cramped, foul-smelling dump. Her breathing labored in the thick stench. With the light from an oil lamp burning, she opened her cardboard box and found a few first aid supplies in a small tin box.

When she was pregnant, she had asked Dick to go to the drug store and buy a bottle of antiseptic, gauze, scissors, and aspirin, because she was not sure if she would be delivering the baby in their boarding room or a hospital. Dick had willingly complied, and she was never quite sure why he had not grumbled about doing so. In the end, Eleanor had not used any of the items.

She surveyed the things. There was not much to stitch a deep wound.

Clara inched into the shanty. She reached under a blanket. "Found it." She pulled out a dark bottle from a pouch.

"What is it?"

"Laudanum. It's for pain." Clara held it up for Eleanor to see. "It's opium."

Eleanor squinted. Grandmother had never used opium when she ministered to the sick or injured, so Eleanor was wary of it.

"That cut needs to be stitched up," Eleanor said. "I'll have to use the gauze for tonight. Tomorrow, if he's still bleeding, we'll need to get him to a doctor."

"You heard Russell, didn't ya? No doctor."

Eleanor sighed, realizing she would just have to use what she had. "I've never stitched up a wound before. We'll need a needle and silk thread, then." She started unrolling the long strip, then said to Clara, "One more thing. Tell Russell we need some whiskey. Something strong. I'll use it to sterilize that gash."

"Fiddlesticks," snorted Clara. "We don't need Russell. I got my own here." This time, she reached under the foot of the bedding and pulled out a flask. "Better make him drink it too."

The next morning, Dick remained too weak to rise. Blood had soaked through the gauze, but compared to the night before, the cut looked like it had stopped gushing.

"At least he won't bleed to death," uttered Clara.

They left Dick to recover.

Eleanor, holding William, climbed into the car with the rest of them to return to the Corbett tomato farm. None of them wanted to go back to work for Robertson, the man who had almost killed Dick. But, living day to day near piles of garbage where rats nested, eating greasy canned pork and beans, collecting water in galvanized pails, Dick and Eleanor needed the money that was due to them.

The family walked toward the field hand. Before they reached him, he called out to the boss.

The tall, lank-of-a-man hustled out of the barn, yelling at them. "Get the hell outta here! Off this property."

"We don't mean no trouble. We're here to finish the job. And get our pay." Russell clenched his jaw and tightened his hands into fists at his sides.

Robertson motioned and shouted to the farmhand, "Danny, call the cops." The boy ran to the house while the boss man snarled at Russell. "Get out. Now. You gotta lot of nerve coming here after that jackass beat up my Paula. Bruises. That's what she's got. All over her."

Seeing no other choice, Russell backed away and dust flew as the five of them scrambled to the car. Russell yelled, "You're a damn crook. I'm the one gonna call the cops. You'll see." He spat on the dry earth as they clambered into the car. Russell started the engine and pounded his foot down on the gas pedal, causing the sedan to spin out in the dirt lot and leave clouds of dust behind them.

"They're thieves!" Russell shouted all the way back to camp.

Eleanor's face scrunched into a scowl because they needed money. They needed food.

∾

Clara doted on Dick. The smell of coffee trailed her as she took a cup of the hot brew to him. Outside, Russell stewed, pacing back and forth from the hovel to his car. "Quit mollycoddling that boy o' yours," he said, ranting and throwing up his arms. "That stupid idiot caused us heaps o' trouble. No pay and now we got to look for new work." He huffed off, walking to the shack near the river.

When he returned about an hour later, he disappeared into the hovel where he told Clara the news. Eleanor, stoking the fire, overheard their conversation.

"There's a broccoli farm that needs pickers."

Twenty-Five

1946

The increasing summer heat of the southern California sun required the Messers to get up earlier than usual. Eleanor didn't mind waking before five o'clock because the smell of crumpled dollar bills and the clanging of coins in her hand was too appealing. With them she planned to buy groceries.

All of them, except Dick, arrived at the broccoli field at five forty-five the next morning on Saturday, July 6. Russell and Sam got their assignment for a field in the distance. Clara, Eleanor, and Betty got theirs nearby. From Eleanor's viewpoint in the field, there were just two other white women. All the rest of the field workers looked like they were from south of the California border. Their brown hair and skin matched the color of the rich, humus soil. As they did in the tomato fields, young kids stayed near the adults. Eleanor walked to her row and caught sight of some children handling the dangerous, sharp knives, and cutting the broccoli heads from the plants. Still others carried, sometimes even dragged heavy baskets down the furrows. She did not like observing the children having to toil.

Eleanor held the weight of the knife in her hands, inspecting what the farmhand had given her. She fingered its dirty flat blade and jagged edge, and considered telling the attendant the knife was too dull and no good. But she reconsidered. She didn't want the Messers to lose this job because of her complaint. It was too important that she earn some money. Surveying both the field she was standing in and the adjacent one, she guessed they could last here for about a week picking the first field and harvesting the second in the distance. Although her muscles had strengthened picking tomatoes, slicing off broccoli heads required stooping lower to reach the plant. By midmorning, her legs, back, and shoulders spasmed in pain. Each swoop with the knife felt like forcing a dull stick through the vegetable stalk.

Eleanor babbled to William, who lay on his blanket in the dirt path. Humming helped her mood, so she made up ditties and sang them to him. Occasionally, she glanced at the woman in the next row. She wore a distinctive yellow and red striped skirt under an apron. Eleanor remembered seeing her days before on the other side of the camp as she drew water from the river. Her coffee-colored hair swept her shoulders, and she had a pleasant face. Throughout the day youngsters flocked around her and chatted in lively conversations as children were wont to do.

"I'm keeping up," Eleanor uttered. She tried to maintain her optimism by singing to her son a little ditty to the tune of "The Farmer in the Dell."

"You and I will go. You and I will go. We'll use the money-oh. And you and I will go."

Then, she whispered, "And, since Dick isn't here, I'm going to pocket my money today. And none of it will go to

Clara." Admittedly, it was only a fraction of what they would need. But Eleanor focused on that goal and held it in her thoughts as a locket keeps a treasured photo.

In the afternoon, Betty visited Eleanor and William. As she did in the tomato fields, she helped pull the basket to the row's end, where Eleanor picked up an empty one.

"That was something, wasn't it?" Betty asked Eleanor.

"What was?" Eleanor plopped a broccoli head into the basket. It landed with a thud.

"My big brother fighting. And you savin' him."

"Sure was." Eleanor nodded.

"He got cut up real bad, didn't he?" Betty didn't wait for an answer but kept on chattering. "He woulda died."

"Hmm. Hard to say for sure."

"You did! I saw you save him. Then made him all better," Betty said. "Least, that's what Ma says. If you didn't go after him, he'd a drownded."

"Is that right?"

"Yep. She and Pa were talkin' 'bout you last night. How you been takin' care of him so good, now he's sittin' up."

After Betty's comments, a warmth glowed inside Eleanor. She was not cheered that Dick was recovering because he would soon beat her again. The glow was from satisfaction for a job well done. Pride was a sin according to Grandmother and the church, but she let it swell in her like bread might rise on a table.

Betty picked up William and settled him in a bit of shade. "How'd you know what to do?"

"Well, it's a long story." Eleanor glanced around the field, ensuring that no farmhand or manager could hear her and Betty talking. The woman in the colorful skirt, who picked next to her, smiled at them. "I learned a lot from my grandmother. She was a nurse aide and took care of sick people in our homes."

"Really?"

"Yep. Then, a couple of years ago when I worked in a fruit packing company in … you know in Millston? In Oregon?"

"Millston?" Betty said out loud. Her face scrunched into a frown as if she were trying to recall the place.

"Anyway, I was working next to a gal who fainted to the ground. Actually, she had a heat stroke … um, she got too hot," Eleanor explained so Betty could understand. "Then, she fell to the concrete floor and cut her head. Ooh, did she ever bleed. And I helped \… like rescuing her."

"How'd you do that?"

"Well, first I—" Eleanor stopped when one of the farmhands walked near their side of the field and hesitated for several moments. "It's another long story," she continued in a quieter voice. "Anyway, after the gal recovered, the doctor told me I did the right things, and that's one of the reasons why I decided I wanted to be a nurse. So I could help people feel better."

Without any hesitation, Betty blurted, "Then, I wanna be a nurse, too."

"I hope you can someday," Eleanor said earnestly in a solemn tone. "I hope you can…"

Eleanor was so involved in telling Betty the story she hadn't noticed the woman in the next row until she finished. The woman's head was tilted; her eyes glanced repeatedly at Eleanor as if she had been absorbed in listening to the tale. Eleanor and she exchanged glimpses and nodded. Each of them concluded that evening when the heat of the day began moderating.

Eleanor collected two dollars and five cents and discreetly

stuffed the dollar bills into her bra and the nickel in her shoe. Nobody was going to take her money.

Upon their return to camp, Dick was sitting outside on a length of driftwood, hunched at the shoulders, and smoking a cigarette.

"You're up," exclaimed Clara with a smile on her face. "How are ya feelin'?"

"Like shit," he moaned.

Clara rushed into the shack and brought out the laudanum. "Here ya go." She gave him a few drops.

"Thanks," he said to her. Then, turning to Eleanor, he asked, "And, what've you done?"

Almost immediately, Russell shot back, "What has she done? She saved your life, you idiot. She trailed you and when you got beat up, she and Betty pulled you out of the ocean. So you wouldn't drown."

Betty agreed, "She's been tendin' you."

"She stopped your bleedin' and been washin' them cuts on you," Russell added.

That conversation unfolded like a mystery. Russell had actually said something nice about Eleanor, who then turned toward Dick. "Let me see how you're doing." She examined his wounds. "Your face is healing."

"Yeah," is all Dick said.

"The swelling's going down," she said. "And, your arm looks better, too. It's scabbing."

Instead of pacing or fidgeting, his usual behaviors, Dick sat quietly. Evidently, the dose of laudanum was enough to daze him, and he forgot to demand the pay she had hidden earlier.

Soon, a car arrived, driving parallel with the ocean's edge on the hard-packed beach toward the river. After it stopped at the third camp, a family got out. The woman living in that shack ran to the car and opened the passenger door. Another young woman who resembled the first got out and they hugged while the men greeted and slapped each other on their backs.

After pouring a cup of coffee for Dick, Eleanor glanced over the fire pit at them. The folks flattened blankets on the sand and unpacked baskets of food from the car.

William napped near Eleanor. Russell had removed a tire and patched it. Clara, as she often did, sat inside the shack while the children explored the receding tide for shells and trinkets. Soon, the woman who lived in the other camp got up from her blanket and walked toward them with two young children in tow.

"Howdy, nice evening, isn't it?" She greeted Dick and Eleanor with a warm smile. Faint lines in her face revealed she was older than Eleanor and younger than Clara. Eleanor acknowledged her with a quick nod.

Clara must have heard her because she flipped the lean-to's tarp up and emerged, turning her attention to the woman.

"I'm Erma from the camp near the river. And these are my nieces. We're having some homemade apple pie with my sister this evening. She's lucky enough to live in town… she's been baking all afternoon. Maybe you saw them drive by. We've got plenty to eat. Would you like to come over and have a bite with us?"

Erma directed her next comment to Eleanor. "And I've heard you singing at the river. Sherman, that's my sister's husband, he's got a guitar and fiddle. How about you come and sing with us tonight? We need a little fun and music to cheer us."

Clara answered for all of them. "That's right nice of ya. We'll come, won't we, Russell?"

Russell nodded his head absent-mindedly as if he wasn't really listening to Clara.

Dick also agreed, "You betcha. We'll mosey over. Much obliged and nice to meet ya."

Before long, Dick tossed out the coffee dregs from his tin cup and ambled over to Erma's. Clara and her family trailed him. By the time Eleanor arrived with William, the evening sky tinged into bands of apricot and ripples of violet. Seagulls' wings flapped above the golden breakers and sandpipers skittled in the shoreline.

Erma's fire crackled. From the look of the folks visiting, Eleanor guessed they had jobs in town. Sherman was clean shaven, wore a pair of pressed khakis and a tan shirt. His wife, whose hands weren't grimy, stood barefoot in the warm sand, slicing pieces of pie, and serving them on scraps of torn newspaper.

Eager to try the still-warm dessert, Eleanor broke off a bit, touched the crust with apple syrup dripping from it to her lips. Then, she closed her eyes and breathed in the fragrant smells. *Mm, cinnamon.* She tipped a morsel to her tongue to taste the essence of its flavors. Satisfied, she slipped the tip of the pie into her mouth and nibbled at it. The sweet pastry tasted like home. Melancholy drifted into Eleanor's awareness as she remembered how delicious Grandmother's pies were.

Dick wolfed his pie down in several huge gulps, as did Russell. Clara ate it hungrily, even licking the paper.

Eleanor brought William to her face and kissed him, so she could share the delightful sugary juice lingering on her lips. He smacked his lips and babbled. Erma noticed and laughed. When Eleanor set him down on her lap again, he fussed for a moment as if he wanted more, but soon closed his eyes and fell asleep. So, she swaddled him tightly and nestled him on the warm sand near her feet.

After everyone finished eating pie, Sherman opened a black leather case and pulled out his fiddle and bow. He stopped, turned the knob to tighten the hairs of the bow, then stroked rosin over it several times. Positioning the fiddle under his chin, he slid the bow across the strings. He tuned the G string first, followed by the D, A, and E strings. Watching and listening to him tune it, Eleanor could tell he possessed perfect pitch. When he was ready, he stomped his right foot in the sand, bowed the first note, whooping, "Who knows, 'So Long It's Been Good to Know You?'"

Erma started singing and Eleanor recognized the tune, humming along because she didn't know all the lyrics. Others joined in. Dick, Russell, and Clara swayed with the rhythm. Then, Sherman, who sported a thin black mustache, waved his bow like a one-armed conductor. They sang, "Don't Fence Me In," "You are My Sunshine," "Oh, What a Beautiful Morning," "This Train," and others. While the grownups sang, the children skipped and danced around the circle of folks.

Eleanor took a break while Sherman put away his fiddle and brought out his guitar. While he tuned it, he said to her, "You're quite a singer. Have you ever thought of performing in a band?"

His question caused Eleanor to flinch, and her cheeks blossomed into a heated blush. Glancing at Dick, who kept his eyes glued to her, she wondered what he thought of Sherman's compliment.

"Well, when I was young, I wanted to be a professional singer. Go to New York and sing in the opera."

"Your voice sure is good enough for it," Sherman said.

Others murmured in agreement.

"What songs do you like to sing?" he asked.

"A lot of different songs." Eleanor shrugged her shoulders. "Songs on the radio. In choir. My family sang hymns. I know a lot of them."

"Good," said Sherman. "We'll sing some hymns." He picked a few notes and said, "Not being disrespectful, but we might have to light a spark under some of them. Don't want to sing death dirges. What do you say to that?"

"That's fine. I can follow your lead."

"Which one?" His smile eased her concerns.

"Oh, golly." Eleanor hesitated while thinking. "I sang "Ave Maria" in Latin as a solo during a choir recital my junior year. I know it in English, too."

"Then "Ave Maria" it is. In Latin, of course," he suggested as his face smiled at Eleanor with a softened, pensive expression. He thrummed the opening chords. "How about this tempo?"

Eleanor nodded. Sitting up straight, she breathed in deeply, filling her diaphragm, and sang the first syllable "*Ah,*" shadowing Sherman's guitar chords and holding that first note for two beats. She thought the other folks might sing along in English. But when she sang "*Maria,*" their voices trailed away, and she was singing by herself. When she finished the last word, "*Amen,*" a gentle hush lingered among the group.

The fire popped. Sparks ascended into the dark. After several moments, clapping broke out.

"Beautiful," said Erma. She dabbed her eyes with the skirt of her dress and lamented, "We just lost my ma, and she loved that song."

"Good God," Sherman exclaimed. "You need to be in the pictures or Hollywood with a voice like that."

"Sing some more," said Erma's husband. "We need your

sweet voice to lift us. Livin' in these damned shacks and pickin' just ain't no way of life."

Erma agreed, "Your music makes me feel better. Hopeful …"

It had been a long time since Eleanor had received compliments on her singing. She enjoyed their praise. Since moving from Wilkes, she only serenaded lullabies to William. Dick ignored her talent. She never knew if he enjoyed her songs or not.

Erma's husband yelled to Sherman, "Hey, where's that beer you told us you were bringing? We need to celebrate."

"I'll get it right now," he hollered back as he strode to his car. When he returned, he passed out bottles of beer to all the men. The only woman who accepted a beer was Clara.

In a matter of minutes, Dick downed his second and started pacing around the gathering.

"One more, Eleanor. Your voice is like an angel. One more," Sherman coaxed as he leaned toward her and winked.

Eleanor shied away, lowering her eyes, and hoping Dick didn't see Sherman's gesture. She knew at that instant she needed to get herself and William back to the shack. She glanced at Dick.

His eyelids squinted with contempt. "Shit. Her voice ain't no angel." Dick spewed his ugly animosity. "She sounds like she's got mush in her mouth. Hear her. Yodels like a sick dog. You should hear her when she's belly-achin'." Dick snorted and laughed.

Although Eleanor sat on the other side of the fire, she could almost smell his rage.

Murmurs followed his remarks.

Erma protested, "That's not so. She has a wonderful voice. I wish I could sing like her."

Eleanor held her breath, keeping her head down and

looking at no one while her right foot started to quiver. She interrupted the conversation. "I need to get our boy back." She quickly stood and picked up sleeping William. "He needs another feeding and his diaper changed."

"Hey, no fun," yelled Sherman.

"Stay longer," suggested Erma.

"Nope. She needs to get that kid of hers with blond hair home," Dick said, curling his right lip into a sneer.

Eleanor picked up William. His blanket flopped open, uncovering his wispy almost-white hair and calm face.

"See, that kid's hair. Funny, ain't it? I don't have a blond hair on me."

Her stomach convulsed and seemed to leap into her throat. He hadn't complained about William's light hair since he saw him the first time in the hospital. Eleanor brushed her dress as if whisking away Sherman's attention. "I must go. Thanks for everything," she said and rushed away from the circle of folks.

As she headed back to their camp, her eyes squinted; she was both angry and nervous that Dick had bullied her in front of the group.

His hideous voice followed Eleanor. "I saw you flirtin' with that dumb shit."

She had hoped he would stay with his family at the gathering. "Hush Dick. Don't cause a scene."

"You're the one who caused a scene. Little hussy."

Eleanor took one more step, then felt a strike to the back of her head. Shards of light sparked before her, causing her vision to blur. Her head throbbed. She struggled to stay standing, holding on to William, but Dick's blow hit her so hard she stumbled and swayed, fell to her knees, and dropped her baby.

"Stop. Stop it. Can't you see I dropped William?"

Eleanor reared up like a bucking horse to rescue him. As soon as she did, Dick shoved her down again.

He hissed the horrible name, "Slut!" Several steps later, he bellowed, "You like that fiddle player?" He stood over her. "Well, you're gonna like this." His menacing howls gnawed inside Eleanor's head as he laughed to the sky. Instead of walking on as she hoped he would, he kicked her arm.

Lying in the sand, William bawled in distress.

"Ahh!" Eleanor screamed. "Help!" No one heard.

Sherman had started strumming a new tune, leading the families at the party in another song.

"Dick. Don't you hear William? He's hurt."

"That bastard? Hurt? I don't give a shit. He ain't mine."

Dick was right. Eleanor had been maintaining the lie for William's sake. At that point she couldn't argue. Before she could get up, Dick grunted, this time like a predator in the wild. His rough, filthy hands groped her.

She twisted and tried to free herself, but he crushed her harder.

Ripping her dress and stripping off her bra, the two dollars she had hidden earlier in the day fell onto the sand. He then clutched her hair and pulled her head back. Before she could scream again, he clapped a sand-filled hand over her mouth and slugged her lower back.

Air whooshed out of her lungs. She tried to breathe, but her lungs wouldn't work. Gasping, she choked on sand and a metallic taste oozed from her lips. She lay limp, unable to inhale or exhale.

Dick dragged her body out of sight into dense scrub, over stones and broken shells that shredded her knees and legs. He stopped near tall grasses. He jumped on and straddled her, stripped off the rest of her clothes, then came hard on her.

Eleanor couldn't move, couldn't fight back.

When he entered her, the misery of his earlier beatings was eclipsed by an excruciating agony she never knew him to inflict. The pain bore as deeply as her final contractions during William's delivery. This wasn't the way Dick usually forced himself on her. His revenge penetrated beyond her deepest despair. She tried to muster strength to shriek. But the only sound she could utter was no louder than a whimper.

Dick whooped in a drunken slur, "We're gonna take a horsey ride. This'll teach ya, you whore."

Dick, after what seemed like an hour, got off from Eleanor and zipped up his pants. A few seconds after leaving the scrub, she heard his voice mock. "What's this? Money growin' on trees?" He stooped and picked up the dollar bills that had fallen out of her bra. "Ha. Ha. Ha." Dick then returned to Eleanor with a swift kick, his foot striking her side before he left. "That last one's for hidin' money from me."

Something cracked in Eleanor's chest. She writhed in agony. Her arms and legs withered beneath her. Gritty sand crushed between her teeth, coated her tongue, and she continued to cough. She looked for her dear baby. Eleanor couldn't see him, but soon she heard his cries. Eventually, she forced herself up onto her hands and crawled to William, whose arms and legs thrashed while he lay on his back screaming. When she reached for him, her strength vanished and she fell face down into the sand, where she lay. Dazed. Concussed. Unconscious.

Twenty-Six

1946

Squawking sea birds woke her before the first light.

"Oh!" She groaned and took a long slow inhale, trying to pull strength into her body. Every breath, every swallow ached. She stretched to find William's warm body still next to hers and relief inched up her fingers. As soon as she touched him, he woke. His jagged sobs told her he was alive, but he smelled of old urine and a full diaper. Eleanor chastised herself knowing he had slept in his waste. It was one thing for *her* to live in the mess she caused. But not an infant. Not her baby. Eleanor shook her head at how awful a mother she was. She wanted to cradle him in her arms and make everything better. She started whimpering as a tear formed, but shortly, she reined in her self-pity. *I have to be strong ... for you, little one. Strong. I can only hope this awful suffering helps me be a better mother.*

Eleanor nursed him as best she could until he turned away from her breast and screamed. Her milk no longer flowed freely. She rose to her knees, then planted her feet in the loose sand while her rib cage burned in pain where Dick had kicked her. She found all her clothes, picked them up, and shook the sand out of them out. Her eyes searched the area for the money that had fallen out of her bra. Then, she remembered Dick had found and pocketed it.

Pigeon-gray shades lightened the sky while Eleanor put on her clothes before anyone could spot her. The torn dress hung around her hips. She gathered up the skirt in one hand, William in the other, and limped toward the stream. Being in her arms, his crying subdued.

Nobody was outside, although Eleanor sensed eyes staring at her. She scanned the camp areas, the shore, and over the tall grasses but did not see anyone walking about. Dick was not around, either. She guessed that he had passed out somewhere.

When she reached the stream, she set her son down in a safe, dry spot of sand. Eleanor then cupped her hands full of the cold water, wishing it would wash away the horror of the attack. But the water only rinsed off the sand and blood. She drank some, hoping it could cleanse her soul and relieve her heartache. Afterward, lowering herself, she tried to sit on a boulder to rest, but she couldn't. Pain screamed within her. Despite that torment, she devised a way to flee. She was desperate; she had to get away now because Dick's actions had escalated too much. Her life and even William's were in peril.

Gathering him up, she embraced William, holding him with what little strength she could muster. "I can't let anything more happen to you. Nothing more!"

The path to the road was an estimated four miles. She observed the terrain and figured she would need to hug the vegetation line so no one could see her. Her box of clothes and personal items were important to her, but in her condition, she doubted she could carry them and William, too. So she decided to leave her stuff behind. Besides, her belongings were in that filthy hovel where Clara and the children slept. Heading south along the underbrush, she walked no more than fifty feet when Dick jumped out of the grasses and startled her.

"Where ya goin'?"

Doesn't he ever sleep? "To town."

"Like hell you are."

"Leave me alone." Eleanor tried to run, but she stumbled, unable to gain any traction on the unstable and loose sand.

Dick sneered at her attempt. "Git back to camp."

"I won't."

"Do ya want a repeat of last night? Did ya like it?" He chuckled to the sky.

"Please, Dick. No. Can't you see I'm limping?"

He snorted and grabbed Eleanor's right arm. His grip was so powerful, she thought he would break her bone. "Now you turn right round. You're walking back to our nice little house." His voice oozed like slime. "You're not gonna make a fuss. Hell, I'll even carry that little bastard o' yours."

"No! You're not going to touch him."

"Ha. Was you surprised last night? That I figured it out? Your big, fat lie."

Eleanor shook her head. "I don't know what you're talking about."

"That bastard, you whore. It takes nine months, ya know."

"Nine months for what?"

I played this dreadful trick for William's and my life. But it isn't working anymore. Dick knows.

"Nine months! For God's sake, woman. You was two-timing me while we was married. Cause you was already pregnant when I came back stateside and found ya waitin' for your lover boy in Wilkes. Weren't ya?"

"You're imagining things. And you're even sicker than I thought you were."

"You watch it," he demanded, taking his grip off from her and waving his arm around her face. "Now, git! I don't know why I keep ya."

Eleanor didn't know why, either. *Why doesn't he just let me go?*

With the meager strength she possessed, she turned around inch by inch, so she didn't fall and drop little William again. Hobbling to camp, she hated Dick more and more. *He* was the bastard.

Why didn't I let him just die on the beach?

Eleanor and William reached camp as Clara was stoking the fire. She glared at Eleanor. "Lord a mighty. What happened to you?"

Eleanor didn't answer.

Dick blurted, "Didn't you see her drinkin' last night? She got so shit-faced, she fell. Poor thing."

His lie caused Eleanor to want to spit on him. For his hurtful story, she wanted to throw a pan at his head.

"Yeah, she's gotta doozy of a hangover."

Eleanor couldn't sit, let alone stand or walk, so she lay in a fetal position on newspapers with William tucked near her.

Monday morning meant picking again. Although Eleanor throbbed everywhere in her body, she got up to get ready for the broccoli fields. Her legs and arms were swollen with purple bruises. Abrasions trailed from her thighs down her shins. Also, an incessant ringing hammered in her ears.

Studying Eleanor's appearance and her injuries, Betty scrutinized her, then looked to Dick and back to Eleanor again as if she were figuring out what had happened. She then walked over and gave Eleanor a cautious hug.

Riding in the car to the fields, clutching William to her broken body, Eleanor tried focusing on the clouds in the east, flaring an encouraging goldenrod and melon red as the sun rose.

By the time the group arrived at their picking spots, those welcoming blushes of daybreak rolled into a menacing aura of pond-scum green. She could not recall ever seeing such alarming-looking skies. A west wind skimmed the dust. Heat spiraled together with heavy air, and she dripped with sweat as if she were standing in a shower of hot rain.

"Damn, it's a hot one today," Dick complained, swiping his shirt sleeve across his sweaty forehead. The back of his plaid shirt was already clinging to him.

Betty stayed with Eleanor. "How ya doin'? Need help?" She pointed to the sky. "Ma says them clouds is trouble. She read it in her cards last night."

"It's just going to rain. Nothing more," Eleanor said, trying to calm Betty. Although Eleanor also knew how fast storms could erupt in such heat. She looked heavenward. The green sky lingered, almost smelling of frenzy. She started her morning's work. Surveying the long rows, Eleanor felt a heavy burden. Knowing she would be stooping and picking for the next twelve hours made her weary.

During the previous day, she had developed a rhythm of slicing the stalks and dropping the broccoli heads into the crates. Slice, drop. Step down the row. Slice, drop. Slice, drop. Step down the row, and glance at William in thanks because he usually slept or occupied himself. But that morning, she could not find her cadence.

After an hour of picking, Betty moseyed back to Clara. Charcoal gray clouds brewed above the fields. Rain drops splattered the parched dust. Eleanor tucked the top-most flap of William's blanket over his face to protect him from the shower. Soon a deluge from the clouds saturated her dress, causing it to hang as if glued to her body. She no longer dripped from heat. Instead, beads of rainwater streamed down her grimy arms, creating tracks to her dirt-encrusted hands. Her hair fell in strings onto her face.

Before long, hail larger than the size of shooter marbles pounded from the dark heavens. The ice particles bounced when they struck the packed earth. When they beat down on her skin, they hurt Eleanor worse than bee stings. William cried. Eleanor swooped him up, protecting him as she crouched in the middle of the field under the downpour. This was no place for them as the hail pummeled, making noises like a herd of galloping horses. When she looked up, the workers were running toward the barn. She shadowed them as shafts of electric blue lightning crackled.

Eleanor had hated lightning storms since she was ten. She remembered a bolt burst under Grandmother's front door in Weston, skittered across the wooden floor, and singed a black hole in the back wall.

There in the field, triple lightning strikes jumped from one cloud to the other and lit the sky. Static bristled the hairs on her arms and legs, while the air snapped with the smell of lightning—a sharp, fresh odor. Branches on a tree near the barn swayed in the tempest until one limb broke off and flew away.

Every time thunder clapped, the ground reverberated in the soles of her shoes. Within minutes, all the pickers, along with the field boss, huddled under the barn's eaves.

As they stood watching, the boss declared, "Shit. There goes the crop. Those heads are ruined now."

It rained so fast, so much, rivulets rushed between the broccoli rows. Hail accompanied by wind blasts beat the tender green flowerets and leaves into the mud. Baskets of harvested broccoli flipped over in the wind, and soon green heads bobbed and floated in the flooding gullies.

The field boss shouted, "No more picking! Line up for your pay."

Since Dick had come along and worked that day, he grabbed Eleanor's pay again.

On the drive back to their camp, Russell grumbled all the way. The hail subsided and the dull skies transformed into menacing slate rivers of rain.

"Watch out!" yelled Dick. "You're gonna run off the road."

"Dammit, I can't see."

It was apparent why Russell struggled. Only the windshield wiper on the passenger side of his car worked, and it barely cleared the waves of water.

"Tell me where to turn," he ordered, jerking the steering wheel, and driving the car away from a ditch. "Judas, the cars in front of me is crawlin'. They's only goin' five miles an hour."

"Good," Clara said. "We don't need to go fast. We're just goin' back to a wet camp," she said, disgusted.

Eleanor wiped the fogged window with the palm of her hand. On the road ahead red lights flashed.

"Cops!" shouted Dick. "His car's straight ahead."

"Shit. Now what? I hate them SOBs," Russell said, snarling belligerently. As he drove closer to the patrol, Russell pumped the brakes to a stop. The engine idled while he rolled down his window.

"The road's washed out ahead," said the police officer, water pouring over the brim of his hat. "You need to turn around. There's a detour up there," he shouted over the shrill wind, pointing. "It'll take you to Cliff Beach." He waved his arm for Russell to move along. Behind the police officer, a palm frond sailed down the road and into a ditch.

"Okay," shouted Russell and tipped his head.

He turned around and drove until he reached town, where he navigated at a speed as slowly as a person walking. Dick pointed toward some buildings. "Looks like all the lights are out. It's dark over there."

Russell crept along the main street and headed south, almost missing the turnoff to the beach. Dick yelled, "The cut-off's a river. Damn thing's flooded. It'll be slippery as snot."

About halfway down the path, the car swerved as if Russell had slammed the brakes and skidded on an icy pond. He righted it until the back tires dug into flood waters and mud. Gunning the accelerator, the tires whirred and spun. But the car did not move.

"We're stuck," moaned Russell. "Get out and push."

"Everybody outta here. We gotta lighten the load," Dick demanded.

"No," Betty complained.

"Now!" Dick shouted.

Eleanor left William in the back seat while the children and Clara got out. Inside, the car had been uncomfortably hot and steamy, but once outside, Eleanor wished she had a warm coat to shield her from the chilly rain. Hair strands slapped her face while the skirt of her dress whipped into a twisted turmoil.

"I'll get on this side," Dick yelled as his shoes sloshed through inches of water. He positioned himself on the left bumper. Pointing to Eleanor, he directed, "You get over on that side. Ma, you get here in the center. Now push. Push."

Pushing the car exhausted Eleanor as a sharp spasm seared within her rib cage. With one hand, she grabbed her chest, her bones feeling like the rain had slashed them with ice shards.

Water swirled up to her shins. She hated the storm, this situation. In eastern Oregon, she had survived winter winds barreling down the Blue Mountains at hurricane forces, but she was not accustomed to torrential floods. Leaves, garbage, small branches, and debris flew at them. She trembled, due to the fear of getting hit in the head and because she was cold. Rain smacked her skin while she and the others shoved the sedan.

The car tires finally budged forward, then stalled again. The access road was washing out. The adults pushed one more time, and Russell was finally able to drive his car to the end of the path, where all of them jumped back in. After Russell turned off from the path, the route that paralleled the shore was compacted enough for him to maneuver.

Their drenched clothing and shoes had tracked pools of water and globs of thick muck into the car. Eleanor's right foot shivered, causing her foot to start its nervous shaking.

Eleanor despised the inside of the shack but decided she would take refuge in it. But as Russell approached closer, they saw that the shack had blown over. The other camps on both sides of the river were ruined, too. The only things remaining were washed up logs, a line of scattered garbage, and dead fire pits where the camps had once been.

One of the poles holding up the front of the Messers' lean-to broke in half, and the canvas tarp flapped in the wind. Russell turned off the engine.

Opening the car door in the battering wind, Eleanor

pushed from the inside with both hands. Even then, it was hard to open. Leaving William on the back seat, she scrambled out of the car and braced herself so she wouldn't topple over from the fierce gusts. Wind howled passed her ears.

Shocked with the initial spectacle, Eleanor stepped back and gasped. It had been a fetid hovel, but it could have been a refuge, of sorts, for Betty and Sam. The only place they had. And now it was destroyed. The shack's wood paneling had ripped off and flown down the beach. Not only had the rain soaked everything, but by the looks of sea foam and rubble, the ocean tide had flowed into the lean-to. The current had strewn blankets, clothes, and socks into a jumble of drenched fabric. Resisting the tempest winds, Eleanor pulled the tarp aside. Upon quick appraisal, her mouth fell open and her eyes widened. Everything was either soaked or gone—washed out to sea.

Unfortunately, Dick still had his wretched knife with him. It was too bad it hadn't washed away, too.

While she scanned the damage, Russell ran to the back of his car and pulled out a toolbox from inside the trunk. Dick grabbed the kit and hustled to repair the mangled metal. After trying to beat and straighten the tin, he threw up his arms.

"Now what we gonna do?" Clara whined.

"We need to leave," Eleanor yelled. Life at the camp was now impossible, so she rounded up Sam and Betty into the car as she picked William up from the seat. Clara limped behind, and soon Russell and Dick followed.

Russell turned the ignition. The engine sputtered, shook, and then stalled. He turned the key again.

"Hurry!" shouted Clara.

"I'm tryin'!" He gunned the gas pedal and tried the key again. And again. The ignition would not turn over. "Shit!"

With the road to the highway flooding with gushing

water, all the group could do was wait inside the car. Through the steamed windows, Eleanor could hardly breathe, inhaling only by taking quick lungs full. The river in the distance surged with trees rolling down it to the ocean.

Eleanor wiped the sweaty windows with the hand not clutching her son.

From inside, the family watched swells as tall as three-story buildings slam into the cliff head. A furious wind persisted as it tossed trashed tin pieces through the air like thrown knives. Wreckage soared in the turbulent maelstrom. Occasionally, surging waves, frothing with foam, lifted and threw logs back onto the beach near them. Once, the ocean's incoming tide flowed under the car and leaked in under the doors. Eleanor got ready to jump out with William but was terrified they'd get washed out to sea.

Stranded, they sat in the car for hours before the chaos subsided. By evening, the sun shone large and golden, hanging near the horizon as if nothing had happened. Earlier, Mother Nature had tormented, now she gloated as if She had always been calm, glorious, and magnificent.

The family finally escaped the confines of the car. William had fallen asleep, so Eleanor did not stir him as she tried to gently get out of the sedan. When she stepped out from the back seat, her shoes and feet sunk in the wet earth. Each step oozed. Slurped. She did not waste any time lamenting. She told Betty and Sam to pick through the mess of branches, wooden house shingles, siding, broken windows, ropes, nets, and detritus, and gather up everything that was theirs and pack them into the trunk.

Mumbling to himself, Dick flitted erratically from one wet thing to another. He dug up a pot from under the rubble of the destroyed hut. He scooped out a half-buried can of coffee from the sand. His anger dissipated until he looked like a ship in fog with no lighthouse for direction. Soon, he squatted on his haunches, stared blankly in front of him, and rocked forward and back while he ranted. "I'll start the day I show up. I'll show 'em. Fix whatever they need. Fix what they need at that airplane factory ..." His voice trailed off and his face froze in a blank expression.

A last gust of wind whipped in from the ocean and startled him. He ducked and covered his head with his arms. "Watch out. They're bombin' us." He clapped his hands over his ears. "Eddie? Where's Eddie? Where are you?"

Clara and Russell gawked at Dick, then glanced at each other with frowns etched into their faces, before turning back to stare at Dick again for untold minutes. His delusions sent a shiver snaking down Eleanor's spine. She believed Clara and Russell were as stunned as she was.

"Lord a mighty. He's havin' a breakdown!" Clara wailed. "Help 'im Russell. Help 'im!"

Russell shook his head as if in disbelief. He still had his wits about him and helped the children rummage. They threw a few salvageable blankets across the bushes to dry. None of the weary group bothered to clean up all the scattered things. They were too exhausted. Clara and the children, along with Eleanor and William, retreated to the car to sleep while Russell found a place near driftwood.

Dark veiled the ocean and the littered beach. While Eleanor nursed her baby, all she could hear were his smacking lips; the family's heavy breathing in the back seat; and the water rhythmically lapping ashore and retreating again. Eleanor glanced once more toward Dick.

In the quiet of the night, they had left Dick sitting alone on the beach to ride out the storm in his head.

Twenty-Seven

1946

Dreaming a fearsome nightmare of tidal waves, wild winds, and Messer swords, Eleanor woke when a woman's whisper roused her. She squeezed her eyes together trying to bring herself to consciousness.

"*Señora. Señora?*"

Eleanor could not identify her voice, but when she opened her eyes, she recognized the middle-aged woman with the brightly colored skirt from the broccoli field. Eleanor turned her legs, then stretched them, and started to silently slide out of the car.

Eleanor had left the four car doors open throughout the night to breathe fresh air and dry out their soaked items. Stepping out quietly so as not to wake the others, she glanced around the beach to see if she could spot Dick. There was no sight of him, so she nodded to the woman, then motioned to her to step away from the camp so they could talk.

The moonlight's glow carved deep lines in the woman's grimacing face. Eleanor could see her soaked skirt clinging to her legs, and her wet shoes squished on the sand. For an instant, Eleanor wondered if the woman was part of her dream.

The woman proved to be real when she said with urgency, "*Ayúdeme. Lumbre.*"

Eleanor didn't understand what the woman said and shook her head. "I'm Eleanor."

"*Sí. Sí.*" The woman touched her chest. "Isabel." She tapped her finger to her forehead and closed her eyes as if she were thinking. She pointed across the river. "Roberto... fire. Arm. Bad," she whispered, tapping Eleanor's shoulder. "*Por favor ayúdeme* ... Help!"

Eleanor did not know her language but was impressed the woman knew a little English. Eleanor knew *sí* meant yes. She asked quizzically, "You need help? At a fire?"

Isabel nodded, then cocked her head. Wrinkles in her face folded graver. "You help ... *Señor* ... dead in ocean."

"Yes, I saved my husband."

"Fire. Roberto... you, um, help Roberto?" she pleaded, with increasingly erratic arm and hand gestures.

Eleanor whispered slowly, "I don't know. I... I guess so. Yes. *Sí. Sí.* I... can... can try." She was not sure what she was getting into. She wondered if this was a trap that Dick had plotted, but in examining the woman's anguished eyes, Eleanor sensed there was no danger in her request. The true danger existed if Dick heard Isabel and Eleanor talking.

"So, Roberto burned his arm." Eleanor spoke in a whisper close to Isabel. "Is that it?"

The woman nodded. "Car." She acted out steering a car. "*Mucha agua.* Water... road."

Likewise, Eleanor used her hands to suggest a car driving, but she could not understand what a car had to do with a fire. "Wait, please." She tiptoed back to Russell's car and lifted William off the seat, making sure to not make noise. She stopped to listen for telltale sounds of Dick or his family. She heard only the constant ebb and flow of the surf.

Eleanor left with Isabel, who grasped her available hand. They wove through the mounds of waste until they reached the river. Gushing and swollen from the earlier storm, the roaring stream had doubled in width and flooded its banks. Logs clogged the river's stream of water. Eleanor planted her feet and stopped hard.

Isabel inched into it, beckoning Eleanor to wade in.

Eleanor stood frozen in fear, sizing it up from one frothing side to the other. How were they going to get through that? The current coursed too fast, too deep. Eleanor eyed Isabel, then the river, and back to Isabel. She speculated on how the woman had crossed it by herself the first time.

Isabel summoned Eleanor again to follow her.

Eleanor shook her head.

"*Por favor…*"

Instantly, Eleanor's emotions rolled like the surf. Duty seized her. Eleanor figured if Isabel had crossed, she and William would, too. Before she waded in, she searched behind them, scanning the destroyed lean-to and Russell's car. She caught sight of Russell sleeping near a driftwood log but still did not see Dick.

Isabel tugged Eleanor's hand, and she rushed in.

Chilly water rushed around her ankles. With each step, she wanted to turn back. But, back to what? Dick?

No, I'm not going back.

Eleanor pressed on. Swift currents pushed at her knees and quickly crept up her hips. She held William high above her heart to keep him dry.

Suddenly, Isabel lost her balance and yelled. Her hand

yanked on Eleanor's arm, pulling her and William deeper into the water.

Eleanor's breath convulsed, and she yelped when bitter-cold water encircled her waist. William howled. She hurried and took a long step, hoping no one had heard their noisy outbursts.

Just then, Isabel let go and screamed as she tumbled into the torrents. Her body and head sank, only to bob above the surface again.

This mishap had occurred so quickly that Eleanor couldn't believe what was happening. "This is a nightmare," she shrieked.

Isabel was being swept away.

"*¡Ayúdeme! ¡Ayúdeme!*"

Eleanor lunged toward her. "Isabel!"

Isabel shot her arm above the rush.

Eleanor leaned, trying to reach Isabel with her free hand, while desperately holding William's little body above the water as much as she could with her other arm. Eleanor launched forward again and grabbed Isabel's hand. She tugged enough so Isabel could find her footing and right herself.

She emerged limb by limb, soaking and choking. "*Gracias.*"

They kept wading through the swift current, then lumbered up a shallow incline until they found solid ground. For several moments, Eleanor had to stand while she regained her jangled nerves and took in deep gulps of air to catch her breath. The pain in her head and rib cage, and the fatigue from the storm had drained her energy.

William was tired also. She comforted his heaving body with a tight hug, then brushed her lips against his wet cheeks. "We're okay, baby. We're okay. We made it."

Soon Eleanor and Isabel rounded the cliff head. They hastened toward Roberto, wasting no time. Isabel pointed to a cabin in a clearing among the beach vegetation. Constructed of wood, it sat back on higher terrain and had weathered the storm. Because of its location behind the head, Eleanor had not noticed it before, or the car parked nearby.

Isabel opened the door and motioned for Eleanor to enter. The dry cabin smelled like comfort as their bodies dripped pools beneath them.

Eleanor looked around. A kerosene lamp lit the room. On the cookstove were two black pots, steam rising from one of them. Next to the stove, two men sat on stools along the back wall. One of them was about Isabel's age, the other a young man. In a corner stood an iron bed with a mattress. In the other corner knelt a woman near a layer of blankets on which a young boy lay. He was about Sam's age. Eleanor remembered all of them from the broccoli farm.

The older man jumped up from his seat, tugged the top coverlet from a different mattress and gave it to Isabel, who in turn, gave it to Eleanor. She thanked them and wiped William and herself as best she could. Then she gave it back to Isabel for her to use. Once dry, Isabel gave a clean cloth to Eleanor, so she could remove William's wet diaper and put a dry one on him.

Eleanor quickly changed her son then looked toward the corner where Isabel gestured toward the young boy. *"Roberto. Ayúdeme."*

When Eleanor saw Roberto, her hand shot to her face in alarm. "Oh dear."

Roberto's eyes glazed in a vacant stare. His skin appeared ashen, unlike a healthy boy who should have had glowing cheeks and vitality. Blisters on the boy's shoulder, traveling down to his wrist, radiated the color of blood and white leather. At the edge of his wound was scalded and blackened flesh. Roberto labored breathing, taking short huffs as he shivered.

Eleanor had never seen a burn so severe. It was definitely more than she knew how to help with, so she stepped back. "Hi," she said as she gave a slight wave to the young woman whose eyes looked as frightened as a grown man caught in a crossfire. "My name is Eleanor."

She started talking, and Isabel translated.

"She Rosa."

Eleanor nodded and smiled at her.

Isabel continued, "Roberto … um …" Her head turned to the man who gave her the blanket. "Miguel?"

Miguel started explaining the incident. "Wind blow. Walls go in. Out." He motioned how the walls shook. "Lamp fall. Fire burn Roberto." He motioned to an empty space on a shelf.

What Eleanor saw when she looked down at the dirt floor was a blackened scorch. Isabel and her family had extinguished the fire and cleaned up the broken lamp. Although whiffs of singed fabric and the odor of charred flesh permeated the cabin.

"Help?" Isabel asked.

"I'm… I'm not a doctor. Not even a nurse."

Miguel asked, "You save man? Yes? The girl talk in field."

"Yes. But…" She shrugged her shoulders and sighed. "Okay, I'll take a look." Eleanor surveyed Roberto's injuries from the doorway, where she still stood. "He needs a doctor."

Miguel answered. "Water too high. Car no drive."

Eleanor held William with outstretched arms toward Isabel. "Could you hold my baby?" He fussed some but soon settled in her arms.

Eleanor stepped toward the boy. "Roberto? I'm Eleanor and I'm going to touch your forehead."

She pantomimed what she was going to do before checking him. "Hmm. He's cool and clammy." Eleanor believed he was suffering from shock. "He needs a blanket."

Isabel passed William to Rosa then took a striped wool blanket that lay folded at the head of the bed and handed it to Eleanor, who rolled it and gently raised Roberto's legs, positioning the blanket under his feet. She had learned from Grandmother it was important to increase blood circulation in patients with shock. With the edges of the blanket on which he lay, Eleanor covered his body to warm him. His injured arm dangled over the side of the mattress.

"I need fresh water, vinegar, and a clean towel. Do you have those?"

Isabel wrinkled her face.

"Water," Eleanor repeated.

Miguel was listening to Eleanor so he could translate instructions to Isabel. *"Agua. El paño,"* said the older man.

Isabel nodded and soon dipped fresh water from a pottery crock into a bowl, then handed it to Eleanor, along with a clean cloth.

Eleanor scanned the shelves. Above the squat cookstove were rows of canned foods, boxes of dry goods, jars of pickled peppers, and other fruits and vegetables. She needed vinegar. Eyes darting frantically, she finally spotted a glass bottle of it.

"There. The vinegar," Eleanor said and pointed to it. Several capfuls of it in the fresh water would cleanse the burn. She concocted the remedy. "I'm going to wash your arm," she said to Roberto gently, Miguel translating for him.

Eleanor moistened the cloth and let the mixture dribble over Roberto's skin. He groaned. She jerked her hand back and hesitated, fearing she had hurt him. She was hesitant to keep going, losing her confidence.

Rosa's sad eyes and expectant expression told Eleanor she needed to continue because she imagined what she would want if her son needed help. Eleanor took a deep breath. What Roberto needed were two aspirin and laudanum to relieve his pain. But whiskey was the next best thing. Eleanor searched the shelves again and asked, "Whiskey? Do you have liquor? Roberto needs it for the pain."

Miguel got up, walked to the shelf, and reached behind boxes. He brought out a clear bottle of colorless liquid.

"Is that liquor?"

He nodded. "*Mezcal*."

"Can you give him some to drink?"

The man crouched near the boy and talked to him softly. He then touched the opened bottle to Roberto's lips. Miguel said something more and the boy took a sip. Shaking his head, he spit it out. The man touched the boy's lips again. This time, Roberto drank sips of the *mezcal* and coughed each time he swallowed. His face winced.

"You're a brave boy," Eleanor said.

Miguel translated, whispering softly to the young child.

Roberto's guttural groans, like an injured animal, became whimpers, and he soon closed his eyes.

After Eleanor finished washing Roberto's wound, she gave the water mixture and cloth to Isabel, and care directions for her and Miguel to follow. "Wash his burn every hour and keep him warm. He needs a doctor."

Miguel acknowledged, nodding his head up and down.

"Tomorrow morning, when the road is clear, you must take him," Eleanor said again emphatically.

Rosa put William back into Eleanor's arms and then touched her hand. "*Gracias*."

She replied to Rosa by bowing her head slightly. "You are welcome." It felt as if Eleanor had not breathed at all while she washed Roberto's burnt skin, and she finally heaved out a huge sigh of relief. At last, she could inhale and exhale again, and recognized she reeked of briny muck from the river. While she eased, she gazed around at newspapers papered on the plywood walls and a wooden crucifix hanging next to a picture of Mary holding baby Jesus on her knee. The hominess of the one-room cabin gave Eleanor a sense of peace she had missed since Grandmother's home.

Isabel caught Eleanor's attention. She pointed at Eleanor's face, arm, and legs. "Hurt?"

Eleanor's blood flushed her neck and reddened her cheeks. She had forgotten what she looked like and tried to cover the scratches and bruises on her legs with her arm. She turned her head away so Isabel and the others would not notice her face, but it was too late.

Isabel persisted with her own concern. "Doctor?"

Isabel scurried to the stove. From one of the cast iron pots, she poured something into a cup then offered Eleanor a hot, milky beverage.

"Mm." Eleanor smiled, the universal language of thanks.

"*Atole,*" Isabel said.

"*Atole,*" Eleanor repeated and drank the entire sweet beverage, since she was as thirsty as she was hungry.

Isabel filled the cup again, and this time, Eleanor shared a sip with William. He smacked his lips and cooed. Even during times of chaos, his sweet baby antics made her smile.

In Isabel's home, Eleanor felt welcome. Even though Dick, the field bosses, and others disdained the families and men from Mexico, Eleanor had a new-found compassion for them. The scorn and racial slurs were deplorable. Eleanor could not understand why the hatred continued; she was so grateful for her new friends. Isabel and Miguel, Rosa and Roberto, they all wanted what she wanted. Loved ones and families. A home. A job to earn money.

Eleanor got up to leave, although she didn't want to. She walked over to the basin and put the cup into it, lingering as an idea popped into her thoughts: *Perhaps this caring family could help me flee.* But, how?

"Miguel?" Eleanor asked.

"*Sí?*"

"Where is the road?" She knew there had to be another road they used, she had never seen them ford the river in their car or drive in front of the Messers' camp.

He pointed. "The road …"

"How far?"

He raised three fingers. "Three mile."

"Where does the road go?"

"Highway."

"Does the highway go to a town?"

He nodded. "San Luis Obispo."

"How many miles to San Luis Obispo?"

"Ten."

Eleanor's shoulders nearly sank to the floor. She felt overwhelmed, but she had to do it. She had to try. "Ten miles," she muttered to herself.

He nodded.

"Thanks… um, I mean *gracias*."

Miguel said something to Isabel. Her expression changed. "*¿Frijoles?*"

Miguel translated. "Eat. We cook beans."

Eleanor did not want to waste time eating. Time was on her side, especially since it was night, but she needed food if she planned to walk.

Eleanor believed that Isabel sensed her hesitation; but she

went ahead and quickly scooped a ladle of thick, spicy brown stew from one of the pots, anyway. "Here, here."

"Thank you!" Eagerly, Eleanor ate the beans and drank another cup of *atole,* followed by a cup of fresh water. She must have looked half-crazy the way she gobbled the food. The meal was more than she could ask for. Their kindness lifted her heart with encouragement, and she touched Isabel's arm as she said, "*Gracias*" to all of them.

Eleanor was anxious to start their escape, but before leaving, she nursed William, hoping it would keep him full for a while. When she finished, she stopped by Roberto's bedside to cheer him on. "I know you'll be feeling better soon."

Then, exiting the warm cabin with her baby son, she looked at him and whispered, "Hopefully we'll all be better soon."

Twenty-Eight

1946

Isabel and Miguel followed Eleanor and William out the door into a cool breeze. Miguel showed her the way toward the path, and mother and son headed north. Eleanor's dress was still damp, and the night air nipped at her skin. She shivered, straining to see what lay ahead in the dark as the clouds obscured the moon's light.

What if I get lost? What if I don't get away?

Stop! Eleanor forced herself to quit panicking or she'd worry herself senseless. "Three miles. Three miles," she repeated out loud like the refrain in a song.

At first, Eleanor walked about ten steps, stopped to listen for sounds around her, then walked another ten steps and listened again. That stop and go pace left her exposed in the clearing around the cabin, so she quickened her steps until she found the path.

Tall beach grasses swished as she inched along, making her way over downed branches, wooden crate slats, palm fronds, garbage, and around rivulets that gushed above her ankles. Although the path was slippery with mud, she waded through the water by shuffling her feet along the mire.

Soon, the ground sloped down to a glade that stretched out in front of them. Apart from knowing they were somewhere between Cliff Beach and the town of San Luis Obispo; Eleanor did not have a clue how far she had rambled. Each step she took seemed to weigh like a hundred-pound gunny sack of potatoes around her neck. It felt like she had already walked all night.

After she plodded across the glade, she found the path leading into tall clumps of beach grass. She pushed apart the stalks then settled on a driftwood log to nurse William again. Eleanor was exhausted and all she wanted to do was rest and cuddle with him under the cover of the vegetation, and then later get far, far away. While William struggled suckling, she gave wings to a fantasy. Flying like a robin and soaring over the terrain, her imagination eventually landed both of them into a freshly made nest somewhere safe. She shook her head, scolding herself for her dizzy thoughts, when what she really needed and wanted was a place to call home.

She had to move on, and Isabel's gifts of food and *atole* provided the sustenance she needed. But she could not stop her worried thoughts. "So many miles?" Eleanor asked William, as if he could answer. "Then what? What will we do without money?"

"Just walk," Eleanor mouthed. *I'll think of something. I have to keep hoping.*

She was finished feeding William and ready to continue their journey when she heard a thud, thump, thud in the distance. She froze, still like a startled deer. *No one could be following me.*

It was too dark. Too far. Too... Eleanor heard another thump and a snap of a branch. She stopped speculating and tilted her head to hear better. The heavy breathing and grunts haunted her. She flinched. Was it an animal? Or, worse yet, Dick? A man's voice groaned.

Stomping footfalls approached from behind Eleanor. She clutched William tighter in one arm, lowered herself onto her knees, then used her free arm to slowly crawl farther into the tall grasses. They rustled and made a swishing racket as she moved deeper into concealment.

Soon, Eleanor flattened her hips to the sandy ground and nestled William to her breasts. Pain in her ribs and the back of her head from Dick's recent beating throbbed with burning spasms. She squeezed her lips together and clenched her jaws, stifling any painful groaning she might emit.

"Eleanor! Where are you?" Dick yelled.

Eleanor's heart beat faster and felt like it lurched into her throat. Beads of sweat trickled down her forehead. One of her eyes twitched. A white flash of terror burned inside her stomach. He must have tracked Eleanor and William to the river and on the other side again. It wouldn't have been difficult because Isabel's and her prints would have been the only ones after the storm.

Moments seemed like hours. Her breathing thinned but quickened. Her right foot jerked from side to side and dread caused her entire body to shudder. She could smell his hostility radiating from him as grasses whooshed near them. William fussed.

No, please stay quiet. William had to stop fussing. She lowered her dress and pushed one of her nipples into his mouth, hoping he would stop whimpering.

"Where the hell are you?" Whack, whack. "I's got my knife. And I's cuttin' down this damn grass to find ya. Then I'm takin' it to you too."

William stirred. She moved her nipple and mashed her

trembling hand over his mouth, worrying she might suffocate him.

Eleanor struggled to breathe, too. She couldn't suck in any air. Spots sprinkled like fleeting fireflies in front of her when his foot stomped just a few feet from her head.

Thwack, thwack. His knife swooshed nearby.

"I know you're in here." His boots pounded the earth so hard the ground vibrated beneath her and into her very being.

"I'm gonna get ya!'" Soon Dick's footfalls tramped away, back toward the beach, and his voice trailed off in the distance.

Eleanor breathed as quiet as a cloud, but her heart pounded so loudly, she was sure he would hear it and turn toward them again. Lifting her hand off of William's mouth, she quietly sighed with relief because he was still breathing. Alive.

She didn't get up for the longest time, listening to their surroundings for what must have been an hour. Before rising, she decided to nurse William again because she couldn't risk him crying. Any sound from them would give away their whereabouts.

Guessing they were out of immediate danger, she kneeled, peering over the height of the grass. No one was around. Only the seagulls squawked overhead. By their flight, she knew daylight was arriving. She stood up, picked up William, and resumed picking her way through what was now scrub grass.

She heard the cars first, reaching the highway soon after. Picking up her pace through the rural landscape as the blue hour of morning emerged, she saw car lights illuminate the road. She panicked as a flatbed truck approached from the oncoming lane. She didn't want to be found. She just couldn't be found. So, she scrambled toward a muddy ditch. While dashing away, she held William tight but stumbled, landing on her one hand and both knees with a jerk. The pain in her ribs seared like a hot burning point, and she screamed. The truck slowed and stopped.

Eleanor froze.

A man rolled down the window in his cab and called out. "You alright?"

Eleanor ignored him, hoping he would drive on. He didn't and climbed down from his seat. A middle-aged man wearing jeans and a cotton shirt exclaimed, "Why, you're just a child. No older than my daughter."

William started crying. The driver looked puzzled.

"I saw you slip in the mud." He reached out his hand to assist. "Here. Let me help."

Eleanor must have startled him with wildcat eyes because he backed away a step. She looked like a mess. Her hands were muddy and wet, her dress and face were dirty. And from William's sour smelling blanket, his cries were becoming howls.

"Here," the man extended his hand again, "I can take you where you're going."

Eleanor held back, assessing the stranger's eyes and the way he spoke. She was wary, but his look of concern and the timbre of his words untangled some of her uncertainty. His intention sounded as good as Isabel's *atole* had tasted. Besides, what was she going to do? Walk the distance to town when she could barely move?

Eleanor considered her options and then agreed. "Thank you."

He nodded and reached behind into his back pocket and

brought out a clean white handkerchief. "Here." His offer was genuine.

"Thanks." Grateful for the small cloth, Eleanor wiped her hands. "But I'm a mess. I don't want to get your truck dirty. And I don't have money to pay you."

"Never mind that. Where are you going?"

"I'm trying to get to the nearest town."

"Heck, I can take you there." His voice assured her, as if that were the easiest trip he'd ever drive. "What happened? Did you get flooded out?"

"Um... yes." That was all Eleanor said before she hoisted William and herself onto the truck seat.

"Well, let me take you to the Red Cross then. They're helping folks who got washed out yesterday."

"That'd be swell."

He pointed. "It's just up the road."

Twenty-Nine

1946

Fearing Dick would find them, Eleanor hid in the morning shadows beside the Red Cross office until a volunteer opened the front door at ten o'clock. Once inside, she explained her story to a soft-spoken woman who listened without interrupting.

At noon, a different volunteer with curly, gray hair drove her and William to the San Luis Obispo train depot. She waved goodbye and reminded herself how lucky they were to be leaving soon on a train. Leaving. Escaping. Eleanor was full of appreciation for the generous strangers who helped that morning. Grateful for Isabel and Miguel, the ride to town, and the Red Cross' gifts. In her hand was a paper sack full of two diapers, a clean baby undershirt, a wool blanket, and a kit she had already used to brush her teeth, comb her hair, and wash William and herself. In her other hand she carried William and slung over her arm hung a small second-hand purse with twenty dollars in it. The money the Red

Cross gave Eleanor was a fortune compared to what she had possessed during the previous year.

Eleanor bought a ticket at the depot. Soon, she and William were headed north on the 12:10 p.m. train to Sacramento. There they would board a different train and travel through Klamath Falls to Portland. The final trip would be to Wilkes, Washington, over 900 miles north.

When the train stopped in towns along the route, Eleanor held newspapers in front of her face so outsiders couldn't see her. Although, if Dick or his family had boarded, they would easily identify her and William. With that nightmare colliding in her mind, she could not sleep or sit at ease.

No one discovered them while the train sped on its tracks and regrets as sharp as a raven's caw stole into her thoughts: leaving behind little Sam and especially Betty hurt. She wouldn't be able to share in Sam's enthusiasm for the shells and rocks he found. Nor could she encourage Betty to fulfill *her* dreams of becoming a nurse. Without a mailing address, Eleanor wouldn't be able to write to them, either. All she could do at that point was to wish them well from a distance.

Eleanor arrived in Wilkes the morning of July 12. As she carried William down the train steps, her shoulder muscles tensed like one of Dick's harsh grips around her arm. The two of them could easily be spotted walking through town and on the rural roads to Grandmother's house. That was, if she still lived there. Grandmother moved around so much. Eleanor hadn't been in contact with her for almost a year, but figured if the dairy had been a success, Grandmother would probably stay put.

After locating a phone booth, Eleanor inserted a nickel in

the coin slot. The nickel clinked into the money box. She dialed Grandmother's number while worries circled in the rooms of her mind about what she would say. Or if she would simply hang up on her. It rang and rang. Nobody answered. The nickel clinked down the slot. Eleanor fished out the coin, and with shaking fingers she inserted it again and dialed the operator because Ernst's number in Millston was long distance. She planned to ask him if Grandmother still lived at the dairy before walking there.

The operator answered and told Eleanor to put more coins into the pay phone.

Finally, the line clicked, and Ernst answered.

"Ernst? Oh, Ernst." Tears tracked Eleanor cheeks. "It's me... Eleanor."

"Is it really you, Eleanor? We've been so worried." His voice elevated, became stronger during their brief conversation.

"Yes. I know. I'm sorry. I never had the chance to call. But I'm back now."

"Good! I'm relieved. Are you okay?"

"Uh-hum. I'm going to see Grandmother. Is she still living on the farm?"

The coins Eleanor fed into the pay phone did not buy enough time for her to tell Ernst her story. She had to cut their conversation short. "So, they're still there. Right?" Her hands trembled as she listened for his confirmation.

"Yeah. Ma and Mattias are there."

A slow smile lifted Eleanor's expression. "I'd like to see you. Soon. I love you and hope you're okay."

As soon as Eleanor hung up, she and William left. She rushed, constantly scanning the foreground, or listening for footsteps behind her, and occasionally turning around to make certain they were alone. She couldn't imagine how

Dick could be in the area, but she didn't want to relax her guard.

Eleanor approached the farm, and the familiarity of the herd's calm lowing in the background nearly made her sob. Clothes and linens hanging on the line fluttered in the summer wind. Grandmother had planted a variety of flowers in a border along the front. Sunflowers, one of her favorites, dahlias, daisies, and a blue hydrangea bloomed into an inviting array. As Eleanor and William got closer to the front porch, Grandmother's yellow roses vined the arbor and perfumed the air. Intermingling with those sweet scents were the barnyard and river cottonwood trees.

She stood at the door and lifted her hand to knock. She paused, smelling the uncertainty of Grandmother's criticism. Would Grandmother tell them to leave, or welcome her new great-grandson and Eleanor? She hoped for mercy because they had nowhere else to go.

Eleanor breathed in deeply, finding courage, and rapped three times. Mattias opened the door and stared. His jaw went slack in disbelief.

He shook his head and stepped aside. "Come in!" Then he called out, "Ma, look who's here."

Grandmother appeared from the kitchen. When they both hugged her and William, their embraces felt like grace. Their warm greetings sounded like a lullaby and reassured Eleanor they were willing to see them.

That afternoon, Eleanor and William tried to nap. She tossed from side to side, unable to sleep and soon woke from nightmares of Dick that tormented her. She relived again his crushing beatings, his flashing knife. Each time, she flinched in pain. Each time she cringed in fear. Would he find them? Of course not. They were safe.

Soon they got up for dinner. After the first real meal she had eaten since Isabel's beans, Eleanor cleared the dishes with Grandmother. Eleanor nursed William while she asked about her and Mattias, and then asked after all her aunts and uncles, and nieces, and nephews, and finally the farm and the herd. Grandmother joyfully shared news about all of them.

"What about Jacob? Do you know how he is?"

"Jacob? You still interested in him?" asked Grandmother, tilting her head. That was when she raised her eyebrows, peered over her gold wire-rimmed glasses at William, then glanced at Eleanor and back to William.

Eleanor squirmed, dipped her chin down as her face and neck blushed.

Grandmother's squinted eyes spoke; she could see that William was Jacob's.

Eleanor gulped hard and hoped Grandmother would not disown her for her transgressions. "Hmm. Just curious about him."

"Let's see … he called once."

"What did he say?"

"He wanted to talk to you. Said he was coming to visit."

"Then what?"

Grandmother gave a quick shrug. "I told him you were married and gone." She turned a hard stare at Eleanor. "We were all worried about you. You didn't come home from work. We didn't know where you were." Her white brows knotted into a deep frown. She hesitated as if she were remembering details or growing angry. "Mattias went looking for you. He drove to the department store. No one there knew where you were. He searched up and down the main streets.

You gave us a terrible fright. Then, you called and said you were with Dick."

Shame wrapped a bitter cloak around Eleanor. "I'm sorry I caused you worry. I didn't want to go. Dick threatened me, and then..." Eleanor stopped before she broke into sobs.

Regret drained her.

Eleanor really *had* wanted to tell Jacob about her foolish marriage. But she didn't. She failed. She couldn't tell Jacob because he didn't deserve heartache.

Grandmother spoke up again. "Then you got a letter from him."

"What'd he say?"

"I didn't open it. It's still here... somewhere." Grandmother turned away from the kitchen sink and headed to the hutch. After opening a drawer, she riffled through a collection of papers. "Let me look... yes. Here it is." She held it up and then handed the unopened letter to Eleanor.

The envelope quivered in her hand. She ripped open the flap and pulled out the letter.

30 September 1945

Eleanor, I hear you got married. Our engagement is off. Don't bother sending back the ring. I never want to see you ...

By the time Eleanor reached the second line, she stopped reading. "*I never want to see you...*" pounded from one side of her head to the other. Her eyes blurred. Blinking, a tear streaked her cheek. She mumbled, "Oh, Jacob ...."

Eleanor plodded upstairs to the bedroom with both William and Jacob's letter. Nestling her son between the sheets on Grandmother's bed, Eleanor muttered to herself, "Jacob, you and I have a fine boy."

Instead of crawling into bed, she pulled out a box from the bottom of the closet. She had carried that box through every move, back and forth, from Millston to Wilkes. Its cardboard was worn. The flaps torn. She rummaged through clothes, a pair of shoes, sheet music, books, stationery, and letters from Jacob. Under all that was the velvet box with the engagement ring inside. Even though Jacob didn't want the ring, Eleanor needed to return it. As hard as it would be, she had to clear her conscience. Tell him of his son... their son.

July 13, 1946

Dear Jacob,

I am sorry, so sorry. I can't forgive myself for not telling you earlier. I didn't want to upset you while you were still serving in the Pacific. And when you came home, I really was going to let you know the night we went to the park, but I lost my nerve. You were so kind to me. I felt I owed you a nice evening. I'm returning the engagement ring. It's yours now.

And I have something else to tell you. I have a son. His name is William and he was born on June 8. He has blond hair and blue eyes like yours. The date of his birth and his features make me believe he is our son.

I know you don't want to see me again, but I had to let you know. I've made a lot of mistakes. Secrets can haunt a person for a lifetime and I'm tired of keeping them. I hope you can forgive me someday, at least for William's sake.

Sincerely,

Eleanor

~

Writing to him caused Eleanor's right foot to thump. She found herself unsettled, unable to sleep. She got another piece of stationery and jotted a note to Janice. Eleanor let her know she was back in Washington and wanted to visit her soon. As she finished the letter, Grandmother's tired footsteps slogged up the stairs. Eleanor decided to write to Fran the next day.

At five o'clock the next morning, Grandmother woke to the clanging of a brass alarm clock. Eleanor nursed William, dressed herself, and met Grandmother downstairs in the kitchen. Eleanor heated thick, creamy milk and stirred oatmeal into a pan on the three-burner electric stove. Then, she served a steaming bowl of mush and a hot cup of Postum to Grandmother in gratitude for her acceptance of their arrival.

Eleanor tried to share a condensed version of her year-long story. "I was helped by a really nice family from Mexico. They fed and…" Eleanor's voice got lost in painful memories. Grandmother didn't press for details, but instead told Eleanor that she and William were welcome until she could get back on her feet again. Eleanor's shoulders slumped as she blew out a deep sigh of relief. Grandmother wasn't going to disown her. For the first time in a year, they were safe.

After Eleanor cleaned up, she and William took a steaming cup of Postum to Mattias. His morning started at four o'clock, when he headed to the barn to milk the sixty cows. The summer's morning began with drizzle. Clouds hung pigeon gray over the river and farm. Dirt on the path became slippery and thick. Eleanor's shoes pulled the oozing mud, making a sucking sound with each step.

She found Mattias in the back of the barn and apologized to him, too. "That was no way to leave," she said and hung her head in disgrace.

Eleanor helped him with barn chores by washing milk cans. She didn't mind. In truth, she slid into an easy cadence and for once enjoyed working near him while William lay bundled and content on a cushion of straw inside the dry barn. Knowing her efforts eased their daily burdens gave her a sense of purpose and helped her regain her frayed dignity.

Staying with Grandmother provided them with a bed—a real bed—to sleep on, food to eat, a bathtub to wash in, and clean clothes. When Eleanor peered into her mirror, she saw that the bruises on her face were fading from purple and blue to yellow. The pain in her chest had also begun to subside. Even better than that, Eleanor could breathe without tight shoulders and tense neck muscles. She felt protected.

Following dinner, a summer storm crackled. Lightning flashed and thunder rumbled. Soon, a downpour rattled the roof. Eleanor came downstairs and wrote a letter to Fran and Pete. Although she had slept soundly the night before, Eleanor felt listless and tired. She worried, wondering if they'd understand. She convinced herself she needed to sound upbeat and, above all, truthful in the letter.

July 14, 1946

Dear Fran and Pete,

I hope this letter finds both of you in good health and wealth. I've missed you so much. During the last year, I was living in southern Oregon and then in California. I arrived back in Washington two days ago and am staying with Grandmother for a while. I have a son named William who is one month old. I've had a few ordeals since we last saw each other. However, I'm determined to work and save money so I can apply to nursing school. I have to keep hope in my heart. Maybe William and I can visit you soon.

In case you'd like to call, Grandmother's telephone number is VI 8 5 5 1.

With love,
Eleanor

After Eleanor tucked the folded letter into an envelope, she helped Grandmother sort the raspberries they had picked earlier in the day. Those that were ripe to eat were dropped into a bowl. The others went into a large pot for cooking into jam. William slept in a wicker laundry basket under the kitchen table. Color had returned to his cheeks and the flesh on his arms and legs filled.

Writing to Jacob and Fran and Pete tangled ragged emotions inside of Eleanor. She was tired of secrets and believed Grandmother had kept a few during the past years. Eleanor wanted to ask her about Mother. She bit her lip. Eleanor had never broached the subject because she wasn't sure how to. What with the commotion of moving like transients almost yearly, Grandmother's incessant work, and Eleanor's reticence, talking intimately with Grandmother hadn't been easy. Eleanor couldn't decide if she should just blurt out with a direct question or try to be subtle. Before she could compose a delicate way to ask, the words tumbled out of her mouth.

"Tell me about my mother."

Grandmother whipped her head around and eyed Eleanor.

Shivers rattled her spine.

"Even though she was my oldest child, I can tell you she

wasn't my first." She turned her attention back to the berries so they wouldn't scorch.

"What?" Eleanor asked. "I thought *she* was your first child."

"She was, but she wasn't the first child I lost. I had a miscarriage. Then, we lost Edward when he was almost one from the influenza. And Virginia nearly didn't make it. She came a month early. So, when your mother died, her loss was almost too much for me. I never expected to live longer than my children."

Eleanor jerked her shoulders slightly back in shock. Grandmother was honestly sharing for the first time Eleanor could remember.

"I'm sorry. I didn't know."

A hard silence overwhelmed the quiet room. During that long moment, the raspberries boiled and splattered out of the pot.

Grandmother finally asked, "Well, what do you want to know?"

"What was she like?"

"Oh, she was smart. Pretty, too. But too smart for her own good."

"Hmm? What do you mean?"

"Well, you're a lot like her."

"I'm not smart." Eleanor snorted. "Look what I've done. Nothing but mistakes." She reflected a moment on Jacob and chastised herself for her thoughtlessness toward him.

"That's what I'm talking about." Grandmother wiped up the spatters with a cloth. "She met Haydon. He's a no-good drunk and beat your mother." She stirred the bubbling mixture. "And he was awful to you."

Eleanor's eyes nearly bulged out of her sockets. Her breath whistled. She wondered if Grandmother knew about

Father's sexual attack on her. Eleanor had never told her. That attack was too shameful and ugly for her to reveal.

"I know what happened. Bernadine told me he bought gifts and then didn't give them to you. She wrote that in a letter a couple of years ago." Grandmother sighed, checked the berries in the pot, then asked, "Do you remember that hearing in the courthouse when you were seven?"

Eleanor nodded, exhaling the breath she had pent-up inside of her. "I sure do. I shook in my shoes. I didn't like standing in front of the judge."

"Me neither. Especially since I didn't know if you wanted to live with him. And I didn't want you to." Grandmother forced the wooden spoon—stained red from the raspberries—into Eleanor's hand. "Here. Watch the jam. I have something for you."

Her heavy footfalls sounded worn-out and scraped the wooden stairs. Eleanor wanted to follow her, but the jam had one more minute to boil. When a timer chimed, she removed the pot from the burner to let the fruit cool. By then, Grandmother was downstairs with a newspaper article and a letter written in pencil.

"When I found out about the car accident and Margarete's death, I took the train to Brentwood." She gazed outside the window. The rain had subsided to a drizzle. "She wrote a letter to me … just a few days before she died. That she was coming home." Grandmother handed Mother's last letter to Eleanor.

She treasured the page in her hand, holding it first to her heart and then to her lips where she inhaled. She wanted it to smell like Mother, but only whiffs of dust ascended from the paper.

"And this article. I've saved them all these years."

It looked and read like the one printed in the Seattle newspaper Bernadine had given her years earlier. This one was shorter in length and had been published in the Brentwood newspaper. Eleanor read the letter first.

Dec. 9, 1927
   Brentwood, Wash.
   1112 Norton Ave.
   Dear Ma,
   I've just visited Bernie and Mike. She looks happy now that they settled into their own place. She loaned me some money because I'm leaving Haydon for good and coming home. I'm taking the train to Pendleton and then the bus to Weston. I should be there by the 14th.
   I got a letter from Uncle Ted. Said if I couldn't get work, he'd send me money to go stay with him in Spokane and help me hunt up a job.
   I don't know what Haydon will do when he finds we're gone. I know he'll be hopping mad that I took Eleanor.
   Love to everybody,
   Margarete

Eleanor's voice drifted thin and weak. "How awful."

"The road was slippery..." Grandmother pushed her shoulders up, standing erect. "But that's not all."

"Not all? What do you mean?" Eleanor tilted her head and eyed her grandmother with curiosity.

"If I knew then what I know now, I wouldn't have let you go for even one minute with that heathen."

Eleanor's brows folded together, forming wrinkles on her forehead.

"Haydon lied." Eleanor was already aware of her father's

deceitful character. Grandmother went on, shaking her head in sorrow. "The truth was covered up. He was in cahoots with the police and the District Attorney. They were all friends. Haydon bootlegged liquor for them. Bernadine told me. She said it was Haydon who ran into your mothe—"

"What!" Eleanor interrupted, her voice rising an octave.

"That's what she said. Haydon all but admitted it recently, one night when he was drunk. Said he was driving after Margarete... to make her go home. He was so mad he ran his car into hers."

"Whose car was she driving?"

"I don't know." Grandmother gave a heavy shrug. "Haydon always was no good." She glanced at the newspaper clipping. "Course, we can't prove it now after all these years." Her jaws clenched.

Eleanor sat wide-eyed and stunned. For as long as she could remember, she had wanted Mother and had wanted to know what happened to her. Grandmother provided some answers. But were they true? And what about that beast? Had Father killed her? At that moment, Eleanor could believe he had. Since he had tried to rape her, she didn't think it was possible to hate him more than she already did, but her resentment grew. He became dead to her.

Later that evening, Grandmother, William, and Eleanor sandwiched together in Grandmother's double bed. Grateful for company, Eleanor welcomed their bodies next to hers.

Eleanor awoke around four in the morning when a lively robin began singing *cheerily, cheer up, cheer up, cheerily, cheer up*. Robin song in the early hours often meant a good day would follow. Hearing the rise and fall in the robin's pitch lulled her back to sleep with that comforting thought. She dipped into a dream where a woman told her to wake up; she remembered Isabel's voice saying the same thing and sensed it was her again. But it wasn't. Grandmother nudged her elbow into Eleanor's side, and she grasped it wasn't a dream.

"Wake up!" Urgency ripped through Grandmother's voice. "Somebody's coming up the stairs. And it's not Mattias."

Eleanor jerked upright in the bed and listened. She shivered from the cool night breeze blowing through the open window. Grandmother was right. That wasn't Mattias' shuffle.

The footfalls came nearer. Whoever it was, walked through the hallway to Grandmother's bedroom.

"Who is it?" Eleanor yelled. "Ernst? Is that you?"

What she heard caused hair to rise on her arms. A laugh. A heinous snicker. Blood drained from her head.

"It's Dick!" Eleanor screamed, letting Grandmother know who the intruder was. "Go away! Or we'll call the police."

"Hah. Do that." His grated cackle broke the peaceful morning.

He shoved open the bedroom door. It slammed against the wall. Eleanor jumped to her feet as Grandmother picked up William, leaped from the bed, and protected him by enveloping her arms around his tiny body. Eleanor switched on a lamp that stood on a small table. Dick's knife glinted like it did the night he waved it in front of her face and sliced through her purse and coat. Like the days he carried it with him and threatened her if she fled.

"Help! Help! Dick's here."

Grandmother turned her head toward the window and screamed. "Help. Mattias. Help us!"

Dick mocked her. "Mattias? That gimp?" He lunged forward, stumbling and slurring his words. "Thish time, I'm gonna... gonna make damn sure you're dead. The whole shtinkin' lot of ya."

"Help!" Grandmother's voice couldn't get enough volume —like she wasn't getting air.

William started a high-pitched wail. Grandmother held him as she backed into the corner. Eleanor stood with her leg touching the bed and Dick in front of her. He swiped his knife, slicing it into the top quilt. Grandmother shrieked. Then he launched toward Eleanor.

"Got it nice and sharp. Gonna shtab ya."

Grandmother tucked William on the floor under the bed frame and jumped in front of Eleanor. "You'll have to take me first."

Eleanor's eyes widened, shocked by Grandmother's self-less undertaking. Dick threw his shoulder into Grandmother's body and knocked her to the floor. Air whooshed out of her lungs. Her elbows and back landed on the hardwood planks. She groaned.

After the assault, Mattias clambered up the stairs yelling, "What's going on?" Once he saw Dick, he shouted, "Get out of here!" Mattias limped into the room and waved a pitchfork he had brought with him. "Get out." His voice boomed.

Eleanor intervened and grabbed the tool from Mattias, whose body listed to his right. It was bad enough Grandmother had been hurt, Eleanor didn't want him suffering, too. Fury engulfed her like a wildfire in dry timberland. Hatred spewed from her mouth, and soon courage filled her.

"Get out!" Eleanor screamed as loud as she could and lunged headlong toward Dick. The tines almost pierced into him.

Each time she yelled; she sprang forward at him.

"I!

"Will!

"Never!

"Run!

"From you again! Never!"

Her knuckles turned white like sea foam from gripping the long, wooden handle. The pitchfork wavered from her shaking arms, but she kept plunging the tines forward. She tried to knock his knife to the ground. "And you're never going to hurt my baby!"

Dick reeked of hatred. And liquor. And stale cigarette breath. He hopped to the left, like a jack rabbit outsmarting a coyote. His knife still flashed.

Eleanor thrust the manure-crusted pitchfork into his shoulder. He grabbed his shoulder and howled, but still managed to hold his knife securely in his other hand.

Eleanor rallied and pounced at him again. He stepped back. Once more she tackled him and prevailed. The fork tines pierced his stomach. Her face scrunched as nausea waved through her, knowing she had punctured his flesh.

His knife fell to the floor with a loud clunk. He grabbed his stomach, pivoting around. He scrambled out of the bedroom, thrashing against the railing and zigzagging into the wall down the stairs.

Eleanor pursued him and shoved the fork toward him repeatedly in irate, yet fearful bursts. "Get out." In the kitchen, she snagged his back.

He toppled and fell to his knees.

She advanced.

Struggling to his feet again, he lumbered out the front door. He ran across the yard, staggering toward the river's earthen berm.

Eleanor stopped running when she ran out of breath. She

inhaled and exhaled loudly. As she regained her strength, the cocks crowed.

Mr. and Mrs. Gray, neighbors across the road, ran out of their house. The screen door slapped its frame. Their German shepherd growled and loped in the direction of the dikes, tracking Dick's steps. The neighbors rushed over to Eleanor just as Mattias dashed out of the back door.

"We called the police. We heard your calling for help," Mr. Gray told Mattias. "What's going on?"

Mattias started to explain but was interrupted by a police car siren's ear-piercing wail already traveling their way. Mr. Gray and Mattias waved their arms to flag the patrol car. Each of them pointed toward the dike. A man, hefty and broad-shouldered in an olive-green uniform, stepped out and toward the neighbor.

"What's the trouble?" he asked him.

Mr. Gray announced, "I heard them shout for help." He nodded his head toward Eleanor. "And I saw some man run away from their house and onto the dike."

"Nearly scared us to death!" said Mrs. Gray.

"He's gone now," Eleanor said, trying to sound confident. Even though she wanted Dick in handcuffs, she hoped to divert the policeman's attention away from the chaos for two reasons. She didn't want gossip flying all over town about Grandmother and Mattias. They didn't deserve any mean-spirited chinwag from townspeople. And, Eleanor had injured Dick. Blood pooled on the kitchen floor. Drops on the ground revealed his direction, and she didn't want to get in trouble with the law.

But Mattias—in uneven breaths—launched into an agitated explanation. "He broke into the house. Swinging a knife. It's still upstairs where he dropped it. And he fought with my ma. And hurt her and tried to kill my niece here, Eleanor, and her baby."

The dog's barking at the top of the dike caught the police's notice. His head jerked in the general direction. "I'll head up there."

"I'll follow you," shouted Mr. Gray.

"The rest of you… go inside and stay there," ordered the officer. He and Mr. Gray bounded toward the Columbia River and soon reached the flat top of the dike.

Mattias and Eleanor hurried into the house. She ran upstairs to see how Grandmother and William were doing. While they had talked with the police officer and neighbors, Grandmother had pulled herself up from the floor. She was picking up William when Eleanor bolted into the bedroom.

"I'm fine. So's he." Grandmother wobbled a bit walking toward the door.

Eleanor steadied her with a firm grip on her arm, and the three went downstairs.

Mattias guarded the back. "I'll watch here. I don't want Dick circling around and coming when the policeman is on the river side." His head moved back and forth with a shuddering palsy while he scanned north and south along the dike.

Outside, men shouted. Eleanor tried to hear what they were saying, but their voices muffled in the distance. Throughout the melee, William fussed. Grandmother rocked him from side to side, humming a soft tune to him. Soon he quieted. Knowing he was safe and not hurt helped Eleanor think easier. She headed to the front of the house and said, "I'll watch out fron—" until loud pops like fireworks interrupted her. Stopping in mid-step, she gasped.

Grandmother cried, "Dear Heavenly Father, help us."

William burst out with a loud wail.

Pop! Pop!

Icy chills raced up Eleanor's back as sunrise crept up the eastern horizon.

Mr. Gray raced over the dike toward Grandmother's house. He yelled, "He's down! Bleeding!"

"Who's down?" shouted Mattias.

Mr. Gray's ragged breathing halted. He shook his head. "The man! I've never seen anything like it. He was crazy. Running with a stick in his hand. He attacked the cop."

The officer sprinted over the top of the dike to his patrol car.

"He needs a hospital," shouted Mr. Gray.

The officer yelled, "I'll call the ambulance."

Thirty

1946

Grandmother and Mattias recounted the story of Dick's attack to Fran. She sat at the kitchen table with eyes as round as fifty-cent pieces.

After the confrontation, Grandmother telephoned Ernst, and he called Fran, who, in turn, phoned Eleanor. Fran offered to take William and her to their cabin in the Blue Mountains. And Eleanor decided that was just what she and her son needed.

Fran had driven to Wilkes and arrived several hours before their Sabbath supper.

While they ate Mattias continued telling the sordid details. "We didn't have to wait inside the house for long."

"After the gunshots, the policeman ran back over the dike to his car," Grandmother added.

Mattias forked a mouthful of the savory lentil loaf that Grandmother and Eleanor had baked.

Fran exclaimed, "Gunshots!"

Eleanor lightly bounced William on her lap, as much to

soothe him as to calm her own nerves. In her mind's eye, she heard again the unsettling pop, pop, pop from the police officer's gun, saw again the disturbing visions of the stretcher carrying away Dick's bleeding body, and recalled smelling the odor of death.

"They took him to the hospital," said Grandmother, "but he didn't make it." She folded her brows together and shook her head like she couldn't fathom that a man was killed near her farm.

"The police shot him in the arm," Mattias said. "But according to the neighbor, Dick was acting crazy. He ran at the policeman with a stick and attacked ... and the cop fired two more shots."

Eleanor turned her head away from Fran and sighed heavily. The reality of Dick's death still stunned her. It left a gruesome hole inside of her, even though she despised him. Death was too palpable. Too close, especially when she came so near to it.

"He was a disturbed man. You know ... it could've been shell shock. His ship was attacked, and he lost a fellow." Eleanor transferred William to her other knee. "Or it could've been... well, I don't know."

The pall of the last several days weighed heavily. Her expression contorted into a grimace, and her body felt as old as her wrinkled face must have looked.

On Sunday morning, July's golden sun dried the dew in the grasses. A few high clouds shimmered in the pale blue sky while the cows lowed peacefully in the barn. Mattias helped Eleanor load her things into Fran's car. He and Grandmother gathered near Fran's new Lincoln Continental. William cooed and practiced waving his arms while Grandmother cradled him close to her.

"How about we celebrate your birthday at the cabin again?" Fran always had a way of looking forward to the good things in life. "Let's see ... you'll be nineteen, right?"

Eleanor nodded.

"Nineteen! That's too much to live through for such a young lady," Grandmother said and gently placed one of her hands on her granddaughter's shoulder.

Eleanor's head tilted slightly. She moved her palm to her chest where a warm sensation, like butter yellow, calmed her. Grandmother's voice sounded as sweet as summer lupines smelled. Her concern touched Eleanor's corded nerves with so much tenderness it cracked open her pent-up desperation, and she nearly wept. Instead, Eleanor wrapped her arms around the woman who had unselfishly blocked her from Dick. Who had raised her as best she knew how, given her difficult circumstances. Grandmother's actions made Eleanor comprehend for the first time that her grandmother genuinely loved her.

Eleanor reflected... Grandmother *had* mothered her. "All these years I wished for my mother. All these years I've made so many mistakes. I realize now how lucky I've been. Grandmother ..." Eleanor backed up and looked straight into Grandmother's cloudy blue eyes, "I mean... Mom. It's a fitting name for you."

Mom's stooped shoulders straightened. The furrows on her face smoothed. She smiled. "You and I... we've had some tough times. We've had to be strong."

Eleanor nodded. "I had to reach down... deep and grab hold of my courage, no matter how hard it seemed. And keep my faith that things would work out."

"Well, I just know things are going to work out for you,

dear," said Fran, fidgeting. "I wasn't going to say anything, but I can't wait to tell you." Her eyes lit up. "Pete has a surprise for you. He has a position in the accounts department at the mill." Her smile beamed from one side of her face to the other. "He wants to offer it to you. And of course, I'll gladly take care of William while you work."

"I can't believe it." Eleanor's face brightened and she smiled, clutching the good news as if she could hold it in the grip of her hand. "Thank you."

While Fran's news was heartening, one sorrow lingered: Jacob.

My only hope is that he'll someday forgive me and want to meet his son. But that's a lot to hope for.

Fran motioned Eleanor toward the car. "Come on, let's go!"

With the promise of better days ahead, Eleanor started singing a hymn she remembered from childhood, "How Can I Keep from Singing?"

Through all the tumult and the strife,
I hear the music ringing.
It finds an echo in my soul.
How can I keep from singing?

Acknowledgments

Eleanor's Song exists due to a team of generous and exceptional individuals. For each of you, I am extremely grateful.

First, I would like to express my deepest gratitude to Ron, my husband, who has supported me in this project and throughout my writing years. I am also thankful for our two daughters and granddaughter. Without all of you I'd be writing words with no meaning.

Thank you to my colleagues, cheerleaders, and cherished friends in Writers in the Grove. MaryJane Nordgren, Anne Stackpole-Cuellar, Paula Adams, Susan Schmidlin, and the late Shannon Brown were early readers, providing suggestions and comments that strengthened the narrative and encouraged me to continue. Also, a shout out to Ann Farley, who shared the names of poetry and literary journals that were seeking submissions, and to Bill Wood's expertise in photography.

I'd also like to thank David Pero, Rigo Loeza, and Kristi-noël Ludwig for your sensitivity read. Your life experiences helped me avoid perpetuating stereotypes and bias.

I could not have reached the publication finish line without Ariane Kimlinger, my insightful editor, who raised the bar with each line she read; Krista Harper, my expert book coach, who held me accountable and answered seemingly endless questions; Gwen Patch, my creative, years-long friend and book cover designer; and Sue Fagalde Lick, who read an earlier version and urged me to publish this story.

I wrote *Eleanor's Song* to shine a warm and healing light on the women who have endured trauma. I hope this work will be a beacon for women in my daughters' and grand-daughter's generations, helping them thrive in the face of adversity and find refuge. Toward that end, I'd like to acknowledge the work that organizations provide to help victims in need.

If *you* are in danger, please see the list of resources below where you may seek help. Because no one deserves to be abused or threatened.

If you are in immediate danger, call 911.

For help and information anytime, contact:

National Domestic Violence Hotline – create a safety plan

www.ndvh.org

1-800-799-SAFE (7233)

TTY 1-800-787-3224

National Sexual Assault Hotline

www.rainn.org

1-800-656-HOPE (4673)

Lastly, I am grateful to you—readers of this book. I cherish the time we have traveled together through this story. Thank you for picking up this book and sharing it with your friends, book groups, and family. May your song be as joyful as "How Can I Keep from Singing?"

≈

A portion of the proceeds from the sale of *Eleanor's Song* will be donated to the Domestic Violence Resource Center in Washington County, Oregon.

Questions and Topics for Discussion

1. The author begins the story, "The women of Eleanor Owen's family cobbled together their hardscrabble lives. For them, history had a way of repeating itself. Like the confluence of rivers, their lives intersected. Adversities flowed from one generation to the next." How does this introduction bear out throughout the book?

2. The Great Depression affected huge segments of the American population—sixty million people by one estimate. What are some of the stories your family has passed down through the generations about their experiences, and how are they similar or different from what the Bowerman family endured?

3. Eleanor, under Grandmother's guardianship, moved twelve times, requiring her to attend different schools and make new friends. Have you ever been forced to move? What was that transition like for you? How did you adapt?

4. How would you describe Eleanor as she struggled after her father's molestation? What changes did you see in her as a result of that insidious act?

5. What are the major and minor themes of this novel? Why are they universal?

6. Houselessness or homelessness, food insecurity, abuse, and economic disadvantage still endanger the lives and futures of children today. What can we do as ordinary people to prevent children from being deprived of safe and healthy childhoods?

7. The author references birds and describes scenery in several different geographic regions. Discuss the role landscape and nature play in this story.

8. What do you think about Eleanor's character as a child, a teen, and a young woman? What do you admire most and/or find the most disturbing?

9. What roles do Fran and Pete play in Eleanor's life?

10. How did Isabel change the trajectory of Eleanor's life?

11. What are your thoughts and feelings about Jacob?

12. How significant were the scenes in which Dick demonstrated what was then called shell shock or is now known as Post-Traumatic Stress Disorder? Was Dick a victim in this story? Why or why not?

13. Eleanor experienced violence in the forms of physical, emotional, sexual, and financial manipulation. Today, abuse also includes digital stalking, sextortion, and institutionalized forced reproductive decisions. Why does the author write a story in which the protagonist suffers abuse when we already live in a broken world?

14. What is Eleanor's relationship with her grandmother and how does it change?

15. There is a faith influence in this story. Why do you think the author included this element?

16. Romans 5:1-11 "... we also boast in our sufferings, knowing that suffering produces endurance, and endurance produces character, and character produces hope, and hope does not disappoint us..." You don't have to practice a faith to understand the development of hope in this context. How do suffering and endurance create Eleanor's character? And how does her character demonstrate hope?

17. Are you familiar with some of the hymns and songs in the narrative?

18. What drew you to read this book?

19. If Eleanor's story were to continue, where would it go from here?

20. What reaction do you have to the title and the cover graphic?

Enhance Your Book Club

In *Eleanor's Song,* Grandmother believed in clean living. In other words, she conducted her life in a moral, righteous, and honest manner. Although, Grandmother's values didn't always sit well with Eleanor. There were numerous references in *Eleanor's Song* that illustrated how Grandmother's character choices aggravated Eleanor. No dancing. No picture shows. No Coca-Cola. But one of Grandmother's traits that Eleanor didn't object to was her fine cooking.

A typical meal for the family would have included lentil stew; homemade bread; fresh churned butter and jam; fresh, dried, or canned apricots; and milk to drink. Grandmother also concocted several types of vegetarian meatloaves comprised of cottage cheese, walnuts, eggs, and legumes. They never consumed pork or beef, and vegetables and fruits were everyday staples.

During the Great Depression into World War II, the family didn't have many resources with which to buy food. With Grandmother's green thumb for growing a garden, milk from their cow Bess, and the chickens they raised, they usually had enough to eat. Some months were very lean, such as the winter of 1935. Some months were plentiful, especially late summer when the vegetables and fruits had been harvested.

Living in the Columbia plateau basin where wheat and other grains grew, Grandmother had access to hard winter wheat for her breads and pie crusts. And from apple scraps, she made apple cider vinegar. During World War II she bartered her coffee coupons with neighbors for their sugar coupons or traded her nursing services for sugar. So, with ingenuity, bartered goods, and these meager ingredients, Grandmother could bake a delicious pie.

Consider how foods connect families and friends across generations. What are special foods that you enjoy that link you back in time to relatives or friends?

Members of your book group might enjoy bringing their special family foods to share at your next gathering.

When you bake Grandmother's Apple Pie, you'll find this recipe is *much* easier than the pies she used to make. Thankfully, today's bakers don't have to churn Bess' cream into butter or gather the egg from the chicken coop. Also, fresh fruit for the filling is available from farmers' markets or the local grocery store.

I hope you enjoy Grandmother's Apple Pie as much as Eleanor did.

Grandmother's Apple Pie

9-inch pie pan makes 8 servings

Pie Crust

3 cups all-purpose flour

1 1/2 cups cold butter (Grandmother never used lard or shortening)

1/2 teaspoon salt

1 whole egg, beaten

1 teaspoon apple cider vinegar

1/3 cup refrigerator-cold water

Beat the cider vinegar with the whole egg until blended and put the mixture in the refrigerator. Cold is your friend when making pie crust. Then, stir together the flour and salt until mixed. A pastry blender is a great utensil, but if you don't have one, two knives and a fork will do. Cut the butter into the flour until the pieces are about the size of green peas.

Pour the vinegar and egg into the flour and butter particles. Mix slightly while adding 1 to 2 teaspoons of cold water at a time. Fold and combine the mixture only until it comes together into a dough and no flour remains. The dough will be sticky, and if it's overworked will become tough.

Gather the pastry into a ball and cut it in half, then shape each half into two balls. Remember how I said cold is your friend? Put the bowl of pastry balls into the refrigerator for at least one hour to chill.

When ready to roll out the dough, take one of the pastry balls from the refrigerator. Shape it into a flattened round on a lightly floured board using a rolling pin. Flatten the pastry to a thin layer about 3 inches larger than the pie plate width. Fold the flat pastry into fourths. Unfold and shape it into the pie plate. Press the pastry firmly against the bottom and sides of the pan.

Voila! That wasn't so hard, was it? Lots of people think making a pie crust is too difficult, so they'd rather opt to buy the pre-made crust from the grocers. That would never have been available to Grandmother, nor would it have tasted as delicious as this scrumptious recipe.

Apple Pie Filling

1/3 to 1/2 cup sugar

1/4 cup flour

8 cups of peeled, sliced thin tart apples (Grandmother

preferred Gravenstein apples. They are a smaller variety, but mighty in flavor.)

2 tablespoons butter

½ teaspoon of cinnamon (Grandmother didn't have access to many spices; they were too expensive. If she had cinnamon, she would have used it. This recipe calls for adding cinnamon to enhance the flavor.)

While preparing the filling, preheat the oven to 425 degrees.

Mix the sugar, flour, salt, and cinnamon in a large bowl. Stir in the peeled apples into the dry mix. Pour the fruit mixture into a pastry lined pan, and then dot with slices of the cold butter.

Remove the second pastry roll that has been chilling in your refrigerator. Roll it out in the same manner as above. Place this second layer of pastry over the filling.

Okay. Okay. This next step takes practice. Fold the top layer of pastry over and tuck it under the bottom layer. Then flute the edges. Using both hands, push your thumb from one hand in between your thumb and index finger of your opposite hand. Or you can simply use a fork. Press the fork onto the pastry to make even lines. Keep your hand light and not too hard or the dough might tear.

Even though Grandmother was strict and short on patience, she possessed an artistic flair. This skill was evident in her pie crusts. She took a sharp knife and etched, into the uncooked pastry, three curved lines to represent stalks. On each stalk she etched short slits on either side to look like grains of wheat blowing in the breeze. You may try this technique or simply cut random slits through the pastry so steam escapes while the pie bakes.

Cover the pastry edges with 3-inch strips of aluminum

foil. This prevents the crust from browning too much. Remove the foil strips during the last 15 minutes of baking.

Bake at 425 degrees for 40 to 50 minutes or until crust is golden and juice begins to bubble through the slits. Let the pie cool to set the juices for at least 2 hours. Serve with a dallop of whipped cream or a scoop of ice cream.

Once you smell the fragrances of the cooked apples and touch the flaky crust to your lips, your taste buds will be tantalized, and you'll be glad you made this pie from scratch.

Thank you for reading *Eleanor's Song*. If you enjoyed this story, please consider writing and posting a review on Goodreads, Book Bub, and Amazon.

About the Author

Susan K. Field is an author of stories celebrating women. Before she started writing fiction full-time, Susan worked in organizational communications, championing the voices of those who could not advocate for themselves: homeless and abused animals, children with special needs, and victims of domestic violence. Based on these experiences, she felt called to write *Eleanor's Song,* her debut novel.

Susan holds a master's degree in writing. Her nonfiction, poetry, articles, and essays have appeared in literary journals, anthologies, commercial magazines, trade journals, and blogs. An excerpt from *Eleanor's Song,* entitled, *A Shadow of a Decision,* won a Kay Snow Writing Award, Short Story category in 2021.

She lives in the Pacific Northwest with her husband and has a penchant for hiking woodland trails.

Made in the USA
Middletown, DE
05 November 2023

41913145R00201